John Pritchard wa... career began with a ... in his local hospita... tion he worked in administration and patient services, and currently helps to manage the medical unit in a large hospital in the south of England. *Night Sisters* is his first novel and he is at work on his second.

'A good old-fashioned tale of battling evil, which turns into a roller-coaster ride to heights of gut-churning suspense and real terror' RAMSAY CAMPBELL

'A taut and fast-moving tale with bags of authentic detail and a slam-bang finale' STEPHEN GALLAGHER

'*Night Sisters* is one of the creepiest and most shocking novels I've read in a long, long, time. The writing is superb. The story is brilliantly eerie, marked by stunning shocks of violence' RICHARD LAYMON

SPECIAL THANKS TO

A number of nursing and medical staff, for their advice and contributions. Any surviving errors are all my own work; put them down to dramatic licence.

Fields of the Nephilim (First Seal) for considerable inspiration – and musical accompaniment – throughout the writing of this.

The Sisters and staff of YCB Casualty Madhouse, where I learned to love working for the NHS.

Sergio Corbucci, Sergio Leone, Clive Barker and Richard Stanley, for further inspiration. Extra thanks to Heather Stewart of the BFI for unleashing The Last of the Western Heroes on an unsuspecting public; Alan Gregory (s/a) for the Django Survival Kit; and Jane Giles of the Scala King's Cross for her dreams-come-true programming.

Tangerine Dream, *The Sisters of Mercy*, *All About Eve* and Mike Oldfield, for keeping me going through the small hours.

And Rachel G (For Her Light)

JOHN PRITCHARD

Night Sisters

HarperCollins*Publishers*

HarperCollins Paperbacks
An Imprint of HarperCollins*Publishers*
77–85 Fulham Palace Road
Hammersmith, London W6 8JB

A Paperback Original 1993
1 3 5 7 9 8 6 4 2

Lyrics from *Ribbons* © 1990 reproduced by kind
permission of Eldritch Boulevard Ltd/EMI Songs Ltd

A version of the opening chapter of this novel first
appeared in *The Dark Side* magazine under the title *On
Her Deathbed*.

A catalogue record for this book
is available from the British Library

ISBN 0 586 21769 X

Set in Linotron Sabon by
Rowland Phototypesetting Ltd
Bury St Edmunds, Suffolk

Printed in Great Britain by
HarperCollinsManufacturing Glasgow

Don't be afraid now:
Just walk on in.

The Sisters of Mercy

TO
THE COMPANY OF BRIGHT ANGELS

(sweet dreams . . .)

PART ONE

Night Casualties

One

They told me afterwards that when Mrs Lennox died, Jenny – who had the reputation of being the most cheerful, most patient, most *loving* nurse on the gerry unit – had been heard to say, quite clearly, 'Thank Christ for that.'

You might find that a shocking sentiment; but the girls who told me it didn't think so, and neither did I. We knew well enough what Jenny had gone through; had seen how that grim old woman had worn down her patience, and turned her bright-eyed enthusiasm into bitterness and tears. And we'd seen more. We'd seen her fear. For all her cool professionalism, she had come to dread that darkened room and its occupant at the far end of the ward. Uncomprehending, her friends and colleagues had shrugged it off: ignored the signs. Only now did we realize that Staff Nurse Jenny Thomas had been truly afraid of entering that room alone, even after its occupant had died. In fact, *especially* after its occupant had died.

It had been a sombre winter afternoon when the doctor was called round to certify Mrs Lennox dead. By all accounts he'd done so as quickly as possible, and left the small, malodorous room with some haste. Jenny had described the old woman to me once, and I could picture her lying there, with that waxen immobility that immediately distinguishes death from sleep. A gaunt face staring up from the pillow, its lines of age contrasting bizarrely with the jet-black of her dyed hair. Eyes still half-open; jawbone slack.

There were no relatives to inform, so at least they'd

been spared that thankless duty. The problems began when Jenny refused to lay the body out.

Sister accepted that the patient had not been noted for her personal hygiene: nightdress and bedclothes were stained and stinking. The body was still damp with the patina of sweat raised by the final struggle against death. Of course it wasn't going to be a pleasant job, but it had to be done, and besides, they needed the bed.

Still Jenny had refused.

She was reminded of the staffing situation – two trained nurses including herself (Sister was about to go off) and a completely inexperienced student, to run a twenty-bed ward. The other staff nurse was starting the drug-round; Jenny would have to do the body, and do it on her own.

A third time she'd refused. The Sister must have been quite nonplussed, getting this from an experienced nurse like Jen: a girl she knew and liked. But she had no option now but to threaten disciplinary action. And finally, reluctantly, Jen had relented, and turned back towards the room where the body of Mrs Lennox lay waiting for her ministrations.

Laying-out is standard procedure, of course. The body is washed, the limbs straightened; the orifices plugged with cotton wool. Not a nice job at the best of times, but when you're doing it alone it can be quite unnerving. Me, I'll find myself talking to them sometimes – explaining what I'm doing, apologizing for the indignities. I still remember that time I rolled a body over and the air trapped in its chest escaped in a long, sepulchral sigh. That was back when I was in my second year. I was shaking for *hours*.

So I knew how Jenny must have felt, washing that cooling corpse in the grey winter dusk; all alone in the room. At one point she'd emerged for a breather, and was talking with the student when abruptly she'd shivered and turned round sharply. The rather startled first year had asked her what was wrong, and she'd said, nothing; but I reckoned

I knew otherwise. With her back turned to the body, she'd felt something – some shift in the air behind her, some coolness on the nape of her neck – that made her feel she was being watched. Maybe she was half expecting the corpse to have moved, be it ever so slightly, since she'd seen it last.

Either way, she'd returned to the job in hand; and after a while the porters arrived with their clanking tin trolley to collect the deceased. The body in the room, shrouded now and wrapped in a sheet from head to foot, was unceremoniously loaded aboard and wheeled off towards the lifts and, via them, the mortuary fridge. Jenny couldn't have been the only person to have thought, *good riddance*.

Shortly afterwards, the same student nurse was sent down past Mrs Lennox's old room to the equipment cupboard in the darkened link corridor beyond it. She'd got what she came for, and was just about to return when another nurse emerged from the ward after her.

That was her first thought, anyway, going by the uniform. But the figure was hunched, and wizened, and coming with slow, shuffling steps. In the moment before her eyes readjusted to the gloom of the corridor, she'd had the grotesque impression of a young nurse who'd aged decades overnight, worn out by the pressure of work. And then she saw the face.

Mrs Lennox's face, framed by the stringy black hair spilling out from beneath the nurse's cap: grinning at her.

The poor girl fainted then: it may sound like a cliché, but maybe you would have too. When she came round, the 'nurse' was nowhere to be seen – and, back on the ward, neither was Jenny. A search of the whole floor proved fruitless.

I don't know at what stage the first, horrible doubts began to occur to people; but eventually someone suggested a visit to the morgue. Perhaps it was just an attempt to placate the student, who was near-hysterical in her account of the dead patient come back to life. So down they went, into the cold room: opened the compartment where Mrs Lennox had supposedly been stored, and pulled out the muffled form within. And even before they'd unwrapped the sheet from around the head, I think they must have realized who they'd find.

It was Jenny, of course, cool and naked in her shroud; her body washed and prepared in the proper manner. Someone had strangled her with their bare hands. Someone with very long and unkempt fingernails.

Mrs Lennox hasn't been seen since. Under questioning, the certifying doctor admitted that he'd been for so long without sleep that he might have omitted to check for all the vital signs, and overlooked some spark of life still remaining. And Jenny Thomas had once told me, in wide-eyed earnest, that the woman was evil. That the woman was a witch.

One of them was right, of course. I really hope it was the doctor.

But now, sitting here in the gloom . . . and listening to the silence of the corridor outside . . . I didn't think he had been.

Two

Maybe I was just in one of those moods.

Casualty was proving quiet tonight. The usual influx in the hour after closing time had long since slowed to a trickle, the last stragglers from the rearguard of yesterday's business – leaving us in limbo to wait for the morning. And you can get to thinking strange thoughts at four a.m. or so, in the emptiest watch of the night, with dawn still several hours distant. I was certainly tired, and slightly edgy: this being my first Night On after returning from sick. Still out of the rhythm. But there was more to it than that.

I'd loved Jenny Thomas – really loved her. And she'd been murdered, quite wantonly, by . . . whom? A geriatric old woman? That I could not believe. Yet who else could have done it?

Or what else?

Silly sort of question, you might think; and only a month ago I'd have given very short shrift to any idea of a supernatural factor in my best friend's death. Maybe in the warm light of day I still would. But now . . . sitting here at my desk, in my dimly-lit office; nursing a mug as I tried getting to grips with next month's off-duty roster . . . my brooding mind kept coming back round to a few uncanny experiences of my own. Things like those limping footsteps I'd heard in an empty ward, back when I was doing my training. Or the sudden drop in temperature one night on Surgical, when a patient passed away.

Or the accident last week that almost killed me.

I'd just been driving over to visit a friend. She lived out

in the sticks, and the town was soon behind me, sprawled like a galaxy of orange suns in the early winter night. The afterglow faded, and there was only the unlit country road, its twists and turns illuminated by my headlamps, and darkness closing quickly in behind. I'd been late, and put on a bit of speed. And as I rounded a bend, a figure had appeared in the road ahead, walking straight towards me: as dark as shadow, and as insubstantial. I remember swearing, and swerving – and then nothing until I came to on my side in a ditch: still strapped into my silent, crumpled Fiat Panda. I'd slumped there, helpless, feeling sick and numb and waiting for the pain; yet part of me had still been able to register the fresh, clean night air wafting in through my shattered window. That, and something else – something I sensed rather than felt, but which set me shivering abruptly. Because suddenly I knew I was being watched from out there in the darkness: watched by something alive, and aware of me; something inexpressibly *cold*. Something which paused for an endless moment, and then passed on, eventually fading altogether into the milder coolness of the night.

I'd been almost hysterical by the time they got me out: delayed shock, of course. After a night in the Obs Ward and some generous medication, I was feeling better, and almost ready to accept that explanation. I'd been dazed: not thinking straight. They reckoned there might have been some concussion – and I was lucky to get away with only that. As for what I'd seen in the headlamps – well, there was no sign of an impact, although it had seemed he would walk into me head-on. Some freak optical illusion, then. Or even a product of stress and tiredness. When *did* you last take a holiday, Miss Young?

So there I'd been, just resigning myself to a week off work, and putting up with the good-natured ribbing of the staff (who found it most amusing to have their own Sister as a patient – though I know they'd been pretty shaken up when the ambulance brought me in), when I got to see a copy of the local paper. My own accident featured prominently, of course – but it hadn't been the only one that night. A number of minor collisions and near-misses had occurred across town, and those involved had all spoken of much the same cause: a shadowy figure glimpsed in the road ahead, walking directly towards the oncoming traffic. Yet no trace of anyone had been found; by the time the shaken drivers had recovered their wits, the street or road had been deserted. It was fortunate, the paper concluded, that only one serious accident had resulted from what had clearly been some kind of reckless practical joke.

I'd showed the article to Karen when she came round to do my obs. 'Told you I wasn't seeing things,' I pointed out, with some satisfaction.

'Maybe not – but you could still use a rest,' she'd answered sweetly – and shoved a thermometer in my mouth.

Round and round my coffee went: a spiralling milky slick. The cubicles stayed empty. The phones stayed quiet. Resus was about as tidy as it was going to be.

A reckless practical joke, the paper had said; but again – somehow – I didn't think so. I could still feel the chill – that icy *presence* in the night. Something cold had passed close by in the darkness, as I'd lain there trapped and trembling. I knew, instinctively, that whatever it was had definitely not been human.

What it *had* been, was anyone's guess. But I also knew, with a sick little certainty, that if it had paused to investigate my car, I would not have survived the experience.

That in itself was a sobering thought – especially for someone as calm and rational as I usually am. But more, it put a whole new slant on Jenny's death: a fresh and unsettling factor for my consideration. For if there really were such things as ghosts . . . and cold black *shapes* that walked the night, even in this day and age . . . then maybe dead people came back to life, too – and strangled pretty nurses.

Of course this hospital has one or two ghosts of its own, or so the stories go; and I suppose I'd enjoyed listening to those stories, and half-wanted to believe them. But it had taken this last encounter, inexplicable and frightening, to really set me thinking.

And now I'd started, it was proving very difficult to stop.

Getting on for four-thirty. Still dark outside, still silent; the town dead but dreaming in its sodium haze. But things would be stirring soon enough: lights coming on in bathrooms and kitchens, and the first commuters and early shift workers driving out on to the empty roads. It had been a quiet night so far, but, who knew, we might be able to fit in a good road smash before breakfast.

The thought drew my lips into a humourless smile, though I scarcely noticed it. Pushing the Off-duty to one side, I paused, surveying the desktop clutter – then reached for this week's copy of *Nursing Standard*, and the article on management in A&E I'd been trying to take in. I picked the mag up; and put it down again. Something else was nagging at me now – reawakened, I knew, by the memories I'd been brooding on. I could always try ignoring it, of course; I'd tried before. But it never seemed to do much good.

Still clutching my cooling mug (Sister's taste for iced coffee was a departmental in-joke), I left the office and wandered down the corridor towards reception – pausing at Utility to look in on Mike and Brenda at their stock-taking. Tonight of all nights I was glad to find them still refreshingly cheerful, even at this ungodly hour.

'Everything okay?'

'Couldn't be better,' Mike grinned. 'We can get on with our work without bloody patients interruptin' us all the time.'

He made a note on his clipboard and resumed his rummaging in the wall unit; the sleeves of his white nurse's coat rolled back to the elbows, and his tie hanging slack. The casual touches somehow made him look all the more professional, but that was Mike for you. 'So laid back he's bloody horizontal', as one locum medic had complained to me: one too full of his own importance to recognize that Michael Shannon was every inch the staff nurse his blue epaulettes proclaimed.

Brenda carried on with her own inventory, smiling quietly to herself. I reckoned the two of them had been making eyes at each other just before I'd appeared – which was fine by me, because Mike had been paying me quite a bit of attention of late, and I'd got the distinct impression he was shaping up to ask me out. He was a nice bloke, too – and I didn't like the idea of him wasting his time.

'Seen Fran?' I asked.

'She's around. I told her she could give the blackboard a clean if we stayed quiet.'

'Michael. We haven't had anyone in for three hours, it's already clean.'

'Well I suggested she could chalk in the numbers, then wipe it again . . .'

Staff Nurse Frances Stansfield was our newest addition. She'd get used to him.

Leaving them to it, I continued on through the department – very aware of the stillness around me, and the bleakness too: that cold hospital aura, honed by bright light reflecting off sterilized surfaces and bare polished floors. I passed the unlit Resus room, and the row of parked trolleys at the ambulance bay, before turning left into the silent reception area – unmanned at this hour, since we're only funded for clerical staff from eight p.m. to midnight.

The front office was in darkness, save for the dim, ghost-green glow of the two VDUs at the desk. Beyond the receptionists' windows, the waiting area itself seemed over-lit and very empty, a long room filled with rows of standard-issue seating — moulded plastic chairs which, as Mike insisted on pointing out, came in the tasteful NHS colour choice of bile green, puke orange, pus yellow and brain grey. Some were still strewn with old magazines from the reading rack: creased *Bella*s and dog-eared *Cosmo*s. At the far end, the night pressed cold against the closed double doors.

I was still trying to kid myself that I was just killing time as I went into the office and took a seat in front of the nearer VDU. I didn't bother with the light; I could almost feel my face soaking up the green-screen glow. And for a long moment I just sat there, staring, as if mesmerized by the endlessly blinking cursor. Then I leaned forward and typed in a name, watching it spell itself out across the screen.

KAUFMANN, JOSEPH

The computer beeped, and flashed up a request for further information. I had it ready, knew it now by heart.

D.O.B. – 29/07/32
ADDRESS – NFA
DATE ADMITTED – 14/06/93

The drive whirred quietly, and in another moment the patient admission data was unscrolling before me. Joseph Karol Kaufmann, age 60, no fixed address, no GP. Admitted by ambulance 21:54. Died in department 22:16.

There was other info too, and various coding references; but that was the gist. Somehow it didn't quite convey the impact of the event. It had all seemed a routine admission to start with, to be sure. But it wasn't. Oh no.

Ambulance Control had given advance warning: collapse coming in, severe chest pains. I'd finished taking the details of pulse and b/p over the phone, and handed the scribbled note to Kathy Jones, who was the doctor on for that night, as we made our way to Resus. From the way she squinted at it, running her free hand back into her dark, tangled hair, I got a hint of just how tired she was; normally she never let it show.

'Is he conscious?'

I nodded. 'Bit delirious, apparently. Look like an MI to you?'

'Um. Probably. We'll get him wired up as soon as he's in.'

The ambulance arrived a couple of minutes later, and I went out to meet it, hugging myself in the chill night air as I watched the crew unload. The man on the trolley looked wasted and gaunt, his face almost paler than the pillow. We wheeled him in through the ambulance doors, bypassing the waiting area's walking wounded; one or two people glimpsed us, and stood up to gawp.

On into Resus, where the routine began to unfold around him with the quiet confidence of endless practice. We transferred him across to our own trolley, and Karen and I sat him up and helped him off with his coat and shirt – from the state and smell of them, the bloke was in off the streets – while Mike and Kathy set about preparing the ECG. I spoke to the ambulancemen as I worked, checking details; Karen kept talking to the patient, softly and calmly, trying to ease the panic that shone in his frantic eyes.

Helen Wright was at my elbow, less the wide-eyed student by now and anxious to help. I gave her the clothes to bag up, calling goodbye over my shoulder to the ambulance crew as they left. *See you again, lads . . .* The electrodes were already pasted to our patient's scarred and bony chest, and Kathy was studying the readout. 'How're we doing?' I asked.

I got the impression she wasn't quite sure. But after fingering her way through the length of readout tape, and listening to his heart sounds again, she nodded to herself, and glanced across.

'MI. We'll make sure he's stable, then get him upstairs to Coronary Care. Will you let them know, Rachel?'

I was already on my way over to the phone, handing my drug keys to Mike as I passed. 'Diamorph?' he asked, and I nodded.

'We think you've had a myocardial infarction,' Kathy was telling the patient, speaking slowly and clearly. 'A minor heart attack. We're going to have to admit you for . . .'

The man looked at her then, and that look left even Kathy lost for words. In the midst of that pale, sweating face, his eyes were glazed and staring – and the despair in them was almost frightening. Deep in his throat, he gurgled.

Here comes the vomit, I thought resignedly, and wondered if Karen would move quickly enough to avoid getting it all over herself this time. Kathy drew back prudently, and I was already reaching for the plastic bowl when I noticed something that made me hesitate . . . and frown.

A thin trickle of blood had started from the corner of his mouth.

My poised hand wavered. For an unreal second we were all of us still as he began bloodily to drool.

I'd seen it all before, of course. Haematemesis and haemoptysis; patients vomiting blood or coughing it up. But suddenly, as I watched that slowly lengthening dribble, strung out with saliva, I felt my stomach go cold and tight inside me. Somehow I'd known that things were about to go horribly wrong.

Kathy turned to me, still awaiting the bowl, and our patient managed one dry heave before coughing a splash of scarlet down her pristine white coat. She swore tiredly, and motioned to Karen to help her support the man as he retched again, convulsing. His mouth yawned open.

And the blood came bursting out.

It was sudden, incredible, horrifying: a niagara of gore that just came and came, dousing him, drenching Kathy and Karen, even spattering me. His body jerked, and jerked again, spraying liquid crimson halfway across the room. For a frozen moment I watched with the numb light-headedness of sheer panic; then lunged forward, jostling with the others as we struggled to stem the flow. Infection-control procedures went out the window: there's no point gloving-up when you're in blood to your elbows, when it's splashing in your *face*. And all to no avail; the stuff kept geysering out. Nothing we did could stop him spewing up most of his bloodstream on to our Resus room floor – a spreading crimson lake that threatened to escape under the doors. And as our frantic efforts began finally to slacken, some cold, detached part of me still found time to picture the reaction of the bored line of patients sitting outside the plaster room opposite, as that creeping bloody tide began to emerge.

So there you go. Joseph Kaufmann, vagrant; died very spectacularly in our department some eight months back. My eyes still on the readout screen, I took a sip of tepid coffee.

Just the basics were outlined here of course; his file contained the gorier detail. Kath had written up the summary: if her usual hieroglyphics were indicative of tiredness, then the scrawl she'd used on this occasion suggested a state of near-clinical shock. I knew: I'd looked through the notes often enough since. Not everything had been recorded for posterity, of course. No mention of Dr Kessler, our consultant, bursting in to demand what the fuck we were doing in there; nor of Mike skidding in the mess and spraining his knee. Nor yet of Helen, pale and shaken, finally crying it all out in the duty room, as Karen and I held her tight.

One thing, however, did come over clearly: the fact that none of us knew what the hell had gone wrong.

There'd been a post-mortem, of course. It confirmed that death had resulted from massive internal haemorrhage — as if we hadn't guessed. As to a reason for the bloodbath, the pathologist had been less forthcoming; but his findings had both puzzled and disturbed him. Not that I've actually seen a copy of his report to the Coroner, of course; but we get to hear these things. And maybe the tale had been distorted slightly in the telling — but the version that reached us said that friend Kaufmann had recently undergone major surgery. Abdominal and thoracic. Maybe he'd had cancer, because great chunks of his intestines had been cut away completely. Organs had been crudely trimmed and grafted. The strain on his ruined system had given him an infarct; and the whole bloody lot had gone together. Like a failed experiment. That was the rumour I heard.

Records had dutifully been checked, and backs covered; but no record had been found, either here in our hospital or anywhere else. If someone really had been attempting to broaden the frontiers of medical science, it hadn't been on NHS time. The police had also made enquiries in the private sector — although no one could really see our meths-reeking ex-patient checking in at his local BUPA clinic. There too they drew a blank.

Back to square one.

Mike said it put him in mind of a particularly nasty backstreet abortion he'd had to deal with in his last job. I took his point, but open-heart surgery was hardly the sort of thing you practised on your kitchen table. It was Karen, in particularly ghoulish mood, who'd suggested that the animal experimentation labs had started dissecting people instead, seeing as the Great British Public was obviously more concerned about animal welfare than the human derelicts on their doorsteps.

We'd had a cynical smile over that one, and a couple

more crackpot coffee-break theories besides. Resigned now to the fact that we were none of us any nearer the truth: no more than we'd been on that first awful evening, when the body had been wheeled away; leaving me standing in a room that looked as if, to coin Mike's phrase, someone had loaded a sawn-off shotgun with spaghetti sauce, and let rip with both the barrels.

So life had gone on; until
  JOHNSTON, MICHAEL
arrived in our department. This was a month or two later, and too many patients had come in through the doors for us to be giving the Kaufmann case more than the occasional thought. Mr Johnston – the late Mr Johnston – had been a more urgent admission than most, having just driven a stolen car full-tilt into a brick wall.

Into Resus he'd come, bloody and wrecked and yet still raving. The ambulance crew had to help us hold him down. The team crowded round in that brightly-lit room, and once again it was all beginning to look routine. We scissored off his clothes and pulled them clear, while the doctor set about checking bones, and wounds, and reflexes: bending in close to shine his penlight in the patient's rolling eyes.

'What's his name?'

One of the ambulancemen supplied it.

'All right, Michael. Michael? can you hear me, Michael?'

But Michael was in a world of his own: a private hell of pain and panic. From his disjointed ramblings, I gathered he didn't like doctors much. Well, he'd come to the wrong place. The doctor – it was one of the locums that night, Sayeed or someone – slipped his stethoscope back around his neck. 'Right . . . I'll need X-rays of left tib & fib, pelvis, chest, both arms . . . and a CT scan. That first of all, I think.'

I nodded, told Brenda to get the duty radiologist on the phone. When she answered, Sayeed conversed with her while we cleaned Johnston up as best we could and prepared him for his transfer to the CT unit on the other side of the building. He seemed quieter now; his eyes glazed over. With everything under control, I stepped outside for a moment, and found a couple of policemen hovering vulture-like in the corridor – par for the course with RTAs.

'You won't be able to talk to him for a while yet,' I pointed out, a little impatiently. 'He'll probably be in theatre for the rest of the night.'

The taller of the two shrugged. 'We'll hang on for a while anyway.'

'Joyriding, was he?'

'Dunno. We get a report of a stolen car, and then whammo. He didn't even slow down, according to the eyewitnesses.'

'You'll want to breathalyse him, presumably.'

'At some stage.' He glanced round. 'Anywhere we can get coffee round here?'

'There's a machine round the front,' I told him, and went on into the cubicle area to see how things were going there.

They managed to get their coffee; they never got their interview. Nor their breath sample. Michael Johnston died at ten past six that morning.

According to the CT scan, his skull was still intact, but his brain had suffered irreversible damage.

And some of it was missing.

Another post-mortem. More puzzles for the pathologists. Because Johnston too seemed to have undergone recent surgery. Brain surgery. Which came as quite a surprise, because the only medical history he'd had with us was one of drug addiction. A policeman who'd spoken to him a week or so before the accident reported that he'd seemed rational enough – yet after what had been done to his cerebral cortex, he'd have been practically a walking zombie, driving that car by sheer desperate instinct alone. There was another finding, too. Though the trephine and lobotomy seemed at one level to have been sophisticated – even audacious – there was indication once again of a certain crudity. And evidence that it had been carried out under conditions that were far from sterile.

'Another backstreet job?' Mike had wondered cheerfully. Me, I was just waiting for the tabloids to pick up on it all with screaming POLICE HUNT DERANGED DOCTOR headlines. And what had Johnston been muttering? Something about doctors, 'fucking doctors . . . still after me. Still coming . . .' Except he hadn't called them doctors but something else – a more specialized term he could only have picked up from professionals.

Clinicians. He'd called them clinicians. A cold word. But I'd wondered why its mention made me shiver.

Three

The phone rang as I was typing in the third name.

Startled despite myself, I reached over the keyboard for it, spilled the last of my coffee, and was still swearing as I brought the receiver to my ear.

'If I'd wanted the Scatology Department,' Mark said mildly, 'I'd have dialled 221.'

'I think that's Pathology you're thinking of, Dr Drew,' I pointed out with completely informal formality: still checking to see whether I'd managed to get any over my uniform. 'And by the way, where are you?'

'The on-call room.'

Which was just up the corridor. 'So why didn't you just shift your bulk round here, you lazy sod?'

He grinned: his voice was full of it. 'It's what the telephone was invented for. But I might stagger round in a minute, if you insist.'

'I won't hold my breath.' After a pause I added: 'You guess where I was?'

'And what you were doing.' Some of the banter had faded from his voice. 'Why don't you let them rest in peace, Rachel?'

That left me nonplussed for a moment. Then: 'What's that supposed to mean?'

'You know. Always poring over the same cases. You know you couldn't have saved them – and the police have got nowhere. So what are you looking for?'

Silently, I had to admit I wasn't sure. Certainly the deaths had been bizarre enough to have a morbid fascination of their own – but it wasn't just that. Something about these particular cases still gave me the strangest feeling. A dull, persistent niggle of unease: like a slow, dripping tap in the darkness of my mind.

He took it upon himself to break the lengthening silence. 'I'll be round in a minute. See you.'

'See you,' I echoed, absently, as he hung up. I'd already guessed that recent events had a lot to do with my digging now. Jenny's baffling fate; my own close encounter. A week's inactivity to brood. And the cases had been weird enough to start with; but now, almost despite myself, I was beginning – just beginning – to wonder who the hell was really out there.

The third death had shaken me the most; and that a week or so before Jenny's own murder. That was a night when the drip ... drip ... drip ... had strengthened briefly to a startling, chilly trickle.

ALISON SCOTT

The full admission summary was unfolding onscreen as Mark stuck his head round the door, then came over to sit in the chair next to mine: wearing his sterile greens like pyjamas, his white coat unbuttoned over them. I gave him a sidelong glance: he hadn't shaved yet, but otherwise looked quite fresh – his sandy hair tidied and brown eyes clear. Then again, he, at least, had had the best part of a night's sleep. He returned my look, eyebrows innocently raised – then followed my gaze back towards the screen. Our proximity was relaxed enough: no hidden agendas. I think he knew I rather fancied him, but he was spoken for already. A purely professional relationship, then – but we liked and trusted each other a lot. And worked together well.

Alison Jane Scott, twenty-two years old, known prostitute, self-admitted with suspected post-operative infection. Died in department 02:20.

This one had been the least messy, but in its way the most shocking of all. She'd wandered in just after midnight, looking dazed and haggard. Complaining of a high temperature, sweats; an unpleasant discharge. An examination revealed she'd recently undergone a gynae op of some kind, and it seemed she'd developed an infection.

She wasn't wilfully unco-operative most of the time; just listless, staring back at me or Mark (he'd been on that night as well) with dull, wary eyes. But when it came to the matter of the operation itself, she'd refused point-blank even to acknowledge it had taken place. Mark had pushed her a bit, clearly suspecting an illegal abortion, but got nowhere. And I'd had the distinct impression, as she'd relentlessly stonewalled, that her silence was born of fear: that the prospect of even mentioning her op was so frightening as to be quite simply unthinkable. It was looking more and more like a backstreet job. I assumed the person who'd performed it had threatened her – terrified her into silence.

I'd been right, too. In a way.

Anyhow, at length we'd given up trying to find someone we could pin the blame on, and Mark decided to get a second opinion from the gynae registrar. While he was out of the cubicle, I rechecked her pulse, and was making conversation in a perfunctory sort of way when her hand suddenly shot out and grasped my wrist: squeezing so tight it hurt. I turned in surprise – and the look in her eyes killed my word of remonstration stone dead. Her face was ashen and gleaming with sweat: I tried to tell myself it was the fever, but those haunted, hunted eyes assured me otherwise. Worst of all was the cold intelligence in them: the fact that she knew exactly what she was saying made the words that followed all the more unnerving.

'Tell them I must be cremated,' she whispered. 'As soon as possible – so there's nothing left for them.'

Somewhat taken aback, I'd opened my mouth and shut it again, before managing: 'Don't be silly – maybe a few days on the gynae ward and a course of antibiotics, and you'll be fine. Nothing to –'

'Forget it. They're here. They're here already. And I can't run any more.' She looked at me earnestly. 'Just leave me alone – or they'll do for you too.'

There was a pause. 'How do you mean?' I asked carefully.

Her patience snapped then: there was an edge of hysteria in her tone. 'You stupid bitch, just leave me alone! *Please . . .*'

I kept very calm. 'Who is it you're afraid of?'

'Them. The Clinicians.' Her voice had faded to a dry whisper again. 'Can't you feel them?'

Clinicians. Again that word. And though I didn't answer her question directly, it did indeed occur to me that the temperature in the cubicle had altered. It hadn't dropped, exactly; but it had . . . subsided. The air felt cooler on my skin. As I stared at her, I realized it was becoming cold.

'Clinicians: you mean doctors?'

'I mean Clinicians. Now for fuck's sake leave me be.'

'All right,' I relented, 'I'll just go and see how the doctor's getting on. Back in a minute, okay?'

I found Mark writing out an X-ray request form over by the desk. 'You know that woman in cubicle two . . . ?'

'Alison Scott? The gynae reg. is coming down to take a look at her: they'll probably want to admit . . .'

'I think you should speak to the duty psychiatrist as well. She's really coming out with some weird things.' And even as I was speaking, I knew she wasn't a psychie case. I just needed someone to assure me that she was.

'Want me to talk to her again?'

I shrugged. 'Might be an idea.'

By the time we'd got back to the cubicle, Alison Scott was dead.

We found her slumped in one corner of the cubicle, all huddled up: her face pinched and wretched with fear. All attempts to resuscitate her proved unsuccessful. The post-mortem results pointed to death from heart failure; the precise cause remained uncertain.

I turned to Mark. 'Remember how cold that cubicle was, when we went back in? And back to normal a few minutes later?'

'So you said,' he came back, a little guardedly; he'd never actually admitted to feeling it himself. 'So what?'

Not having told him about the eeriest aspect of my road-crash experience, I just shrugged. 'Just seemed strange, that's all.'

But he'd begun to pick up on it now. 'So what are you suggesting? That she saw a ghost? That she was scared to death? Come *on* . . .'

'Look, I'm not suggesting anything. Okay?' It came out sharper than I'd intended.

He held up his palms. 'Sorry. But that girl was suffering from the early stages of septicaemia . . .'

'It doesn't kill you that dramatically.'

'Okay, point taken. We don't know why she died so suddenly. But you can't let it obsess you like this. Same goes for those other cases. Maybe there are some things we can't explain; but we just have to carry on. I know you've had a rough time recently, but . . .'

He tailed off awkwardly, but I knew his unspoken thought was that Jenny's death was getting to me. And so it was – but I still reckoned I was rational. We see it all in this place: all the misery and mess. But I hadn't seen fear like those three showed before.

Something was wrong, I knew it. Out there. In our town. Something was *wrong*.

But dawn was creeping up on us now, fading in through the double entrance doors; and it seemed that the hospital, an island universe through all the long hours of the night, was joined to dry land once again. A last dark thought dripped down against the stone of my scepticism; and then the mental tap was closed. I screwed it tight. It stopped.

I checked my fob-watch and managed a smile. 'Soon be time for bed.'

He seemed to accept that the previous subject was now closed. 'Glad to be through your first night back?'

'You bet I am.' I pressed the exit key, and the VDU screen cleared as data – and dark memories – returned to the disks where they'd been stored.

The night ended as quietly as it had begun. With handover completed and the early shift of day staff settling in, I stopped off in the toilets to splash cold water on my face: clearing the muzziness that was settling over me – and snapping me out of my more disturbing night thoughts. The sun was fully up now; the outside world alive and awake once more. Back to the world of dreams, Sister Young.

I studied myself for a moment, there in the mirror. Fatigue didn't do me any favours, but I reckoned I still looked the professional I sometimes didn't feel. You might think of Sisters as older women, with years of experience behind them, but I'm twenty-six, and Ravensfield General is my first senior post. I've been a Trauma or Surgical nurse ever since I qualified, and I've seen a lot; but actually running the place is a different proposition entirely. Sometimes it scares the shit out of you.

While I was at it, I decided I wasn't looking too bad altogether. Maybe a little waif-like, what with my pale complexion and wide blue eyes, offset by the dark straight hair that hung to my collar; but I'd heard my smile called winsome, and I knew that I was pretty. In my own quiet way.

On to the changing room, where I divested myself of my uniform dress, tights and sensible shoes, in favour of blouse, sweater, jeans and trainers; chatting with Fran as she shrugged out of her own work clothes. She seemed to have settled in well over the last couple of weeks; a pint-sized and perky young Scouser, blessed with the essential A&E prerequisites of cool head and keen sense of humour. I reckoned she'd make a good member of the team, which was a relief: your face has to fit, in a department as close-knit as this one.

Outside in the corridor, Mark called goodbye as he went through to a meeting with Kessler; and as I left, Steve — one of the night porters who'd covered us for the shift — made a point of mentioning how good it was to see me back. I was feeling tired but happy as I walked across to the bus stop. The thoughts that had gnawed at me through the night seemed distant and insubstantial now — fading back into my subconscious beneath the bright cold morning sun.

Behind me, the buildings of Ravensfield General Hospital loomed up dour against the sky: great blocks of sixties concrete grafted on to dark Victorian brick. Row after row of windows watched me: ward-floors stacked up one on top of the other. We had beds for nearly six hundred patients here — though the cutbacks meant that some were never used. That wouldn't have been obvious to the rather awestruck casual observer, of course — unless they passed the hospital at night, and saw that while the windows over-looking the road were brightly aglow, or showed at least the muted glimmer of night lights, the upper floors of the old north wing remained in darkness. We had several wards and a couple of theatres closed up there: slowly gathering dust behind locked doors.

I knew myself that it made for a vaguely ominous sight: that slice of shadow and silence cut into the brightly-lit evening bustle of the hospital. And of course there were staff who'd claimed to have seen ghosts up there, and heard old, shuffling footsteps in the gloom. But it was daytime now, and I was going home to sleep in a flat with sunlight pressing against the drawn curtains, and the ordered life of a quiet, leafy suburb going on around me.

Whatever vague unease still lurked within me, it could wait until dark.

Four

The next two nights were nearly as quiet. Minor injuries:
cuts and cracked bones. Bread and butter stuff for us. The
high point (relatively speaking) was Adrian Bell asking me
out again.

That was Friday – or Saturday's small hours. He'd been
chargehand porter for the shift, and come down to keep
an intimidating eye on one of our more aggressive customers. After the latter had wandered sullenly off, back
into the night, I'd returned to my office to catch up on
some reading; and was halfway through the accompanying
cheese and pickle sandwich when Adrian stuck his head
round the door.

'Caught you.'

'In-flight refuelling,' I pointed out, mouth impolitely full.

He made a show of nodding, his eyes amused. 'All okay
now?'

'Fine,' I told him gratefully. 'Thanks for coming down.'

'No problem.' He paused for a moment, looking
thoughtful; not quite meeting my eye. Then: 'Listen . . .
what are you doing next week?'

'Oh. Well . . .' I smiled, and let my own gaze drift while
my mind went into fast forward. 'I'm not sure of my Off-
duty yet . . .'

The nursing equivalent of *I'm washing my hair*, and he
knew it. Accepted it too, with a rueful smile of his own,
and left it lying. 'Fair enough. By the way . . . how's Danny
getting on?'

Our departmental porter. I pulled a face which probably
spoke volumes.

34

His smile became a grin. 'Not that bad, is he?'

I hesitated, feeling suddenly almost guilty. 'Well, no he's not. He's all right, actually. It's just . . .'

And that was it: there was nothing I could put my finger on. No aspect of his work that I could fault. He was off tonight, but he'd have handled that drunken loudmouth competently enough. A tested member of the team, now: conscientious and quiet. I just didn't like him. For no good reason, he gave me the creeps.

Mea culpa, I suppose. Nobody's perfect.

'He'll settle in soon enough,' Adrian predicted drily: his tone suggesting he knew what I meant. 'You get any problems, let me know.'

I nodded.

'You know . . .' he added musingly. 'If I was to have, like, a cardiac arrest right here . . . you'd be duty-bound to start resuscitating me, wouldn't you? Mouth to mouth, and . . .'

I grinned. 'Oh, I'd probably have to shove an airway down your throat first – make sure your breathing wasn't obstructed. Then cannulate a nice large vein . . .'

'Mm. On second thoughts . . .'

'. . . and zap you with a couple of hundred joules on the defib . . .'

'Yes. Good job I'm feeling fine, really, innit?' He winked. 'I'll see you, Rachel.'

I gave him a cheerful little wave, and listened to his slow departing footsteps; then took another bite of sandwich, and returned my attention to *Burns and Their Treatment (Illustrated)*.

Saturday night was probably going to be busier (much busier, knowing our luck) but I was off, so it wasn't my worry. I woke up late on the Saturday afternoon, and just slouched around in my T-shirt for a bit, enjoying the peace and quiet of having the flat to myself. Not that I begrudged

Sarah her share of the place: she's my flatmate – bright, slightly scatterbrained, works on Surgical – and good company as well as someone to split the rent with. I get on with her well enough – and in fact, with her working days and me on nights, we're not tripping over each other that often. But there are times when you do need space to yourself, without heaps of ironing on chairs, half-cooked meals in the kitchen, or strange boyfriends wandering out of the bathroom when you least expect it.

For my own part, I'd started sleeping regularly with Wendy again. I'd thought it was all over; but now I found I was needing the company more and more. Someone to snuggle up with. Someone to hold on to in the dark. She was still in my room, lying lax on my unmade bed – an outsize rag doll, smiling brightly at the ceiling. I'd won her in a kids' unit Christmas raffle: years ago.

The cat sidled up to rub itself against my leg as I made myself some toast and coffee. We call him Trinity, which is different, I suppose. Ignoring his wheedling on the grounds that he'd already been fed twice today, I stared out of the window at the neighbouring rooftops and back gardens. The sky was overcast: sullen with cloud. Someone was working on his shed, but other than that it was all quiet: the stillness of a winter afternoon. For no particular reason, I found myself recalling Saturday teatime when I was a kid: my dad and older brother watching the football results while mum and I made the tea and toast, cosy in the kitchen as the outside daylight cooled and faded.

A quick glance under the grill told me the bread was just as white as it had been thirty seconds ago, and I turned back to the window. The radio was chattering happily to itself in the background, and I was ignoring that too, scarcely noticing as the commercial break faded into the local news – but the lead headline put a hook through my idling attention and drew my head round sharply.

Murdered.

36

That word registered at once; the rest of the sentence took a moment to make sense around it.

'. . . *a man has been found murdered in a derelict house in* . . .'

Our town. Suddenly I felt my thumb between my teeth.

'. . . *multiple stab wounds. A post-mortem examination* . . .'

Now there was a rarity – even for a place as big and rough as this one's getting. We were promised coverage of a scheduled press conference in the next bulletin, and the reporter passed on to other matters – but he left me well behind, still worrying his words – running them through my mind again, and then again. Of course I knew that most murders happen within a family, or circle of acquaintances: the chances were this was just some private, vicious settling of scores. Over and done with. The idea of some maniac walking around – catching people alone and slaughtering them for the hell of it – flitted quickly through my head, but without conviction. That sort of thing might happen in films, or even America; but not *here*. No; the slightly sick disquiet I suddenly felt came from memories of mutilation I'd seen myself. Not the rough and random mutilation of the car-smash, though, nor even the crude carving of a knife or broken bottle. Rather the precise and pitiless intervention of surgical steel – and outcomes in terms of a heart burst open, a brain top-sliced; a uterus scarred and sterile. Over the past year, someone with detailed medical knowledge had done all that, and maybe more – and maybe he was a maniac, at that. Or maybe something worse.

Much worse. I sensed where my thoughts were going, and almost shook my head to clear it. *Pack it in*, I told myself flatly: *no more nightmares*. It was daylight, after all, and the real world was all around me. And there was evil enough in some of the human beings out there, without me having to invent spectres of my own . . .

Murdered . . .

I became aware of a sharp reek in my nostrils then: the toast had burned black, and was starting to smoulder.

With Sarah away for the weekend, I had an uninterrupted, empty evening in front of the TV, and an early night. But Sunday was a better day: brighter; clearer. I knew it was a day to visit Jenny.

I took the first bus of the afternoon, travelling across town to the Milston Road cemetery through streets that were quiet and all but empty, apart from the occasional car or someone walking his dog. Getting off by the corner shop just down the road, which really did seem to be open all hours, I bought a modest bunch of flowers (their selection wasn't that great) before walking slowly on to the open iron gates, and through them into the sunlit silence of the graveyard.

It was an ideal afternoon, fine and crisp; the twigs and branches of denuded trees standing out sharply against the clean, cold blue of the sky. The lawns were tidy as ever; the whole layout of the place spoke of restfulness and calm. I walked past the ordered plots without hurrying, making the most of the atmosphere . . . the peace . . . and enjoying the refreshing keenness of the air. But perhaps there was a certain reluctance too that made me tarry: a lurking unwillingness to reach the place I was heading for, and face its reality once again.

At length I got there none the less – the youngest corner of the cemetery, where the long, narrow mounds of earth had yet to be concealed by slabs and headstones. In a way they seemed the better marker: the natural brown of turned soil, offsetting the vivid splash of colour here and there where someone had placed fresh flowers. Much more moving than the ornate monuments of stone and marble all around me. But I knew how it was: how the earth had to be left to settle before the headstone could be erected. And *settle* meant subside, as the rotting coffin lid finally caved in, and dark earth slithered through to engulf its occupant's remains.

So how could I picture that happening to Jenny, whom I'd last seen six weeks ago, vivaciously alive, her blue eyes shining – surely not the same person who now lay, cold and still, six feet beneath the mound I'd paused before?

Still not quite believing it, I crouched and laid my flowers on the bare earth.

Silence. No voices or traffic; not even birds. I quite wanted to pray, but my mind just wouldn't focus. I just sat on my heels there, my coat brushing the dirt, and felt the hot, stinging wetness force its way into my eyes and nostrils. I couldn't keep it back. I didn't try.

After I'd finished, I sniffed, and wiped my cheeks, and blew my nose; and felt a little better. More time passed. Finally I gave a small sigh, and rose to my feet; walked over to a nearby bench and sat down.

I knew there were some things about her death I would never fully come to terms with. The shocking senselessness of it; the unanswered questions. But as I sat there, soaking up the atmosphere of calm and stillness around me, I reckoned I was slowly learning to live with it. The cry had done me good, cleared away a lot of pent-up grief and confusion. I still didn't know why she'd died – but the turmoil inside me had faded now, leaving a sort of resigned acceptance. I did know that I'd loved her very much – and that was a memory I could treasure, and always carry with me.

Letting my gaze ease off across the cemetery, I found myself musing that she probably wouldn't have wanted a burial – not a free-thinking, practical girl like Jenny. A clean cremation with minimal ceremony would have been much more her scene. I think the church service and the more permanent resting place had been for her mum's benefit: she'd wanted it that way. It had been a nice service, though. I'd cried then, too.

Still, there were worse places to be remembered. My eyes kept roving over the neatly regimented headstones – picking out the bright patch of a fresh floral tribute here and there; pausing briefly on the occasional fellow-mourner among the graves. Coming to rest on the tramp standing beneath a yew tree some fifty yards along the roadway.

Watching me.

I blinked; frowned slightly. I couldn't make out his face, not clearly, but I was sure he was watching me. He stood motionless, hands buried in the pockets of an old gabardine coat. His hair was long, and straggling. I got the impression that, if the wind changed, I would smell him from here.

His appearance wasn't unusual, of course: over the past two years the number of homeless in the town had increased quite markedly, with people being attracted down here by empty promises of work. We had our share of squatters, and people who slept in doorways; and related problems like alcoholism and addiction too. We certainly dealt with the members of this underclass in Casualty often enough – not least the late Messrs Kaufmann and Johnston. What really made me angry was the truth behind Karen's black joke about human experimentation: the fact that people didn't seem to give a damn.

I hoped that I did: I certainly felt the shortcomings of the society in which I lived so comfortably, and felt them keenly. But ideals are easy; the acid test is how you relate to the individual vagrant, and all his dirt.

He was beginning to make me nervous.

I looked away, back towards Jenny's grave; then across to the other side of the cemetery, contemplating the view with a show of interest.

After a minute or two, I looked back. He was still there. He hadn't moved at all.

When I looked away this time, it was to see if anyone else was nearby – and close enough to lend moral support, if need be. But this part of the cemetery was deserted. Of course there were one or two other people around, but they were occupied with their own grief: heedless for a time of the wider world's concerns.

The atmosphere had gone: the peace was sullied. And though loath to break off my communion with Jenny, I suddenly felt a pressing urge to get away, well clear of this empty place, and back where there were people round me. Rising to my feet, I glanced his way again. No reaction. I turned my back on him, and started walking towards the gates, with a briskness of stride that I hoped was suggestive of irritation rather than flight.

I got about ten yards before giving in to the temptation to look behind me. I had to see if he was following.

He wasn't. He'd disappeared.

I stopped, and glanced round quickly. No sign of him, which I found vaguely unsettling – although there was the odd clump of bushes around that could easily provide cover, and he might even have gone to ground amid the headstones. The fact that he was no longer there was hardly a reassurance; the reverse, if anything. It's like when you discover a large spider lurking motionless in your bedroom (if you're an arachnophobe like me, anyway): so long as you can see it, you know where you are; but then your attention wanders, and when you glance back at the wall, it's not there any more, and you've no idea where it's gone to. But it's around somewhere: and you've got to sleep in here tonight.

I hastily resumed my walk towards the gates. Reaching them, I turned back one more time. But the graveyard was as empty and unthreatening as it had been when I arrived, and the tattered man was nowhere to be seen.

I kept on walking, thoughtfully: a bit uncomfortable with my reaction, now that he was gone. Knowing bloody well I'd reacted like that before – and would do so again.

Take that time the other week.

It had been something of a fraught night. With the clock unhurriedly edging towards midnight-thirty, the department already reeked of sour alcohol; there were people just wandering around. Patients, relatives, a stray policeman. There was shouting and laughter; voices drunkenly amplified. Someone had just puked on the floor in cubicle six. Kathy was keeping amazingly calm, considering.

Most of the noise stemmed from a bunch of off-duty squaddies waiting in reception while one of their mates got his hand stitched. They were all in scruffy civvies, but there was still a depressing uniformity in their cropped scalps and loud, livid faces. They were uniformly pissed, as well.

It had been hard enough to concentrate with just that row going on; we didn't need chatting up as well. Eventually Mike (whom no one tried to chat up) managed to usher them out along with their patched-up friend, ignoring shouts of 'you Mick poufter' and similar valedictions. I'd caught Brenda's eye, and we'd shared a heartfelt sigh of relief.

Mike came back, muttering something about the bloody IRA never being around when they were needed.

Five minutes later, there was a dog in the department.

Bren almost dropped the tetanus set she'd been preparing as the Alsatian stuck its nose around the utility room door before padding off down the corridor. I was trying to keep order in the cubicles, and turned at the sound of her surprised little gasp – looking in through the opposite doorway. I saw, swore, and went after it – but someone down at reception was already shouting 'Carl! Heel!', and the dog – it was an awfully big dog – was disappearing back in that direction even as I reached the main corridor. Determinedly I followed.

By the time I got there it was back with its owner, sitting at his feet as he stroked its dirty fur. The man was slouched in one of the chairs – they were mostly empty now – and looked me challengingly in the face as I came through. And I stared irritably back at him, taking in the state of his clothes – the patched, faded flak jacket; his stubble beard, and unwashed hair, drawn back into a ponytail. I guessed he was one of the Travellers.

We'd been having problems with the Travellers of late. Or the hippies, as some called them; or gyppos, or worse. It seemed they came and went with the seasons; wandering in and pitching camp; being evicted and moving on. Quite a crowd had decided to winter in our town this time around; people were starting to complain.

'Look, if you can't keep that dog under control, you'll have to leave,' I told him, tightly.

He shrugged, didn't reply. His eyes hadn't left my face.

'Can I help you?' I went on: quite formally, but with no politeness at all.

'You're really welcoming tonight,' he muttered.

'We're busy: have you got a problem or . . . ?'

I felt his gaze drop to my throat, and the crucifix I wore there.

'You a Christian?' he asked suddenly.

I blinked, and almost said *None of your business*; then nodded.

'You could have fooled me,' he said evenly.

That stung.

For a moment I was really tempted to say *Well sod you, mate* – even if not in so many words. I was in the wrong, and knew it, and buggered if I was going to admit it. So it took quite a struggle before I was able to draw breath, manage a smile, and murmur, 'Sorry.'

He held up one hand, palm outward, revealing an oozing gash. 'Did this on some barbed wire.'

I nodded. 'Looks nasty.' I picked up a casualty card from the front desk and came back. After a moment's hesitation – I knew he'd noticed – I sat down beside him.

'Don't smell very nice, do I?' he said drily, and glanced across.

I met his gaze. 'You were right: it shouldn't make any difference, should it?'

But it had, of course. And still I hadn't bloody learned.

The Sunday bus service being what it is, I decided I'd walk at least part of the way home. I knew a few shortcuts, and it was still light enough to take them – though the sun was getting lower and colder all the while. From Milston Road I took the footbridge over the ringway, and on through the Stoneham Estate towards the town centre; scenting a foretaste of dusk frost on the air, along with the cooking smells of Sunday tea that wafted out from warm bright kitchens. I missed the bus at the corner of Clarke Street and had to cut across through Lamborn. That's one of the older parts of town: a lot of the houses are empty, boarded up. But I was halfway down Stone Road before it dawned on me that yesterday's murder had happened here – in one of these derelict buildings I was passing. The realization brought me up short.

I don't think it was fear I felt, even though the shadows were lengthening on the street. Rather, it was a macabre curiosity. The news reports on last night's TV had taken every opportunity to emphasize the gruesome nature of the killing: apparently the poor bloke had been cut to pieces. I tried to remember if they'd actually mentioned which of the empty houses the remains had been discovered in – number eighteen I decided, after a moment – and here it was just coming up on the left. I stopped again.

It was getting chilly. There was no one on the street. I knew I should be pushing on for home, not hanging around; especially when I was lingering in the fresh footsteps of a murderer. But the house exerted its own grim fascination. Two storeys high, with slates missing from the roof and windows blocked off with chipboard: one empty slum in half a terrace of them. I stood there before it, scanning its impassive façade; trying, almost despite myself, to visualize the darkened rooms within – and what had happened there.

And then the front door swung gratingly open, and I almost jumped out of my shoes.

A uniformed policeman, buttoned up in his anorak, appeared in the doorway. The surge of adrenaline had left me feeling sick and giddy, and I could only stand there getting my breath back as he eyed me with some disdain. Obviously he'd been detailed to keep the place secure until the forensics and scene-of-crime teams had finished; and to discourage the morbidly curious, like me. The cold must have driven him indoors from his exposed position on the front step; he'd probably been having a cup of tea in the back or something.

'Would you mind moving on, miss? Nothing to see here.'

Actually it was Bill Roberts, who was regularly up at our department on some business or other: last week it had been an argumentative drunk. He hadn't recognized me, and was putting on his most patronizing voice-of-authority tone. I couldn't help smiling, in the circumstances.

After a moment, recognition dawned, and he relaxed, grinning apologetically. 'Afternoon, Rachel – sorry, didn't recognize you in civvies.'

I'd heard it suggested, rather unkindly, that he wouldn't recognize a thief if the man walked past him wearing a mask and carrying a sack with SWAG written on it. But he was a decent enough bloke, when he wasn't throwing his weight around, and I could at least try and find out what he knew.

'They finished in there yet?'

He shrugged. 'I dunno. Might have. Shit, but the guy was in a mess . . .'

45

'So I heard.'

'You haven't heard the half of it.' He paused then, clearly wondering whether he should say more. I raised my eyebrows in mild enquiry; and after a moment he decided that this was one professional to another, and continued.

'You remember that RTA, beginning of November?'

I knew which road traffic accident he meant: I was still trying to forget it. I nodded.

'Well this was worse.'

Must have been bad. 'How do you mean?' I asked, interested.

'Well, this guy had been all split open too — only not torn this time, but cut, all neat and clean. That's what makes it worse, it was so cold-blooded: sort of *clinical* . . .'

Clinical. The word lodged and grew cold inside my head; I felt my stomach shift uneasily. My gaze strayed to the open doorway behind him — a gaping entrance into blackness. The blinded windows stared down at us, and were they really so unseeing? Abruptly I found myself struggling to suppress a shiver.

It must have shown in my face, for he looked at me quizzically. 'Hey, you okay? Sorry, I thought you Casualty nurses were used to this sort of thing.'

Used to what? I thought dully; my skin still recalling the chill of Alison Scott's cubicle. I could still see the fear in her fixed, dilated stare as well. And smell the sickly sweetness of her post-operative infection . . .

Cutting. Cold. *Clinicians*.

I grimaced, and glanced away.

The nearby streetlamp came on: sputtering pink that steadied to a deepening rosy glow. I looked at my watch, and was about to make my excuses when a car turned into the street and drove up to park at the kerb close by me. The man who got out wore plain clothes but was obviously another police officer, and this time it was he who recognized me first.

'Hi, Sis – how are things?'

Joe Davies, indeed: I'd last seen him a couple of months back, when he was still in uniform. About the same age as his colleague (about the same age as me, come to that), he was cooler, sharper, with straight fair hair, and pale restless eyes behind designer specs. On the beat, he'd always been careless of the finer details of uniform dress: you could count on noticing a button undone here, a scuffed toecap there. Now he was plainclothes, this tendency had been allowed to develop further, so that, though he wore a suit, his shirt was unironed, and his tie hung slack beneath an open collar.

His question had been rhetorical: without waiting for an answer, he turned to Roberts. 'All quiet?'

The PC grunted.

I gave Davies a quizzical look. 'Thought I heard you were with the vice unit these days.'

He grinned. 'You heard right.'

I waited for him to elaborate. When he didn't, I nodded towards the house. 'So?'

For a moment he was reticent, as Roberts had been before him. But I knew he'd come round. When it comes down to it, everyone trusts a nurse.

He shrugged. 'It'll be in the papers soon enough, I suppose. The dear departed was a pimp, and probably into drug pushing too. We'd been watching him for quite a while. Bit of a bastard, by all accounts.'

I felt a sudden warm tingle of relief go through me. After a moment my mind caught up, and realized why. 'And you reckon this was just a sort of gangland thing – drug pushers falling out?'

Again he shrugged. 'Who knows? Maybe it was more personal – he used to beat his girls up regular: I think you had one come in to you not long back, but she wouldn't press charges. Maybe one of them had a big brother with a nasty temper . . .'

47

'Very nasty,' Roberts put in, with feeling.

'Anyway,' Davies continued, ignoring the comment, 'we'll probably know more once we get the results of the p-m. The official one, I mean.'

I hesitated. 'There was an unofficial one?'

'Yes. Oh yes.' He gave me a chilling little smile. 'It happened right upstairs. Every organ cut out of him, and not a knife-stroke out of place. The best pathologist in the business couldn't have sliced him up better.'

'Oh,' I said faintly, and relief died like a candle in the cold.

Of course they would go on looking, for vicious drug dealers, or violent people pushed too far; but now I knew they'd be wasting their time. Something way beyond the imagination of your ordinary copper had come to this dark and mouldy house – and murdered once again.

Another *drip* against the stone. Cold water. Or colder blood . . .

And Davies, as he turned towards the house, couldn't resist adding one final grisly detail. 'When the Home Office guy did his preliminary examination up there in the bedroom, he reckoned there was a possibility the poor sod was still alive when whoever it was began cutting. Still alive, and still conscious . . .'

He nodded a farewell and went on into the dark doorway. Roberts smiled, half-apologetically. 'I shouldn't let it worry you too much, Rachel. Probably just dealers settling scores . . .'

'I know: don't have nightmares, right?' I couldn't help the edge of sarcasm in my voice, but he didn't seem to notice.

'All the same . . .' He glanced up at the cold, colourless sky. 'I'd be getting along if I was you. Soon be dark. Safe home, eh?'

'Yeah. Thanks.' I watched him re-enter the house, closing the door behind him; then turned and continued along

Stone Road. And though I was glad, very glad, to get to be able to put some distance between myself and number eighteen, having to turn my back on that grim, befouled place didn't make me feel better at all.

After a minute, I began to walk a little faster.

Five

Monday night it was back to business.

I'd prepared for it in the usual way: late night on the Sunday, and as much sleep as I could get during Monday. It had been another bright day, and oblivion hadn't come easy – not with the sounds of everyday life filtering through the curtains along with the sunlight. I was lucky this was a fairly quiet street, with only the occasional car and a few kids playing. Oh yes, and the sodding ice-cream van rolling up at three o'clock playing *Greensleeves* in a peal of loud, distorted chimes.

It was well dark by the time I caught the bus up to the hospital: several other night-shift workers were already aboard, or got on with me, and most of them I knew. I swapped anecdotes with Janice, a nurse from Theatres; and cheerfully endured the jokes of Ken, a security man at one of the sites on the neighbouring industrial estate. But some of my attention was inescapably caught by the sight of the hospital itself, looming darkly into view against the dimness of the sky. Like a black fortress in the night, with many windows dark, or dimly-curtained, but others watchfully ablaze. I've always loved the life of Nights, the wakefulness in a sleeping world – the atmosphere of a place that's never sleeping; merely sedated. But a hospital at night has its eerie side too; its sinister shadows. It was that aspect that struck me most forcibly now.

It wasn't even that I was thinking particularly about the murders and mysteries of the past few days, and weeks, and months. Routine's the great comforter; and the prospect of a busy night in Casualty was enough to clear the excess mental baggage from anyone's mind. I knew I still had fears lurking there below the surface; but real life went on. It had to.

The bus pulled in across the forecourt from our department's brightly-lit canopy, and I disembarked. At least there weren't any ambulances parked askew outside the doors, blue lights still pulsing, so I hoped I wouldn't be pitched straight in.

I changed into my uniform in the locker room: fastening the close-fitting navy dress up to the collar; unzipping the cuffs and rolling the sleeves back to my elbows. I was still trying to fix my cap on with one hairgrip too few when Judith, one of my counterparts on Days, came in and joined me at the mirror.

'Rachel. It's good to have you back.'

Sister Parsons — Judith, but never Judy. Despite her silver-grey hair she was still in her forties; and her vivid blue eyes were those of someone younger still. A northerner with a brisk — some would say brusque — manner, and I knew some of the students didn't get on with her: but that was their loss, for she was everything that they aspired to be: competent, calm and compassionate. I reckoned she mothered me sometimes, but I didn't mind. Sometimes I needed it.

'Busy shift?' I asked, through a mouthful of protruding hairgrips.

'Not too bad. One RTA in for observation; a few cuts and bruises. One OD — a bottle of paracetamol and maybe half a bottle of vodka. And she didn't look a day over sixteen, poor girl.'

I grimaced. 'Bet the wash-out was fun. She okay?'

'We hope so. The Medical team admitted her, anyway.'

'Let's hope it stays quiet.' I finished adjusting my cap and stepped back to admire the result; then turned and grinned at her.

'You're settling back into the routine, then?' Her own

smile was fond. 'But then you've always been able to adapt. Some people your age would find being on permanent nights just impossible to adjust to. But you love it, don't you?'

It was true: as I said, the atmosphere grows on you. Maybe most women my age would prefer the more ordered social life of a day job; but not having a partner or any family commitments made this option just as easy for me. Unsocial hours make for good rates of pay; and besides, the social life in this town is practically non-existent anyway.

I adjusted the fob-watch pinned over my breast, and she glanced down at hers. 'Parker's doing handover tonight . . .' – I placed the face, nodded – 'Apparently she still remembers you telling her to get her hair off her collar on her first night down here . . .'

I remembered it too: she'd seemed quite nonplussed, getting that attitude off a girl only three years older than she was. 'It was rather a heavy shift,' I pointed out, defensively.

Judith's smile widened. 'Well it did the trick, anyway. And niggles aside, she's turning into a damned good Casualty nurse. She's got another block of nights coming up next month; you can really start polishing her up then.'

I nodded again – and realized how good it felt, being treated as a fellow-professional by the nurse I most respected; sharing together in the development of our staff. She was right, Staff Nurse Joanna Parker was going to go far. I hoped I'd be able to bring out the best in her along the way.

Nice to be back, Judith.

Karen came in at that point, already in uniform apart from her cap and belt. We all said our hellos, and Judith left us to finish getting ready, as the clock eased round to the start of one more working night.

*　　*　　*

The department was still fairly busy, and Joanna had perched herself on the doctors' desk by Cubicles to give report; I was sure Judith wouldn't have approved, but she was behind a curtain helping with somebody's dressing. Me, I didn't mind. I'd done the same often enough.

'Right,' she said, glancing down her page of notes; her stethoscope still slung around her neck. 'One RTA in Short Stay for overnight obs; Darren Allen, age 24, query concussion. Bloke with a gashed leg in Cubicle Four . . .' And so on down the list: those patients in their various stages of treatment, and those who'd been clerked-in but had yet to see the doctor. The last couple of hours seemed to have been heavier than Judith had let on, but Joanna seemed to have come through it all cheerfully enough. No tinge of tiredness in her fresh, freckle-dusted face, and her voice was bright and lively.

She was wearing her mousy hair well off her collar, too. '. . . Query pneumothorax in Six, Mrs Jean Fowler, 51 . . .' And Mike and a couple of students stepped aside to let the Medical Houseman get at the X-ray viewing box, slapping the black film up under the clip. The white, eerie glow lit up the image, outlining the shadowy lungs. One was obviously distorted. One more bed filled; or were they full up already, and phoning around? From the grimness on the doctor's face as he studied the X-ray, I guessed it might well be the latter.

That might make for some fun later on, if they started backing up into here.

I looked back to Joanna as she finished. A routine workload, then; nothing dramatic. Nothing life-threatening. Mike, Karen and the rest had taken down what notes they'd needed, and began dispersing with a general murmur of thanks. I thanked her too – with a compliment that brought a pleased little smile – and went to get the drug keys off Judith. 'I'll leave things in your capable hands, then,' she said as she handed them over; then gave an exaggerated sigh, and smiled afresh. 'Right: time to see if Jack read the instructions right, or if he's burned his supper again. At least the traffic should be better than it was this afternoon . . .'

We said goodbye; and as she went on down towards the changing room, her parting shot was *Have a nice night*.

She really meant it, too – which just goes to show how worthless good wishes sometimes are.

We had a fairly steady throughput of patients – all walking wounded – to start with; but by half-past midnight things had quietened down considerably – so much so that I reckoned we could take our staggered meal-breaks up in the canteen (sometimes when it's busy we have to send someone up with a trolley, and we eat off our knees down here in the duty room). It was getting on for one when my turn came round. I unclipped the bunch of ward keys – the true symbol of authority – from the safety pin on my lapel and passed them to Mike, and Karen and I went up together. I was still carrying the departmental bleep, tucked away under my cardi: any crises and I'd be right down again.

Half of the canteen was in darkness; the rest was bright, and fairly busy, with nurses filtering down from the various wards, and a huddle of porters round one of the window tables. Despite the mediocrity of the food, the place always gave me a strangely upbeat feel: an island of light at the very heart of the dark and dormant hospital. Karen and I loaded up our trays and joined the queue; I was first past the till, and nodded towards the table by the Coke machine, where Anne O'Brien from ENT was already tucking in.

She looked up, smiling, as we joined her. 'Hiya. Quiet tonight?'

'Apart from the twenty-eight-car pile-up,' I said airily. 'We're putting a brave face on it.'

Karen unclipped her belt with a grateful little sigh, tucking the ends into the pockets of her dress. 'How's the curry?' she asked, studying her plate without enthusiasm.

'About two spoonfuls short of critical mass.' Annie wrinkled her nose in a mischievous grin, and set about raking up another forkful. She was halfway through eating it when her eyes suddenly widened, and she leaned forward with a (slightly muffled) exclamation of interest. 'Hey, is that the ring, then?'

Karen glanced down at the gold circle with its small, bright diamond, fastened to her dress with the clip of her fob-watch so as to leave her hands clear for work. Her smile was tinged with the hint of a blush.

'Yeah. He gave it to me tonight – just before I came in to work. Can't wait to wear it proper . . .'

Staff Nurse Karen Kane: three years younger than me, and very much in love. It wasn't surprising, she was attractive enough, in a bright-eyed, slightly nervous-looking way. She'd been seeing Steve, her bloke, for nearly a year now, and he'd finally popped the question a week ago. Not surprisingly she was over the moon about that – though she hadn't let such distractions affect her professionalism, and remained as clear-headed and competent as ever. A good nurse and a good friend, and I enjoyed working with her on both counts. I didn't get the chance as often as I'd have liked, because she was normally on Days, with stints of Nights according to the department's internal rota. But with the purchase of a house now looming, she'd been working extra nights in anticipation of the mortgage.

'Named the day yet?' Anne asked; but before Karen could answer, the bleep on my belt went off with a rapid staccato of pips, and we all tensed. Cardiac arrest group alert: with a forkful of chips poised halfway to my mouth I waited for the voice-over.

The message came crackling over the channel a moment later: '*Cardiac arrest, Coronary Care . . .*' It repeated four times, but we were already relaxing, the instinctive surge of adrenaline thinning out. Not one of ours, not this time . . . One of the porters at the window table had got the call too, on the cardiac bleep, and left at a sprint, ready to assist upstairs.

Karen glanced after him, then back at me. She shrugged.

'Anyone notice what was for pudding?' Anne asked.

'Fruit pie.'

'Meaning rhubarb?'

'Usually.' I grimaced. 'Among other things.'

She decided to risk it anyway, and while she was paying, the two of us moved on to speculate whether Staff Nurse Mike Shannon was likely to get off with Staff Nurse Brenda Griffiths. Karen doubted it, but on balance I reckoned they'd go well together; apart from anything else, Mike was Irish and Bren was Welsh, so there might at least be an element of Celtic solidarity there. Mike was in his thirties, energetic and cheerful, his rather boyish good looks tempered by the premature grey in his dark hair and beard. Brenda was more Karen's age, very demure and quiet-spoken; but her smile was as spontaneous as sunshine, and it rarely failed to lift our spirits.

'So when are we going to get you fixed up, then?' Karen wanted to know, an impish little sparkle in her eyes. 'No eligible young medics around? How about that Dr Wright?'

I grinned. 'I don't think so, somehow. He's a nice bloke, but . . .'

But I'm not ready to get hitched yet, Kaz. Still too restless . . .

Break was over all too soon. Finishing our cigarettes (you'd be surprised how many nurses smoke), we said goodbye to Anne, picked up our bags and made our unhurried way back downstairs to the department. The waiting area was still nearly empty — just a couple of people slouched in the chairs, and a girl standing over by the drinks machine, head down as if counting her last pennies.

Apart from a long brown scarf and gloves, she was dressed, rather scruffily, in black from the boots up: tight jeans, long threadbare coat and a flat-brimmed cowboy hat. The Gypsy Goth look, I decided. My cursory glance took in the fact that her dark hair was cropped close to her skull, with a single braid curling down below her collar. And even indoors, in the dark small hours of a winter's morning, she was wearing shades.

I assumed she'd been clerked-in, but checked with Mike anyway as I retrieved my keys. He raised his eyebrows.

'Far as I know we've just got two blokes waiting – a cut hand and a sprained wrist; plus the guy with Graham in Suturing now . . .'

I glanced down the corridor towards the suturing room. 'What happened to him?'

'Argument in a nightclub – *Ramon's*, I think; it usually is. Some charmer smashed a glass in his face.'

'Bad?'

'Pretty superficial – more blood than damage. But he'll need a good few stitches.'

And Dr Graham Hancock doing the needlework. Lucky man. Graham was one of our less charming doctors, short on patience and especially surly in the small hours. 'Who's helping him? Helen?'

He nodded. 'Good practice for her: how to put up with an SHO who reckons he needs his beauty sleep.'

I smiled at that. 'How about the sprained wrist: he been X-rayed yet?'

'They should be about ready for him now. Shall I . . . ?'

'I'll take him round if you like.' This from Karen, just back from locking her bag away. She still wore her blue cardigan: it was at least one size too large, giving her a slightly forlorn look.

'If you would, thanks.' I fastened the clinking bunch of

keys back on to my lapel. 'And I'll go find out what our latest customer wants.'

She was sitting down when I re-entered the waiting area, holding a plastic cup of coffee in both shabby-gloved hands. I guessed she was making the most of its heat; to judge by the state of her clothes, she was currently living rough – or maybe in a squat, if she was lucky. Everything looked dirty and ill-fitting: the coat nearly ankle-length; the grey jersey beneath it reaching halfway to her knees. Even her high-laced boots were stuffed with thick socks. Her cropped, easy-clean hair suggested much the same thing. And I could smell her from here.

Another Traveller, then. Or one more real example of the destitution which our local politicians spoke about in such airy, abstract terms.

She was contemplating the drink as I came over, and didn't look up until I was standing in front of her and clearing my throat. Close to, her grubby face looked pale and very young – but I sensed an underlying hardness in her expression: a suggestion that this girl might be young in years but was old, old beyond measure, in experience. Bitter experience. Her eyes might have told me more, but they remained hidden; the black shades were impassive and vaguely unsettling.

'Excuse me *(miss? I left it hanging)*. . . can I help you at all?'

For a long moment I thought she wasn't going to reply; and, as I waited, became aware of the silence of our two other patients. I felt the tingle of their watchfulness on my back – and suddenly realized they were nervous. Two healthy, previously garrulous young lads had made sure there was a wide space between them and a solitary girl – and now sat stiff and uneasy in their chairs. In a way I didn't blame them. It was getting hard to face down that cool, eyeless gaze, and I broke the contact briefly, my attention switching to her hands, her chewed-down gloves; the glint of silver rings against her knuckles. One of them bore a pentagram sign. Another formed the double-mask motif of the theatre – except that both the faces were skulls, one leering, one grimacing: both staring emptily up at me.

I looked back to her face.

'I'd like to see the doctor, please,' she said in a low, slightly hoarse voice.

'What's the problem?'

'I've been sick ... past few days. Got the runs too. Liquids is all I can keep down.' She took a sip of coffee as if to prove the point.

'Have you been to your GP?'

She shook her head. 'Don't have one. I'm just ... passing through, you could say.'

I could indeed: we'd had her type in here often enough. The dog-handler had been the most recent example – and at least he'd presented with a genuine injury. Some of them came seeking shelter, however temporary; others hoped to be fobbed off with medication – free pills, if they could get them. In general, it was departmental policy to give such people short shrift; but then again, she didn't exactly look the picture of health; and who knew what lurking medical condition we might be turning away?

Better to be safe than sued (to put it realistically). And it would keep Graham on his toes for a while longer. With that not unpleasant thought, I relaxed slightly. 'All right. The doctor will take a look at you as soon as he can. In the meantime, can I just take a few details ... ?'

I sensed her gaze follow me suspiciously to the desk as I walked over to get a caz-card. 'Like what?'

'Just your name, address, date of birth – that sort of thing.' I had my pen poised, and was trying to be as conciliatory as possible. It was difficult. Someone else in need of a sympathetic face perhaps, but that was the last thing on my mind. She was giving me a chill.

'McCain,' she said, after a moment's hesitation. 'Carol McCain. No fixed address.'

'Date of birth?' I prompted hopefully.

She smiled then, albeit faintly. 'I'm older than I look,' was all she said.

I was back behind the desk making a Fracture Clinic appointment for our supposed 'sprained wrist' when her name was finally called. She rose slowly to her feet and followed Mike through towards the examination area, giving me a sidelong glance as she passed. I didn't realize how fixedly my eyes were following her until the waiting youth muttered: 'Getting to you, too, is she?'

I blinked. 'Sorry; where were we . . . ?' Returning my attention quickly to the clinic sheet; but he was still looking up the corridor, frowning slightly.

'Something weird about that one,' he said softly. 'Something really . . . *weird*.'

I wondered if he'd tried chatting her up or something. He gave the distinct impression of someone who fancied himself, as well as anything in skirts. Perhaps her rebuff had been unexpectedly cold. Yet there wasn't the tang of sour grapes about his attitude; rather a puzzlement that bordered on unease . . .

'We do get some odd customers at this time of night,' I allowed, neutrally. 'You get used to it after a while.'

Famous last words.

I finished writing up his booking, and watched him walk off into the night clutching his appointment card, his forearm encased in plaster. The two patients who'd needed stitching up had also departed; a couple more minor injuries had joined the queue. It was proving to be an average-to-quiet night on the whole. I started back up the corridor, and met Graham halfway. He was looking tired, his plump face pale and slack.

'Just another three,' I told him mercilessly, and he cast a wistful glance towards the duty room, where the plasterman on call was just about to brew up.

'What've we got in One?' he asked with resignation.

'Bad case of D&V, apparently: says she hasn't been able to eat for a few days. She's been sleeping rough . . .'

He gave me an exasperated look. 'Rachel. She should see a doctor in town: sign on as a temporary resident. This is supposed to be a department for accidents and emergencies, for God's sake . . .'

I shrugged. 'Well she's here now, and we're hardly rushed off our feet, are we?' He opened his mouth to protest further, and I added: 'And besides, who's to say it's not something serious? Come on, Graham, you might as well take a look at her.' *So we can get rid of her as soon as possible,* I almost added.

'All right, all right.' He yawned, and glanced at his watch; then again towards the duty room, where the first hissings of the kettle could now be clearly heard.

'Don't worry, we'll leave some for you,' I assured him. He gave me another look, as though – for some reason – unconvinced by the sweetness of my smile; then muttered something under his breath, and turned back towards the examination area.

I wandered into the duty room, where Dave, the plaster technician, was studying the dented kettle as if willing it to boil more quickly. 'He's in a good mood tonight,' he observed drily.

'Isn't he always?' I sat down in one of the low, shabby chairs, feeling the webbing sag beneath me. Unlacing my shoes, I slipped them off and leaned back, flexing my stockinged feet.

'I've seen firemen with shorter ladders,' he said, without appearing to look.

'Piss off.'

He grinned at that, watching me crane forward to

61

examine my tights. There was more to Our Dave (as we called him, to avoid confusion with one of the regular ambulancemen) than met the eye: a quirky sense of humour lurking behind that placid exterior. I was settling back in my chair again when Mike stuck his head round the door.

'Hey, Raitch . . . How many Goths does it take to change a lightbulb?'

'None, they all prefer sitting in the dark,' I said comfortably. 'Go away.'

'Damn, she's heard it before,' Karen muttered in the background. The two of them wandered disconsolately back towards reception.

Dave nodded towards the kettle as it bubbled towards climax. 'Want one?'

'Please. Coffee if you're making it.'

'How about his lordship?'

'I think he might appreciate it.' And to be fair, the man had been on duty since nine o'clock the previous morning.

'Tea, coffee?'

I wasn't sure: it had been so long since he'd last deigned to take tea with us. 'Hang on, I'll go and ask him.'

I put my shoes back on and went through into Examination, a long, over-lit room fairly wallpapered with charts for instant reference: toxic substances, advice on Hep-B (*All blood is guilty until proved innocent*), Wallace's ubiquitous Rule of Nines for the assessment of burns . . . Ten trolley-beds formed a row down one side, individually curtained-off into examination cubicles. Only the one was in use at the moment, furthest from the door. I walked down past the sinks and the X-ray viewing boxes and the desk for writing up notes, glancing into each of the empty cubicles to check that all was tidy and in order; if not it would give us something to do if things stayed quiet. Thus occupied, I had almost reached the last cubicle before it registered that there was no sound of voices coming from behind its drawn curtains — and for no logical reason, I suddenly hesitated. And the silence persisted.

I could understand a few moments' quiet to ponder a symptom; but an examination is more than anything a verbal process — the doctor's questions, the patient's replies. Yet the stillness was total: I couldn't even hear any movement in there. And I realized then that my nerves had begun to tingle, as though sensing something ominous and threatening, separated from me by no more than the thickness of that plain green curtain.

My overactive imagination again, of course. More likely she'd wandered off somewhere and Graham had gone looking for her. I drew back the curtain anyway.

In that first split-second I glimpsed enough: the white-coated figure on the floor beside the trolley, the black-clad figure bending over it, and straightening as I came through; the glint of a drawn knife in the harsh light. And I'd been on the Control & Restraint courses, knew all about how to reason with a knife-wielding patient — but as those sombre shades came round all I wanted to do was turn and run. I got as far as the turn. Before I could run, or even shout for help, her fist was in my hair and dragging my head back, stretching my throat so I choked on my cry and could only gawp soundlessly as she hauled me back into the cubicle. Desperately I threshed at the end of her arm, struggling to get free, to stop the white, ripping pain in my scalp: arms bent back, both hands scrabbling at hers now, trying to pry those fingers loose. But effortlessly she drew me in. From the corner of my eye I caught the gleam of the knife, and with a last frenzied effort managed to twist half around and lash out, knocking the glasses from her face.

I glimpsed eyes that were a cold and bleached-out blue, in the instant that the bright light struck them. The pupils reacted immediately, contracting to pinpoints, and with a snarl that was partly pain she jerked her face away.

Photophobia: she couldn't stand the light. And before I could even think to take advantage, she'd wrenched me right round by the hair and slammed me bodily against the back wall. Winded, I gasped aloud. The fingers in my hair loosened and withdrew; I felt her grasp my shoulder and turn me slowly round to face her.

And a quick, sickening punch to my midriff dropped me in a heap at her feet.

For a moment everything was just a queasy blur; my head echoed and spun, and I didn't even have the strength to retch. Then I became aware that she was sitting on her heels beside me.

She'd put her shades back on and pushed the wide-brimmed hat to the back of her head. The knife was cradled in both hands now, as though she was doing no more than idly weigh it, testing its balance. I managed to focus on the weapon, and it was a vicious-looking switchblade: cold, clean steel, and grips that looked like they'd been carved from bone. And for all the easiness with which she handled it, the point was still angled down towards me.

'I had questions for your doctor,' she told me, in the same dust-dry monotone she'd used before. 'He wouldn't answer them. I was about to show him the error of his ways, but . . .' She inclined her head, studying me thoughtfully. 'Perhaps you will answer them for me.'

Oh shit, I thought. Aloud I managed to ask: 'What . . . questions?'

'A young girl was brought into your department this evening: she'd overdosed – tried to kill herself. What happened to her?'

I swallowed. 'She was admitted . . .'

'Which ward?' And as I hesitated, with the instinctive reticence of someone for whom patient confidentiality was second nature, she leaned forward and hissed: 'Don't even dream of lying: I'll see it in your *soul*.'

I believed her, too: the shock of that icy gaze still

throbbed within me. It was fortunate that I was in a position to answer her, having browsed through the admissions ledger earlier in the evening. 'She went to Jenner Ward: that's Medical . . . second floor . . .'

She absorbed the information in silence for a moment; then reached slowly out with the knife and used the point to snag the silver chain of my crucifix, and lift the pendant clear of my collar. She spoke again, even more quietly than before.

'This. Is it just a trinket . . . or something more?'

Again I swallowed, trying to lubricate a mouth gone bone-dry. 'It's what I believe in. *Who* I believe in . . .'

She nodded, and let it fall back into the hollow of my throat. 'You'll need to,' she promised softly – and even her breath felt cold.

And with that she rose swiftly to her feet and was gone.

For a long moment after the curtain had flopped closed behind her, I just slumped there, eyes wide with disbelief. Then reaction set in – a sick and chilling surge that left me shivering. But despite the weakness that came with it, I began struggling to my feet.

I was halfway there when Mike stuck his head round the curtain to see how we were getting on: the shock that blanked-out his cheerful expression was so abrupt it was almost funny. 'Rachel – what –'

My legs nearly gave way at that point and I had to clutch at the trolley for support. He moved quickly forward but I waved him away: 'Okay. I'm okay. What about Graham . . . ?'

There was the sound of movement from the floor on the far side of the trolley, and a stifled groan. I leaned over. Graham was trying to sit up: his face paler than ever, and streaked with blood from a gash on his temple. I never thought I'd be so relieved to know he was still with us.

'What happened?' Mike was asking, even as he stooped to help the doctor up.

'That girl – she's a nutter, she's got a knife.' I paused for a gulp of air. 'Need to fast-bleep the porters, tell them she's after the girl on Jenner – the OD – ring the ward too. And the police . . .'

Karen was approaching by then, and detoured straight to the wall-mounted phone. I returned my attention to Graham, seated on the chair now, as Mike set about examining his wound; but when I glanced back at her, I saw the worried little frown creep over her features. She punched in the emergency number again.

'I can't get through – something's wrong with the phone, it's just whining . . .'

'Shit! Try the one in my office.' She hurried to do so, and I stumbled after her. I was more or less steady on my feet by the time I got there – but the expression on her face as she looked up from the phone was enough to stop me short.

'Same again – it's interference or something. Now I can't get a dial tone . . .'

'Oh my God . . .' I couldn't believe it: not another switchboard failure, not now. And that crazy woman with a knife was on her way up to a sleeping ward – and about to arrive without warning . . .

Mike had come up behind me, and was about to echo my disbelief when I turned and grasped his coat. 'Come on. We've got to go after her.'

He nodded, and we began to run. It was sheer instinct that prompted me to relinquish my keys, and I swung back round to toss them towards Karen; behind me, getting further away by the second, I heard Mike shouting, 'Danny. Where's Danny? Someone find the lazy sod!' And then I was racing after him, down past the treatment rooms and Suturing and Minor Theatre, and on into the dimly-lit corridor that led to the lifts.

Six

In that claustrophobic tunnel, the noise of our footfalls on the linoleum floor swelled and rebounded and echoed around us, effectively masking any sound from up ahead. Maybe she'd already reached the lifts, of course, or was fast approaching them; but perhaps she'd paused, and was lying in wait for any pursuers – especially ones as reckless as us. That thought occurred to me just before we reached an angle of the corridor, where it bypassed the plant room, but I was going too fast to stop now, and with the breath rasping in my throat I couldn't even voice a warning. Mike went round the corner first, and the adrenaline surged through me as I lost sight of him. But a moment later I'd followed suit, and had him back in view, still running, his white coat-tails flying – and beyond him a straight stretch of empty corridor, with the lift area at its end.

We ran for it, reached it, and skidded breathlessly to a halt, our eyes scanning the indicator lights. There were four lifts serving this end of the building, and two were still on our level, empty and unused. The third was out of order, which was par for the course.

The fourth was on its way up.

The indicator still showed our floor, but that was just the mechanism catching up. Even as we watched, it clicked up to the next level. Mike swore, and made for one of the waiting lifts; but I already had the door to the main stairway open, and turned to shout.

'Stairs! Come on, it's quicker!'

It is, too. This end of the building might be relatively modern, but the lifts are fast approaching the end of their natural, with a tendency to judder and grind and stop at floors you have no wish to visit. Whenever I'm in a hurry, I take the stairs.

So up the stairs we went: clattering, panting, grasping the banister rails to swing ourselves around the corners; passing the doors to the first floor, and going faster all the time. Reaching the second floor, we fairly burst through the fire-doors into the deserted reception area — and saw the lift we'd been racing standing empty before us. As we stood there, gasping to refill our lungs, the door slid smoothly closed again, an automatic function that seemed almost mocking.

'Oh . . . *sod*,' I murmured, 'she's up here.'

Mike walked quickly to the set of doors leading through into the central corridor, and pushed them open. The thoroughfare beyond was in semi-darkness: just doctors' offices and storerooms, all deserted at this hour. To left and right at this end, more fire-doors sealed off the access corridors to the first two Medical wards, Harvey and Radcliffe. Likewise at the far end, for Lipscomb. And Jenner.

I moved up to follow him through; still a bit unsteady on my feet after our sprint up here. Still short of breath, too — but I struggled to keep my panting as shallow as possible as I peered into the gloom ahead of us. Where nothing stirred.

We went on down the corridor, quickly and quiet. The door to the seminar room was slightly ajar, and Mike paused and pushed it open; I watched with my heart in my mouth as he reached in to switch on the light and survey the room — but it was empty. We hurried on.

Welcome to Jenner Ward said the sign over the closed double doors that came up on our right. Through their wired glass panels I could see on down the dark passageway, dimly-lit beneath the tubular hoods of the nightlights; past bays and side-rooms asleep in shadow, to the single desk lamp at the nurses' station. There didn't seem to be anyone around. Warily, I pushed the doors open, and we slipped through.

With no idea of which bay our would-be suicide was in, we made straight for the desk; drawn also, instinctively, by the warm glow surrounding it, for the dreaming darkness of the ward was unsettling; *unquiet*. I heard ragged breathing in the gloom, and coughs and mutters; the ghostly respiration of the sick. Of course I'd worked my share of night shifts on inpatient wards and was familiar with the atmosphere. But I'd never quite got used to it, and always found it eerie. Tonight, with the prospect of a deranged intruder with a knife lurking somewhere in the shadows, the restless dark was positively scary.

We reached the station without incident, having glimpsed nothing untoward in the bays we'd passed, nor in the sluice room either. I reached over for the nursing cardex, a ringbinder of notes on all the ward's patients, and had started leafing through it before realizing I'd forgotten her name. 'Bloody hell . . . Jones . . . ?'

'James,' Mike prompted calmly, still glancing round. 'Angela James.' He'd obviously been browsing through our admissions register as well. I quickly found the relevant entry, and saw she'd been put in one of the side-wards, the four single-bedded rooms back near the doors. We'd already passed her by, without knowing it. I had the sudden, sinking feeling that her pursuer might not have overlooked her so easily.

We turned to retrace our steps, and one of the nurses was just emerging from the end bay, pushing a commode. She raised her eyebrows. 'Hi . . . can I help you?'

I hesitated for a moment; then, trying not to make it sound too melodramatic, I said: 'We've had a patient-emergency down in A&E . . . think she might have found her way up here. She was talking about one of your patients, Angela James, and . . . er . . . she's got a knife.'

That took the colour out of her cheeks somewhat, but

she retained her composure admirably. 'Have you bleeped the porters?'

'Not yet — none of our phones were working . . .' And no fault of mine, but I still felt myself flush at her disbelieving look. She went over to the desk and turned the phone around towards me. 'You'd better do it now, then.'

Smarting, I moved to do so — while Mike turned to the distinctly unimpressed-looking Staff Nurse. 'I think we'd better check that Angela's okay, right now,' he suggested evenly, and the two of them set off down the corridor. I watched them go, tucking the receiver under my chin as I punched in the number. There was a crackly pause; then the dull whine of number unobtainable. *Fuck*, I mouthed, and tried again; frowning in disbelief as I got the same result. It seemed the phones were playing up everywhere. I slammed the receiver down — belatedly realizing there were people trying to sleep all around me — and was wondering what to do next when there came a rustle of movement from right behind me. I spun round.

The girl who stood there looked about fifteen — though she must have been older, or they'd have put her on the kids' ward. She was wrapped in an overlarge hospital dressing-gown that made her seem even frailer than she was. Her face was pale, with dark shadows around the sunken eyes, and her fair hair hung in strings. She looked as if she was feeling really awful.

'I've been sick again, nurse,' she reported miserably; and as I stared at her, I realized who she was, who she must be.

'Angela,' I ventured, 'we . . . er, thought you were asleep.'

She actually smiled at that — if smile was the right word for the rictus that spread across her thin features. 'No . . .' she almost whispered. 'No, I'll not be sleeping again. Not safe to sleep . . .'

I gave an understanding sort of nod. 'Where were you?

The toilet?' I glanced down the corridor to see if Mike had re-emerged from her room yet. And as I did so, something caught my eye – a shift of shadow in the darkness of the bay beyond her. Someone was on their feet in there, and coming out. *Another patient needs the loo*, I found myself hoping with surprising fervour – but in vain. Because the figure who emerged was fully-dressed, in dirty black. And wearing shades.

Angela might have sensed the movement at her back; she certainly saw the horror on my face. She turned quickly – and recoiled against me with a stifled sob. And the woman who'd called herself McCain stepped fully into the corridor – her clothes still blending with the gloom, but her face as calm and pale as a cadaver's – and extended a gloved hand towards the girl. Palm open, like an offer to a drowning man.

'Angela. Come with me now. It's not too late . . .'

Me she ignored completely, as if I wasn't even there: although Angela was rigid against me, and my hands had instinctively gripped her shoulders. The two of them might have been alone here in this darkened ward: sharing in a secret tryst while the lesser world slept. But as I slowly eased the terrified girl backwards, away from her visitor's slow-paced advance, I glimpsed something slip into McCain's dangling left hand – and a moment later, with a sinister click, the blade of her knife licked out and locked.

'Never too late to follow me,' she breathed, her blank stare still not acknowledging my presence.

I risked a fast, frantic look down the corridor – but it was empty: no sign of Mike or the Staff Nurse, though they must surely have discovered that Angela was out of her bed by now. At any moment they'd reappear, and see, and come sprinting to my rescue; but I knew that even the very next second would be one too many.

Spinning Angela round, I grasped her wrist, and ran.

Round the corner we went, and on down the link

corridor towards Radcliffe Ward, feet thudding on the carpet, dimly-glimpsed doorways and bed-bays veering madly past on either side. *Just like a crash-call*, I thought breathlessly; and an old nursing phrase flashed with idiot incongruity through my mind. *A nurse should only run in cases of fire or haemorrhage . . .*

Behind, McCain was coming at a walk. My fleeting look saw her stride increasing. When I next glanced back a moment later, she was running.

. . . haemorrhage . . .

We fairly crashed through the set of fire-doors separating the wards and raced on through Radcliffe. A Staff Nurse and a student were sitting at the desk, writing quietly by dusky lamplight. Both heads jerked up as we appeared, the unison so perfect it should have made me laugh. No time to explain, of course; nor to call for help, nor even shout a warning. We just kept running – Angela stumbling now, but even if she'd fallen I'd have dragged her – and the woman with the knife was at our heels. So let them call the porters. Let them find a phone that fucking worked.

Please, God. Jesus. *Please.*

Round the next corner and back towards the central corridor now – and suddenly there was someone in our path, shuffling across from toilets to bed-bay. A grey-faced old man in a faded dressing-gown, mobilizing laboriously with a walking frame. His head was slowly coming round, but nothing had time to register. I slowed for just a second, and swerved past him, and yanked Angela with me through the gap.

McCain hit him full on.

The two of them went down together, with a rattle of metal and a sickening thud. The sound made me wince: despite myself I slowed again, glancing round. My every nursing instinct cried out against leaving the poor guy gasping there on the floor, his rheumy eyes rolling as he fought for breath. And even as I hesitated, I saw Mike appear at the far end of the corridor, pushing past one of the stunned ward nurses, and come racing towards us. There was surely no need to keep on running; we could corner her here; restrain her. But McCain had already struggled to her knees, her knife still glinting through the gloom, and now she lifted her head and looked at me, and bared her teeth in a vixen grin.

We kept on running.

Through the next set of doors, and the next, and we were back in the Medical Unit reception area. That left us with a choice of the main stairway up or down. For a moment I could think of nothing but Mike back there, maybe tackling that mad bitch, struggling to disarm her – and then I saw that one of the lifts was open wide and waiting.

Someone must have just used it – maybe a nurse trailing back from the fag-end of Break, or returning from delivering specimens to the lab, or whatever. It didn't matter. We ran for it, as behind us we heard the doors of Radcliffe Ward burst open.

Over the threshold, past the photoelectric beam, and I jabbed the button, any button, and held it down.

Nothing happened, of course.

Wrong button, I realized after a stupefied pause, you're pressing for this floor, *shit*. And I put my thumb to the ground-floor button with all my weight behind it as Carol McCain shoved her way through the last set of doors into the reception area, and saw us.

The door began to close, so painfully slowly that for a horrible moment I thought it would fail to connect properly and automatically reopen. And McCain came running any-way, aiming to get her foot into the narrowing gap and block the beam. I shrank back against the far wall, pulling Angela with me, and the last I saw of McCain was a glimpse of her frustrated snarl as the door closed in her face.

Stillness for a second. Then the lift lurched, and started to descend.

I let my breath out in a gasp that left me drained. My legs were suddenly kitten-weak, and I had to slump back against the wall to save my balance. Beside me, Angela James was weeping silently, the tears rolling down her hollow cheeks; but I sensed she still had all her wits about her – primed with adrenaline, and ready to run again.

But who the *hell* was she was running from?

I'd ask her later, to be sure; but right now, as the lift reached ground level, we both had other things to think about. I knew there was no way I could stop the doors opening. If necessary, if she was already waiting down here, I'd punch the button for the top floor and throw myself against her, forcing her back until the doors had closed behind us and Angela was safely on her way. What that might cost me I didn't pause long enough to consider: I knew my hesitation would be fatal for both of us if I did.

The lift steadied itself, lined itself up; there was another pause. I thought I couldn't get any more keyed up – but my stomach still lurched as the door slid smoothly open, and I saw –

Nobody there.

Nobody in sight, anyway. I glanced at Angela, and swallowed, and moved slowly forward to peer out.

The foyer was empty.

And even as we hesitated, unsure what to do next, I heard footsteps from down the corridor – several people, walking quickly; and voices I recognized.

They reached the lift area a moment later: Adrian, who was clearly chargehand porter for tonight, and three of his lads – including Danny from our department. His eyes widened as he saw us.

'Rachel – we just got a call from A&E, said you'd gone off chasing some nutter with a knife . . .'

Well at least the phones were working again. I nodded

urgently. 'Yeah, some woman got up on to the Med floor, she must still be up there now. Have they called the police?'

They had. The Duty Nurse Manager as well. All the wards were in the process of being alerted. I nodded again, thankfully, and gestured to Angela, who was keeping close beside me, hugging herself in that outsize dressing-gown.

'This is Angela. The girl she was after. I want to get her sat down and with a cup of tea, can someone come with us?'

It was Danny who volunteered, and the three of us went back down the corridor towards Casualty; my arm round Angela's shoulders now, soothing her as the shock began to set in. I reckoned it would be more private round by us, rather than in the canteen or wherever. Part of my mind was still very much on what must be happening upstairs – that woman still loose, still armed and dangerous; and what had happened to Mike? But I realized that right now this girl needed all my attention, so I forced the other thoughts and fears from my mind and concentrated on her. Speaking softly. Guiding her steps.

A cup of hospital tea. I'd just been looking forward to one when all this had started. Maybe ten minutes ago. Maybe a lifetime.

Seven

'Want to tell me about it?'

She looked warily up from the mug that steamed in both her hands. 'About what?'

'Who she is.'

She glanced down at her drink again, and didn't answer.

I didn't push it. The police were already here, and would be asking their own questions soon enough. I could hear the WPC on the phone in my office, just across from the duty room where we were sitting. One of her male colleagues was hovering in the corridor outside, his handset picking up occasional crackles of conversation on the open channel. More officers were still searching the building; the intruder had not yet been located.

Mike was sitting in with us: a much-recovered Graham had obligingly sutured the laceration in his side, and decided he didn't have concussion. He was off sick as of now, of course — but the police would want a statement from him too, and he was nursing a coffee while he waited.

I caught his eye now, but all he could do was shrug. He'd been lucky, and he knew it. She'd slashed and kicked him brutally as she'd struggled clear: the realization of how close death had come was there to see in the paleness of his face. The two of us had been through some sticky situations together since I'd joined the night shift; I well remembered that time he'd disarmed a bottle-wielding drunk and could still make a joke of it afterwards. I'd never seen him as subdued as he was tonight.

Death had come close. But McCain had come closer. And, like me, he must have felt her coldness, the icy insanity beneath her calm exterior. I knew that this was what had really unnerved him; knew just how he was feeling.

And she was still in here with us: somewhere in this warren of echoing corridors and shadow-filled wards. Even with the police in A&E, I didn't quite feel safe. It's a big department, after all, divided into half a dozen areas: trolleys, cubicles, theatres . . . Tonight it was empty – and the bright lights only made it all look emptier, and emphasized its silence.

I sipped some more coffee. Still warm, but what the hell.

They questioned Angela first, with me still present at her request. Not that she was about to tell them anything, either: it was all shrugs and monosyllables. From the line the policeman was taking, they obviously thought she was involved in street crime of some description: drugs or prostitution. McCain was clearly acting on behalf of some pusher or pimp – perhaps she was one herself. Angela, chalk-faced, did not deny the possibility – but I knew they'd got it all wrong. I didn't intervene, though; nor did I mention my suspicions when I came to give my own statement. What did I know about it, after all? Nothing – except that I'd looked Carol McCain in the face, and heard the things she'd said; and knew that whatever had brought her here, it was nothing so sordidly simple as drugs or sex.

When the police had finished with me, Kessler was waiting; something like this was worth dragging even a consultant out of bed for. He saw me in his office, and sat me down, and seemed quite concerned. Too restless to sit still, I was fairly hunched forward in the chair as I gave a more or less comprehensive report of what had happened. When I'd finished, he asked me if I wanted a cigarette – which, considering his views on smoking, was quite a concession. I nodded gratefully, fumbled in my bag for my packet of

Players and lit up. Drawing in the smoke, I closed my eyes, and began at last to think of relaxation. When I opened them again, he was watching me levelly.

'You're all right to carry on?'

I nodded again, almost urgently, and he smiled: it was the answer he'd expected. Kessler was a good bloke to work for, on the whole: he knew his stuff, and wasn't above getting his own hands dirty once in a while. And though he could be a bastard at times, abusing the staff remained his prerogative alone: he was fiercely protective of our interests whenever they were threatened from above. Or at times like this.

'Have they . . . caught her yet?' I asked.

He shook his head. 'Last I heard they were still looking.'

I glanced down at my fob-watch, and saw it was nearly three a.m. Kessler was removing his glasses to pinch the bridge of his nose. His hand moved up to rub his forehead, below the dark, receding hairline; he was probably a lot tireder than he looked.

I breathed out shallowly, so as not to pollute the air too much.

'Since we're here, Rachel,' Kessler resumed, 'there's something I have been meaning to discuss with you – and tonight would seem to be as appropriate a time as any.'

I shrugged, waited.

'You remember those syringes disappearing from the utility room?'

That had been a while back. I nodded.

'Nothing like that's happened since, has it?'

'Not since they reviewed the security.'

His turn to nod. 'As I thought. But there's renewed concern, apparently. Someone's been scavenging round by the waste skips: they think some of the sharps buckets have been taken.'

'They must be desperate.' Desperate enough to filch used needles from the very bins in which they awaited incineration: the yellow plastic tubs sealed with Biohazard stickers and the legend *Danger of infection*. Danger of Hep-B, danger of AIDS ... I grimaced at the thought.

Kessler nodded. 'They are. You know how bad the drug situation's getting round here; the police were up to see me just the other day, warning about addicts on the prowl for needles and syringes. Improved security or no, I want you all to keep your eyes open; make sure things are all accounted for and locked away. And we could do with less of this department being used as a public thoroughfare, too; people just wandering round ...'

'Am I to take that as a criticism?' I asked, my tone even.

He smiled thinly. 'It applies to all the shifts, Rachel – perhaps yours less than most. Just keep the clientele in line is what I'm saying.'

'And if the clientele comes wading in with a knife? What are we supposed to do then?' My temper was on a shorter fuse than I'd thought; I swallowed and glanced away for a moment, then looked back at him. 'Sorry. But are we any nearer getting a second porter on nights; or a panic-button system?'

Kessler met my gaze. 'You know I'm still pushing night security,' he said quietly. 'After tonight, I'll be pushing all the harder. Admin's pleading financial constraints; but I think we're getting there.'

'Well it won't be too soon,' I muttered. Oh, it was starting to get to me now, all right, as it had to Mike already: the realization that I could have died tonight. Could have *died*.

Kessler shrugged. 'I couldn't agree more. Anyway ... that's what I wanted to talk to you about.' He paused for a moment, watching me finish my cigarette. 'You coped admirably tonight, Rachel. It won't be forgotten.'

I thanked him and left. Mike was hanging around by the duty room, ready to go now, but not before he'd said goodbye. I really felt like hugging him and just holding on:

what we'd been through tonight had left the both of us shaken up. I think it was only the fact that I'd had Angela to worry about that had kept the real shock from setting in much earlier.

'How is she?' I asked, looking past him into the empty room.

'They've taken her back to the ward; the WPC's going to sit with her. Poor kid wanted to wait for you, but upstairs were anxious to have her back and under obs.'

'I'll look in on her before I go off,' I said, feeling rather warm and pleased inside to know my efforts had been so appreciated: not just by Kessler but by the girl whose life I'd saved. I noticed one of the policemen then, still lingering at the far end of the corridor, and that put something of a dampener on things. 'Oh, don't tell me they haven't caught her.'

'Afraid not. Though they reckon she must have done a runner, got well away. This is just precautions.'

'Well I hope they're right.' Because the place was a honeycomb of places to hide – from cleaners' cupboards and service corridors, to the empty wards up in the north wing. And whoever the woman McCain really was, I knew she'd try for Angela again. And possibly for me.

'Anyway . . .' Mike said, interrupting my thoughts. 'I'll see you, Raitch.'

'Yeah,' I said, snapping out of it; smiling. 'See you, Mike. God bless.'

Eight

I promised I'd just be a minute, and the Staff Nurse showed me into the side-room where Angela lay. Despite the fatigue apparent on her pale, drawn face she was still awake – struggling to raise herself as the door opened. She relaxed visibly when she recognized me, though still unable to manage a smile, and lay wearily back once more.

'Hi,' the policewoman in the bedside chair said. 'You just off?'

I nodded. The night-light was still on, but the sky outside had already faded to a pre-dawn grey. I was still in uniform, apart from my cap, and wearing my long black nurse's cloak – just the thing to encourage that unkind rumour that Night Sisters have to be back in their coffins before sun-up or they'll crumble to dust. I approached the bed.

'Hello again. How are you feeling?'

She made a noncommittal sound. Something told me she wasn't going to say much at all with the policewoman there; maybe she did have criminal connections at that. I glanced at the WPC – a pretty, cheerful-looking girl with short blonde hair and a freckled nose. 'You've been keeping her company, then?'

She nodded. 'We haven't exactly talked the night away' – she smiled across at her charge – 'but it's best not to be alone on a night like this. I keep telling her to get some sleep, but she won't listen – will you, Angela? Won't consider a sedative or anything.'

Angela confirmed this with a silent shake of her head.

'She's right,' I told her, 'you'll feel so much better for

it.' And as she miserably returned my gaze, I recalled what she'd said to me the last time.

I'll never sleep again. Not safe to sleep.

'Actually . . .' the WPC said, getting to her feet and stretching, 'if you don't mind staying with her for a minute, I'll just go for a wee.'

I waited till she was out of the door, then sat down on the end of Angela's bed. 'So how are you? Really?'

She just stared at me for a moment; then moistened her lips. 'They didn't catch her, did they.' It was more a statement than a question.

'Not yet, no. But I think they will soon. And anyway, there'll always be someone here to look after you.'

Tiredly, she shook her head. 'Forget it. If she wants me, you won't be able to stop her.'

'So who the hell is she?' I insisted. 'Look, I won't tell anyone, I promise . . . but she could have killed me and two of my friends tonight; I just need to know *why*.'

'She wants me to come with her,' was her indirect answer. She rolled her head on the pillow, staring out of the window at the promise of day; then turned her shadowed, haunted eyes towards me once again. 'And I want to. I really do. But I'm so scared.'

That left me speechless for a moment. Then: 'Come with her . . . where? I mean, doesn't she want to harm you, then?'

She shook her head. 'She says she wants to save me, and I believe her. I have to. But if they find out . . .'

'Who? Who would she be saving you from?'

But the last of the colour had gone from her face now, faded down to the bone, and she shook her head. 'Look, forget I said that, all right? Please?' The quaver in her voice confirmed it: she was scared all right. She was terrified. Despite her plea, I was about to pursue the point, when a sudden recollection shut me up. Alison Scott had been terrified too: scared into silence by something that later killed her right downstairs in my department. Scared of the Clinicians . . .

And the word was suddenly on the tip of my tongue. I wanted to say it aloud, see what reaction it got. I moistened my lips . . . and didn't speak. Perhaps because I didn't want to trouble her further; perhaps because I was afraid of her reply. It was so much easier to believe that this was all some squalid vendetta between vice gangs, and nothing more. People capable of hideous cruelty, to be sure; but people none the less.

'All right,' I told her. 'I won't say anything if you don't want me to. But that woman . . . She's ill. You'd be crazy to go with her . . .'

Angela said nothing; I was suddenly afraid she'd clammed up on me completely. But then she murmured: 'Oh, she's ill all right. At least . . . I hope she is.'

I waited, not quite understanding. The WPC would be back in a moment, if those weren't already her returning footsteps.

'Because she thinks she's an angel,' the girl continued dully – and looked me right in the eye. 'She thinks she's the Angel of Death.'

Not surprisingly, I found it hard to get to sleep when I got home; just lay there, snuggled up beneath the duvet and staring at the ceiling. For all the familiarity of my surroundings . . . despite the sunshine outside, and Sarah on a day off and quietly knitting in the living room . . . the gnawing unease just would not go away. A new thought had entered my head on the bus home – and plummeted straight to my stomach, where it rested now like a cold lump of lead.

If someone was mad enough to believe they were the Angel of Death, maybe they were crazy enough to live out the fantasy – and dissect some poor sod with a very sharp knife.

So had McCain committed that atrocity? Had I come

that close to the psychopath the police were seeking?

Close enough to feel her breath . . .

Shit. S. H. I. T.

I rolled over one way; then another. Turned the radio on. Turned it off. Wondered if she could possibly trace me home . . .

Oh for God's sake . . .

I tried pushing my mind in other directions for a wasted while; then gave up thinking altogether, and just fixed my mind on *feel*. It was a trick I'd tried before on stale and sleepless nights (and days): wiping out my racing thoughts with sheer physical sensation. Curling up warm and comfy, I slipped my arms under my T-shirt to embrace my naked breasts. And began lazily caressing.

Slowly I relaxed; gently massaging my tired flesh: stroking and soothing, until it let go its grip on the waking world, and dropped backwards into deep, delicious darkness.

After a while, I began to feel cold.

Maybe I'd kicked off the covers or something. I clung to the dark for as long as I could – but the growing chill on my skin was enough to fade my dreams, and I realized I was beginning to wake up. The sense of loss was just the same as always: a sinking feeling even as I rose towards the surface.

The air kept getting colder.

I shivered, opened my eyes – and almost gasped with the shock of finding myself in a long and whitewashed room. The place was bleakly sterile; brightly lit. And freezing. It was a place I'd been before, and often. I knew it was the morgue.

Somehow I was fully dressed again: in uniform, even wearing my cloak. It didn't make me any warmer. Hugging myself, still wondering what I was doing here, I turned around – suddenly not wanting to have my back to the row of heavy doors that sealed the fridges. And then I saw that one of the doors was fractionally ajar.

For a moment I just stood there: staring. And then the thought was in my mind that I'd have to close that door before I could safely walk away from this place. Shut it fast – or something might get out . . .

Slowly, warily, I walked over. The closer I got, the tighter my stomach shrank. At last I was standing beside the door, close enough to grasp its cold metal edge.

And swing it fully open.

My body seemed to do that of its own volition, acting independently of my horrified mind. And now I saw that there was a body occupying the middle tray of the compartment beyond: wrapped in a soiled white sheet, its muffled head towards me.

I tried to fight the urge to uncover the face. I tried so hard. But to no avail. Heart in mouth, I reached out and pulled the sheet clear. Clear of the corpse's face, and bare shoulders and upper chest.

Jenny. It was Jenny.

She lay there before me as though asleep. Except that no sleeper is ever so pale, so breathlessly still – nor has the bruised fingermarks of strangulation mottling throat and neck.

My whimper was all but muffled as I pressed my fist against my mouth: holding back tears, or nausea, or maybe both. I turned away.

And a cold hand shot out and grasped my trailing wrist.

Squealing, I swung back round. And saw that her eyes were open. Lacklustre now, their sparkle dulled; but staring at me – and pleading.

'Please, Rachel,' said Jenny's corpse. 'Please don't leave me. It's so cold here. So *cold* . . .' And she dragged me bodily towards her . . .

*　　*　　*

85

I was instantly awake: breathless and drenched with sweat. For a few minutes more I lay quite still, not wanting to move and feel the wetness of the cotton against my skin. The daylight against the curtains was duller . . . greyer. A glance at my alarm clock told me it was already nearly four o'clock.

The way I felt right now, the sooner I got back to work the better.

Twenty to nine. I finished fastening my uniform, and gave myself a brief once-over in the mirror, checking that every detail of my navy uniform was neat and in its place: the fob-watch and name-badge, the RCN pin on my lapel; the insignia of the London teaching hospital where I'd trained and qualified . . . Scissors and pens all ready in my left breast pocket. My sleeves unzipped and rolled back. The silver-buckled belt cinched in tight round my slim waist.

Still hatless, I walked down the corridor towards my office. There was one call I needed to make before I got stuck into – and hopefully absorbed in – another night's work. I wanted to know how Angela was faring.

Someone answered on the eleventh ring; perhaps they were busy up there. She certainly sounded brusque enough. 'Jenner Ward, Staff Nurse.'

'Er . . . hi, it's Sister in A&E here. We had a girl come through here yesterday, went to your ward . . . There was a bit of trouble later on. Angela James, her name was . . .'

'What about her?'

'Just wanted to check how she was . . .'

A pause; sheets of paper rustling. Then: 'No, she's not on this ward.'

I'd had the phone tucked between shoulder and chin, as though forcing myself to act casual; speaking as I made the final adjustments to my cap before pinning it on. Now I felt myself tense, frowning.

'What . . . you mean she's been transferred?' Perhaps even admitted to the psychiatric unit, which would explain so many things so conveniently . . .

'No,' the Staff Nurse said after another pause, 'she's gone; took her own discharge this afternoon.'

For a moment I was lost for words.

'Is that all?' she asked – rather impatiently, I thought.

'No, I . . . Didn't they try to stop her, then?'

'Discharged against medical advice; the form's signed and in the notes.'

'And what about the police protection?'

'I've no idea. Now if you'll excuse me, Sister, we are quite busy at the moment . . .'

'Yeah . . . yes, sure,' I said absently, and she hung up.

There's no way you can detain a patient against their will, of course – not unless it's under the provisions of the Mental Health Act. And though it would have been so much easier to believe that Angela was simply a mentally disturbed young woman, I didn't think she was, and neither, obviously, had the doctors. Some of our would-be suicides do accept voluntary admission to the psychie unit. But Angela had wanted only to get out.

And go where? To follow in the footsteps of Carol McCain? Or to find somewhere quiet where she could finish the job she'd botched the first time round?

A glance through the admissions register confirmed what I already remembered well enough: Angela James had been of no fixed address. She was out there somewhere now, in the cold and the dark – perhaps still searching for a refuge for the night. I remembered how small and frail she'd looked in her hospital dressing-gown; the prospect of her wandering the streets, alone and vulnerable, made my stomach sink. But what really left me feeling sick was the thought of who or what might be stalking her through the shadows. A vicious pimp, perhaps. A vengeful pusher.

Or something worse.

Something or someone she knew about already. Someone or something that had scared her half to death. Death by suicide . . .

Somewhere in the night, the Clinicians were waiting. They were waiting for her. And McCain – whoever she was, wherever she fitted in – was out there too. Wolves, lurking in the darkness: waiting for the lamb to come tiptoeing fearfully by.

Nine

After Wednesday, I was Nights Off until the weekend.

On Thursday I went looking for Angela.

I was tired; the past few nights had been busy. I'd had only a few hours' sleep after I got in on Thursday morning. But I knew I wouldn't be able to rest – to sleep deep enough to do me any good – until I'd at least tried to find her.

So as morning faded into cloud-dulled afternoon, I set out for the shopping precinct, where a lot of the homeless tended to hang out. It was somewhere to start, anyway. Afterwards, I could try the bus station . . . or the squats down Heath Lane . . . or even the hostel they'd recently opened on Greville Road, although something told me she wasn't about to wall herself up in there. The prospect of deliberately putting myself in the way of the town's grimiest inhabitants didn't fill me with delight – but I knew she must have gone to ground among them, which left me no option but to follow. And besides . . . I'd paid enough lip-service to ideals like a more just society, a better deal for the poor; agreed with all that stuff that makes you feel guilty in the *Guardian*. Well here the poor were, waiting. Perhaps it was time to put my money where my mouth was.

The precinct was fairly quiet, and I saw no one who even resembled a vagrant. Maybe the security guards – the *Volkspolizei*, Mike called them – had moved them all on. I went on towards the bus station. The sky was beginning to glower, now, and I felt a few spots of rain on the wind that sent litter rustling ahead of me across Market Square.

I saw him as I turned the corner: a grey-haired, grey-faced man in a shabby greatcoat, sitting on the paving with his back to the wall, just along from the chip shop. Even as I watched, I heard him mumble something to a couple hurrying by. They ignored him.

My first instinct was the natural one: to do likewise. To avert my face, avoid catching his eye; hoping to be past before he'd even noticed me. Then I remembered why I'd come here in the first place; realized he might be able to help. I slowed my pace, and he looked round hopefully.

'Got any spare change, darlin'?' Irish, what a surprise. He didn't actually have a bottle in a paper bag beside him, but I wouldn't have been surprised at that, either.

He grinned as I fumbled in my purse. Fifty pence, why not? I let him see the coin, then palmed it. 'Wonder if you can help me? I'm looking for a friend . . .'

'Would've thought a young lady as pretty as yourself would have lots o' friends already,' he beamed.

Don't try the blarney on with me, you old bugger, I thought drily. Aloud I said: 'She's about sixteen, fair hair, quite skinny. Called Angela.'

'And what would you be wantin' with a girl called Angela?' he asked in a reasonable tone.

I shrugged. 'Like I said, she's a friend.' After a pause, I added: 'I think she's in a bit of trouble.'

He studied me for a moment; it struck me how bright his green eyes looked against his grizzled, wind-burned face.

'Aye. Maybe more than a bit, at that.' The words came out curiously soft. I heard them with a twinge of unease; waited for more.

'Could be you are a friend of hers,' he continued after a moment. 'And if y'are, then listen. The best service you can do that poor girl is stay well clear. There's them as we don't speak of out for her blood, and she needs to lie low.

I know she's the one you mean; and there's nothin' you can do for her now.' He tipped his head back, still studying me. 'I'd not be tellin' you any o' this, y'understand,' he added; ''cept that you've got an honest face on you. And honest eyes.'

I stared back at him in silence for a moment. Then: 'Who's after her?'

He shook his head. Stonewall.

I shrugged again. 'Okay . . . well, thanks anyway.' I was about to toss the fifty down to him when it dawned on me how demeaning a gesture that would be. So I squatted down before him, meeting him eye to eye, and handed the money across. 'Thanks.'

He took it, fisted it, grinned once more. 'Thank you, darlin'. Money's cheap; respect's a gift worth a whole lot more.' And as I began rising to my feet once more, he reached out, tugged my sleeve. 'You watch out now. There's bad folk about. Worse than ever you dreamed.'

There was genuine concern in his voice, and on his face. Concern for me. Coming from a homeless vagrant, that really made me nervous.

Not quite sure what to do next, I wandered on into the bus station, a suitably grey setting for a bit of sombre thinking. I didn't doubt his words, not for a moment. Whatever was going on, it was out of my hands now. Yet how could I walk away? How could I ever rest easy again, knowing what I did? Imagining what things might be lurking in the shadows of our town . . .

I was convinced the same Clinicians who had murdered Kaufmann, and Johnston, and Alison Scott, were after Angela now: they wanted her dead. I knew it for certain, but who'd believe me? I had no evidence to go on. Even if I went to the police, and played down the weirdness enough for them to believe I was sane and sincere, what could they do? Where could they start? What would be the point?

So what would *I* do, if the Clinicians came to suspect I knew of their existence, and decided to deal with me too . . . ?

So many questions. No answers at all. Deep in my thoughts, I was startled back to reality by the rattle of coins from close by. Coins in a paper cup, held out in the hand of a beggar.

Wearily I turned, still undecided whether I should pay up this time or not.

The beggar grinned.

I froze.

It was McCain.

I just stared into the reflecting blackness of her shades, and felt my stomach drop away. Sickening adrenaline flooded my system, priming me for fight or flight – a total waste, since I was too petrified even to think of either.

She was dressed as scruffily as when I'd seen her last – but no hat or coat today. Nothing to attract a second glance – apart from the glasses, which gave her the unsettling look of a blind girl begging for pennies. One who saw and judged everyone who passed her by.

Her long and filthy jersey was veed at the neck, with a black wool shirt beneath it; and I noticed a small leather pouch on a thong around her throat: probably some weird New Age amulet. Her silver rings looked tarnished in this light. She held her cup left-handed, her right dangling loosely at her side. I knew, with a cool, tight certainty, that her knife could be out in less than a second. Out, and into my stomach. A couple of people were sitting on a bench a dozen yards away; they'd blink and miss it. No one else was close.

'Any spare change?' McCain asked, with mocking cheerfulness.

'You've got a nerve,' I managed, after a moment.

Her smile widened. 'Think someone spotted me? Maybe remembered my description in the paper? Called the police?' She shook her head. 'Don't hold your breath, Rachel. They won't even come close.'

Someone was coming towards us, walking down past the empty bus bays. I thought about appealing for help, but knew it would be useless. She'd kill us both. Easily.

She even took a casual step around me as he passed, and held out her cup. 'Spare some change, mate? So's I can eat.' But he ignored her. She stared impassively after him for a moment, and I wondered if he'd ever know how close to death he'd come. No, of course he wouldn't. Lucky sod.

'You know, you quite impressed me, the other night,' McCain said conversationally, turning back. 'You did well. Did your best for Angela. You mustn't blame yourself.'

I frowned uneasily. 'Where is she now?'

'Still in the canal, I expect. They won't have found her yet.'

It was the casual matter-of-factness of her tone that really hit home; for a moment I was speechless – dumb with cold horror. Then: 'You . . .'

She raised her eyebrows. 'Me what?'

'Bloody hell, she . . . she was only a kid.'

'She was old enough.'

'Murderer,' I hissed.

'Yes.'

'Well sod you.'

'I didn't kill her,' McCain said.

I rubbed a hand across my forehead, and back into my hair. 'No? Then who did?'

'She killed herself. Drowned herself.'

'You drove her to it, though, didn't you?' I accused – not really caring whether I was provoking her or not. 'She was trying to get away from you.'

She shook her head. 'I could have saved her, Rachel. And she knew it. But she was just too scared.'

I remembered what Angela herself had told me, and maybe McCain was telling the truth, at that. But before I could press her further, she'd touched a fraying-gloved finger to her lips. 'It's over, Rachel. For you it's over. Just forget you ever met me, or her. Believe me, it will be better for you.'

She turned, and began to walk away.

'Who're the Clinicians?' I said.

She stopped, and looked back. 'Oh Rachel, Rachel,' she said, and her tone was almost pitying. 'You don't want to know. You really don't.' And with that she kept on walking.

Ten

'Rachel? What'll you have?' Mike asked.

I glanced at my watch: last orders, and I still wasn't drunk yet. Not drunk enough, anyway. 'Another G&T, please.'

'You all right?' Karen said, casually enough, as her Steve volunteered to help bring back the drinks.

'Yeah. I'm okay.' I managed a smile. 'It's been a long week . . .'

'Too true,' she murmured, glancing from me to Mike as he headed for the bar. 'Shit, you were lucky.'

I nodded; we knew that all too well. And of course I had a whole lot more on my mind – though I wasn't about to mention that to anyone.

It had been Mike's idea that we go out for a Friday-night drink – an all too rare off-duty get-together, to help us over the past week's events: McCain's attack, and now Angela's subsequent suicide. The suggestion had been welcomed, and those of us who were off tonight had spent a cheerful enough evening in the hospital's local. Both Mark and Kathy had been able to make it, but Graham was on call. I wondered if even he might have accepted the invitation otherwise.

In the midst of such busy, companionable surroundings, it was that much easier for me to shove darker thoughts to the back of my mind, and concentrate on enjoying myself as best I could. The alcohol helped, of course: though still sober, I was beginning to feel warm and bright-headed, with a tendency to giggle at the feeblest joke. All around me there were people – normal men and women, drinking and chatting and relaxing after the week's last working day – who knew nothing of Clinicians, and cared less. Maybe I should take McCain's advice and join them.

Maybe if I got really pissed, I'd forget the dull unease that still weighed down my stomach.

The blokes came back to our table clutching the drinks. Steve handed me mine, then squeezed in beside Karen again: he kissed her smartly on the cheek, and she smiled delightedly up at him. The engagement ring was on her finger now, the diamond catching the light. They made a nice couple.

Kathy, who was driving, sipped her fruit juice. 'I hear you're off next week, then?' she said to Mike as he sat down. 'Going anywhere?'

Having heard Mike extolling the joys of walking in the Brecon Beacons quite often enough this week, I let my attention drift over to Mark and Fran, who were discussing some film or other. Mark, with a fresh pint now in front of him, was already quite amiably plastered: to look at him, and hear his cheerfully profane comments, you wouldn't have guessed he was a doctor. Then again, I suppose the rest of us didn't look like nurses, either. Perhaps the public we deal with don't often think of us as having a life out of uniform. But this time tomorrow night, we could be struggling to save the life of any one of the people now drinking around us.

Strange feeling, sometimes.

'Rachel, Rachel,' Mark was saying. 'You've seen that film, what was it . . . ?'

'*The Untouchables*,' Fran prompted drily.

'*Untouchables*, right. Fucking good film, actually . . .'

'It was,' I agreed. A bit bloodthirsty for me, but still . . .

'Anyway . . . the person who played Al Capone, right. I reckon it was Danny DeVito, and she . . . this person, right' – indicating a grinning Fran – 'says it wasn't.'

'She's right,' I confirmed. 'It was Robert de Niro.'

Mark blinked: possibly he was trying to focus. 'No. No, I'm sure it was Danny DeVito. Little guy . . .'

'Though of course de Niro wasn't the original choice for the part,' I said airily, drawing on a snippet of information I'd picked up from some magazine in our own waiting area. His eyes lit up. 'Ah. Yes. That's what I meant, of course. The *'riginal* choice for Al Capone was . . .'

'Bob Hoskins,' I smiled.

He just gawped at us, looking from me to Fran. ' 'S a conspiracy,' he decided indignantly after a moment, extending his appeal to the rest of the table. 'A fucking *conspiracy*, I tell you . . .'

The rest of the table found this hilarious.

Still smiling, I reached for my handbag. 'Mark . . .'

'Fuck . . .'

'Mark. Watch your language, there are ladies present.' I ruffled his hair on the way to the loo.

'You're a fine one to talk, Rachel,' he hooted after me, speaking loudly enough for half the pub to hear. 'I remember that time we had an arrest come in without warning, and you wandered out saying, "What have you brought us this time, then?", and the ambulance bloke goes: "Cardiac arrest!", and you go: "Oh fuck!" in front of everyone . . .'

I managed to gain the safety of the ladies' before my face got too red. God, the man was an embarrassment sometimes. And I still wouldn't have anyone else treat me if ever I got admitted to Casualty again . . .

When I re-emerged, I found Mike had posted himself at one of the fruit machines by the door, as if waiting to catch me on my return. He looked a little awkward. Suddenly I realized why.

'Rachel,' he said, as I tried to get away with a passing smile. 'Can I . . . ask you something?'

I paused, shrugged. 'Sure.'

'I was . . . ah . . . wonderin'. After I get back: maybe we could both go out for a drink together . . . ?'

Not like our Mike to be so tongue-tied; I hesitated just long enough to let him see I took it seriously.

'Thanks, Mike. Really. But it wouldn't be a good idea . . .'

Oh, it crossed my mind to say yes, too, and see where we got: both good friends, after all, and unattached. But where Adrian's fishing had been amiably casual, Mike looked a little too earnest. And to start something I wasn't going to finish just didn't feel right.

Besides, it's not the wisest thing to start going out with one of your staff. Especially if it doesn't work out.

He mananged a smile back. 'Okay. Sorry.'

'I . . . thought you and Brenda had something going, anyway,' I said, trying to smooth things over. I'd seen this coming a while back, and still found the words weren't ready.

He shook his head. 'Nah. Not really . . .' There was a slightly uneasy pause. Then, just as I was about to extricate myself, he gave in to temptation again. 'Someone else, is there . . . ?'

Mark laughed out loud in the background.

'No,' I said firmly, 'there isn't. Listen, Mike – we're a team, you and me. I really like working with you. Why not just leave it at that?'

He nodded unhappily, and returned his attention to the fruit machine; but I could feel his eyes on me again as I made my way back to the table. And my principles told me that 'no' should be answer enough, even for a friend; but it still hurt to see his discomfort. Yet what more could I tell him? Only that I was saving myself for the real thing: whenever I found it. And that, deep down, I've always been an independent sort of girl – and sometimes jealous of sharing my inner self at all. A sign of insecurity, perhaps; or common sense. I still wasn't really sure.

Downing my drink, I picked up my coat. 'I'm off now,'

I announced with forced brightness. 'See you all Sunday or whenever . . .'

'How're you getting back?' Kathy asked.

'Bus.'

'You sure? Your stop's quite a way, isn't it?' A look of concern crossed her face as she watched me buttoning my coat. 'Look, let me give you a lift, Rachel. The streets aren't safe these days . . .'

'I'll manage,' I said evenly, and turned down Karen's offer too. Right now I just wanted my own company for a bit. I said my goodbyes, and was almost at the door before Mike caught me up.

'I hope you're not going to offer me a lift as well,' I muttered.

'I'm not,' he said; 'but the others're right, you know. It's not safe out there: there was a murder the other week, remember? There's no need for you to leave; I'll go if you want . . .'

I turned to him, and smiled, and shook my head.

'It's all right, Mike. Really. Have a great holiday, okay?' I touched his arm. 'I heard the main drawback of walking in the Brecon Beacons is tripping over dead SAS men. Look after yourself.'

He managed to smile back, and I went on out into the orange night.

The street, largely residential, was empty at this hour. I stood there outside the doors for a moment, breathing in the cool, refreshing night air: letting it clear my head. Then I turned left towards the lights at the far end of Yateley Road, and the bus stop just beyond them. A hundred-yard walk or so.

I'd covered just over half that distance when I heard the sound of someone's footsteps following.

Eleven

Cold unease uncoiled in my stomach; I felt suddenly sick. It wasn't fear yet, though — not quite. Right up to the last moment, you always believe it's never really going to happen to you.

For a moment I even hoped it was Mike, making one final try. But I knew it wasn't. Mike was wearing trainers — and these were heavier footfalls altogether.

Keeping my eyes resolutely to the front, I kept on walking. Just a little faster. Perhaps I was imagining it, anyway. And perhaps if I ignored it, it would go away . . .

The footsteps followed.

You read it in the papers time and again; you see it on the news. And still you tell yourself it only happens to others; convince yourself it's only a luckless or imprudent few — not ordinary working girls like you. But the phrases they always use were racing through my mind now. *The body of a young woman has been found . . . been sexually assaulted . . . police are appealing . . .* There had been a case on *Crimewatch* only last week, a teenage girl up in Rochdale. Raped. Murdered. And I knew that in her final moments she'd been thinking just the same as I was. It can't happen to me. He wouldn't . . . He won't . . .

But he had.

And she'd been a real person too: a cheery, pretty girl, brought up by loving parents, with seventeen years of richly-textured life behind her, and everything ahead. And all of it lost on one dark night — snuffed out for no reason at all.

That was the worst bit: the utter senselessness. How can

you guard against something that strikes at random?

The bus stop was just ahead, but I didn't even pause. The houses on either side were in darkness, and I wondered how much screaming it might take to rouse somebody from sleep. Or maybe I should simply run . . .

The footsteps seemed to have dropped back a little way.

Forcing myself to stay calm, I turned into the next street. My stomach lurched as I realized that some of the street-lamps were out, leaving great pools of shadow in between those that still glowed warm and amber. But I couldn't turn back, not now. I stepped up my pace once more. All I had to do was keep on walking. I'd walk all night if need be.

I heard the scrape of a boot on the pavement as whoever was following me reached the corner. I kept going, into the first patch of stifling gloom. My skin began to crawl then, as if the dark was something tangible. Something physically cold . . .

I could hear nothing now between the rhythmic clack of my own high heels. I shrugged deeper into my coat, thrusting my hands into the pockets, chin tucked in. Back into the light, and as the silence behind me persisted, I felt the first faint stirrings of relief. It was as I entered the dark halo of the second outage that the urge to look back finally proved irresistible. As if the shadow would somehow mask me from any pursuer, and he wouldn't see my brief, betraying glance.

My stride faltering, I turned.

There was nobody there: the street behind was empty.

I smelt his breath first, a gust of sour alcohol; before I could even flinch, I felt rough hands seize me, strong arms wrap round me, squeezing the breath from my lungs as I was dragged bodily back into much deeper darkness. And now the fear came, the sickening burst of adrenaline, but all too late. Too late to tell me that this time it was going to happen to *me*.

He'd been lurking in the alleyway he was hauling me down now, an unpaved, unlit access to the garages behind this block of houses. Lying in wait – no doubt alerted by the sound of my heels, carrying too far on the still night air. And in seeking to evade an imaginary pursuer, I'd walked right into him.

I struggled and threshed in vain, my screams trapped deep in my throat by the iron pressure of his arm. Back into the garage yard we went, enclosed by the black outlines of lock-ups looming up against the stars. And the stars were our only light – so distant and cold – as he swung me hard against a concrete corner, and threw me to the ground, and dropped heavily across me.

His fingers slid over my face and into my hair; his face, unreadable in the gloom, was very close to mine. He was breathing hard, the stink fanning my cheeks. I felt a wetness down the side of my aching skull, and realized it was blood.

'C'mon, love,' he hissed. 'Don't muck around, now. I'll give you a good time – and that's what you're after, isn't it? You want it really: I know you do . . .'

No I bloody didn't. But with his weight crushing my chest I was breathless to protest; I could scarcely move. And now he leaned in close to whisper in my ear.

'I won't hurt you if you're quiet. But if you try screaming, or scratching, I'll fucking murder you, understand? Do you?'

I sobbed, nodded.

He drew back, and began to fumble with my clothing.

There was a crunch of boots on gravel, right behind him.

Before he could even begin his awkward turn, a dark shape was rising up to tower over us, a scarecrow against the stars: reaching down to grasp my attacker and drag him off me. A second figure was already moving in from the left. Even in the throes of dizzy, gasping shock, I smelt the aura of foulness they brought with them, the reek of dirt and urine. The stench of the streets.

Vagrants, I realized numbly. I'd been rescued by bloody vagrants.

And as I lay there, disbelieving, the vagrants produced blades of steel that sparkled in the starlight. Ignoring my assailant's dazed resistance, they bore him down, held him helpless on the ground. And began to cut.

Began to dissect him before my eyes.

I made a small, horrified sound. It tasted of bile in the back of my throat.

He didn't scream: the sound was choked to a gargle in the blood of his sliced throat. His killers worked on in silence, opening him up – cutting out organs that glistened blackly beneath the sky. I smelt the stink of his violated entrails now: the noxious gas escaping, the bitter whiff of excrement . . .

As I began silently to shake, I became aware of a third figure, crouching down beside me. I wanted to shriek, to squirm away – but all I could do was whimper as he punched a needle deep into my arm. I glimpsed the syringe, felt the tingling pressure of its contents entering my system.

And a sudden, aching blackness sucked me down.

I awoke on a hard surface, in a darkened room.

For long minutes – so many they might have made an hour – I lay motionless, and listened. I was on my back, and some surreptitious flexing of muscles confirmed that all my limbs were free. I was still dressed too, including my coat – which offered some protection against the dank, chilly atmosphere of the room. Judging by the wood surface beneath my spread fingertips, I reckoned I was lying on a table.

Whatever drug they'd floored me with, the effects still lingered: I felt dazed and detached, as though on the brink of some out-of-body experience, and my head throbbed dully. I couldn't think straight: it hurt to try. But a vague memory of what I'd seen just before I'd lost consciousness still lurked down there in the depths, and my stomach responded to its presence with the occasional sluggish heave.

I stayed absolutely still, not even blinking; not daring to move. I couldn't sense any presence in the surrounding gloom, but they had to be somewhere close. They. I hadn't the strength to think it any further through; knew only that something dreadful was out there in the dark, and patiently biding its time.

Unconsciousness welled up around me once again. I struggled briefly, and sank.

When I next came to, there was a familiar smell in my nostrils, the spiky aroma of disinfectant. I felt something clammy move across my forehead, brushing my hair aside. Then gentle, dabbing pressures against my left temple, soothing the soreness there.

I remembered the fall then; the cut, and the blood. Now someone was cleaning the wound. I squeezed my eyes open, and saw the yellow latex of surgical gloves just inches away. Relief flooded through me: I was back at the hospital, being cleaned up. Then a quick tetanus jab, and . . .

But then I realized that the air was still heavy with damp and cold, and the room only dimly-lit. No bright, aseptic blaze of Casualty lighting here. No comfortable trolley either. I was still lying on the table: and now I saw that my attendant's sterile gloves ended at the cuffs of ragged greatcoat sleeves.

He straightened up, and had turned aside before my eyes could focus on his face. The sight of his clothes was unsettling enough: the coat was torn and filthy, and his dark fedora begrimed with pale dust. His gloving-up had been a mockery. I was being tended by a tramp.

His attention had switched to something beside me: he was poring over it, and in the dimness the shadow of the hat-brim hid his face completely. Uncomprehending, I rolled my head to one side to follow his gaze.

A second, smaller table had been drawn up at right angles to the one I was lying on: its surface draped with stained green linen. There was a metal kidney bowl on it, into which he'd tossed the used cotton-wool swab; and an array of surgical implements that gleamed faintly in the subdued light. Scalpels, mostly, along with some scissors and a hook-bladed stitch cutter . . .

The sight of those sharps, along with the shabby figure now fingering his way through the selection, brought memory hurtling back: the empty streets, the footsteps following; the near-rape, the rescue, the ripping . . . I sucked in air with a horrified gasp, and he turned and looked down at me.

I very nearly screamed.

He had a face like worn-out leather: gnarled by high cheekbones and a sullen brow. Short fair hair curled lankly down from beneath the hat; blond stubble roughened his jawline. And he was wearing a pair of welder's goggles that masked his eyes — made his stare opaque and blank and yet all-seeing. That's what really scared me: those dark and eerie lenses, above his slow and leering grin.

From the other side of the table, a dry voice in the dark asked: 'She is conscious?'

'Now she is,' the tramp answered: still fixing me with his blind gaze. His own voice was monotonous, almost machine-like — but with a grim, gravelly undertone that no computer could have imitated.

'Good: it will make examination easier. Proceed.'

I tried to speak; swallowed and tried again. 'Examination?' It came out sounding so small and afraid.

But they ignored me. 'The abrasion to the forehead is minor,' the tramp reported drily, going through the assorted implements as he spoke; while my cowering mind made unwilling connections between that hospital surplus hardware and the recent spate of disappearing sharps bins. 'There is some bruising to the throat and sternal area . . .' He selected a metal spatula; pocketed it. 'Did actual intercourse take place?'

'That we will need to determine.'

The tramp had picked up another instrument, and was turning it experimentally in his pale-gloved fingers. I recognized it at once, and felt my stomach contracting like a fist. It was a speculum, a gynae tool: a hinged metal funnel that opened up the vagina for inspection. With my disbelief unable to stifle a growing dread, I watched him carry it round to the far end of the table. I tried to struggle up, at least to my elbows, but it was useless: I had no strength left in me, no co-ordination. Every attempt to move just short-circuited my nerves. I couldn't even cry my protest when he laid the instrument aside to grasp my ankles and pull me bodily down the table, until my legs were mostly dangling over the end; then he pushed them apart and moved up between them.

The first implement he produced from his pocket was a scalpel.

One glimpse of that and I did begin to struggle, trying to thresh clear with reserves of strength I'd never guessed existed: a final reservoir of tight-mouthed desperation. But the shadowy second man moved in close to hold me down – the reek of his clothes almost smothering me – and after a frantic moment my energy ran out and I was helpless once again. I could only whimper as the first tramp carefully sliced off my Marks & Spencers knickers with that cold, sharp blade, and discarded them into the darkness. I felt the cool caress of air as he lifted back my skirt.

'Oh no,' I whispered. 'Oh please don't . . .' But the speculum was back in his rubber-sheathed fingers now, and without further preamble he bent forward and began to examine me.

Intimately.

I just lay there, and stared at the ceiling until the tears blinded me completely, welling up in my eyes and over-flowing; trickling down to wet my hair. With cold, inhuman thoroughness he explored me – his blunt, sterile spatula chilling the living warmth within me wherever it touched; the latex-skinned fingers pushing and prodding at my tenderness. It wasn't as if his probings were particularly vicious or rough; rather that his examination was so dis-passionate, so uncaring of the distress it caused. He didn't speak again, and I couldn't. And nor could I find the cour-age to raise my head and watch the ragged figure at work between my legs, my deepest secrets laid open to the sombre scrutiny of those goggles.

After what seemed an age of misery, I felt him withdraw his implements and straighten up. His footsteps creaked across the floorboards as he came back round to the instru-ment tray beside me. I risked a look, my vision still a wet, stinging blur: saw him drop the spatula into the bowl, along with the vaginal swab he'd taken, and select another fine-bladed scalpel from the range available. Then he turned back towards me.

My stomach cringed.

I couldn't make out his expression; and when that grim voice sounded in my ears again, I didn't want to. For the first time he was addressing me, and his tone told me enough. So mockingly solicitous. So coldly insincere.

'You have been fortunate: there was no penetration. If it had been otherwise, there would have been danger of . . . infection: we would have had to operate. A clitoridec-tomy might have sufficed; or a hysterectomy, to ensure there was no risk of an unwanted conception.' My eyes were clearing now, as I blinked away my tears; despite my wishes to the contrary, I saw his smile. His eyeless grin. 'Of course, we have no tradition of anaesthesia here . . .'

I almost choked then. My gaze locked on to the sharp, glinting blade in his gloved fingers: a surgeon's tool, such as I'd seen at work so many times before. But everyday life was a world away from this icy, shadowed room, which I now shared with someone insane enough to cut my womanhood from me while I was still awake to scream. And no reason for any of it. They knew well enough that the poor sod — I actually thought of him as poor — who'd attacked me had got his come-uppance before he'd had a chance to do anything; and since when was major surgery a remedy for rape? No: what I'd just gone through had been humiliation for the hell of it — a sick but simple exercise of power. That, in far more than an abstract sense, had been the real violation I'd suffered tonight.

The dawning realization brought anger with it, a bitter upsurge of rage. Which evaporated instantly as the man to my right, who'd eased off during the examination itself, leaned suddenly forward and gripped my jaw, forcing my head round to meet his stare. And this new face was so black with grime it seemed born out of the surrounding darkness; but his eye sockets were darker still — pits of shadow in which I could see nothing.

Again the parody of concern. 'Your eye: some bruising . . .' And with his free hand he fished up a penlight from his pocket. A moment later he was shining it into my right eye, the fingers of his other hand pressing into the skin around the socket to force it wide. I stared blindly back into the glare, still helpless to resist. 'Please,' I murmured, desperately, 'I can see fine, really . . .' But once more I was ignored. A moment or two later the light clicked off again, and he straightened up; glanced across me to his companion.

'It is possible she has a detached retina,' he said, as though I wasn't even there. 'It would need immediate surgery.'

The other man moved quietly out of my field of vision and round to the end of the table; sliding back into view again as he craned forward to see for himself. And then, with slow, clinical precision, he brought the gleaming scalpel down . . . down, until the point was hovering a millimetre above the conjunctiva, my eyeball's invisible skin. I couldn't focus on it; but beyond its metallic blur, I saw his face dip down towards mine, with a yellow-toothed grin beneath those empty lenses.

I gawped up at him, awash with terror: afraid even to blink, in case that blade slit my eyelid clean in two . . .

For a moment more the nightmare tableau held; then the blade was slowly, almost grudgingly withdrawn, and the goggles drew back into the gloom.

The second man leaned in close, laying his hand against my face: the tight glove leprous with patches of trapped air. He spoke very softly in my ear.

'You will whisper nothing of this, Rachel Young; or we will perform such surgery on you as you never dreamt to feel. We are Clinicians. We will speak with you again. Remember us . . .'

The other was back at my side again, and lifting a syringe before his blanked-out stare. A thin jet of liquid squirted upward from the needle: bright as quicksilver in the semi-dark.

'Sweet dreams, little angel,' he crooned – with a grin to waken nightmares. And with that farewell in my ears, I felt a deep, sharp needle-stab in my limp left arm – and my mind went out like a lightbulb.

Twelve

Dawn.

I sat there and watched the sky beyond my office window: watched the pale pink light becoming gold as the invisible sun approached the horizon. It didn't make me feel the slightest bit better.

Day was coming, dispelling shadows. That should have been a reassurance. But dawn also meant another night's work was almost over – and I'd have to unhook from the rhythm and routine of the department.

And start remembering again.

My mind had tried hard enough over the past few days to shut it out: the gory horror that the following morning's media had trumpeted as 'the Backstreet Butcher's' latest murder; and my dark, *unclean* encounter with the men who'd called themselves Clinicians. I'd certainly felt a moment of giddy unreality, reading about my would-be rapist in the paper: an office worker with a wife and small kid, grinning almost shyly at the camera in the snapshot they printed. An ordinary bloke called John Lester. It threw me completely: having to reconcile that smile, those homely details, with the shadow-faced snarl of my attacker. Like what had happened afterwards, it went beyond belief. But it had all been real – and the images were still there behind my eyes to prove it: perpetuated by the sick weight I still felt in the pit of my stomach. The knowledge beyond doubt that they were watching me, and would come for me again.

As promised. It had been just as clear a dawn when I'd stumbled home on that morning after. Wherever they'd dumped me, I'd been up and walking before the drug had fully worn off; moving on autopilot, driven by fear. When I'd finally made it, pushing the front door closed again and leaning heavily against it, Sarah had glanced at my wan face on her way through to the kitchen and remarked innocently: 'Looks like it was some party . . .'

Unable even to think of a riposte to that one, I'd made straight for the bathroom, knelt to contemplate the depths of the toilet bowl, and waited for all the bitterness in my stomach to come surging up.

And as I waited, I'd heard a single, stealthy footfall just outside the door.

It wasn't Sarah: I could still hear her singing snatches of some pop song in the kitchen. Just down the corridor, but she might as well have been a million miles away — separated from me by a gulf of cold, inhuman silence in which something alive was lurking.

I knelt where I was in frozen fear, but heard no further sound. There had just been that one footstep: just the one. After a while I heard Sarah leave the kitchen and come on down the corridor to her bedroom. Helplessly I waited for the screams. There weren't any. She walked back towards the kitchen, still humming softly to herself.

After a while longer, I'd finally worked up the courage to unlock the door. My sickness was forgotten, now: I'd gone beyond mere nausea. Warily I peered out . . . then re-emerged from the bathroom. Nobody there, of course. My heart still in my mouth, I looked into Sarah's bedroom, and then my own. There was nowhere for anyone to hide. And no one could have left the flat, however stealthily, without Sarah noticing.

I'd imagined it, then. I must have.

Must have . . .

(. . . *sweet dreams* . . .)

It was Brenda, wandering into the office, who broke into my reverie. She must have noticed my paleness, because her smile faded into a look of some concern. 'You okay?'

I nodded, and even managed a weary smile of my own. 'Yeah. Just tired. Didn't get much sleep yesterday . . .' That was certainly true enough. Maybe I was safer in the daylight; I didn't feel it.

'White as a ghost, you looked,' she admonished, still half-serious. But that sprightly North Welsh intonation of hers brightened my own smile, and suddenly, without really thinking, I said, 'Well you'd know, wouldn't you? Superstitious lot you are . . .'

She giggled at that, and walked past me to the window. I thought the topic would peter out there – and suddenly realized I didn't want it to. 'Seriously, though . . . Do you believe in that sort of thing? Ghosts and such?'

She turned, and looked at me quizzically; I kept smiling, as if this was just idle curiosity, and after a moment she shrugged.

'Do you know, I'm not sure. I mean . . . part of me says, of course not, I'm a professional young woman, both feet on the ground, all that. But another part of me remembers what it's like: on the wards, at night . . .'

I nodded: I remembered too. Oh yes.

Bren leaned back against the windowsill, looking thoughtful; then glanced at me again.

'My *Taid* – my Granddad – used to tell me stories when I was little. I can see him now, sat in his chair by the fire, and me and my brother sitting on the rug listening. And we'd be spellbound, you know? All the superstitions they had. Like, people used to talk about the "corpse candle", which was this light that was seen at night, going up to the door of a house where someone was about to die. Gave me the shivers, that did.' And she grinned a little self-consciously.

'Go on,' I prompted quietly. 'I'm interested.'

She shrugged again. 'I remember one time he told us

about something that happened when *he* was a kid. His family and another one had met in the street, and the parents were talking – this was in broad daylight, right – when suddenly the other family's little girl pulls on her mother's sleeve and asks, "Did you see the funeral passing? Just then?" sounding like a full cortège had just gone past, horse-drawn hearse, the lot. But nobody else saw a thing. And she just kept on asking whose funeral was it, and who was dead . . . ?'

She paused then, as if mesmerized by the memory; then snapped herself out of it with a mock shudder. 'Great one for ghost stories, my Granddad. I suppose it came naturally to him: he used to walk miles to work – leaving home before dawn and coming back long after dark. And walking those lonely country roads at night . . . It'd be enough to give anyone the horrors.'

'And . . . have you ever seen anything strange yourself?' I wondered; it must have been clear by now that I had more than a passing interest, but if she noticed she didn't pick up on it.

'No . . . Not really. Though a couple of times I think I've felt, like, an atmosphere – when someone's just died on a ward and had a hard time of it. Nothing you could put your finger on, but . . .' She looked at me seriously. 'I'll tell you one thing, though: no way are you going to catch me up by the closed wards on my own after dark. No *way*.'

I nodded, with feeling; and this time let the subject go. In a strange way it had helped, a bit: talking like that. Of course I couldn't tell Brenda or anyone else about what I'd been through; but knowing I wasn't the only one aware of the *weirdness* in our world was somehow vaguely reassuring.

Bren checked her watch. 'Nearly there. Want a lift home?'

'Thanks, but no. There's someone I want to see upstairs, before I go.'

'A patient?' I nodded. 'Friend of yours?'

I nodded again. 'An old friend . . .'

Seventy-three years old, to be precise.

Miss Morgan had been our next-door neighbour since we'd moved into our current flat. She'd seemed a little crabby at first, but I'd cheerfully persisted, and helped her out with her shopping on occasion, and we'd managed to strike up quite a friendship (not so Sarah, who still tended to refer to her as 'that daft old bat'). She'd been an inpatient on one of the Medical wards for a week now; I understood the prognosis wasn't good.

The ward was well awake by the time I got up there; the big meal trolley was parked with doors open at the angle of the corridor, and breakfast smells hung heavy in the air. There was a group of nurses standing or sitting around at the desk, waiting for the day to get fully into its swing. I knew a couple, and said hello. Visiting time didn't start officially until much later in the morning, but since I was staff they let me skip such limitations. Still in uniform – cloak and cap and all – I entered the six-bedder bay and went over to Miss Morgan's bed.

She was lying propped up with pillows, her eyes closed; her face sagging. The meal on the overbed table was almost untouched.

'Miss M?' I ventured softly. 'Are you awake?'

Her eyes fluttered open, focused on me. She smiled then, and with surprising warmth. 'Rachel . . . how lovely to see you. Please, sit down.'

I did so, almost tentatively. She sounded weak and worn out – so different from the sharp, severe old woman she'd seemed when I first met her.

'So how are you?' I asked.

'As well as can be expected, I suppose. Isn't that the phrase you use? Everyone's been very thoughtful, very kind

'. . . but I somehow doubt that I'll be leaving here again.'

I opened my mouth to protest – then saw the look in her eye, and shut it again. She nodded approvingly. 'That's it, Rachel. You're an intelligent young woman: you know it wouldn't be any use.'

I shrugged, conceding the point. 'Is there anything you need?'

'I think I have all I want.' Again she smiled. 'To know that someone still thinks of an old woman like me is perhaps the most important thing.'

I smiled back, a little modestly. She'd been in hospital before, and visiting her had sometimes been a chore; but if a sense of duty made me do it, I'd sometimes found our conversations more rewarding than expected. And how could I not visit now, when she was dying and knew it. I was glad it would probably happen here, too, in the Medical Unit, and not the grimmer, dingier Geriatric Unit in the older wing. Not that there weren't good, compassionate nurses aplenty working on those hard-pressed wards. But one of them had been Jenny Thomas – and she'd been strangled by a patient already certified dead.

I hadn't been able to face the gerry floor since that day.

We talked for a while longer, about this and that. And I was about to make my excuses when she calmly asked me: 'What's wrong, Rachel?'

I blinked. 'Wrong?'

Miss Morgan nodded. 'You're not yourself, are you? Usually such a cheerful, loving, Christian girl; but something's troubling you.'

I just stared at her for a moment; and a cold little voice inside me said, *well actually, Miss M, I almost got raped the other night, only he got disembowelled before he could do anything, and then a couple of psychopathic tramps took me to a house somewhere, and tortured me, and said they'll call on me again . . .*

And something else told me that, even if I did tell her

everything, she would listen, and believe, and give me whatever help or advice she could . . .

But of course I said nothing. Just shrugged, and made noncommittal noises as she gently pressed me further. At length she accepted I had reasons to hold my peace, and we said goodbye.

On my way back to the lifts, I couldn't help recalling her opinion of me: such a Christian girl. I wished I felt that I deserved it.

Thirteen

I was into a seven-night stint, now — and never more grateful for a seventy-hour-week slog. Because for the next few nights running I would not be alone after nightfall; not be asleep after dark. And as the week progressed, I'd sleep better during the day: much too tired to dwell on the horrors that seethed in my mind whenever it was idle. Seven nights on would be followed by seven off, of course: but I'd deal with that period of enforced idleness when I came to it.

In the meantime I put my head down and got on with the job. So long as we were busy, I could hang on to the real world. And sometimes — like tonight — the compassion I felt for the sufferings of others quite overwhelmed my private fears.

It was Wednesday: my fourth night on. There'd been a bad RTA just outside town — two carloads of teenagers, probably racing each other, and one had gone off the road. One boy was killed outright; Mark had just gone wearily out to certify him in the ambulance. Another boy was in Resus, and not doing very well; one of the registrars from upstairs was with him now. Two more kids — minor injuries, but pretty shaken up — were being made comfortable in the cubicles. And I was in the Quiet Room with the relatives.

The dead boy's parents hadn't been contacted yet. So far we had the mother and father of the one in Resus, and the mother and sister of one of the others. All of them pale and tense, asking broken questions; no tears as yet. The traditional cups of hospital tea had dutifully been provided.

The air in the tastefully furnished little room was thick with cigarette smoke.

'Can I see him yet?' the critical boy's mother asked again.

'He's with the doctors now, Mrs Wilson,' I assured her, 'they're doing all they can. We'll let you see him as soon as possible . . .'

She nodded numbly, moist-eyed now. Maybe she knew. Perhaps mothers always do. Or perhaps she'd simply seen through my calm and noncommittal answers, and realized I wasn't telling them the whole truth.

The whole truth being that I thought he was going to die. He hadn't been breathing when the ambulance got here, and his heart had stopped twice since then. We certainly were doing all we could – I glanced down as we heard someone run past outside, probably going for some more bags of saline – struggling against death itself in an attempt to get the lad stabilized for transfer to ITU. But my experience told me that this wasn't one we were going to win.

Experience. Something these stolid, middle-aged people seemed to find hard to credit in a girl young enough to be their eldest daughter. They'd been quite put out to find me in charge; it had taken me a little while to convince them I knew what I was doing. I didn't mind, though: you can't really take offence with people as frightened and confused as they'd been. Mark would be in to speak to them shortly. I hoped he'd volunteer to break the news when the time came.

Mr Wilson put an arm round his wife's thin shoulders; he was eyeing me grimly. Not feeling up to denying the obvious for much longer, I rose to my feet. 'I'll just see how they're doing . . .' I murmured, and slipped quietly out.

By the time I got to Resus, it was all over.

Mark had returned, and was conversing with the other doctor beside the trolley. Karen was taking down the drips.

Our late patient, all of seventeen years old, lay supine and still, almost ignored now; the blood and bruising standing out vividly against the paleness of his skin.

'Oh shit,' I said, resignedly.

June Smith came up behind me. 'The police are here: they're waiting in your office.'

I almost swore again. Things weren't finished yet, of course: not by a long way. After the news was broken, the relatives would need to formally identify the body, then answer questions for the Coroner's report. I thanked June – one of the day staff just starting her night rotation – and walked over to Mark. He raised an eyebrow, waiting.

'Want to tell them?'

He sighed, and glanced towards the doors. 'Not really. But . . .'

I tugged his sleeve. 'Come on. We'll do it together.'

Whatever they might have dreaded previously, they knew now. They knew as soon as we came in.

'Mr and Mrs Wilson . . . This is Dr Drew. I'm afraid he . . . we've got bad news.'

And Mrs Wilson began to cry: silently shaking as the tears spilled down her twisted cheeks. I went quickly over and knelt down beside her chair, on the other side from her husband: putting my arm round her too, the two of us supporting her as she sobbed convulsively. I spoke to her softly, trying to comfort, to convince her he hadn't suffered, while Mark answered the father's hoarse and halting questions with similar assurances. The other relatives – friends of the family, it turned out – looked on in wretched silence, on the verge of tears themselves.

At length Mrs Wilson asked: 'Will you let me see him now?'

'Of course,' I said, and swallowed. 'Of course. You both can. Let me just explain what we need to do next.' I told them about the Coroner's procedure, the formal ID. At least they'd be able to do it up here, rather than in the grim, chilly confines of the mortuary. I knew the team were cleaning him up even now; wheeling the trolley into one of the treatment rooms where there'd be a bit of privacy. Maybe placing a single flower on the sheet, if they could find one. I was just getting to my feet to go and see if the police officer was ready, when Mrs Wilson took hold of my wrist. I looked down, into the pain of her hazel eyes.

'Please . . . will you come with us? Stay with us till it's done?'

I nodded, covered her hand with my own.

'Of course I will,' I said.

There are times when I think the job's made me hard. There are times when I know it has. You can take only so much pain and distress and death before a part of you has to switch off – or compensate by making very sick jokes. But some things still get to you. Tonight it had been the waste of two young lives and the shattering of two more that left me feeling particularly down.

It was one a.m. now, and we were quiet again. The relatives had all gone home, as had one of the lightly-injured kids; the other was in for overnight obs. The police still hadn't been able to contact the parents of the other fatality: the ambulance had unloaded him at the mortuary, as was usual with DOAs, and his body now awaited morning in the darkened fridge. His mate would be joining him soon enough; now that the Wilsons had finally left, we could send him down too. The policeman on the case finished his paperwork over a coffee with Karen and me: like us, they get to treat these things as grim routine soon enough. We said our goodbyes and I saw him to the door, watching as he walked across the ambulance bay to where he'd parked his car. It didn't even occur to me to tell him about what I'd suffered last Friday night. I knew there was nothing he or anyone could do to help me.

I went back into Resus, where June and Brenda had just finished bagging up the bloodied clothing they'd cut off the late Ian Wilson. Jeans. T-shirt. Underpants (soiled). Shirt. Socks. Training shoes. June went through Bren's handwritten inventory, and countersigned it before slipping it into the big blue plastic carrier. The clothes made a smallish bundle at the bottom. It's details like that that bring you down to earth sometimes.

Last offices was all there was left, and Brenda and I did them together: working in silence, rather than chatting like we usually did when sharing the job. Last time we'd been idly discussing the prospect of holidays; but tonight she'd caught my eye before we started, and seen that I really wasn't in the mood.

Finished, she glanced at me again, before going quietly out. I stayed staring down at Ian; thoughtfully stripping off my gloves. After what I'd been through at the hands of the Clinicians, the feel of rubber against my skin still set my mental teeth on edge.

There was a squeak and rattle from up the corridor outside: a trundle of wheels on the lino.

Pulling off my pinny, I crumpled it like a binliner, and bagged it. My hands were sweaty from the gloves, and I went over to wash them at the basin, elbowing the long-handled tap open and closed. When I turned round again, I found Danny watching from against the wall.

He leaned back as though he'd been there all along: his expression quite without guile, but I glimpsed a flicker of his amusement as I visibly jumped.

'God, Danny . . . Don't sneak around like that, all right?'

'Sorry, Sister,' he murmured, straightening up with a quiet smile. I'd given up trying to get him to call me Rachel. 'I've got the trolley outside. If he's ready.'

I nodded, and went over to hold the door as the long,

lacklustre metal box was wheeled in. Danny unclipped the chain and swung it open on its hinges; Ian Wilson's limp, shrouded form was transferred across. The lid came down again, and locked.

'How come you've got to do this on your own?' I wondered. 'They can't be that busy . . .'

'They are,' he answered matter-of-factly. 'Lot of sickness in Portering at the moment, and the night shift's right down. Adrian says they can't spare anyone right at the minute.' He straightened up, his gaze unblinking. 'I can manage.'

I shrugged. He certainly wasn't popular with a lot of his workmates, I knew that. Maybe he was used to going it alone.

How long had he been with us now: three months? I still felt I didn't really know him; certainly not as well as Adrian and the other pool porters who covered for us on Danny's nights off. I could talk to Steve Wheeler about politics for hours – and Jim Yates was always good for a laugh, even in the long, empty hours before dawn. But young Danny kept his counsel all to himself. That was his privilege, of course, and I didn't begrudge him it; but I still sensed that, behind the placid exterior and sparse conversation, there was something more that didn't meet the eye. And whatever it was, I didn't like it.

From what Adrian had said, I gathered he'd dropped out of college or something; maybe that explained the air of quiet superiority he still gave out. But from time to time, I caught a fleeting glimpse of something colder: like contempt . . .

'Tell you what,' I said. 'I'm going to Break, so I'll come down with you, bring the property, if you like.' I suddenly found myself hoping quite fervently he'd say no to that suggestion; but I knew why I'd made it – and why I'd have to follow it through. Partly it was one more effort to get to know the bloke a little better; but mostly it was because I hadn't been down to the mortuary since my dream of

Jenny's speaking corpse. And despite the all-too-real horrors I'd encountered since, the memory of that dream still haunted and distressed me, and I knew I had to exorcize it somehow.

Those cool, enigmatic eyes stared back at me for a moment; then it was his turn to shrug. 'Sure. If you want to . . .'

I nodded and, feeling a little hollow inside, went back to Resus to collect the dead boy's clothes.

The mortuary was tucked discreetly away in the northeast corner of the basement: quite convenient from our point of view, and we were linked by a lift and service corridor unused by the general public. Danny pushed the trolley along at a smooth, steady pace, and I walked briskly to keep up. The first of my reasons for coming didn't look as if it would find fruition: we hadn't exchanged a word since leaving the department.

As for the second . . . I felt my mouth drying out as we came to the wide double doors with their stencilled legend *Strictly No Admittance, Authorized Personnel Only.* Danny fished out the key and unlocked them; I pushed one open and held it while he rolled the trolley through into the darkened annex corridor beyond.

I could feel the cold upon my skin; I breathed it into my lungs along with the heavy smell of formalin.

'Light switch to your left,' Danny said calmly. I fumbled for it, found it, flicked it on. A bright – though hardly warm – glow bathed us as we proceeded on down the corridor, past the locked-up office, to the next set of doors which gave on to the body store.

More darkness; deeper cold. I remembered where the switches were for in here, and felt my way over to press them. The overhead lights buzzed and came on, flooding out the long, bleak room with their reassuring glare as Danny pushed the trolley in and manoeuvred it past a linen skip to the nearest set of fridge doors.

I stayed exactly where I was.

My fingers still on the switches, I was staring fixedly across the room towards what I'd glimpsed in the instant before the darkness disappeared.

A line of light beneath the post-mortem room door.

'Anything wrong, Sister?' I heard Danny say. Ignoring him, I moved slowly away from the wall and began to cross the room. I couldn't see any light from in there now, of course; but I saw something else – a dampness on the tiles, edging out from under the door. A spill of water, tinged rosy pink with diluted blood.

But they don't do p-ms at one in the morning – apart from the odd forensic job, and I knew this wasn't one of those. I swore silently, turned to Danny –

And he was standing close behind me now, arms comfortably folded: watching with a faint smile on his face. The same amusement that I'd glimpsed before: but darker.

'Don't be afraid . . . Rachel,' he said softly. 'You know who's in there.'

I did, too, suddenly: and I was bloody terrified.

'They often come in to work here at night,' Danny continued, like one conspirator sharing a secret with another. 'There's not much chance they'll be disturbed; and the facilities are perfect for their needs.' His voice was as quiet, as calm as ever, but there was an edge like a razor's to his thin smile now.

'These are the masters of the house, Rachel,' he added, voice still hushed. 'And they've been waiting.'

I just stood there, staring helplessly back at him; feeling as trapped and alone as when I'd been on that table and under the knife. There were *Clinicians* in here – separated from us only by the thickness of the door. And Danny, who knew of them also, and served in secret, seemed to think I was in this with him now: a new initiate into whatever awful cult this was . . .

'Go on in,' he urged me then. 'They have . . . such sights

to show you.' From the dreamy dilation of his pupils, I guessed he'd been shown a few himself.

I knew if I got any colder, I'd start to shake. My body temperature had plunged, my skin was crawling. He must have seen the horror on my face – but he misread it.

'It's only right to feel awe in their presence, Rachel: we all do. But there's no need to be afraid. Go in. It is expected.'

I found my voice. 'Wuh ... Won't I be ... uh ... disturbing them, or –'

He shook his head. 'Like I said: they've been waiting for this. Waiting for you to come of your own free will. You will be welcomed.'

I wanted to scream, but no one would hear me; wanted to run, but I'd never reach the outer doors. I knew that walking into that room would be like stepping blindfold into Hell – involving me in some black and bloody ritual that even my soul might not survive. That the Clinicians were evil was beyond all doubt; but now, after months of slow suspicion – that drip ... drip ... dripping in the dark – I was suddenly plunged into cold black water, out of my depth and over my head; the freezing lake of fear that all those drops had formed. Fear that their evil was more than merely human. They might be carrying on Satanic sacrifice in there for all I knew. And I, who'd not been to church or confession in far too long, felt no strength left inside me to resist whatever I was going to face; no deep inner convictions any more. No *faith* ...

Danny was already turning back to the morgue trolley. 'I'll just get him stowed away, and then I'll leave you to it,' he said over his shoulder. 'Don't worry about locking up: I'll be round to do it later.'

I took a small, wary step towards the p-m-room doors.

I could hear muffled sound from within now: a running tap. The pool of dampness on this side of the door was spreading. I gave Danny a last, miserable look. He nodded encouragingly.

With my heart thumping in my throat, I pushed the door open and stepped inside.

Fourteen

The p-m room was ablaze with harsh white light, reflecting from the scrubbed and sterile surfaces round me: gleaming on worktops and white tiles; glinting on the steel of equipment and implements.

Glistening on blood and guts.

There were three high, metal dissection tables in the room, and the central one was occupied. A corpse was laid out on it, face upward, one arm dangling towards the floor. It was a middle-aged man, and he'd been partially disembowelled: I could see red and yellow offal in the raw chasm of his opened body cavity. More viscera, still oozing with blood, had been dumped in a large plastic bowl on the floor beside the table. There were splashes of red on the surrounding tiles, and down the sides of the solid-based unit. His eyes were still wide open. Glazed and empty, they stared up into the glare from the lights in the extractor hood above the table.

There was no one else in the room. The door now closed behind me: I was alone with that cadaver. One more victim of the Clinicians, and doubtless he too had still been alive when they'd started to slice. I noted the grime on his skin, the ragged trousers he still wore. Another of our down-and-outs, of course: prey to the monsters that hid in their midst. And if I failed to please them, I'd probably be next.

The mix of fear and nausea churning up in my stomach made me feel light-headed, and I had to lean back against the door for a moment until the urge to throw up had subsided. I kept glancing nervously round the room, but there was no sign of whoever had inflicted this latest horror. A door on the far side of the room – the pathologist's office, I guessed – was half-open, but the room beyond was in darkness. The only movement anywhere was the tapwater still streaming into the overflowing sink in one corner, dripping on down to the floor and rippling across the tiles towards me. I felt its wetness under my shoes as I stepped forward.

Slowly, almost resignedly, I began to walk across to where the grizzled, grisly corpse lay waiting; wrapping my long cardigan closer round me, though it brought neither warmth nor comfort. Still tight-lipped with nausea – but unable to deny a certain morbid curiosity.

It was no one I recognized, of course. The grim, bony face seemed frozen in a rictus of horror. I could see his heart had already been removed, and his lungs and larynx. Wrinkling my nose against the stink, I turned away, and almost brushed against his rigid, dangling arm.

Some of the implements they'd used on him were arrayed across the adjacent table, dripping blood through the grille top into the channels below. Here were scalpels and lancets and surgical shears . . . and other sharps as well. A straight razor. A hypodermic syringe . . .

I kept on walking, as though on eggshells, towards the blackboard that took up much of the far wall. Normally used for recording things like weights and measures during autopsies – but tonight someone had chalked a weird, occult-looking design on it: a broad series of concentric circles, interwoven with runes and symbols and scribbles of indecipherable script . . .

I stared at its details, trying to puzzle out its meaning. Some words looked vaguely familiar – I lingered on VNDSN for a moment – but it was no use. There was something singularly ugly about it, though, and I turned away with a little shiver.

And saw that the cadaver's open eyes had followed me across the room.

For a moment I just stood there and felt my mouth stretching to accommodate the scream that must surely come.

The gutted, butchered corpse began to twitch. The dangling hand I'd passed so close to was slowly being raised.

And Carol McCain said drily: 'You've no idea how hard it is, to kill a Clinician . . .'

She'd emerged from the darkened pathologist's office and was watching me now with the ghost of a grin on her pale face. As ever she wore her shades; and the black hat, pushed carelessly to the back of her head. One breast of her coat was spotted with blood; one sleeve bespattered. Her switchblade was glinting in her hand.

The corpse's struggles had slackened. Now it lay still once more. McCain turned her attention towards it.

'Please,' I almost whispered, 'who are you? What do you want?'

'Did Angela never tell you?' was her soft reply. 'The Clinicians will. Their name for me is . . . Nemesis.' And she walked over to the table and, bearing down on the body's chest with her free hand, she bent forward and began to cut again.

The corpse jerked: its dangling arm flailed out, but uselessly. Now the liver was out; here came the duodenum. And still it spastically resisted her.

I was shaking my head. 'No no no no NO . . .'

'*Yes*,' she hissed back, looking up from her red work. There was a droplet of blood on one cheek now, like a tear from behind those blind shades. 'You wanted to know what Clinicians were − well here's one. And there's but one sure way of killing them. Dissect the bastards, and burn the offal. It's the only way to disperse their life-force. Otherwise they just keep coming . . .'

The corpse's resistance was becoming weaker. The body

cavity was almost empty now, revealing yellowish bone amid the crimson. McCain turned from the table, glancing around.

'What . . . What're you after?' I managed.

'Bonesaw,' she said grimly, still looking.

'Bone . . . saw?' I realized why, of course, but I still had to say it.

'Need to take his stinking brain out,' McCain explained, baldly. She paused then, and looked at me. 'You'd better get right out of here. Out and back to your work. I know how impossible that sounds after this, but you have to try. If that porter asks you anything, just ignore him: he won't pursue it. He doesn't know what really happened here . . .'

I gave the corpse a fearful glance. 'And what if –'

'Don't worry: the others won't have sensed this, not yet. He came alone – I lured him here. You'll be safe for the rest of your shift.'

'And afterwards?'

She'd found a saw now, was weighing it in her hand. She looked at me again, and smiled: the perfect psychopath.

'We can talk about morning when morning comes,' was all she said.

Somehow I made it: I made it through to the end of my shift. If anyone noticed how pale I looked, or how silent I seemed, they didn't mention it – perhaps putting it down to distress at the death and grief we'd had to deal with. When I finally got into the locker room, I even managed to change clothes calmly enough – but my uniform dress, still whiffing of formalin, was bundled to the back of my locker as soon as I'd got it off. That was going twice through the laundry before I ever wore it again.

Outside in the cold, grey daylight, I glanced around uneasily before making for the bus stop. The dawn chorus was in full flow now; but the lights were still on throughout the hospital, as though the wards were almost reluctant to believe that day had finally come. One of the fluorescents under our canopy was winking fitfully on and off.

There was only one other person waiting by the bus shelter. It was McCain.

I recognized her on sight, of course, but made no attempt to avoid her. Whatever was going on, she had answers. And she knew how to kill Clinicians. Where else could I go?

PART TWO

Night Watchmen

Fifteen

The silence was beginning to get on my nerves.

'Well?' I prompted. McCain smiled thinly.

'I'm just wondering where to begin,' she said.

'How about the beginning?'

We'd caught the first bus into town, and now sat facing each other across a table in one of those dingy all-hours cafés by the station. At least she'd cleaned the blood off her coat; the smells of formalin and disinfectant mingled with the more normal street stink to create an interesting cocktail of aromas. People weren't fussy in this place, but even so I noticed we seemed to have the corner very much to ourselves.

'The beginning was a long time ago, Rachel. A very long time. There are some things I need to establish before we start there.'

'Such as?'

'You believe, don't you? In God, I mean.'

Silent now, I nodded.

'And if you believe in a power for good, then you also, presumably, believe in one for evil?' She waited for me to nod again, more cautiously now, before continuing. 'But do you believe in evil in the real world? In demons and black magic?'

I hesitated for only a moment. Six months ago I'd have probably had to say no. Two weeks ago I'd have said maybe. This morning, after our nightmare encounter with that unquiet corpse, I was ready to say yes.

The corner of her mouth lifted in the faintest smile of

satisfaction. 'Good. Because there's none blacker than the sort you're going to have to face.'

Verbally, I didn't reply. Mentally, I cringed.

'It's a form of sorcery that's been practised for centuries,' McCain was saying, as if to rub it in. 'But by only a few: a chosen handful – and all of them doctors. A strand so esoteric that barely a whisper of it escaped outside their secret circles. You won't find it mentioned in any book on the occult. There's only one allusion to it I can think of, in some obscure Renaissance manuscript on the practice of medicine. There's a veiled reference to "the Black Physick". A warning . . .'

'Doctors . . .' I stared back at her, wide-eyed. 'You mean medics here at the hospital? Like . . . a coven or something?'

She shook her head. 'Not the way you're thinking. Occasionally they might choose . . . disciples from among the terminals, as they call you. Or servants, like that porter of yours. But new initiates are rare. No . . . we're dealing with much older practitioners of the Art.'

There was a pause before I ventured: 'Like . . . how much older?'

She eyed me levelly. 'Like about three hundred years.'

I absorbed that in silence. After what seemed half an hour, I said: 'You were going to start at the beginning . . . ?'

Again that eerie little smile. 'All right. How good's your history? What do you know of the Knights Templar?'

I frowned; considered it. 'Weren't they crusaders or something? Warrior monks?'

She nodded. 'A mysterious – some say mystical – order of knights; the defenders of Solomon's temple, as they called themselves. Very fanatical, very dedicated. None holier than they, you might have thought – but in the fourteenth century their Order is suppressed, their wealth seized, their leading members tortured to death. And the reason given is that they have betrayed their faith, and fallen back on the practice of sorcery and ritual magic.'

I frowned, not quite seeing the relevance of this twist in the conversation. 'So?'

'So the chief movers behind their condemnation and destruction . . . according to some . . . were a rival order – the Knights Hospitallers. Heard of them? A martial order of monks themselves, but with a special interest in healing, in caring for the sick.'

'The Knights of St John?' I couldn't help smiling at her look of slight surprise. 'Yes, I've heard of them. It's where the St John Ambulance take their name from, isn't it?'

'They do. Hardly descendants of them, though. And certainly not of the faction I'm going to tell you about.'

I waited.

'The next bit is a little obscure,' McCain admitted (as if the foregoing hadn't been). 'Some versions have it that the accusations of sorcery were a slander – a pretext for the destruction of one of the most powerful – and therefore, to some, the most threatening – orders in Christendom, and the theft of their lands and riches. Others imply that the suppression of the Templars was engineered by those who wanted their secrets for themselves: who wanted to possess whatever canon of occult knowledge the Order had amassed.'

'So were they into black magic after all, or – ?'

She shrugged. 'No one really knows; though legends say that Solomon was himself a worker of magic, and bound demons to his will. I'm just telling you what I suspect. Because not long after the Templars were eradicated, the rumours start – and we hear the first whisper of a new faction arising within the Order of the Hospitallers. A very obscure one, though – and again referred to only cryptically, even in the more apocryphal works of the time. But we know its members took the title of *Iudex Medicus*. The Order of Clinical Judges . . .'

I wondered who "we" were, but didn't pursue it. 'And they were doctors?'

'Not exclusively, not then. But as the Hospitallers faded in their turn, and the medieval practice of medicine moved onward, the adepts of this new Order – its Black Physicians, if you like – were drawn more and more from the medical profession, until it became their exclusive domain – a dark, secret knowledge handed down from one doctor only to another.'

'Until today?' I was mesmerized, I had to admit it. Unlikely it might seem – but no more unlikely than a cadaver that tried to resist you even as you dissected it.

McCain shook her head once more. 'No: like I said, there are no new initiates, not now. The Order is almost extinct; most of its adepts over the centuries have dwindled or been destroyed. In England they were all but burned from the soil by Lord Cromwell and his witchfinders: a few truly guilty victims among the scores of innocent. Only a handful have survived to see today: a last cabal.'

I shifted uncomfortably. 'What did they do, these ... Black Physicians? Sacrifice their patients or something?'

'Again, not in the sense you think.' McCain sat back, her eyes unreadable as ever behind those dark lenses. 'Two ironies, Rachel. At the beginning, I believe they even sought to use their power to do good: to bring life and healing. But they gradually became corrupted – and drew on power for power's sake.

'The second irony is this: even now, they do not believe that power is supernatural.'

It seemed bloody supernatural to me. 'How can they not?'

'As a state of mind, it's had centuries to develop. Listen. From the start, their obsession was with learning, with knowledge – no matter how ancient or how forbidden. The quest for absolute truth, if you will. It became their idol; became their god. Some of the eastern mysticism they inherited was thousands of years old even then: remedies and rites from Old Sumer.' She paused. 'Heard of that?'

I glumly shook my head.

McCain smiled like someone truly in her element. 'The oldest civilization ever known, Rachel: and the first to bring forth medicine out of magic. But their physicians were sorcerers as well: they believed in demons that brought disease; in spirits to be placated or expelled. The Clinicians embraced the rituals, believing they enriched the powers of the mind; but they came to disbelieve in demons, and reduced them to meaningless words. Such superstitions were beneath them. Or so they thought.'

Eyes downcast, I listened; watching my untouched mug of coffee growing cold.

'And as they embraced pure Science,' McCain went on softly, 'so they lost their faith in anything outside it. Everything lay in the absolute power and wisdom of man – if they could only find the key. Even the occult powers they came to possess and wield . . . the powers their ancient ancestors called demonic . . . could be rationally explained: made to fit the natural law of a cold, dead universe. Hinted at in the earliest of writings; ignored or forgotten by later, lesser mortals . . .'

Her voice grew suddenly intense. '*It's not magic to them, Rachel.* It's natural power, to be tapped and used by those with the learning and the skill. Nor is it evil, for that idea means nothing to them. Neither does good. All that matters is their science: their endless pursuit of *knowledge.*

'One consequence of this: the notion of faith, especially religious faith, in things unseen and unproven, is anathema to them; it's a concept they simply cannot grasp. So they hate it – and fear it.'

'Fear it?'

'Yes. Oh yes. Because real faith makes them doubt.'

There was silence then. Instinctively my fingers crept to the crucifix at my throat, as though to check it was still there. I twisted it gently on its chain, rubbing it between forefinger and thumb.

'So how many are left?' I asked; and my mouth was suddenly dry as I added: 'And what do they want? What do they want with me?'

McCain leaned forward again, putting her elbows on the table; resting her chin on the backs of her folded hands.

'When I came to this town I found five. There may be others elsewhere; there may not. Once, they will have had human names; but those are long-forgotten, like their humanity itself. The names by which they call themselves now are these. Melphalan. Altiplaz. Glaukostyx. Vindesyn. Vokaine.'

They sounded curiously familiar. After a moment I realized why. 'Drugs. They're the names of drugs.'

'Developed from them, yes. Who knows what different things they've called themselves down the centuries? And believe me, they've lived that long: since Cromwell's time, or even earlier. Using and abusing their fellow-men. Torturing; murdering. Resurrecting. Endlessly experimenting, to further their knowledge; probing the deepest, darkest secrets of spirit and flesh . . .'

I remembered the cryptic scrawlings on the mortuary blackboard: the word I thought I'd recognized. VNDSN. 'The one you killed last night, that was . . .'

'Vindesyn,' she confirmed.

'And . . . that bloke they found autopsied in Stone Road . . . ?'

'Altiplaz.'

'The police said he was a pimp, a drug pusher.'

'Living among you, they take on many guises. Especially ones that let them profit from human degradation.' Experiments with whores and junkies; I slammed the door on the thought before it could develop further. 'As to their plans for you . . . I don't know. Not yet. Believe me, Rachel. But I suspect they require an accomplice of some sort – someone else within the hospital. I think they've sensed your strengths of character – and of will. Those are powerful qualities – which can be just as powerful when turned to the dark side.'

I stared despairingly back at her. 'Look, how do you know all this? All about them? And why are you taking them on?'

'So many questions, Rachel. I'm here to kill them. To wipe them out for ever. What more do you need to know?'

I recalled what Angela James had said of her: that she believed herself to be an angel. A fallen angel. A destroying angel. 'Your name,' I murmured. 'It's not McCain, really . . . is it?'

Her smile was so cold it nearly made me shiver.

'Isn't it as good a name as any? But you're right: my true name is something else. Another drug-name, before I took it as my own. *Razoxane*.'

I nodded: it seemed appropriate, somehow. *Razor*-sounding . . .

A sip of tepid coffee, while I studied the oh-so-normal outside world for a moment. Then: 'So what do I do now?'

'Watch. And wait.'

'For what?'

'They think they've got their hooks in you: they told their slave as much. They've no way of knowing you were involved last night. Sometime soon they'll come and speak with you again. Let them. Find out what they want. Pretend to play along.'

I grimaced at the prospect. 'The one last night . . . Vindesyn. You're sure he's . . . ?'

She nodded. 'All his guts were ashes before we met this morning. His soul – if you can call it that – had nothing left to cling to. The Void sucked it down.'

'You mean . . . Hell?'

'That's one name for it.'

'And what happens when they find his body?'

'That's already taken care of. He's all neatly sheeted

141

up in the fridge now; the ledger's been altered and the paperwork's all in order. They're that busy in your morgue, they probably won't suspect a thing. Just another unclaimed corpse, to be disposed of at public expense . . .'

'Right. All right.' I was fingering my crucifix again. 'And while I'm acting all interested in joining him, where are you going to be?'

'Somewhere close.'

I remembered her words as she'd sliced up her victim: *I lured him here.* 'You're using me as bait, aren't you?'

'I'm protecting you, Rachel,' she countered evenly. 'They chose you, and they'll come for you – whatever I do. But together we can destroy them, don't you see?'

I nodded heavily. I saw, all right. I hadn't asked for any of this, but I'd got it all, and there was only one way out now.

'Look . . . Just make sure you stay really close, okay?'

She just put on her hat, and settled it squarely. I glimpsed more than a hint of irony in the gesture; but it was practical clothing for all that. Just as her long coat kept her warm, so the hat's wide brim kept the rain off her face. And maybe the sunlight too.

It was her shades I couldn't hack. The eyes are windows to the soul, or so they say, and mine are clean and clear. But hers had been glazed with ambulance glass, and showed only my reflection. I could feel the watchfulness behind them, though. The gaze of her warped and grinning mind.

'Of course, Rachel,' she almost purred. 'I'm your protecting angel, after all . . .'

Because I couldn't see her eyes, I couldn't really tell if she was joking.

But somehow I didn't think she was.

Strangely enough, I slept quite well that day. Perhaps I was beginning to believe it, too.

Sixteen

Even before I'd left the flat to do some shopping, late on Friday afternoon, I knew where I was going to finish up.

I'd still been a bit dopey – six hours' sleep hadn't really eased the weight of the hours I'd worked so far this week. I felt knackered, basically. But even so, I managed to wander all round town before finally, fatalistically making my way down Lenton Street towards The Magick Eye – our town's alternative bookshop.

I'd never been inside before, though I gave its windows a curious glance whenever I passed. From what I'd seen, and heard from others, I gathered they specialized in New Age-type stuff: astrology, weird religions, the occult – even 'green' issues, with an earth-magic sort of slant. And despite my protestations of scepticism – and a certain Christian primness – I had to admit the place had a certain fascination. There was a vague, and vaguely seductive, sense of the forbidden about the subjects it dealt in.

The forbidden is always fascinating. Even St Paul says that.

After a quick, almost guilty glance around, I pushed open the door and went inside.

There were a couple of other people browsing, plus the bloke at the till: a long-haired young man with a pentagram ring on one finger. He gave me an incurious glance as I entered, then went back to reading his dog-eared paperback. I walked deeper into the shop and tried to look as if I knew what I was after: I didn't want anyone taking an interest and trying to sell me something. I made a show of studying a shelf of books on tarot and divination, before making my way over to the section marked *Magick*.

Christ, but they had it all. Mysticism. Magic. Witchcraft. Guides to ritual; books of spells. Strange, unsettling titles. Authors with exotic-sounding names. *The Book of Egyptian Magic* was here, and *The Power of Babylon. A History of the Golden Dawn. Wicca Work. An Introduction to Black Magic.*

Shit.

I reached out almost tentatively for this last work: a fair-sized paperback with a black cover (of course) and an upside-down pentagram on the front. My mouth dry with apprehension – or anticipation – I began to thumb through it.

Latin liturgies. Strange symbols. Invoking the pentagram. Rituals of summoning. Rituals of banishment . . . Already feeling I'd somehow seen too much, I closed it again, swallowed and replaced it on the shelf.

And glanced furtively around – the way I've seen blokes do in a newsagents after flicking through the girlie mags. Making sure that no one they know's just walked in.

Maybe some of them feel just the same as I did now. Afraid of being caught in the act, doing what society calls shameful. And unable to quite shake off that feeling of having dirty hands . . .

Back home, I went straight to my room and over to the bookshelf. My Bible was there, crammed in among the romances and the thrillers; I hadn't opened it for months. But I took it out now, and turned it over in my hands, as if it was some talisman with protective powers. It was a New English version, with a leather cover and gold-edged pages – a present from my parents when I'd left home. I turned to my mother's writing on the flyleaf: *To Rachel, with lots of love – Mum & Dad*. Reading that brought a burning surge of homesickness as I hadn't felt in years

– not since before the road-crash that had killed them both. That had really brought me down, of course: I'd been in my first job, working on a London casualty ward, and suddenly the everyday grimness we learned to live with was brought shockingly home to me. So sudden; so senseless. At least they'd lived to see me qualify: to become the nurse I'd always dreamed of being.

I still missed them; sometimes still felt lonely. But never more alone than I did now.

After a moment, I placed the Bible on my bedside table – within easy reach. Maybe having it there didn't make me any safer; but I felt a bit more comfortable knowing it was near.

Friday night I got a phone call.

I was in my office making some changes to the Off-duty when the phone rang. The internal phone, not the special direct line they save for major accidents and suchlike. Still writing, I reached out casually and picked it up.

'A&E, Sister.'

'Hello, A&E Sister. Remember me?' A quiet voice. Cold. McCain. Or Razoxane, or whatever she was calling herself.

My whole body tensed: I felt as if I was going into rigor mortis. 'What do you want?'

I hadn't seen her since our talk in the café; we'd finished our coffee and gone our separate ways. I assumed she'd been keeping an eye on me since then. I hoped she had.

'About that idea you had,' the soft voice said. 'Using your seven-day break to take off somewhere – stay with friends or whatever. Let me pass on a word of warning.'

It was certainly a possibility I'd considered; as the end of my stint approached, I'd begun to think of it more and more. 'What?' I asked uneasily.

'You were going to take the train? Somewhere between here and the next station, you'd be found in the toilet.

Locked in. Ripped open. Your heart stuffed into your mouth.' It wasn't a threat, it was a statement of fact: something as inevitable as sunrise. I almost gagged.

'See you around,' Razoxane said, and hung up.

And I just sat there, open-mouthed, the receiver at my ear. Not even knowing if she'd been predicting the Clinicians' reaction – or her own.

Seventeen

My working week finished quietly, with a low-key Saturday night. I was pretty much on edge, and knew I sounded irritable, but people seemed to put it down to tiredness, and gave me room. Mark asked if I wanted to go out for a drink with him and a couple of the others next week sometime; I made noncommittal noises. Karen wanted to know if I'd go to aerobics with her on Tuesday; I said I wasn't sure.

Danny gave me one or two knowing looks; I tried to smile back, despite the chill I felt inside.

The flat seemed very quiet when I got in. Sarah and her latest boyfriend (this week's boyfriend) had left the previous day on a week's skiing holiday. A little warily I explored the place, but everything was as it should be. And though being on my own made me more than a little nervous, I felt I needed to be alone – to think things through, get them straight in my mind. And to face whatever nightmares might come. Nightmares that would slice me up without a second thought . . .

I knew it would take me a little while to get used to getting my sleep at nights again; I was still a bit muzzy by Monday. But the monthly departmental meeting was being held that afternoon, and I decided to come in on my own time for it. It was a chance I had all too rarely, and the night staff could do with the representation; but of course my need to stay in touch with the sanity of the real world had something to do with it, too . . .

It was strangely disorientating: seeing the hospital by day. The corridors were busy; the Outpatients' Department overflowing. Casualty itself seemed a different world in the afternoon sunlight – so far removed from the bleak and echoing labyrinth it had come to feel like on Nights. I walked through the half-full waiting area, passing as just another patient in my jeans and sweatshirt; which was just as well, since the advertised waiting time was now two hours, and a couple of people seemed to be looking around for someone to complain to. I went round beyond the desk, smiling hello to the receptionist and a middle-aged Staff Nurse I rarely got to work with, and walked on down the corridor to our pocket seminar room.

Kessler was in full flow when I slipped in; aware that I was a little late, I gave him a quick nod of greeting and eased into the nearest chair. With the ghost of a smile he kept on talking: adding to the diagram on the whiteboard. Strategy and budgets for the coming year. I took out my notepad and began to write.

There were about ten of us around the table, including Dr Khan the Senior Reg., our Service Manager Miss Wright, and most of the Day Sisters. Judith, also in mufti and seated across from me, caught my eye and winked encouragingly.

Kessler droned on, his voice punctuated by the squeak of his marker pen across the whiteboard. Questions were asked; comments made. One of them got a good laugh, and automatically I smiled along, though I hadn't really been listening.

Halfway down my first page, I'd already started doodling.

Normally I'd have been concentrating, interested: anxious to hear how we were planning to meet the months ahead. But today my mind just wouldn't stay still. My thoughts flitted about, as though afraid of staying in one place too long. In case the memories caught up again.

I was trying hard to keep Razoxane's warnings out of my head. I wasn't succeeding.

'. . . with us, Rachel?'

I blinked, glanced up. Kessler was looking right at me, pen still poised.

'Uh. Sorry . . . ?'

'I was asking if you were still with us,' he asked evenly. I flushed, and felt like cringing. 'Er, yes, sorry.'

He held my gaze for a moment longer, then returned his attention to the board. I sat back, and bit my lip, and felt absurdly like a schoolgirl caught daydreaming by her teacher. Dr Ivan Kessler had that effect on you sometimes.

People didn't call him Ivan the Terrible for nothing . . .

The briefing went on; and now I felt sufficiently stung to pay attention, and contribute to the discussion. I got quite absorbed in it, too: so much so that for a while I forgot my worries – just as I'd originally hoped. We broke up just after four; Kessler came over as I was packing away my notes.

'Good to see you here, Rachel. We need more input from the night staff at these meetings. And thanks for your contributions: they were helpful.'

I nodded back, smiled – and breathed a small inward sigh of relief.

Judith was waiting outside. 'Fancy a coffee?'

I certainly did. The two of us went up to the canteen together. 'So how're things?' she asked as we settled down at an empty table; her tone as casual as befitted a polite enquiry – but her shrewd, steady gaze leaving me in no doubt of her concern. I shrugged, not trying to evade the scrutiny; right now I really needed someone watching out for me. Part of me even wished she would somehow see right through, into the shadow behind my eyes – so I wouldn't have to bear its burden on my own any longer. But she was blind to it, of course. And how could I begrudge her that blessing?

'. . . Fine, thanks.' I let my eyes wander, my chin in my

hand: then looked back to her. 'Last week was pretty heavy, but . . .'

But I knew she was digging deeper than that, in her careful way: wanting to be sure I was over our little crisis with the intruder. With Razoxane. Neither of us alluded to it directly as our easy chat continued; but I think I managed to convince her I was coping. Easier than convincing myself.

Smokes followed drinks; and just before we were finished, she leaned forward, and made the only mention.

'Kessler's really proud of you, you know that? Not the type to say so, I know; but I've worked with him long enough. I can tell.'

I just smiled, and nodded, and watched my cigarette smoulder.

And thought: *Oh Judith, what am I going to do? What the bloody hell am I going to do?*

That night I woke in warmth and darkness, to the tingling pleasure of someone tickling my foot. Mischievous fingers, gently stroking its sensitive sole; teasing between the toes. Sending ripples of delight through my sleep-dulled system.

I stretched in luxurious doziness: savouring the sensation for the thirty-odd seconds it took me to remember I was alone in the flat this week. And cold sweat drenched me in an instant stinging sheen as I jerked my foot back and fairly hurled myself against the bedhead, sustaining jars and bruising I didn't feel for many minutes.

Silent darkness pressed into my eyes as I huddled there, feeling my T-shirt soak up my sweat; my heart thudding faster than a drumroll. Outside the feverish overdrive of my motionless body, nothing moved in the room.

I waited.

I waited through all the rest of that long, long night: frozen and staring blindly into blackness. The small hours crawled by with wretched slowness, minute by minute, until it seemed the dawn would never come. And then I became aware of a colourless glow beyond the window, fading gradually in behind creeping dark clouds; and some of that light began to thin out the gloom in which I crouched. Walls became discernible . . . the shapes of furniture . . . and finally I could see clearly enough across the room to realize it was empty. I was alone. The door was still firmly shut; so were the wardrobes. And though I couldn't quite summon up the courage to lean over and peer beneath my bed, I knew it hadn't been Trinity. The cat had already been asleep, curled up in his basket in the kitchen, when I turned in.

Perhaps I'd dreamed it, then. Just another nightmare.

I didn't think so, though. Not for one moment.

My car was back on the road by this time, and on Tuesday afternoon I just went for a drive: steering at speed through the various intertwined estates at the fringes of town; following one road, then another, with all my mind on my driving and none of it left to dwell on the empty flat I'd left behind. I needed the workout anyway – I'd been half-afraid I'd lost my nerve – but the exercise perked me up altogether. Waiting at the lights at Mason Street, I thumbed an *All About Eve* cassette into the tape deck, and drove on with Julianne's gorgeous voice filling the car. I felt a bit better by the time I got home. It was nice while it lasted.

Part of me had wanted just to keep driving, of course: to put my foot down until the whole place was well behind me. But there was no such easy escape, I knew that. It might take them years, but they'd find me in the end. Or she would.

*   *   *

I made damn sure the flat was secure before I went to bed.

It was well past midnight when I finally gave up channel-hopping from one uninteresting programme to the next (and back again); sitting curled up there on the sofa, toying restlessly with the remote. I thumbed the off button and the picture winked out with a crackle, leaving just the gleaming red dot on the console. I padded over and switched it off completely, then straightened up and stood quite still. Listening.

The flat was silent.

With my black sweatshirt and leggings I felt I was almost one with the shadows as I gave the place a quick once-over. Front door chained and bolted. Windows locked. I ventured into the darkened kitchen, where only the small blue flame of the water heater's pilot light stood out in the dimness. I could just make out Trinity's sleeping form in the cat basket under the table. I checked the window locks there too, before retreating – partially satisfied, but still reluctant – to my room. I locked the door and quickly undressed; then got into bed and fumbled through my Bible, trying to find some words of comfort – something I could concentrate on: anything to keep my griping fears at bay.

After a while I felt a little calmer, but not much. I laid the book on my bedside table, where I could reach it easily, and squirmed deeper in under the duvet. I left the main light on.

I'd considered not sleeping at all, of course: keeping vigil all through the hours of darkness, hoping against hope they wouldn't catch me by surprise. But I was tired enough after last night, and still not fully recovered from the past week's grind. I had to get some rest, recharge my batteries, or I'd be easy prey. I'd thought of reverting to my worktime sleeping pattern, too – sleeping during the day, while the sun was up, so I could be awake and watchful through the night. But the fact was I needed to be out and about among other people for as much of the day as possible: in cafés, shops and pubs. Only then did I begin to feel safe.

The worst thing was not being able to talk to anyone about it: I knew that anyone I involved, no matter how indirectly, would almost certainly be killed. By one faction or the other . . .

Sleep didn't come easily. I tossed and turned for what seemed like hours. But eventually, with the duvet pulled right up to shield my eyes from the light, I felt myself slipping away . . . down into the welcoming dark.

When I awoke, there was daylight filtering through the curtains, diluting the glow of the electric bulb. I lay still for several minutes, listening to the silence of the flat; then propped myself up on one elbow and glanced around. My room was undisturbed. No one had been in here with me while I slept.

Nothing happened the next night either.

The night after that, I dreamed that I was dying – and woke to find I was.

It was a stifling dream, a blur of suffocation: like being sucked to the bottom of the deepest, coldest sea. I groped blindly towards wakefulness – that half-imagined light beyond the darkness; grasped it, and hauled myself in. Back into my body. I awoke.

But I still couldn't breathe.

Or see, or even scream. Something soft was pressing down across my face, crushing my nostrils closed; sealing up the dark behind my eyelids. I tasted cotton in my mouth, smelt Persil – and knew it was my pillow.

My arms flailed out in panic – and struck something solid. I clutched at cloth, felt flesh and bone; lost my grip, and groped again. Squirming and squirming, but I was on my back, defenceless, and my skull was throbbing now, my lungs beginning to singe and smoulder; and suddenly

I had his wrist. Cold skin and matted hairs, and more bones close beneath them. Bones like iron. They wouldn't budge.

I felt my consciousness begin to fade. My chest was bursting, as if I'd swallowed a sun, but even that agony was greying out around the edges. I heard muffled, shapeless sounds inside my head, and knew they were my final gasps for breath. And then the pillow was yanked away, and I was left there like a landed fish – fairly whooping to refill my aching lungs.

I hadn't left the light on this time: the darkness above me was total – and filled with a chill so heavy it seemed to soak into my T-shirt. There was a smell in it, too: a stink of filth and formalin, like a blocked drain in the morgue. And as I lay limp and helpless, too drained to do anything but pant, I realized there was movement.

A rustle of clothing; then the sound of fingers fumbling with my bedside lamp, so close and loud they jarred me like nails across a blackboard. The dusky-yellow glow clicked on to reveal a tall, ragged figure standing over me, motionless beside the bed.

I shrank back as if crushed by some invisible weight, flattened down against the mattress; quite speechless with horror.

His clothes were dark: a long wool coat, stiff with dried stains, worn open over shabby waistcoat and trousers and wrinkled shirt. The wide-brimmed hat he wore was black, and, like the clothes, looked old. Centuries old. His figure almost blurred into the gloom beyond the lamplight – apart from the face, which stood out mask-like in the dimness. Staring down at me.

It was a grim face that might have once been handsome. Haggard now: hardened. His beard and collar-length hair were black, but I saw the odd reflecting glint of grey. The eyes that studied me were deep-set and dark, and deathly cold.

154

He still held the pillow in his free hand. After a moment he dropped it casually aside; and spoke in a dry, quiet voice.

'Understand this first, Rachel Young. Your life is in my hands now. I can take it whenever it pleases me to.'

I just stared up at him, petrified; still sucking air. My lungs weren't halfway full yet.

'Yes: you fear me,' he observed, nodding. 'You are wise to. Yet I can also be your friend: give you power and pleasures beyond your sweetest dreams. Consider that terror you felt, on the threshold of death. You can follow me, and never feel its like again.

'The choice is up to you.'

He drew up the chair from the dressing-table, and slowly sat. Down on a level with the lamp now, and its glow caught his gaunt cheekbones, and kindled sparks in the depths of his eyes. He nudged his hat up his forehead, almost casually: and I saw that he too wore the sallow rubber of surgical gloves – as if I was some infectious case, unclean to touch . . .

'Permit me to introduce myself,' he continued, with empty courtesy. 'My name is Melphalan. I am a Master Practitioner of the Order of Clinical Judges. Some men have given me the title *Lord* of Physicians.'

There was something almost mesmerizing in that voice: a rich yet rasping tone that held my attention as rigidly as his stare.

'You might protest that some of what I have to tell you is beyond belief,' Melphalan said. 'But I think you had already begun to suspect that we existed – even before we revealed ourselves, in order to save you from your assailant. We have watched you, Rachel: for a long while. And every time one of our subjects survived long enough to reach your department, we sensed your suspicions grow. Oh, you tried to persuade yourself otherwise, did you not? But slowly you became aware of us – and what we are.

'Yet how could you ever have guessed the true nature of our Order?'

I lay there, hugging myself as I stared back at him; still unable to speak.

'We're deathless, Rachel,' he almost whispered. 'We've lived for centuries. When first I entered the Order, this nation was still at war. Civil war. The blinkered physicians of the age still killed more often than they cured. But for those of us with the wisdom and the will, the power to regenerate the flesh was there for the taking. I mastered it in my turn: I have aged not a day since then. And that is now a gift I have to give.'

It dawned on me then that, for all his watchfulness, he knew nothing of my meetings with Razoxane: was unaware that she'd explained things to me already. Having this advantage over him, however small, gave me something to cling on to. But I knew I mustn't let him even glimpse it: if he realized I'd been got at, he'd kill me now.

So, finding my voice, or a husk of it, at last, I said: 'That . . . isn't possible.'

His lips parted in a mirthless smile, and showed his teeth. 'You believe I am insane, of course.'

He said it calmly enough, but cold instinct warned me not to try out my psychie training just now, and I shook my head urgently. 'No. No. It's all just . . . so hard to believe . . .'

He nodded understandingly. 'Our powers are not easily comprehended by the common mass of humanity. They never were. Even those who witness our works fall back on primitive explanations of magic and sorcery. Yet all can be explained through the ancient wisdom which your so-called scientists have long forgotten. The power to pro-long life . . . to restore life . . . those are the secrets we have discovered. Powers that can benefit all mankind.'

I thought of their victims we'd seen in A&E: the fear

and mutilation and needless death. 'So why do you kill?' I said dully. 'Why cause so much suffering?'

Melphalan chuckled softly: almost indulgently. 'Rachel,' he admonished, 'are you so innocent? Wisdom is life's greatest treasure: it must be bought at a price. In order to know fully the spirit and the flesh, we must persist in our investigations. Down to the last cell and nerve-end. There is always something new to be learned. Some deaths will be inevitable to further this cause: that has always been the case, and always will be. And what better use can we find for those degenerates who grovel in your gutters, or sell themselves for money?' He spoke the last sentence with what sounded like genuine contempt.

Once more I remembered what Karen had said, when we'd mopped up after Kaufmann. The vivisectionists were after people now . . . It had seemed blackly funny then; it didn't tonight.

I swallowed.

'So . . . what do you want with me?'

Once more the hint of a smile on the half-lit face before me.

'Have you not guessed it, Rachel? We seek your help.'

'Help?' I blurted in disbelief. 'That night . . . You *tortured* me.'

I broke off immediately, and for a moment thought I'd gone too far. His hooded eyes regarded me in silence: unblinking as a lizard's. And then Melphalan shrugged.

'That was unfortunate,' he conceded – sounding about as regretful as a speak-your-weight machine. 'I charged my brothers with your protection: they felt obliged to ensure you had not been harmed . . .'

Like hell, I thought back grimly. *Like fuck.* Despite my dread, I had to grit my teeth for fear I'd spit it out aloud. Because I knew damn well they'd done what they'd done to degrade and terrify me – to reduce me to a nervous wreck. To break down my defences and let them in . . .

And Melphalan knew that I knew: I heard the sardonic edge of humour in his voice as he continued.

'You must forgive their enthusiasm. Nearly five centuries have passed, but Vokaine my brother still has the mind of a medieval field surgeon — which is what he is.'

I couldn't quite keep the grimace off my face at that.

'Help you how?' I asked it warily enough, but my voice was steady: the very fact that I was able to talk rationally with my awful visitor helped me get some sort of grip on myself.

Melphalan paused to consider his reply.

'You will understand that we and our kind have always been misunderstood: and shunned. Strangers and wanderers upon earth, your Bible calls us. You see how even we are forced to live. Since we came to this city, we have been confined to backstreet premises which scarcely do justice to our skills . . . constantly moving from place to place to avoid detection. Yet your hospital has unused wards where no one ever goes; operating theatres forgotten behind locked doors. Where better for us to continue our researches? But in order to establish ourselves in secret, we require the service of someone who already works within its walls . . .'

'But why me?' I insisted, almost desperately. 'Danny Wright works for you, doesn't he? And how many others? Why do you want *me*?'

'Remember what I told you, Rachel,' the Clinician said calmly. 'We have been watching you for longer than you know. We like what we have seen. Your intelligence, your sensitivities . . . your strength of will. They are qualities we value.'

Qualities just as powerful when turned to the dark side, as Razoxane had told me. I tried to keep my revulsion concealed as he continued.

'A woman like yourself can serve us well, Rachel Young.

For once established, our practice will need its gatekeeper. You understand my meaning?'

I nodded stupidly: knowing what the name meant in NHS terms, at least. Someone to filter the demand for a doctor's services – to ensure that the most appropriate cases went through for treatment . . .

'I shall make it clear for you,' Melphalan said. 'Your department sees thousands of people in a year. Some are treated and discharged; others admitted to the wards beyond. You will be in a position to assess the patients who come in through your doors: to identify which will make the most appropriate subjects for our attention.'

If any colour had remained in my face, it drained away now. 'How do you mean . . . appropriate?'

'You will recognize this quotation from the Christian mythology you flirt with,' came his reply: '*It is not the healthy who need a physician but the sick*. Many who seek out your department suffer not so much from physical ailments as from spiritual ones: sickness of soul. They are lonely, frightened, disturbed – and vulnerable. As human beings they are worthless. As citizens, they will not be missed. The dregs of this town come to your doors, Rachel. You will refer them on to us. If they have been discharged, we can arrange to make house calls . . .'

The way he said it confirmed my suspicion: Melphalan had a sense of humour. A hideous, evil, gloating sense of humour.

'If they have been admitted to the wards, we will visit them there. Do not suppose the night staff can prevent us: they will not even realize we have been.' He leaned forward again, interlacing long and bony fingers. Latex gleamed. 'We come and go as we please. Just as I entered your flat tonight without sound or hindrance. The superstitious might think we walk through walls, but it is altogether simpler than that. What power we do exert over certain material things is as nothing compared to the powers we have over the human mind. The very psyche is a malleable thing for those with the knowledge, Rachel. If I had chosen to visit you at work, your colleagues would believe they saw nothing more than a patient's relative speaking with you in your office . . .'

I nodded still, but I wasn't really listening. My mind had got hung up a while back, snagged by a memory awakened at his description of the gatekeeper's role. A memory of a documentary film I'd seen once, with interviews of Auschwitz survivors. One had spoken of the infamous Dr Mengele himself, waiting at the railhead to examine the disembarking damned – assessing them, to decide which would live a little longer, and which would be handed over to their exterminators. Those judged as worthless went straight to the gas chambers. And now they wanted me to play that role . . .

Nauseated, breathless, I still recalled Razoxane's instructions. *Pretend to play along.* Despite my disgust, I managed to say 'So what's in it for me?' and almost sound convincing.

'Everything you ever wanted,' was his snake-smooth answer. 'We can fulfil your every desire: your every lust. You'll learn undreamed-of secrets. You'll live for ever.'

I moistened my lips. 'And . . . how much time have I to decide, or –'

'You have no time at all, Rachel. But who would need to think twice when made such an offer?'

I stared hopelessly back at him. Once again Razoxane's words came whispering through my mind. *Pretend to play along . . .*

'No,' I said.

His expression didn't change. 'You refuse our offer?' he said evenly.

I felt terror begin to rise inside me: one more step and I'd be past the point of no return. And maybe I'd be the next one they found autopsied alive. But some fundamental instinct told me I had to resist: *had* to resist. It wasn't something I could rationalize; the sense of evil in this room was now so strong that the last of my consciously religious thoughts had been overwhelmed, despite Razoxane's assertion that Clinicians could be unnerved by sheer faith. It was with no hope of salvation that I shook my head once more.

'Get out,' I whispered. 'Get away from me, please, just go.'

And Melphalan rose smoothly to his feet. He stood over my bed, looking down; squaring his hat again, as though what must follow required a grim formality.

'I thought you were wise,' he said, almost regretfully. 'It seems I was mistaken. But there is yet time for you to see the error of your ways.'

And then his hand lashed out — but only to sweep the lamp from the bedside table. The bulb burst, and Melphalan vanished in the darkness. A moment later, I realized the room was empty again, and I was alone.

Only then did I begin to cry.

Eighteen

I went to see Miss Morgan again next day; I had nowhere else to go. Alone and frightened though I was, I couldn't face my friends and their blissful ignorance – still less endanger their lives. Not that I was about to unburden myself to Miss M, either; but we'd be sharing something none the less. For she too knew what it was like to have come to the brink: to the edge of darkness.

I could tell as soon as I saw her that she wouldn't linger there for long. Her face was quite without colour, and its lines of age and pain were smoothing out: she looked at peace already. After a quiet word with the nurse in charge, I came and sat beside her bed, and watched her sleep. There was no need to disturb her, no need for us to talk; it was enough that I was there. She'd be out of it soon enough: free of this life and all its nightmares. The way of all flesh . . . even mine. Right now, I found the prospect almost insanely reassuring.

There were visitors at a couple of other bedsides; a low murmur of conversation filled the bay. It was turning into quite a nice afternoon outside: warm sunlight spilling in to brighten the ward's drab decor. I heard the drugs trolley trundled past; a student nurse clarifying some point of medication with her mentor. The voices faded towards the next bay down. The phone on the station rang several times before it was answered.

Just another Late on the workaday ward. I remembered it well.

I realized that Miss Morgan's eyes had fluttered open,

focusing on me. It seemed to take her a moment to realize who I was. Then her weak smile came.

'Rachel . . .' Even after that she paused for breath. 'So glad . . . you came to . . . say goodbye.'

I smiled back, a little awkwardly. To ask how she was seemed rather pointless. 'Have you . . . got everything you need?'

'Peace . . . of mind,' she answered after a pause. 'That's all . . . any of us . . . need.'

I nodded: I knew that all too well.

She swallowed, and stared at nothing for a minute or so. Then she continued, in a slightly stronger voice. 'I'm not afraid of it, Rachel. Not afraid. It will be my last and longest rest. I've had . . . a long life, and a good one. And now I'm tired, Rachel. So tired . . .'

I reached out, took her hand. 'Sleep well, Miss M. You've earned it.' After a pause, I added quietly. 'It's a beginning, not an end; believe me. You'll wake up young . . .'

She smiled again. 'That's more my Rachel. I'm afraid I've . . . lapsed a little, as you know. I'm not sure I still believe all this . . . business about an afterlife. But . . . say a prayer for me, if you would. I'd be grateful . . .'

Silent now, I nodded; a little surprised myself at how fervently I'd spoken.

She was about to say more: I saw her hesitate, struggling with the words. Then she gave a little sigh – and as I watched, her eyes began to glaze. I glimpsed the tinge of blueness creeping into her slack, pale skin, and knew her heart had faltered to a stop.

Sheer instinct prompted me halfway to my feet, sucking in air for the warning shout: the reaction ingrained in every nurse. A word was all it needed, and the crash bell would be tripped, the ward alerted, the medics summoned from all corners of the building. And that word died in my throat as another, deeper instinct intervened to override my training and drop me back into the chair.

Let her go, my impulse said. *She's worn, and tired, and hurting. Let her go.*

I sat motionless, wide-eyed, to watch her die.

Someone stepped up close behind me then; I knew without turning that it was one of the nurses. 'Miss Morgan . . . ?' she ventured, in the second it took her to realize what was happening. Then I heard her shrill voice call 'Cardiac arrest, bay two!', and felt like cringing.

The words brought a surge of adrenaline that swamped the ward; I tasted its sourness myself. Patients and relatives tensed up around us. Staff dropped what they were doing and came running, faces stiff with instant stress. The nurse who'd shouted was already pulling the curtains closed around the bed, talking quickly even as she moved: 'You'll have to leave now, the crash team will need room . . .' I nodded dumbly and stumbled clear. Another nurse brushed past me. Glancing down the corridor, I saw the first of the doctors come sprinting, his white coat flaring around him.

Back at the bedside, one of the nurses had started heart massage. Through a gap in the curtain, I saw Miss Morgan's limp body jerking with each thrust. Her slack mouth seemed almost pleadingly agape.

I had this crazy urge to wade back in and pull them off: to tell them that this wasn't what she wanted, not now. Instead I stepped back as the crash trolley was wheeled into the bay, bearing its load of drugs and equipment and ECG monitor. Another doctor — as out of condition as the first, to judge from his rasping breath — went in after it, closely followed by a porter lugging the defib box. If all else failed, they'd use that on her: press its charged paddles to her frail, flat chest and slam the current through her.

I stood there, helpless, and watched the too-familiar routine unfold with tears in my eyes. Her peace was all shattered now, her dignity gone; an airway forced down her throat, the front of her nightdress ripped open for electrodes to be pasted on. The crash team crowded round her; someone recommenced heart massage with rib-cracking force. One of the doctors would be hunting for a vein, thrusting a needle into her flaccid arm so they could get a drip up. She'd been slipping away, and now they were dragging her bodily, mercilessly back, neither knowing nor caring whether she wanted to come. My reeling mind locked on to a joke a squaddie told me once: *No one here dies without permission* . . .

The anaesthetist on call arrived, still in his theatre greens, and went in to confer with the first doctor. A couple of medical students were in there too now, hovering at the back; all part of their education, after all. I wanted to shout. I wanted to scream. But of course they'd have ignored me.

One of the auxiliaries, who'd been going round comforting the other patients in the bay, came over and laid a hand on my arm. 'Come on, love. There's nothing you can do here.'

I glanced at her kind, lined face. 'Why can't they leave her alone?' I blurted without thinking.

She shrugged. 'They're doing their best for her. As long as there's life there's hope, isn't that what they say?'

Hope for what, I thought, but didn't say it. With a last miserable look at the frantic activity round the bed, I let her lead me over to the station. They'd left a third-year student to man the phone: I recognized him from his stint down in Casualty last year, when he'd done a week of nights. 'Hello, Steve.'

His look was as unhappy as mine must have been. He waited until the auxiliary was out of earshot again, then murmured, 'It's not right, is it?'

I shook my head tiredly. 'She was ready to go. She wanted to. And now . . .'

'Baxter put *Not for Crash* in the notes,' Stephen confided evenly. 'Pity he didn't make it clear to his enthusiastic juniors.'

'Nor to you lot, presumably.'

'Oh, we knew, all right. There's been an . . . understanding for a while. That nurse was Agency – the one who shouted. But we couldn't just ignore her, could we?'

I made a face, and glanced back towards the heroics in bay two. 'So how long do you reckon they're going to jump up and down on her chest for, then?'

'God knows. We had an arrest the other week, and lost him, but not before they'd put enough electricity through the bloke to light up a *city*. By the end the medics were queueing to have a go . . .'

'That's the trouble though, isn't it,' I said drily: thinking aloud as much as anything. 'The way they're trained. Like death is always a tragedy, something to be avoided at all costs. Doctors are trained to believe that dying's the worst thing that can happen to you . . .'

'And it isn't.'

Sarah was back when I got in, looking tanned and fit and generally pleased with life. She was midway through unpacking when I looked in to say welcome back: putting as brave a face on things as I could, but she picked up on my glumness straight away.

'Oh, Rachel, what is it?' She followed me through into the kitchen. 'Come on, something's up.'

I busied myself with the kettle, trying to sound casual. 'I was visiting Miss M from next door, and she's in a bad way: arrested twice this afternoon. They transferred her to Coronary Care.' In my mind's eye I could still see her being wheeled past on her bed: unconscious, intubated, catheterized; festooned with drips. Trapped inside a dying body. Condemned to linger . . .

That seemed to take the wind out of her sails somewhat, even though the two of them hadn't really got on. 'Do they think she's going to make it?'

I shook my head.

She didn't know quite what to say to that – no matter how many deaths you've seen, it's always different when it's someone you know. I thought I'd better change the subject before we both got depressed. 'Coffee?'

'Mm? Oh . . . yes, please.' She took out the milk, sniffing the carton as she did so – an instinctive gesture which, she'd told me, stemmed from having lived for a year in a nurses' home without a fridge.

'So come on, tell me,' I prompted. 'How was the holiday?'

'Brilliant, thanks. I really enjoyed it.' And as she proceeded to enthuse about it – and about Terry, her latest conquest – her perky sun-in-the-eyes grin was back again soon enough. I was glad to see it.

I had mixed feelings, really: relief that I wasn't alone any more, to be sure – but a slight, sick feeling of unease as well. Now that Sarah was back, what if she too should encounter the grim physicians who came and went at will? As she chattered away, I wondered, unwillingly, how that airy innocence would fare against a demonic torturer from out of the dark.

I managed to suppress a shudder, but only just.

Yet at the same time, I had the feeling that life was suddenly back to normal: as if the past week had been no more than an empty nightmare, or bout of black depression. Sarah's cheerfulness brightened things up no end; the flat felt alive again. Watching her cuddling Trinity as we watched TV that night, I actually began to let myself believe that Melphalan and his unholy cohorts would take no for an answer and leave me alone.

*   *   *

My sleep that night was restless and fitful, but otherwise undisturbed. During one of my lying-awake periods, I tried rationalizing it all out. The Clinicians clearly needed people who would serve of their own free will – and I'd rejected everything they had to offer. They might try again, but it must be clear that I wasn't about to change my mind. Maybe the fact that I was a Christian (or trying to be) upset their calculations too. Yet Melphalan had let me live. Of course, no one would ever believe anything I said about my nightmare encounters: I represented no threat to them on that score . . .

Maybe they'd decide I just wasn't worth bothering with. Maybe.

During the following day, I took to wondering – nervously – when Razoxane would next pay me a visit. I'd defied her instructions to play along with the Clinicians; she might not be too happy about that. And yet where had she been when Melphalan was at my bedside? Why use me as bait if the trap was never sprung?

But I received no visitors – by day or night.

On Saturday night I rang the CCU. The nurse in charge ascertained who I was, then regretfully informed me that Miss Morgan had died in her sleep that afternoon. I thanked her and hung up with a feeling of profoundest relief. She, at least, was safe now. And at peace.

By Sunday, despite some lingering trepidation, I was looking forward to an uninterrupted night's sleep again. Apart from anything else, I was exhausted – worn out by the strain I'd been under, the hours of wakefulness. I'd be back at work from tomorrow night, and wanted to feel as refreshed as possible – ready to slip back into the rhythm.

Sarah was staying over at her boyfriend's, so I was alone again – but I felt calmer and altogether more confident now. I'd tried to get back into the habit of saying my prayers before bed, as well. I found that helped, a bit.

I said them on my knees tonight. And my fingers sought the reassuring, keen-edged outline of my crucifix as I slipped under the covers and snuggled down. The silence of my room was deep, unthreatening – a womb-dark stillness into which I gratefully sank, closing my tired eyes.

Nineteen

'Bloody lights aren't working,' I found myself muttering, dry-mouthed, fingering the switch again.

'Don't worry,' Danny whispered at my elbow. 'They're all waiting for you. Just walk on in.'

I hesitated on the mortuary threshold, peering into the gloom. There was no sound from within: just the silence of a score of corpses. The air was heavy with disinfectant, cold upon my skin. I felt the gooseflesh creeping up my bare forearms.

I took a cautious step forwards, over the edge and into the dark. I could almost feel the weight of bright light from the corridor on my back, pushing me in beyond its fading reach. I glanced around, straining my ears to hear above the sick, numb pounding of my heart – then looked back to where Danny's silhouette was slowly closing the doors behind me. I just stood there, helpless, as the sterile dark swallowed me whole.

They'd be waiting in the p-m room, of course: at least there'd be light in there, though I could see no trace of it now, as I tripped and fumbled my way down the line of fridges. I came to one that was ajar; another was open and swung wider as I blundered into it. The refrigeration units hummed tonelessly in the gloom; icy air wafted out of the open compartments. Swallowing down the beginnings of a scream, I blindly kept on going. I'd almost made it – almost reached the door by my reckoning – when it happened: from out of the darkness ahead came a sigh, harsh and cold, and so close that I felt its breath upon my face.

Instant panic engulfed me, sweeping all thought away;

but before I could even recoil, a hand had grasped my shoulder, strong fingers squeezing tight, though I twisted and squirmed to break free. Fear rose like vomit within me, bringing screaming hysteria up with it, and I was helpless to stop it. Helpless. And in the midst of my struggles I awoke with a start, and found I was back in my own rucked-up bed, in the glow of my bedside lamp, and Jenny was leaning over me, face full of concern. It was her hand on my shoulder, shaking me awake.

Reality reasserted itself around me, and I slumped back with a gasp, feeling my body begin to generate a chilling sweat as reaction set in.

'Easy ... easy now,' Jenny was murmuring – as gently as if I'd been a scared and sleepless patient. And yet even as I stared up at her, I felt a cool tickle of unease in my stomach – offsetting a vague, confused notion in my mind that for some reason she shouldn't be here. It wasn't just the fact that we didn't share a flat: this was something far more fundamental. But my mind was blurred, and memory an aching blackness. Whatever the cause of my disquiet, I couldn't focus: couldn't find it in the gloom ...

She looked as if she'd just woken up: her long hair tangled, her eyes still sleepy. I was suddenly reminded of my training, and the nurses' home at 6 a.m.: those of us on the Early making our dopey, dishevelled way towards the washrooms while the Lates slept in. A reassuring memory: an ordered and familiar world. I felt my stomach begin to settle.

Sitting forward on the bed, Jenny pressed her palm to my moist forehead, and frowned afresh. 'Rachel, you're burning up ...' Her hand slid on down my cheek. 'Just relax: let go. I'm here ...'

Suddenly I wanted to hug her and hang on tight: let her haul me back from the precipice of sleep, and what I'd dreamed there. I sat up clumsily, and felt her comforting arms slide round me. 'Nothing to be afraid of now . . .' she whispered in my ear.

I nodded; but something was still back there, in the tired shadows of my mind. Something about her. Something I really ought to know . . .

It cut through slowly; but it came. Even as she soothed me some more, I felt a growth of coldness in the depths of my stomach. My body remembered before my mind – but my brain caught up in the end.

It hit me like a low punch: winding, sickening – throwing me back against the pillows. Jenny Thomas had been dead these past two months – her soft, familiar accents caught and crushed for ever inside her throat; her beauty long since sullied by decay. She was sleeping in the cold earth now: tonight. And there was a ghost in my bedroom: *touching* me.

Freezing fear immersed me: icing up my heart, my lungs, my gut. For a moment I couldn't even think, let alone move; and still her bright eyes watched me. The absence of any threat encouraged my mind to risk itself above the parapet again: it fed me the hopeful thought that not all ghosts were evil, or even frightening. But it was too late for that: I had already realized that this could be no ghost – she was warm and fragrant flesh and blood.

So who – or what – was she?

She leaned forward. 'Please don't be afraid, Rachel. There's nothing to be scared of, I promise . . .'

But my aching fear remained – and struggling in its grip, I hastily crossed myself: fingers finishing on my lips, and sticking there, as if moist saliva had suddenly become adhesive . . .

And Jenny flinched.

I stared back into her widened eyes, and saw something crawling there: something dismal and disgusted. And somehow afraid.

The only prayer my stunned mind could grasp at was

one that came ready-made: the simple formula of words I used to mouth at Mass each Sunday. Words that had come to seem dulled by repetition, but which came to me now with their purest force: the words of an angel and a saint, and I gasped them out not as set liturgy but a fierce assertion, a focus of faith.

'Hail Mary full of grace the Lord is with thee –'

And the thing with Jenny's face drew back, her sweet smile faltering.

'– blessed art thou among women,' I went on relentlessly, 'and blessed is the fruit of thy womb *Jesus*.' And I don't think it was the words themselves that forced her retreat, so much as the defiance in my voice and in my eyes, born of the belief – the desperate hope – that I suddenly wasn't facing her alone . . .

'Holy Mary mother of God pray for us sinners . . .' But she'd backed away towards the corner now, and my voice tailed off as I seized the chance to scramble hastily off the bed and over to the door. I never took my eyes off her, and now shouted, 'Go away! Just go away, leave me in peace . . .' And I realized I was sobbing, the tears beginning to stream down my cheeks.

My visitor just stood there, hugging herself: looking so forlorn that I felt a twinge of pity. I suddenly couldn't face the reproach in her eyes, and turned away, out of the room: going on down to the kitchen. I clicked the wall-switch – there was a moment's dim, buzzing anticipation before the striplight came on – and walked shakily over to the sink, bracing both hands against it, waiting with head bowed until my breathing had eased.

After a moment, I heard her come in behind me.

'Please . . .' I muttered, without looking up. 'Please, whoever you are, just leave me alone.'

But she came cautiously over, her bare feet quiet on the linoleum. My muscles tensed as I sensed her there, right behind me. I suppressed a shiver.

'Please, Rachel –' I felt her lay her hand on my shoulder.

Something snapped inside me. Fear and disbelief boiled over. I can't have been thinking rationally in the moment when I snatched up the kitchen knife on the drainer and spun around to push it deep into her stomach.

Maybe I'd half-expected her to vanish into thin air; but she didn't. Her mouth and eyes opened wide in surprise and horror; then the eyes closed as she grimaced, and groaned with pain, hunching forward. There must have been horror on my own face too, oh yes – standing there facing her, the knife in my grip buried so deep in her flesh that I thought I'd felt it grate on spinal bone.

I jerked it free.

Blood – scalding, human blood – splashed over my midriff, dyeing my T-shirt crimson. She gasped deep in her throat – and then slumped against me, her face pressed to my breasts. And as her knees buckled, so she slid down me, breathing her last against my stomach, my groin, her head resting between my thighs for a moment of ghastly intimacy before she fell sideways, and was still.

Silence in the kitchen. I let the knife slide from my nerveless fingers, and it clattered on the tiles beside her body. The blood was already spreading, pooling beneath her. I swayed, sagged back against the edge of the sink, and now reaction was stoking up: in violent, breath-racking shudders that turned the sweat on my skin to ice. I looked down at the pretty young woman I'd just murdered, and believed I must surely go insane.

After a few minutes of sheer, mindless panic, I managed to pull myself together enough to straighten up and stagger back into the hall – giving her corpse a wide berth. The toilet loomed up invitingly: I lurched in, and threw up copiously into the bowl, slumping down on to my knees to spit out the last bitter bile.

As I knelt there, lost in my own misery, I heard a sharp popping sound, and the light from the kitchen went out.

Immediately I became aware of a sudden coldness on my skin – this time generated from without. I froze, listening to the silence; and in the silence, movement.

My legs felt like jelly, but I managed to struggle to my feet, a new rush of adrenaline urging me on. The noises were coming from the kitchen. Slowly I turned around. I didn't want to look, of course; I wanted to curl up in a corner and die quietly. But I knew I had to see.

A wash of blue-grey moonlight tinged the kitchen: by its glimmer, I could see a face being slowly lifted from the floor. But it wasn't Jenny's sweet, martyred face. Oh no. This face was male, and caked with grime and dried filth; the hair around it plastered with mud. But in the midst of that dark, grim mask, the deep-set eyes were gleaming.

It was strange, but now that I knew exactly what I was up against, I wasn't particularly afraid any more. There was just the sick numbness of resignation.

The Clinician was climbing to his feet, his malevolent eyes never leaving mine. It was one of the two who had examined me in that dimly-lit room. His befouled and tattered trenchcoat gave off a stink that turned my stomach. What heady hallucinations he had conjured up to disguise that reek as Jenny's perfume, that dismal face as her beauty; those bony hands as her loving touch. Despite myself, I gagged – and backed away, retreating into my bedroom, the only oasis of light left in a desert of darkness.

Unhurriedly he followed; tugging off his fleabitten, fingerless gloves as he came. As I watched, mesmerized, he drew a pair of latex surgical gloves from his pocket and pulled them on, drawing the pale, sheer rubber tight over the knuckles – a mockingly token gesture of sterility. I had my back to the wall by the time he opened his coat and held one side wide, revealing a fearful array of surgical instruments, their burnished glint contrasting bizarrely with the squalor of the garment that concealed them. He selected a wicked-looking scalpel, and brandished it wordlessly towards me, the blade agleam with cold, reflected light.

His slow advance ceased: for a moment we were a tableau, frozen still. And then he came for me, crossing the room in three strides. Forget those slow, shambling monsters in the movies: speed is the real terror, something coming so fast you don't have time to think and there's just the white-out of pure panic. I threw myself aside, and the scalpel slashed wallpaper where I'd been standing. I fetched up on the bed, and rolled off as he came at me again. The blade moved in a blur of blued steel, superhumanly fast, hacking up the pillow like a chainsaw: taking Wendy's beaming face clean off. It seemed almost a pre-programmed sequence of movements, for his face was coming round to snarl at me while the knife was still slicing. I was trying to get clear as fast as hands and knees would take me, but that wasn't nearly fast enough. The third time, he was on me. I felt the rubber-skinned fist clench in the roots of my hair, and then he was pulling my head up, dragging it back to expose the throat. The point of the scalpel pricked my flesh; horror enough if it was a used blade. Forced to rear up and backwards, there on my knees, I waited for the final cut.

It didn't come. Instead, after a long moment during which I heard the dry breath rasping in his throat, and knew my life teetered in the balance, he withdrew the blade, and slung me contemptuously to one side.

I lay still where I had landed, huddled on the carpet, afraid to move: breathless and nauseous. Because for the first time I'd seen a Clinician enraged: the cold, dispassionate veneer cracked open. My instinctive assertion of faith had blocked him at first – repulsed him as Razoxane had said it would. But then I'd had the temerity to stab him, and fury had blotted out his unease – while I'd been too demoralized to focus that faith against him. I reckoned it was only dread of Melphalan, his Lord, that had stopped him slicing me to bits.

He was fingering his stab wound now: its foul, necrotic discharge oozing down the front of his coat. The blood soaking my own front felt as greasy as vomit: a clammy, clinging mess. Then he raised his eyes to me once more, and they were almost luminous with hate.

'Stick a knife in me . . .' he muttered thickly. 'Stick a fucking *knife* in me.' I got the impression he couldn't quite believe it.

My fingers closed around the crucifix at my throat, and for all my fear I managed to meet his gaze: my spinning thoughts focusing on that touch of cool silver. He'd come to seduce me, body and soul, and I'd repelled him: I'd actually managed to drive him back. And I suddenly realized I could do it again. And again.

He saw my movement, and took a step towards me – but only one. 'You will suffer, Rachel Young. I promise you that.' He gestured with the scalpel. 'Your superstitions won't save you . . .'

But they were keeping him at bay. I'd made a fist around my crucifix now; tightly clutching that tangible reminder of things not seen. 'Get out,' I whispered.

He seemed to hesitate. The scalpel glinted in his hand.

'Get out,' I said again, louder this time: feeling a sudden icy calm come over me. 'In the name of all that's holy, get out of here.'

'It isn't over,' he growled, as he began to back away. 'It has barely begun.' I watched his reluctant retreat: watched until he was gone through the door and I was alone. After a minute, I felt the temperature begin to rise almost imperceptibly back towards normal, and knew he'd left the flat.

I lay where I was. Eventually, the pain of the crucifix digging into my palm persuaded me to open my hand, and let the pendant slip down on to my chest again. It had left deep, red marks in my flesh.

Slowly I struggled to my feet.

Reaction had left me breathless and drained; my heart still thudded painfully. But a fierce rush of adrenaline kept me moving. Ignoring the unstuffed pillow – its feathers still afloat on the air – and the tatter of torn wallpaper, I went on through into the kitchen, and stood staring down at the pool of bile-dark blood still spreading across the moonlit floor.

I'd stabbed one of them. I'd hurt him. And I'd driven him off.

I realized I wasn't afraid any more. Instead there was just a flood of deep relief – and a feeling of triumph that left me almost light-headed.

Twenty

The door creaked drily open. For a moment there was silence. Then a whisper came out of the dark, and grew to a whirring of wings as a vulpine storm of vampire bats burst forth from the room and filled the corridor, squealing with evil hunger.

'Bloody hell, Mike,' I said through a mouthful of crisps. 'This is crap.'

'It was the only one left in the shop,' came the defensive reply; but in the light from the TV screen I reckoned he looked suitably abashed.

'You can see the *wires*!'

'Shush,' said Karen, 'it's good.'

I shrugged and settled back in my chair, dipping again into the bag of crisps in my lap. What the hell; things were dead quiet tonight, and we'd just recently had the video donated by the local Round Table, 'for the enjoyment of patients and staff', so we'd decided to put the thing to good use. Asking Mike to choose the film might not have been such a good idea, but still . . .

It was a chance to relax, at any rate: I had my shoes off, and my stockinged feet, crossed at the ankles, were resting on an adjacent chair. Karen was sat next to me, sipping a Coke; her eyes wide. Mike was next to the door, where he could keep one eye on the corridor. Also with us in the darkened duty room were June and Helen, and Kathy too, though we'd insisted it was past her bedtime. Danny was mooching round the department somewhere: he claimed he'd seen it before.

That suited me fine. His company I could do without.

In fact I was feeling really good at the moment: still on a high after repulsing the Clinician. Nothing had happened since; in fact I'd slept surprisingly well. Some sober corner of my mind was trying to bring me down to earth again, whispering of retaliation and revenge, but I was managing more or less to ignore it. They must know I was useless to them now, I kept telling myself; and more than that, they're scared — scared of what I believe in. It makes them doubt . . .

As ever, work was helping: bringing me face to face with people who had troubles enough of their own. Tonight it had been a young, quiet bloke who'd got a faceful of gravel coming off his bike; just one more casualty, until he'd turned to watch me prepare the trolley and calmly said: 'I'm HIV positive. You ought to know.'

I was going to glove-up anyway; but when he told me I just reached out and touched his shoulder: squeezed it briefly. No words, no meaningful glances. Just a moment's contact, skin to skin, for someone so very alone . . .

The buzzer sounded, down at reception.

'Whose turn is it this time?' Helen murmured.

'Mike's,' I said cheerfully. He gave me a mock-pained look. It was good to be working together again: the other week's embarrassment felt as good as forgotten.

'Gosh, can I tear meself away?' he wondered, getting up.

'Shhh,' Karen insisted, 'you're spoiling the atmosphere . . .'

'. . . about as much atmosphere as a Berni Inn . . .' we heard him mutter as he left.

I glanced at my watch: nearly two o'clock. This would be our first customer in over an hour. I had another crisp.

Several drama-packed minutes later, Mike returned and resumed his seat.

I glanced up. 'Who was it?'

He shrugged. 'Dunno. Some drunk.'

There was a pause.

'Well?' I prompted, ignoring another anguished shriek from the TV.

He feigned surprise. 'Oh, yes, sorry. Cubicle two, Doctor.'

'For God's sake, Michael,' Kathy groaned, good-naturedly enough. She began extricating herself. 'How is he?'

'Quite happy, by the looks of it. Couple of coppers brought him in – not even D&D or anythin', but he's got a dirty-lookin' cut they reckoned wanted seein' to.'

Kathy sighed. 'Do tell me what happens.' She paused at the door. 'If he vomits down my dress,' she added, with studied calm, 'I shall be *very* cross . . .'

Mike followed her out, still grinning.

The rest of us continued watching the film. After a couple of minutes, Mike put his head round the door again. 'You haven't seen him, have you?'

I grimaced. 'Oh, don't tell me he's wandered off . . .'

'Hey, I only left him for a minute, and he was pissed as a fart anyway. Just sat there, grinnin' to himself. Weirdo.'

I got resignedly to my feet, and pulled my shoes on. 'Come on then, let's find him. This lot can tell me what happens.'

'Have fun,' Karen murmured as I stepped over her legs.

Outside in the corridor, Kathy was already walking down towards Resus. I glanced the other way, up towards Theatre. No sign or sound of anyone.

While Mike pushed open the door of the Quiet Room to peer inside, I went round towards the treatment area: not that I thought he'd somehow overlooked the bloke or anything, but it was a logical starting point. Some of the lights were off in the cubicle section – this month's directive on saving energy – but Kath had left the X-ray viewing box over the desk switched on, and its bleached white glow tinged half the room. She'd left a film clipped to it, too: the one of the head injury we'd had in earlier. Walking down past the empty trolleys and through that cold spill of light, I felt my gaze drawn uneasily to the luminous image of the patient's cranium: a ghost-skull, staring down at me. I made a quick detour to switch the viewer off. Waste of electricity . . .

In the moment's stillness that followed, I could clearly hear my fob-watch, ticking quietly away on my breast.

Mike had gone up the theatre corridor and was waiting outside Suturing. He shook his head. 'No sign.'

'Damn. Let's try down the reception end,' I told him. We started back down the corridor together, but then I veered off towards the central utility room. 'Carry on; I'll just make sure he's not helping himself to the drugs cupboard.'

'You can't miss him,' Mike called back as I pushed through the door into Utility. 'A real scruff, and wearing *goggles* . . .' He said the last word almost gleefully as he walked off; he didn't see me come completely to a halt inside the room, sucking in air with a gasp.

The bottom had just dropped out of my stomach.

I remembered the goggles, all right: remembered them staring down at me; a blind grin. Scalpels and speculum and cold rubber fingers. Oh *shit* . . .

I felt suddenly, hideously vulnerable in this cold, bleak, brightly-lit room. I swung around, yanked open the door –

And Danny was standing there, blocking the doorway: that faint, sneering smile was back on his face.

I just stared at him for a moment: stared up at him, for he was taller than me. Then, without quite knowing why, I murmured: 'I'll scream . . .'

And his smile widened. 'You *will*,' he agreed pleasantly.

Then his hand lunged out, fast as a striking snake. I flinched away, but he'd already got what he wanted: grasping my crucifix and snapping it from its chain . . .

I teetered, off-balance – but he ignored me, brushing past to stride over to the worktop. There was a sharps bin there: a big yellow bucket where we dumped used needles and blades.

He dropped my crucifix down the red-rimmed port in the lid.

I stood and watched, my eyes widening with horror. And as he turned to me again, I realized how naked my throat felt now. How naked *I* felt now . . .

Danny was grinning. 'Thought you were so clever, didn't you, Rachel? Thought you were so bloody clever. And now you'll find out just how stupid you've been . . .' And with that he was gone – disappearing through the opposite door.

My first impulse was to get back out the way I'd come, and run – despite the instinct that baulked at leaving the crucifix behind. Find Mike; grab Kathy. Lock ourselves back in the office if we had to. I was a pace from the door when I heard a scraping, stealthy footstep in the corridor outside. And felt the cold.

I couldn't scream. My throat was dry as dust. As dusty death . . .

I fairly threw myself across the room, towards the worktop, towards the sharps bin. I could have tried following Danny, of course: he'd probably be waiting, but I was ready to fight tooth and nail. And yet I knew it would be in vain: without the cross, I didn't have a chance.

Not that it had power in itself: I realized that. Just a symbol in silver – but it gave me something to clutch at, cling to. It focused my thoughts. It focused my oh so fragile faith.

I peeled off the plastic lid. The bin was half full of sharps, a thicket of glinting needles: all of them used, some still sullied with blood. And one was from the tetanus shot I'd given the bloke with HIV.

Which one? Which bloody one?

My crucifix was right there in the midst: silver in a nest of steel.

I swallowed, and glanced back towards the doorway. It was empty.

I could feel him coming.

Slowly, gingerly, I reached into the bucket, groping for the cross with trembling fingers.

The temperature *plunged*.

I gave a little sob, but didn't dare look back again. My hand was shaking so much, I almost stuck myself: my flesh was already tingling in expectation of that first, fateful jab. But I had it now – caught between my first two fingers. And though my co-ordination seemed shot to hell, I managed at last, unbreathing, to fish it out.

I swung round as he took his first step across the threshold.

It was him, all right: the one who'd examined me. His gaunt grin was a death's head: I had the chill impression of only empty sockets behind the goggles. The wound he'd come in with – a thin, raw scar down one grizzled cheek – was glistening with gobbets of pus.

The scalpel in his hand glinted sharp and cold and unforgiving. His advance was almost insolently slow.

'No, Melphalan said you need me,' I gabbled, still fumbling with the crucifix.

He shook his head, still smiling. 'Melphalan has no use for fools.'

I tried to brandish the cross at him, but my mind was a whirl, a useless blur of terror. Even the memory of my previous victory seemed suddenly unreal; and when I tried launching into the Our Father, the words were dry and lifeless in my mouth. Appalled, I backed away – still trying desperately to latch on to some formula of words, a rite of exorcism, *anything*. 'I command thee, foul spirit,' I ventured, and thought he was going to laugh. 'Begone, leave us . . .'

'You feel the *doubt* now, don't you?' he leered back. 'You don't *believe* . . .'

My mind was a blank as I pressed back into the corner:

the crucifix still extended, but almost slipping from my nerveless fingers. I was going to die, I suddenly realized; I was going to *suffer*. My mind recoiled from that awful, inescapable fact – and in so doing unleashed a surge of emotion that was almost outrage. Bitterness rose within me, clearing my head: sharpening my terrified mind.

'Get away from me . . .' I whispered.

He kept on coming.

Something inside me snapped.

'In the name of Jesus Christ FUCK OFF!'

That stopped him.

I was trembling, my face wet with sweat. The crucifix wavered – and I thrust it aggressively towards him again.

He didn't move.

I couldn't see his eyes, of course; couldn't read whatever feelings showed there. But I got the impression that he suddenly wasn't so sure of himself any more.

Real faith makes them doubt.

I was standing there before him, defenceless – and abruptly unafraid. Defying him. It was irrational: it threw him. The ghost of the grin still lingered on his face, but he was tensing up. 'There's no god to save you,' he insisted grimly, and I saw his grip tighten on the scalpel.

I took a step forward.

He took one back.

I couldn't quite believe I'd just done that. I took another.

He backed warily away, towards the door.

I couldn't summon up the nerve for a third step; I hoped I wouldn't need to. We stared at each other across that cold, empty room, each taking the other's measure – and suddenly a scream came ripping down the corridor, a shriek of human anguish. The shock may well have released fresh adrenaline into my system, but I was already OD-ing on the stuff, so I didn't notice.

I listened – we both did – as the scream became a whimper, then a gurgle, and finally silence. I knew it was Danny's voice. The Clinician had reached the door now, and was peering into the corridor. His movements betrayed a new unease. Lingering on the threshold, he turned to me once more, and extended the scalpel; snarling his hatred back at me.

'You'll *weep* for this,' he promised. '*Weep* for this.'

And with a rustle of his stinking coat he turned and was gone.

I stayed where I was for what seemed like many minutes: I was pretty sure I'd fall over if I tried to move. Then I heard someone running down the corridor, and glimpsed Mike as he passed the door. Despite my expectations, I found I was still able to walk, and stumbled out after him.

I caught up with him by Suturing. It wasn't difficult: he was standing rock-still. I glanced up at him, saw the pallor of his face – and followed his line of sight. Then I wished I hadn't.

Danny was lying sprawled on his back just inside the suturing room. He'd been quite spectacularly disembowelled. Blood and bits of offal splashed and stained and littered the floor. In a matter of seconds someone had turned him into an anatomy lesson.

'Oh Holy Mary Mother of God . . .' Mike said weakly. There was sweat on his brow; he was breathing in short gasps. I knew how he felt: experienced Casualty nurse or no, I wanted to heave as well.

Danny's eyes stared sleepily at the ceiling.

Kathy and June were approaching down the corridor; I waved them back. 'No . . . You don't want to see this.'

'What's happened?' Kathy asked.

'Danny's . . . been murdered.' It sounded so inadequate, somehow.

That brought them up short, not surprisingly; but after a moment Kathy said, with commendable calm, 'Well I suppose I'd better certify him then . . .'

'Oh shit. Yes, of course.' I stepped aside. 'June, get the

others here where we can see them, now, okay? We've got a nutter loose.' *Again,* I almost added. So much for our quiet night.

I wondered who'd done it – another Clinician? As Mike walked over to the nearest wall-mounted phone, I glanced nervously into the treatment area. There was no one in there, and nowhere to hide – except behind the half-drawn curtains of cubicle two, where Mike had unsuspectingly left his 'patient'.

And even as I watched, while Mike put out his emergency call and Kathy knelt tight-lipped beside Danny's vivisected corpse, that curtain was twitched aside.

It was Razoxane standing there, of course: the self-styled angel of death. Her knife still dangled from bloody fingers, dripping crimson to the floor. She smiled at me: a knowing, sinister smile – and let the curtain slip back into place once more.

I turned away and sagged back against the wall, hugging myself as I watched Kathy going through the motions.

From now on, I knew, it was going to be war.

Twenty-one

When I finally got home that dark, wet morning – after we'd answered all the questions the police could think of – Razoxane was already waiting.

I should have guessed, of course; even as I closed the door, and chained it, and leaned my forehead wearily against it, listening to the silence of the flat behind me, I should have bloody guessed. But I still felt cold shock spike my belly as I wandered through into the unlit kitchen and found her finishing her breakfast.

She was head-down over a bowl of my cereal, her grimy hat brim hiding her face as she spooned the stuff hungrily into her mouth. The smell of her coat and clothes befouled the room. She hadn't even taken off her half-unravelled gloves.

I just stood there in the doorway, watching her eat; trying not to breathe too deeply. I knew she knew I was there.

Eventually I said dully: 'Why do that? He wasn't . . . one of them. Just someone they used.'

She finished chewing her mouthful, swallowed – and slowly raised her head. And I saw that at last she'd taken off her shades; her blue eyes were so pale they seemed almost luminous in the gloom.

'Sometimes they'll give powers to their servants,' she answered evenly. 'I have to make sure of their extinction.'

Well she'd done that all right: not much chance of a resurrection with your heart gouged out and slashed open to spill its contents across the floor; your last scream ripped from your throat, along with your larynx and trailing lungs . . .

I know I hadn't liked the bloke, but still . . .

'He tried to kill you, after all,' Razoxane pointed out. 'Set you up for Vokaine to slaughter.'

Which was true enough. Too drained to debate it further, I drew out a chair and sat, while she resumed her meal. I'd already slipped too deep into this mire – this black morass beneath the pastry-thin crust of everyday life – to register the bizarreness of it all: a scruffy, smelly young vagabond eating muesli in our neatly-ordered kitchen. Nor did I feel more than moderately cold at the thought that the woman across the table from me had already hacked and sliced three people to bits – two of whom, admittedly, had no longer been truly human. Insane she might be – perhaps it was the only way she'd been able to come to terms with the horror of what she stalked – but at least she was consistent, and always coldly in control. I felt no threat from her any more; in fact I felt almost safe.

'Are you . . . going to stay close now?' I asked haltingly.

Her spoon scraped the milk-slicked bottom of the bowl. She wiped her mouth, and looked at me again.

'I'll be there when you need me.'

I remembered how close Melphalan had got; how close his scalpel-wielding cohorts had got. I shuddered.

'Because they don't want to use me any more, right, they want to kill me.' I heard my voice rise towards panic, and paused, swallowing, until the surge of fear had passed. 'He told me I'd weep for this,' I continued, more quietly. 'He promised me that.'

She shrugged, apparently unconcerned that I hadn't followed her instructions in the first place. 'Either way they'll come for you, Rachel; and they'll find me waiting.'

I sat back. 'You'd better be,' I murmured.

Razoxane reached for her coffee mug, and didn't bother to reply.

Still fidgety, I glanced around the kitchen – but it wasn't till my gaze had come back round to her that I finally registered the worn leather satchel lying at her elbow on the cluttered table. I leaned forward again. 'What's that?'

She looked down; then up again, a thin smile on her face. 'Something I took from his lodgings last night ... before the policemen arrived.' She pushed it across to me. 'Take a look.'

Gingerly I reached out to unfasten the flap. There was a sheaf of papers inside. I glanced questioningly at Razoxane again.

'They're not dangerous,' she said drily. 'Not in themselves. Go ahead.'

With instinctive reluctance I drew them out and began leafing through them. Some were pages photocopied – or torn – from books; others were handwritten, or covered with geometrical symbols. Magical symbols, I realized after a moment.

'That's one of the signs by which they can be recognized,' she said, gesturing. 'A Babylonian heptagram.'

I studied the thing for a moment. 'Is it?'

I sensed the ghost-smile in her voice as she elaborated. 'Something they inherited from their ancient forebears: a focus for their powers through incantation. See the names?'

There were certainly several words in the complex, interwoven star-shape before me: a sort of pentagram, only with seven points. The scripts varied in size and style. Some of them I couldn't read at all. But some I could.

'Namtar?' I ventured.

Razoxane nodded. 'A Sumerian demon: the bringer of plagues. And Nergal – their god of death and desolation. The physician's oldest enemies. All just mantras to them now, but . . .' Her smile faded. 'Names can have power, Rachel. They open doors.'

At least I recognized the symbol at the centre, encircled by those sinister words: a staff and coiled serpent. The ancient mark of the physician.

A lot of the other pages looked like extracts from antiquarian medical works: the sort of yellowed tomes they'd kept under glass in the library of my old teaching hospital. Woodcut illustrations and calligraphic script – but some of the scenes they portrayed made me grimace and grit my teeth. Ritual mutilation. Explicit anatomical dissection. Images somehow more shocking because of the textbook detachment with which they'd been sketched. And the way the written commentaries were laid out suggested incantations: rites or spells. Some were in English – often old-looking English – the rest in a mixture of Latin, French and German. The modern languages I'd done at school, and could make some headway; but something about them looked wrong. Words were half-recognizable; crudely misspelled. *Faictz que vouldras*? I glanced up at Razoxane.

She leaned forward to check. 'Renaissance French,' she explained, in answer to my unspoken question. 'Some of that stuff's even older. Medieval . . .'

I just stared at her. 'He was a porter, for God's sake. He used to read the *Sun*!'

'You really shouldn't judge by appearances, Rachel,' she told me softly. 'The man clearly had hidden . . . depths.'

Still grimacing, I turned up another diagram: a pentagram within a circle, again with the serpent and staff motif at its centre. I frowned. 'Wrong way up, isn't it?'

She shook her head. 'Not for them. The pentagram is a figure of power, right; it encompasses the four Elements, and the single point upward represents the higher, spiritual plane – the Divine Presence. Point downward, all that's turned on its head. Material reality is all that matters. It's a challenge to God.'

'I thought they didn't believe in God.'

'Oh, they don't. Not in any conscious way. Religion to them is mere superstition, something they hate and despise; the sign of the inverted pentagram subverts it. But deep inside – in whatever human remains they have within them

– they've got superstitions of their own . . . as I believe you've already discovered.'

I nodded, half-understanding. 'You mean they're afraid of the cross and things?'

Once more she shook her head. 'The cross doesn't frighten them, Rachel; and prayers won't hold them off. Remember what I told you. It's the faith of the person holding the cross, or speaking the prayer, that gives them pause. A cross is just a symbol, and prayers are just words – but if you use them to articulate and concentrate the faith you can feel, you can direct it at them – and drive them back.'

I absorbed that in silence. Then: 'But if they use all this occult stuff . . . how can they not believe in the super-natural?'

'I told you: it's a part of their arrogance. They will accept *nothing* as unknowable. Everything can be explained by science, by human wisdom. Confront them with evidence of the supernatural and they'll always think their way around it: put it down to undiscovered natural phenomena, or untapped powers of the mind, or whatever. And some-times they're right, of course. Like someone wise once said: the universe is weirder than you *can* imagine.'

'So how come you know all this?' I asked at length. 'How come you know them so well?'

'I've stalked them long enough,' she answered calmly. 'Them and their kind. The land must be purified.'

I swallowed. 'Look . . . Who are you?'

'A sorry guest on a darkened Earth.'

That was helpful. 'For how long?' I persisted, a little warily; for all I knew she could be right on the edge.

She shrugged. 'Who knows? Since before the man you now call Isaiah began to preach. Long before that. Before Abraham, and Moses. Before their Stone Age tribes had even dreamt of God . . .'

I knew I shouldn't have asked her that.

'I have no sense of time, Rachel,' she continued, quite matter-of-factly. 'Not any more. I exist: I destroy. I cleanse the Earth, and when it's done, He'll take me back. But the work is never over. Never . . .'

I just sat there, nodding dumbly. She wasn't the first psychie case I'd had to deal with, of course. Most Casualty departments get their share of oddballs; and I'd done my three months on a psychiatric ward during training, too – an eye-opening period during which I'd met Jesus, Napoleon and Adolf Hitler. I'd never got used to psychie: never got used to patients whose sickness lay in something as elusive as the soul. People who looked normal, and talked rationally, and walked a ghostly landscape of their own.

And now here I sat, passing the time of day with the Angel of Death. Only this time the subject was on the streets, and armed with a knife, and pledged to living out her fantasies in all their gory detail. And just to complicate the matter, her victims were all she claimed they were: a cabal of dark, demonic killers, creatures beyond rationale or reason, whose very existence made me wonder if I wasn't in need of psychiatric help myself.

As I stared at her, thinking how absurdly awkward the silence felt, as though we'd merely run out of small talk, my mind touched briefly on one other possibility: as warily as fingers reaching out for fire or ice. The possibility that she wasn't mad or self-deluded. That she really was an angel: a heavenly being beneath that grim exterior. A nightmare fallen from God. One fleeting touch. Then my mind recoiled, and shrank away.

Razoxane smiled, as though she read my thoughts.

'I must be going, Rachel: I have things to do.'

'Like what?' I asked, suspiciously.

But she didn't answer; merely pulled her shades from the pocket of her coat, unfolded the arms one-handed and slipped them on to mask those chilly eyes once more. She got to her feet.

I changed tack. 'What if they come back? Where'll you be then?'

'Around. But don't be afraid, Rachel. You have the power to defy them now, and they know it. They will be wary.'

I'd just realized how tired I was beginning to feel. 'And what if I'm asleep?'

'They won't come for you again — not for a while. Trust me.'

I shrugged helplessly. I had no option but to trust her.

Trinity was under the table now and rubbing himself against my leg; blissfully unaware of life's darker realities. So long as someone fed him, he was happy. Absently I reached down to stroke his fur.

As Razoxane reached the door I asked: 'When will it all be over?'

She paused, looking back. 'Soon,' she promised. 'For all of us.'

And then she was gone, leaving me sitting in the murky light of morning, in a kitchen that smelled like a station waiting room after they've just turfed out the drunks.

Despite my tiredness, I decided I'd have a bath before turning in. Opening the kitchen windows to let the damp air in would do something to disperse the smell Razoxane had left behind her; but on the way home I'd already smelled myself. The sweat of fear that had soaked my underwear and pasted my uniform to the skin of my back was slowly, sourly drying. Besides, I still felt stiff and tense, too restless for sleep. A hot, relaxing soak was what I needed now. With luck, it might wash even memory away — at least for a while.

I checked the door was chained again, and the rear window locks in place. Not that such things would keep Clinicians out, of course; but they might slow them down a bit — discourage them somehow. I was clutching at straws, and knew it — but didn't care. What kept me going was the thought that maybe Razoxane was right, at that: maybe it wasn't just physical barriers now keeping them at bay.

Finished, I went into the bathroom and turned on the taps. Once hot and cold were running in the right proportions, I put the plug in, poured a capful of Sarah's herbal bath stuff into the downpour, and retreated to the doorway: lingering there where I could watch the bath fill up while still listening to the silence of the flat, straining my ears above the thumping roar of the water. I heard nothing; sensed nothing. At length I locked the door, and quickly undressed.

The water was deep and hot and fragrant as I slid into it and settled down. It took my weight as my taut muscles slackened; swirled sudsily up and over me. I lay back, my breasts awash, and closed my tired eyes.

My mind quietened. After a while, it began to drift away.

What brought me fully awake again was a sound of scratching at the door.

I sat up, splashing; one hand closing around the damp metal of my crucifix as I hugged myself instinctively. I waited, huddled there; breathless, motionless. And as the slopping water quietened, I heard the sound again — and realized it was Trinity.

Relief.

I let my breath go gasping out, and slumped back down once more. 'Trinity!' I almost yelled. 'Don't *do* that to me, okay?'

The cat kept scratching: it sounded like he was sharpening his claws out there.

'Look, go away,' I said loudly. 'I'm not feeding you again.'

As if in answer, there came a frantic scrabble of claws against the door, and I heard him hiss, and spit and begin to squall. A cat-fight, now of all times: some other moggie had got in through the cat-flap, and they obviously weren't getting on. I sighed, and sat up again, reaching for the towel. 'Oh for God's sake . . .'

I never knew a cat could make a noise as hideous as the one I heard then: an eldritch screech that pimpled even my warm flesh with instant goosebumps. And before I could even blink, the blood came splashing under the door.

It came in a single gout, sprayed at high pressure through the narrow crack — spattering across the floor almost to the base of the washbasin. All sounds ceased on the other side of the door.

I just sat there, wide-eyed, my mouth a perfect O.

They were here. In another second they'd smash down the door and come for me, and here I was, naked and helpless, my mind an utter blank.

But they didn't come.

I could sense them out there: could feel their evil, so intense that my body registered it as a sensation of physical cold. But after lingering for an endless minute, the presences began to recede. I felt them fade. Almost unwilling to believe it, I realized they had gone.

The bright-red blood continued to soak into the bathrug. I stared numbly at it, until my vision blurred over and I began to cry. After struggling for a moment, I sagged back down into the water, and just let go. I cried my eyes out.

Razoxane had promised they wouldn't come for me, and so they hadn't. They'd come for Trinity instead. And their slaughter of our cat had been message enough. A grim assurance that they hadn't forgotten.

And wouldn't forgive.

Twenty-two

'I've left June in the duty room,' Fran said. 'She's a bit weepy.'

'She OK?' Mark asked, tucking the phone under his chin. Fran nodded. 'Just last week getting to her I think.'

'It's been getting to us all,' Mark muttered – though not without sympathy. He returned his attention to the phone as the person he'd been waiting for came back on. 'Okay . . . right, see you in a while then.' He hung up noisily, and fumbled for a pen. 'We've got all fucking night, after all.'

'I'll go and talk to her in a minute,' I suggested to Fran. 'It's time she got it out of her system, anyway.'

'You've coped with all this really well, Raitch,' Mark said, writing; he sounded quite impressed.

I shrugged. True, it's not every day you find your departmental porter brutally disembowelled – but as far as I was concerned, he'd been one of the opposition, and I wasn't losing any sleep on his account. I was losing quite enough on my own.

I could still smell that night; phantom whiffs of it still caught me unawares. The shitty stink of Danny's entrails . . . the smell like dustbins on a hot day that Razoxane had left behind her . . . the sticky reek of Trinity's last meal, half-digested in his mangled guts . . .

'You just wonder what this whole world's coming to, I suppose,' I murmured, noncommittally.

He nodded. 'Hell of a thing though, wasn't it?'

That was true enough: it had got us national media coverage (BUTCHER CLAIMS THIRD VICTIM bawled the tabloids) and round-the-clock police protection. Some of the reports had compared the latest killing with the events following 'Carol McCain's' first visit to our department; in that, at least, they spoke truer than they knew. Knowledgeable speculation about vice wars was still way off-target, though.

'How're we doing, anyway?' I asked Fran.

'The bloke with the cut hand's just waiting for his TT booster. The girl with the gynae pain's comfortable ...'

'Their reg. is coming down to look at her,' Mark put in, still scribbling.

'... And the Colles fracture's being plastered now. Otherwise, we're open to offers.'

I glanced down at my watch. 'Quiet tonight.'

'Shhh,' she grinned as she walked off.

Five days had now passed without sight or smell of Razoxane and the Clinicians. I'd even begun to wonder if their weird private war hadn't climaxed somewhere else, and they'd maybe wiped each other out. Three against one seemed pretty long odds – but even if Melphalan's firm had realized they were themselves being stalked, they might not be able to outsmart their human pursuer so easily. A girl with a slaughterer's skills, and a mental age as old as time, was one formidable opponent. I thought that almost enviously.

It wasn't just their last, vicious calling card that was weighing on my mind now, though. I'd been to visit Jenny again; and someone had been there before me.

When I'd got to the cemetery, late the previous afternoon, the sky had been low and heavy, the air fresh with the aftersmell of rain. I'd walked in through the gates and down the puddled road, clutching my bunch of flowers in one hand and my rolled brolly in the other. The dismal day did nothing to alleviate my sombre mood.

I wasn't quite sure what had drawn me here today; I'd more or less accepted the fact of her death, and was willing to let her rest in peace. Maybe it was because I felt so alone now that even her memory would be company; and maybe – as with Miss Morgan – I found the very thought that she was dead, and far beyond all human misery, strangely comforting.

I'd almost reached her grave before I noticed the flowers already on it. Not mine: I hadn't been for weeks. But they must have been there a while, because they were dead. Dead, and withered, and beginning to rot.

I studied them, grimacing faintly. It wasn't just that they looked unsightly; there was something vaguely unsettling about them. Perhaps her parents had been down to visit, of course; but I knew that her mother was not a well woman, and they couldn't make it often. Maybe one of her friends from the ward, then. Or someone she knew from outside work. All were obvious possibilities; but they didn't make me feel any better. Something about those flowers looked wrong. I had the uneasy impression they'd already been dead when they were left there – as if to defile the grave . . .

With an effort, I shrugged off my unease and knelt to place my own, bright flowers upon the soil: gathering the dead ones before getting to my feet again. I stood for a moment, gazing down at the plain wooden marker.

Maybe the Clinicians had put them there: a macabre reminder for me. The thought slipped into my mind unbidden, and I found myself glancing nervously around. There was no one else in sight today: a wet midweek afternoon wasn't anybody's favourite time for visiting graves. For all I knew, there could have been unseen watchers anywhere around me, amid the gravestones or in the bushes; but today, for once, I didn't think so. Despite its grimness, its deathly connotations, the cemetery was calm, a place of peace. I felt I was alone here.

As I returned my attention to the cross before me, I remembered the tramp I'd seen that time before; an encounter I'd all but forgotten. But thinking on it now . . . it could have been Melphalan himself, or one of his cronies. Studying me, as he'd said they'd done. Learning of the bond that still existed between me and poor, dead Jenny.

So perhaps this was one more way of getting to me; sullying her final resting place. But if they'd hoped to scare me, they hadn't succeeded – I felt a sudden surge of sharp, offended anger.

Leave her out of it, you bastards. You can't touch her now.

I became aware of a noise in the silence then, a distant sound like metallic thunder, creeping closer as I listened. After a moment I realized it was a helicopter.

I looked up with idle, instinctive curiosity, studying the slow-moving greyness of the sky until I'd spotted the thing, still a couple of miles distant: a tiny insect-shape, bejewelled with a bright speck of light. As I watched, it came drifting closer.

I realized it was a police helicopter at about the same time as I heard the sirens; I looked over towards the new sound, and glimpsed the pulse and flicker of blue cop-lights between the houses on the far side of the cemetery. Several vehicles, travelling fast. I wondered what the drama was, and whether the day shift up at the Department would end up getting involved.

The sirens seemed to be congregating in the Lamborn area; the chopper was over there now, and hovering. After a pause, it occurred to me to wander over there, and find out for myself.

By the time I got to Copleston Road – just a couple of streets away from where Razoxane's first victim had been discovered – part of it had already been cordoned off. There were a lot of police in evidence.

I joined the small crowd that had gathered at the tape barrier. The street ahead was strewn with patrol cars, some of which had been parked askew and in a hurry; a couple still had their lights going. Officers on foot were going from house to house, presumably warning occupants to stay indoors. A few more stood close by the barrier, keeping an eye on the public. Their handsets were busy, crackling with crosstalk and static.

'Any idea what's going on?' I asked a woman next to me; she shook her head, but someone else volunteered the information. 'It's the Butcher – they reckon they've got him this time . . .'

There was a general stir of excitement among the crowd; I felt my stomach tighten. Was it Razoxane they'd cornered, then? Had she stuck her neck out too far this time? And if they did manage to take her – after God knows how many of the town's fresh-faced young coppers had been cut to bits trying – and put her in the secure psychiatric unit where she certainly belonged . . . what would happen to me? Who could I call on when the Clinicians came again . . . ?

I leaned forward, straining to overhear the messages coming over the police radios. Maybe it was one of the Clinicians themselves who'd been spotted, of course; it was after all Vokaine's description that had been circulated nationally. But I couldn't see them showing their faces in daylight, somehow. Nor being caught so easily.

One of the policemen was coming over, and I saw it was Bill Roberts again. He was met with a chorus of questions, which he fended off with deliberate vagueness. He'd just finished assuring us there was nothing to see when he caught my eye.

'Rachel. Hello again.' I could almost see the wheels go

round as he thought back to our last meeting. 'Live round here, do you?'

'I've ... got a friend round here,' I answered, economically.

His handset gave a squawk at that point. '... *three-one-three* ... *No sign of anyone down this way, over* ...'

'You reckon it's the bloke who did the Stone Road one?' I prompted, in a conversational sort of way.

He glanced at the others – we'd moved a little way clear of them now – then back at me. Just like last time, he hesitated a moment, while his instinctive reticence was won over by the desire to share an insider's knowledge with someone else. Then he lowered his voice.

'I shouldn't be saying this, but ...'

But being the operative word; the man could not keep his mouth shut. Who knew, maybe he fancied me or something, and was trying to impress.

'... we've found a body in one of the lock-ups round the back there; still warm. Stab wounds. Some vagabond type was seen loitering in the vicinity, so we were scrambled. No sign of him now, though.'

He nodded to an unmarked van parked at the far end of the street. 'The firearms unit's in on this one: no half-measures this time.' He paused, looking abashed. 'Look, Rachel, don't spread that around, okay? I'm sure it'll be covered in the press conference, but ...'

I nodded absently; my mind already racing. Had she nailed another, then? Three down, two to go? 'Had he been ... carved up?' I asked carefully.

'Not as bad as the others – though the pathologist hasn't had a chance to examine him yet. We think we know who he is though. Local villain. Small-time, but a nasty piece of work.'

That could have been just another of their disguises, of course: and if Razoxane hadn't been able to finish the job of dissection, he'd be up and about again before they knew it . . .

'I don't know, Rachel,' Roberts was saying. 'What's happening to this town, eh? Used to be just traffic offences and burglaries and a couple of assaults at the weekend; and now suddenly we've got Jack the Ripper walking round out there.'

'Is that what you reckon, then: that it's some nutter?'

He spread his hands in a gesture of bafflement: 'God knows. A lot of the lads agree with the papers – that it's some kind of gang-war thing. You know how bad things have got round here . . .'

I nodded, recalling a recent article in the local rag: the one that had berated the police for letting prostitution and the whole drug scene get right out of control. 'Mm,' I agreed, tactfully enough.

He seemed content to keep on theorizing; and maybe he needed to. I guessed he was still trying to rationalize it all, get it straight in his mind – this flood of urban horror that a stolid, unimaginative copper had never dreamed to deal with.

I sympathized, I really did.

'The first one was that pimp . . . who was also a dealer. Then that bloke Lester, who was into computers . . . God knows what he'd been up to . . .'

I knew what he'd been up to, all right. But I kept my peace.

'Then your porter, who was maybe nicking drugs or something . . . and now this guy. Maybe it's a takeover, or something. Maybe the heavy mob are moving in.'

'What about that bitch who ran amok in our department the other week? The one with the knife.' I was curious to know if they'd fitted her in somewhere. 'Reckon she's involved?'

'Maybe. The witness ended up in the canal, after all. Yeah, we're still looking for her, all right.' But not for the crimes of the Backstreet Butcher, I reckoned: she was a mere woman, after all . . .

His radio crackled again. '. . . *two-two-four again . . . if he was here, he's not any more . . .*'

Into thin air, I thought.

Roberts glanced back down the street. 'I can see them cancelling all leave at this rate,' he predicted gloomily. We both looked up as the chopper clattered overhead, sweeping in a wider circle now.

His gaze came back round to me. 'I'll tell you one thing for nothing, though,' he said, an uncharacteristic, sombre flatness in his tone. 'Whoever is doing it, he's a nutter all right. A fucking psycho. 'Scuse the language, Rachel.'

I smiled faintly. 'I've heard worse.'

We watched the police officers begin filtering back towards the central control point, grim-faced and empty-handed. And maybe luckier than they knew.

'Anyway . . . nice to see you again,' Roberts said. 'Things well with you? You were looking a bit down . . .'

I shrugged. 'Our cat died last week.'

He managed not to smile. 'Sorry. Miss him, do you?'

'Mm,' I said, noncommittally.

Slight concern crept into his expression. 'Hey. You really do, don't you?'

'It's not just that; it's the way it happened. Some wildcat got in and . . . well, ripped him to bits actually.' That's what I'd told Sarah anyway. She'd been too upset to query it.

He shook his head. 'Rotten old world, sometimes, isn't it?'

I nodded. It certainly was.

I looked up from my quiet chat with June as our police guard for tonight stuck his head round the duty-room door. 'Any chance of some more tea?'

204

'Help yourself. Kettle's just boiled.' I heard the phone in my office start ringing as I spoke.

I went across, but Fran had beaten me to it. 'Do we know anything about injuries?' she was saying. 'Right . . . when will they be here?' *RTA* she mouthed at me as I appeared in the doorway.

Bloody hell, I mouthed back. She almost giggled.

'Two-car accident down by the Elliston Estate,' she confirmed when she'd hung up. 'Three coming in, one head-injured and unconscious. Five minutes.'

'Right, let's get ready.' It felt good to slip back into the routine once more – emptying my mind of less immediate concerns. Walking down towards the front doors, I made an effort to concentrate on the job in hand: the reception of casualties – their assessment, treatment and care. And it wasn't really so hard.

I could hear the sirens already, whooping it up out there in the night.

Life goes on, after all. Because death never lets up.

Twenty-three

I was Nights Off and doing my shopping when Razoxane appeared to me again.

I'd been making my unhurried way back from Tesco's, lugging a carrier full of groceries; my mind idling. Down I went into the damp, dingy underpass beneath Talbot Way, and she was waiting there for me: lounging casually against the wall halfway along. The definitive phantom vagabond.

I hesitated; it crossed my mind to turn and walk away. But what would be the point? So I pursed my lips and kept on going, my reluctant footfalls echoing ahead of me down the dank passageway. She straightened up as I drew level, and flashed an empty smile of greeting. She was hugging herself, the old coat wrapped tight around her: one hand concealed beneath it. I gave her a pinched look of acknowledgement, without breaking stride. 'Well?'

She fell easily into step beside me. 'Well what?'

'Have you killed them all yet?'

'Patience, Rachel,' she chided. 'It's a waiting game, remember.'

I glanced uneasily over my shoulder: no one was following. Eyes front again, but no one was ahead of us either.

'The cops are still looking for you, you know,' I muttered. 'You're hardly unobtrusive dressed like that.'

'People notice what they choose to notice,' she answered drily – sounding as if she too had a say in the matter. 'I wouldn't worry.'

That reminded me of something Melphalan had said: something about having power over the human mind, so that people accepted bizarre sights as unremarkable . . .

'Look what I've got,' Razoxane said, like a little girl.

I turned and looked as she held one half of her coat open – and saw she was holding a gun there against her ribs. I thought it was a rifle for a moment; then realized it was one of those pump-action shotguns, oil-black and ugly. I knew right away that it was the genuine article. I felt the breath go out of me.

She closed her coat again, like a flasher, and grinned at me.

'Where the *hell* did you get that . . . ?'

'I bought it off a man,' she said matter-of-factly, as we emerged into the sunlight again. After a moment she added: 'I had to kill him first, though.'

Oh, God. 'The bloke they found over Lamborn way? That was you, wasn't it?' The police had been a bit cagey about details, but they'd admitted that the murdered man had been found with a couple of hundred pounds' worth of used notes stuffed into his mouth and slashed-open stomach. It had livened up the gang-war theory no end.

She nodded. 'His fault. I'd come prepared to do business – a straight sale – but he seemed to think it was all pretext, and I was really just a weird girl who got turned on by guns. So: I had to show him his error. But I paid for the shotgun; that was only proper.'

'So . . . he wasn't one of them, then?' She shook her head. 'Then why . . . The papers said there'd been . . . some mutilation – like the others . . .'

She shrugged. 'We can't be too careful, Rachel: their servants are everywhere. To be safe – I cut out his heart, and burned it.'

I gave her a sick, sidelong look. Her paranoia was getting worse, all right. And who would she next decide was a servant of the enemy, I wondered. Which of our fellow-citizens was next in line for vivisection or cremation . . . ?

And she had a gun, now. An automatic bloody shotgun.

'What're you . . . planning to do with it?' I asked cautiously.

'It's my equalizer,' was her reply. 'It evens the odds. You couldn't kill them with one of these; but you could damage them, badly – slow them down. Gives you the chance to get in close with the knife, and finish the job.'

Feeling nauseous now, I could only nod. Bill Roberts had wondered what the town was coming to. He'd seen nothing yet.

But a part of me, deep down, felt something else: a pang of cold excitement. We were going to take the bastards on. And we were going to win . . .

We parted company at the car park, and I watched her walk casually away: watched passers-by glance distastefully at her scruffiness, without recognizing the woman whose description had been so widely circulated – and without ever guessing what violent death she carried beneath her coat.

I managed to get about two hours' sleep that night before something – some eerie, inexplicable sense of *presence* – awoke me once more. For a moment I lay quite motionless, hopelessly hoping that whatever it was would just go away. I waited, listening to the silence, until I could stand the crawling of my skin no longer; then opened my eyes to find cold moonlight filling my room – and Razoxane waiting patiently at the foot of my bed.

'Bloody hell . . .' I murmured, squinting irritably back at her.

'Come with me, Rachel,' she said softly. 'There's something I want you to see . . .'

'Look . . . what time is it . . . ?' I rolled over to peer at my alarm clock; and froze.

The clock wasn't there: no comforting digital readout

floating in the dark. Instead, in a patch of moonlight, I saw an antique-looking hourglass, its frame sculpted to resemble twin skeletons, one upright, one inverted: each a mirror image of the other. A jewel in the uppermost skull's eye winked knowingly back at me.

The sands were running out.

'Time enough,' came Razoxane's calm voice.

Not *another* bloody dream, I thought dully. And maybe it wasn't, at that.

Maybe I'd have preferred it if it was.

The weird, disembodied feeling was the same; but recognition failed to snap me out of it – and the details were so unsettlingly vivid . . . As I reluctantly sat up, I remembered again about powers over human minds, and gave her an accusing look.

'You're . . . in my head, aren't you? Interfering with my mind . . . You're making me see this . . .'

Razoxane smiled faintly, and didn't answer.

'Just leave me alone, let me sleep . . .'

She just held out her hand; and I realized there would be no denying her. I climbed out of bed (the cold felt real enough) and walked over, and she reached out and took my hand.

'Come on,' she almost breathed, and opened the bedroom door. I went out after her – and found we'd stepped straight into a medieval dungeon.

That's what it looked like, anyway: grim, dripping stone walls rising up around us, with stark metal fixtures glimpsed here and there . . . and human bones scattered in the shadows beneath them.

Everything was tinged by a glowing downspill of moonlight from the night above us, funnelled into the chamber by the chimney-like walls. It seemed almost focused at the centre of the room: highlighting the seven-pointed star etched out upon the flagstones – and throwing the seven dark figures who stood around it into black relief.

Clinicians screamed my mind. My mouth might have followed suit, but for Razoxane's grip tightening on my hand.

'Don't be afraid,' she hissed in my ear. 'This isn't here, or now.'

One of them stood at each point of the heptagram, facing inward; unmoving, as though lost in silent contemplation. They were all wrapped in long coats, as though to ward off bitter chill; their faces shadowed by the sort of wide-brimmed hats I'd seen in pictures of Puritan times.

'What . . . what is this?' I asked her: whispering instinctively.

'A convocation,' she answered evenly, not taking her eyes off the gathering. 'Melphalan's cabal of seven. What your modern doctors would call his "firm" . . .'

And as if on cue, the Lord of Physicians began to speak.

He was across the circle from us, and I only knew him by his voice; his face was a pit of shadow. One closed hand rested thoughtfully against his chin. The moonglow just caught the silver ring on his third finger.

'Our minds are one, and open,' he said solemnly; 'the wisdom is ours for the taking. And the power. What news from the north point? Are all things now ready?'

'They are,' another Clinician answered.

'And from the east: are our subjects prepared?'

'They are,' a third man confirmed; I realized they'd been identified by the points of the star at which they stood, as though the whole design was some occult sort of compass rose . . .

'Excellent,' Melphalan said. 'Tonight we shall loose the souls in their purest state . . . capture them . . . and study their secrets. Their energy will become our own . . .'

I glanced at Razoxane; but Razoxane was peering almost apprehensively upwards, into the frost-blue glow. It reflected from the lenses that masked her eyes (*Moon-*

glasses, I thought dumbly. *Moonshades*), and bleached her face like bone. As I watched, her mouth grew grimly tighter – as if she sensed something descending towards us: coming in from the cold . . .

'We will enrapture the women first,' Melphalan was saying, his voice growing in intensity. 'Their spirits are stronger. We will focus them by fear – and purify with pain . . .'

Razoxane tugged at my hand. 'Come on, Rachel. We've seen enough . . .'

I let her draw me back through the doorway; I really didn't want to see what happened next. Back we went into the safety of my bedroom.

But my bedroom wasn't there.

I almost clutched at my throat: the jolt of shock had left its muscles achingly constricted, and in that instant I thought I'd choke. We'd stumbled into another chamber, smaller than the first, and dingier: lit by oily lamplight rather than the clean, cold moon. There was a long wooden table at its centre, with the body of a man stretched out upon it. And sombre figures gathered all around.

As I gawped, I felt the cold redoubled, like a blast from an open freezer. It raised the fine hairs all along my fore-arms – and turned my nipples button-hard beneath my flimsy T-shirt. I wanted to shrink away and shiver; but Razoxane's hand had slid into my hair, and fisted there – forcing my dazed head forward.

'Watch,' her voice commanded flatly. 'Listen. *Learn*.'

The bloke on the stained table was strapped down tight, like an inmate of old Bedlam. I glimpsed his spasms, his twitching fingers, rolling eyes – and realized, with a helpless plunge of horror, that he wasn't mad at all; just out of his mind with dread.

The madmen were those who stood around him.

Melphalan was waiting at the table's head: hatless and in his eighteenth-century shirtsleeves. His hair was short and neatly styled; his beard trimmed. A picture of gentility; but his cold black eyes belied it.

His brother Clinicians had turned to watch him. The faces I could see were gaunt, severe; the yellow lamplight turned their paleness sallow. But I could feel their eagerness: it filled the room – and chilled it even further.

'And so . . . gentlemen,' Melphalan said; the heartbeat's pause making me wonder if he sensed the irony himself. 'Our subject is ready; and so are we.'

The subject's panting filled the moment that followed. His mouth gaped for breath enough to fuel the engine of his fear; he looked long past screaming now.

Someone else stepped forward – and with a start I recognized Vokaine. No goggles here: his eyes were a piercing blue – standing out bright in his weathered, bony face. He was wearing a leather apron over his clothes: something that made my stomach draw back even before he'd picked up the knife from the table top and turned it to catch the light.

It looked like a cheese knife: forked into two points. As Vokaine looked from it to the subject's bloodless face, Melphalan leaned smoothly forward to take the latter's head in a two-handed grip, and hold it rigid.

'The soul must first be sealed up,' the Lord of Physicians said – the edge to his voice hinting at the force he was exerting, as though seeking to crush his victim's skull. 'Immured within the body. So we begin . . .' And Vokaine bent forward, and started with the subject's staring eyes.

The screams raked my eardrums; drowned my own whimpers. I tried to twist my face away, but Razoxane's grip was unrelenting.

Vokaine laid the oozing knife to one side, and selected a long metal probe from the implements arrayed along the table. Sharp and slim as a knitting needle. He stooped again, to one side of the keening subject, and aimed his thrust.

Another shriek. Another.

With that fist in my hair, I couldn't even shake my head: the only protest I had mind enough to manage. Before my helpless eyes, the bloody probe was replaced by a wicked-looking pair of pliers, and Vokaine – face still quite expressionless – was bracing one hand over his victim's mewling mouth, and starting work on the centre of his face.

A wet, tearing sound. The pop and crunch of cartilage. And whatever this was, dream or vision or bloody nightmare, my tears were real enough – I felt them on my cheeks and tasted their salt on my tongue.

Razoxane's fingers in my hair; her voice in my head. '*Watch*.'

Sight. Hearing. Smell. And now Vokaine was wielding a hooked set of tongs, and prising the subject's mouth open to get inside.

Another ripping sound. My tears had gummed my eyelids open: they *wouldn't shut*. I glimpsed a fragment of something pink being dropped into a bowl held out ready by another Clinician. And as Vokaine drew back, and glanced up, it seemed our eyes met for just an instant – and held each other. Terror sank its teeth into my stomach; and the moment passed.

Only touch was left now. And as I watched, panting, they took that too. Melphalan himself did the honours, twisting the bloody, bubbling head until the cervical spine gave way: the dry crack seemed to split the silent room. The body twitched spasmodically. I saw Melphalan fingering for a pulse – and nodding with satisfaction as he found one.

I felt on the very edge of fainting: as if only Razoxane's grip was holding me upright.

'. . . is completed,' Melphalan was saying smoothly. 'The subject soul insulated from the world outside. Free from all sensory contamination. And now we shall wait, gentlemen. And when the soul is as pure as only insanity can make it . . . we will begin.'

I became aware of a tugging behind me: Razoxane

pulling me back from this awful brink once more. I stumbled after her, into swallowing blackness, and blue moonlight beyond it.

We were back in my room again; the sudden shift combined with my leaden-bellied nausea to leave me swaying. I grasped the door-jamb, and glanced breathlessly at Razoxane. She'd released me and drawn back: looking thoughtful.

'O God . . .' I managed, and swallowed. 'What was all that in aid of . . . ?'

'A taste of all I'm up against, Rachel,' she answered, as though preoccupied still. 'Old enemies. Ancient enemies . . .'

'What we're up against,' I reminded her dully; and now she looked at me.

'Yes. It occurs to me, Rachel . . . perhaps I should spare you this.'

Oh please, I thought.

'How . . . ?' I began; and the instant click of her switchblade made me jump – my first and last reaction before she pushed the cold blade deep into my left breast. My T-shirt never slowed it, of course; but for one timeless instant I felt the elastic resistance of my skin before that gave way as well.

My mouth opened wide on a horrified gasp as I stared downwards, disbelieving. Then Razoxane twisted the knife with all the strength in her slim wrist.

I gagged – and it was daylight.

I found myself curled up in bed again, alone.

Shit.

I actually went so far as to feel myself, frantically checking for pain – or blood; but I was unharmed. A glance at my alarm clock told me it was back in its place; the time was 9:25. Drained, I lay back again, and stared at the ceiling.

Razoxane. Damn you. Get the hell out of my head.

After a while I slid out of bed and padded wearily through to the bathroom, tugging my T-shirt over my head.

I stayed under the shower for a long time: sluicing out my very brain, or so it felt like. Finished at last, I dried off and pulled the T-shirt back on; I couldn't be bothered to get dressed. I went into the kitchen and made myself a coffee, taking it through into the living room to have a look at the weather. The morning was overcast; the light muddy. I grimaced, and sipped my drink.

Behind me, Razoxane said casually: 'Morning, Rachel. I thought you were never getting up.'

I yelped, and dropped my mug, flinching back as it broke and splashed hot coffee over my toes. I rounded on her. 'Jesus *Christ*!'

Stretched out comfortably on the sofa, she looked behind herself. 'Where?'

I would have said more, but the shotgun registered then: propped upright within easy reach. I took a painful swallow of air.

Her unseen eyes came back round to me. 'Have you been here all bloody night?' I asked hoarsely.

She nodded. 'It was cold; and I got tired of the streets. Don't worry, I didn't disturb your flatmate. And she went off on her Early at half-six . . .'

'You were playing tricks with my mind, weren't you?' I broke in tightly. 'Giving me dreams . . .'

She looked at me closely for a moment; then shrugged. 'Maybe I did, Rachel. Or maybe you were sharing mine . . .'

Whatever she meant by that. I thought again of how the dream had ended; thought of the knife beneath her coat. Glanced at the gun, which looked as if it could probably fire on its own . . .

'I'd get myself another coffee if I were you,' Razoxane said idly; recrossing her booted ankles on the opposite arm of the sofa. 'You look like you could do with it.'

I nodded dumbly, and walked back out; but the first place I went was my bedroom, to put on my dressing-gown

– wrapping it round me and belting it tight. As if the extra layer would somehow offer more protection if the knife came out . . .

Back in the kitchen, I was spooning coffee into a clean mug (I still hadn't got myself sufficiently together to clear the first one up) when I realized Razoxane had reappeared in the doorway. I risked a look.

'So what do you dream about?' I muttered warily.

'So many things, Rachel,' was her soft answer. 'Sins and shadows: past and future . . .' She'd retrieved her hat from the coffee table and was examining it pensively: as though looking for one specific grain of dust amid its coating of grime.

'You dream of the Clinicians?'

She nodded again. 'They're always there: images of them, and what they've done. Lest I forget. Or forgive . . .'

'This dream I had . . .' I said carefully. 'There were seven of them. You called them Melphalan's cabal. But five now . . . ?'

'I killed my first Clinician nearly three centuries ago,' she explained: as casually as a girl discussing her first boy-friend. 'An apothecary turned alchemist – dissecting people's brains in search of some chemical that would aid his quest. I did as much for him, and more: I was learning all the time. But he was of Melphalan's cabal – and from that day on the feud has been one of blood between us.

'I've hunted other Clinicians since – and killed more than a few. But it's less than a hundred years since I picked up the scent of Melphalan and his firm again. We skirmished once or twice; they tried and failed to trap me. I lost them in turn, and the hunt went on. I finally snared the second out of seven in Germany, just before your Second War . . .'

She really believed what she was saying, that much was clear. And worse, I believed it too. A fresh chill tickled my spine as I recalled what I'd thought when Melphalan first met me: that grim idea of the *gatekeeper* . . .

'Germany?' I broke in, and suddenly it seemed so horribly obvious. 'You mean those Nazi doctors – Mengele and people – were Clinicians?'

But Razoxane shook her head.

'No, Rachel. Oh, I suspected it too, of course, and came looking; but they never knew of the Order of Clinical Judges. And yet . . . for all that . . . the thought-world's just the same. Human beings with absolute freedom to do what they want; the absolute power of life and death. Absolute corruption always follows . . .' She lapsed into silence.

The kettle boiled and bubbled.

Razoxane turned back towards the living room – then leaned in again. 'Black, no sugar,' she added, with an unnerving little smile.

I trailed through after her, and handed her a mug. Sipping from my own – swallowing down heat into my cold and hollow stomach – I forced my thoughts back on to the visions she'd made me see.

'That . . . awful thing last night. That experiment. What did they think they were doing . . . ?'

Razoxane contemplated her drink for what seemed quite a while. Then she said: 'Melphalan is afraid.'

I almost hooted. '*He's* afraid?'

'Oh, but he is,' she continued quietly. 'Afraid of death. Afraid of hell.'

'But you said he –'

'This is the hell that Melphalan fears: to die, and linger in his dust for all eternity. Unable to see, or hear, or feel, or move – but still *aware*. Souls never perish: he's discovered that much. But his science leaves no room for an afterlife – so they've nowhere to go.

'The Clinicians have always fought to defeat death. Firstly for the sake of others – then only for themselves. The early attempts – mystical and medicinal – all failed. There were internal haemorrhages; collapses of the immune system. Cancers so virulent they were practically *carnivorous* ...' A vindictive smile played briefly at her lips. 'It took until the late Middle Ages for them to find ways to fix the life cycle – and so prolong it. But they're still not immortal; and one day death will catch the last of them.'

I was nodding, fascinated; the mug already cooling in my cupped hands.

'It is Melphalan's belief ...' Razoxane continued slowly, 'that, if only he can understand the nature of the soul, he can move ever onward, from one body to the next – and so stay one step ahead of death, for ever. That's his specialty, if you like. Trying to catch souls at their purest. Experiments like the one you saw – cutting minds off from the outside world completely. The rest's just casual research: window-dressing in a butcher's shop. But it keeps his cohorts happy.'

'So ... what's Vokaine's specialty, then ... ?' I ventured.

Razoxane smiled. 'Pain thresholds.'

I nodded quickly, and took a gulp of coffee. I hadn't the nerve to ask what Glaukostyx was into.

After a minute, I just shook my head.

'What?'

'They started out as *doctors*, Razoxane ... So where did it all go wrong?'

She gave me a thoughtful glance. Then: 'You're a Catholic, aren't you?'

I blinked; then shrugged. 'Sort of.'

'You know *Ecclesiasticus*?'

'Not personally, no.'

'Got a Bible?' she asked drily.

'In my room,' I said, and followed her through. She picked the book up from the bedside table – while I just stared at the twisted sheets, and realized how much I'd sweated last night – and thumbed through it to the page she was after. 'Chapter 38,' she said, handing it across.

I read.

Honour the Doctor for his services – for the Lord created him. His skill comes from the Most High, and he is rewarded by kings . . .

I glanced up, and saw her nodding.

'That's the real irony of it, Rachel,' she said, as calmly as ever. 'There's no one more worthy of honour than the doctor. No one. The skill to ease pain, and prolong life: every civilization has prized that above all else. The man who wrote that reckoned it was a gift from God . . .'

There was something in her voice I couldn't quite pin down: a sort of wistfulness. 'But Melphalan's lot started playing God?'

She nodded. 'The doctor has great power – and a choice along with it. Two paths, right or left. To give of himself, or just to take. At the beginning, the Clinicians even thought they were following the right-hand path. But they were wrong.'

We were back in the living room by now. I finished my coffee in silence.

Razoxane set down her own mug, and reached for her hat. Then for the shotgun.

I hugged myself instinctively: keeping my forearms pressed to my breasts even after she'd tucked the weapon under her coat.

'Where'll you be?' I asked in a low voice.

'Ranging over the whole earth, from end to end,' she smiled thinly. 'Book of Job,' she added, seeing my puzzled frown.

'Right. See you . . .' I watched as she went through into the hall; listened, as she let herself out.

Then sat heavily back on the sofa she'd so recently vacated, and rested my weary head in both my hands.

After a while, I yielded to temptation and went back

into the bedroom for the Bible. Book of Job. And I found her mocking little reference in the very first chapter. Words ascribed to the Devil himself, in his most chilling role of all: as God's Accusing Angel.

Well thank you, Razoxane, I thought grimly. *Thanks a bunch.*

The next day I got a phone call: in the afternoon, when I was trying to get some sleep before work. Sarah answered it, and came and knocked gently on my door. 'Raitch? Are you awake?'

I was; I'd been lying there contemplating the ceiling for a while now. Sleep didn't exactly come easy these days.

'Who is it?'

'Dunno. She says it's important.'

I sat up quickly, feeling my stomach flip over with anticipation. 'Hang on, I'll be right there . . .'

She'd left the receiver lying beside the phone. I picked it up, glancing round to make sure she'd returned to Daytime TV, and held it to my ear for a breathless second before saying cautiously: 'Hello . . . ?'

'Rachel. We need to meet.'

'What, again?'

'I think I know where they've been hiding,' Razoxane elaborated calmly. 'And we've got some help now.'

I had the phone tucked in between chin and shoulder, and was nervously scratching my bare elbows. 'What sort of help?'

'You'll see. Do you know Fenner Street?'

'Uh . . . yeah.' Most people in town did, if only by reputation. Once in a while the police would bow to local complaints and mount a purge to thin out the kerb-crawlers, but that area was still the nearest we had to a red-light district.

'You need to get down there tonight. Go to number

thirty-six. The people there are friends, and can be trusted. I'll meet you there. Okay?'

For a moment my mind was blank, as I groped frantically for an excuse. Any excuse. 'And then what? I mean . . . I've got to be in work tonight.'

'Phone in sick.'

I wasn't about to do that. 'Look, what is this?'

A pause; then she seemed to relent a little. 'All right. We need to make plans, but it shouldn't take too long. If you can be there at six, we'll get through it as quickly as we can. Believe me Rachel, you need to be there.'

I chewed my lip uncertainly. In the background I could hear the soundtrack of whatever vacuous Aussie soap opera Sarah was watching.

'You'll be quite safe,' Razoxane insisted. 'We're not going to go after them tonight or anything.'

'Right. All right.' I nodded, though she couldn't see it. I'd go along with anything that got this nightmare over sooner rather than later. 'Six o'clock then. Number thirty-six.'

'See you there,' she said, and hung up, leaving me listening to the purr of the broken connection: once more bereft of my guardian angel.

Twenty-four

I got propositioned twice before I made it to number thirty-six Fenner Street.

Both times it was blokes in cars. I heard them pulling in close behind me, and instinctively quickened my pace as they drew level, leaning across to speak through their passenger windows.

'How're you doing, love?' the first one asked.

I considered ignoring him altogether, then gave him a frosty little smile and said, 'I'm sorry, you must have me confused with someone else.'

He raised his eyebrows in a 'touché' expression, and drove on.

The second was more persistent.

He followed me most of the way down James Street with his wheels in the gutter, mixing unnervingly fake small-talk with enquiries about what I offered and how much I charged. I walked on with my head down, feeling my cheeks burning with humiliation and embarrassment – and my stomach knotting up with fear. It was a very empty street.

Eventually he seemed to lose patience with my playing hard to get.

'Look: fifty quid for it without a condom, what do you say?'

Piss off seemed a bit risky; I contented myself with: 'Just leave me alone, okay?'

'Fuck you, then,' he muttered, and accelerated away.

'You should be so lucky,' I gritted after him, watching

his car turn sharply left into the next street and disappear, its engine noise gradually fading to silence.

I still didn't feel safe then.

I knew this was hardly a wise area for 'respectable' girls to visit alone, of course; especially at this hour, with the sun already down and the dusk beginning to settle on the streets. But I still found it really scary — the thought that any woman still out and about was somehow fair game to the prowlers in cars. I'd tried to dress as unprovocatively as possible under my raincoat: a floppy cardigan over my blouse, and one of my long skirts. It didn't seem to be doing much good.

When I reached the end of Fenner Street there were already a couple of women standing around on the corner: both in tight skirts, and one wearing a red blouse under her coat. They both gave me a suspicious look, as if I was competition. I ignored them, and walked on, and wondered what the hell I was doing here. A nice well-brought-up girl, as my Mum used to call me proudly, walking alone down a street like this.

There was a third woman waiting near a lamp-post, a bit further along; the red spark of her cigarette end pricking the dusk like a feeble challenge to the flat, pink glow above her, which popped on as I watched. She struck a sombre as well as solitary figure — her jacket was black, and her long hair just as dark; but her fishnets and short leather skirt suggested she was in the same profession as the others. She was younger than them, though, and better-looking, with a rather wan prettiness that suggested she hadn't been on the game for long. She gave me an incurious glance as I came closer, then returned her attention to the roadway as a car cruised speculatively past. Her hands slid down on to her hips and she posed herself, and grinned: it made her look even younger. I reckoned she was maybe nineteen.

The car didn't slow down. She looked after it, and shrugged.

Her eyes came back round to me again.

I was glancing at the numbers. Thirty-two. Thirty-four . . .

She was standing right outside number thirty-six.

Unsure of quite what to do next, I passed her and paused, looking up at the house: a three-storey Victorian job, looking rather the worse for wear; its small front garden overgrown. The weathered paint was flaking like a bad case of eczema. I could almost smell the damp.

None of the windows was lit. They watched me mournfully.

'Help you?' the girl behind me asked, and I almost jumped.

'Er . . . I'm meeting a friend here . . .'

'You're Rachel?' Scots accent: soft one.

I nodded dumbly.

She stared back at me for a moment, tight-lipped, and I thought she'd grown a little paler. Then she nodded towards the front door. 'You'd best come in, then.'

'Whatever.' I followed her through the gate, and watched as she fished the key out of her shoulderbag and unlocked the door; glancing quickly up and down the street before pushing it inward. The hallway beyond had a stale and mouldy smell, creeping deep into my nostrils as I crossed the threshold. The passage through to the back of the house was already clogged with shadows.

And the silence settled over us like a shroud.

More to break it than anything else, I asked: 'Are they bedsits here, or what?'

She gave me a sidelong look, then shook her head. 'We're all together. Me and some friends.'

Presumably her fellow-workers. And maybe her pimp.

The uncarpeted staircase creaked beneath her high heels and my own ankle boots as we ascended through a haze of grey to the first floor. The smell up here was stronger: the odour vaguely familiar, like rancid cheese.

She pushed open another door on the landing, and led the way into a sparsely furnished bedroom. I lingered just inside the doorway, glancing around: noticing the patches of damp, the wallpaper beginning to peel. I wondered if the punters noticed too; and if they cared.

She'd gone over to the window, gazing out at the last of the light. Then she turned back to me.

'You can wait here if you want. It won't be long.' Her voice was lacklustre now: she sounded tired, resigned. I wondered how she'd got involved with Razoxane – and how long she'd lived the same nightmare as I had. She'd lost colour, all right: I could tell that even by the ashen light from the window. The confident, sexy exterior was all gone, now; her sparkle wiped away. She just looked scared.

I shrugged; and tensed as I heard a door open, and footsteps in the hall below us.

'Trish?' A man's voice. 'She here?'

'Yeah,' she called back, and added to me: 'That's Paul.'

Whoever Paul was. I waited for him to come on up, but he didn't: I heard him moving around down below, and caught a murmur of voices. 'Who else is there here?' I asked.

She didn't reply for a moment: just stared into my face, as if wondering if I could be trusted. Then she made her decision. 'Just the four of us. Me, Paul . . . Steve and Colin. We've been together for a while.'

Strange set-up, I thought. Maybe they're on the dole or something, and she's selling herself to help them pay the rent (they'd sure picked the right area in that case). But it was people like this the Clinicians preyed on, after all: the ones at the bottom of the heap. And now, it seemed, these particular victims had decided to start fighting back.

Much good would it do them – or me – without Razoxane's help. I hoped she'd get here soon.

The girl, Trish, had sat wearily down on the edge of her

bed: she looked as if she'd had a hard day. I watched her kick off her shoes, and stretch, and stifle a yawn. There was a long, pale ladder in one of her stockings. When she looked up at me again, her kohl-rimmed eyes were wide: as if with wonder.

'You don't know how lucky you are,' she muttered. 'You really don't. Any of us said no to a Clinician, they'd rip our guts out. I . . . had a friend, called Alison, she was on the game too, working for them. She got pregnant, and wanted to keep it; she tried to get away. They caught her, and did the termination on a kitchen table – without an anaesthetic. She died in hospital . . .' She held my gaze, though her eyes were getting very bright, and I knew she was seeing me through a film of tears. I just stared back at her in awkward silence, and remembered Alison Scott, prostitute, who'd survived her backstreet abortion only to die of terror – or despair – in our department.

Trish sniffed, and glanced away.

'You said she was working for them . . .' I ventured. 'How did they . . . use her?'

'Same as they use me,' she almost whispered. 'We're bait: we lure the lonely . . . find out which ones are suitable material . . . and then they take care of the rest. It's a Judas kiss, all right.' She giggled then: it was too bitter to be hysterical.

'That's a bit like what they want me to do,' I told her – suddenly anxious to show I sympathized, and knew what she was going through. 'I work up at the hospital . . . They want me to turn my patients over to them.'

She looked back at me. 'They must want that pretty badly, Rachel. You wouldn't be alive now otherwise.'

That's what I'd thought myself.

Come on, woman, where the hell are you? I realized I needed the loo quite badly: all this standing around feeling keyed up. 'Where's the toilet – through here?' I asked, and was walking back across the landing towards a likely-looking door before she could answer.

'*Rachel*. Wait a minute . . .' I heard her getting to her feet, but before she could say more I'd pushed the door open and found myself in the bathroom, looking at the bath.

The bath was full of blood.

That was the nightmare first impression, anyway; it took me only a second to realize that the thing was empty, apart from a thick crimson scum along the bottom. But the whole bath was coated with blood, great smears that had splashed up the sides and dribbled down again. The white enamel beneath was barely visible. And there were *bits* amid the gore, clinging to the sides or afloat in the ooze. Bits of flesh and hair and . . .

Horror hit me like a punch in the guts: I took a lurching step backwards, pinching my lips tight shut as my stomach threatened suddenly to overflow. The bathroom's pent-up stink came after me: the thick cheesy smell of rotting tissue, diluted by a miasma of bleach and disinfectant that clung to my face like chemical claws. I glimpsed the wrinkled shadows of rubbish sacks in there, and industrial gloves – and a rack of knives and cleavers above the bath that would have done justice to an abattoir . . .

Their backstreet butcher's shop; their secret surgery. The Clinicians were here, they worked here, this was their hiding place.

And I'd just walked right into the lions' bloody den. I almost whimpered. And as I stood there, petrified, I heard Trish come up behind me – and then her arm was round my shoulders. But not to restrain me, I realized dimly; she was trying to comfort, quietly insisting: 'Don't look, Rachel. Don't look. Come away now. It's all right.' And she drew me back against the far wall, hugging me close as reaction caught up and left me shivering. '*Shhh*. It's all right . . .'

Oh, it wasn't all right. Not at all. But I still found time to think how strange it felt, being comforted by someone several years my junior.

'It's horrible, I know,' she was saying, and clearly meant it. 'We just don't think about it — what goes on in there. You have to shut some things out, Rachel, you'd go nuts otherwise . . .' She hesitated — then continued in a flattened, toneless voice, as though finally unburdening herself of a weight she'd endured for far too long. 'It's for disposing of the bodies . . . and they always make Paul do it. Always. Because he used to be into peace, and non-violence, and not eating meat. They make him *carve*.' Another pause, while she helplessly stroked my hair: seeking comfort as much as offering it now. 'He used to live on the road, you know,' she added dully. 'Paul. He used to be one of the free ones. And now he's walled in with the rest of us . . .'

I let her hold on until I'd managed to get a grip on myself; then eased off, swallowing, and glanced jerkily around. 'The Clinicians. Are they . . . here now?'

She shook her head. 'One was here earlier today, but none're here at the moment. They got your message, though — that you were coming in. Someone'll be back tonight.'

Oh, Razoxane, I thought. You bitch. You *cow*.

She'd set me up, of course. And here we'd been, talking at quite crossed purposes, right in the Clinicians' lair: me and one of their servants — who served them still, however reluctantly.

I had to get away.

My gaze strayed past her towards the head of the stairs: a descent into deeper gloom, but then only the front door between me and the street. But she saw, and shook her head once more: almost sadly.

'It's no use having second thoughts,' she said, as if she'd read them. 'They'll only take so much, Rachel. You defy them again, they'll make you suffer. You'll scream yourself to death.'

As I stood there in the shadows of the landing, staring hopelessly back at her, it came to me that I'd been here once before: in this dank and dismal house. They must have brought me here that first night. Examined me in one of the rooms . . . The memory of that vile invasion turned me cold all over – and now here I was once more, back in their hands – betrayed by the only person who could save me.

I was still wearing my crucifix, somewhere under cardigan and blouse. I didn't even realize it. All I felt now was despair.

Trish reached out, and laid a gentle hand on my arm.

'Come on. Come downstairs. I'll get you a drink.'

And as I followed her down the squeaking staircase, she glanced back at me, and forced a smile. 'When I was little, you know, I used to have bad dreams about haunted houses. I never thought I'd end up bloody living in one . . .'

One of the blokes was waiting in the doorway of the unlit breakfast room; he gave me a cursory glance, then looked at Trish. 'How's it going?'

'Quiet,' she muttered, sounding relieved; then turned to me. 'Rachel – this is Steve.'

Steve grunted, and glanced at me again. I reckoned he was about her age, or maybe older: tall and scrawny in a stained grey coat. Greasy black hair and beard framed his pallid face, and he wore a cheap pair of wire-rimmed specs.

'Come on in,' he said to me after a moment. There was an edge of mockery in the invitation. Heart in my mouth, I followed Trish through.

The others were both in there, waiting; as shabbily-dressed and underfed as the first man, and looking edgy. Presumably on tenterhooks for the return of their lords and masters.

These were the truly homeless, I'd realized that: still

members of that rootless, shadowy underclass, for all the roof over their heads. Trish was in better shape than the others – presumably her controllers took care to keep her as alluring as possible. But somehow I got the impression – as her friends welcomed her back with evident relief, like a younger sister – that the three of them were prepared to give up their own food if need be: going hungry so that she could have enough.

I wondered vaguely how the Clinicians had got their claws in. Drugs, maybe; or simple desperation. These would have been normal, cheerful young people once, and maybe not so long ago. And what sort of existence was left to them now? While Trish opened herself to all comers, I guessed the others worked at lugging bodies, scavenging hospital waste – and mopping up after bloody operations.

A glimpse of bright yellow caught my eye, over in the corner. I took a step closer, and saw it was a sharps bucket, still sealed with Biohazard tape; one of them had probably nicked it from the skips last night. There was a box of latex gloves on top of it, and someone must have helped themselves from hospital stores to get their hands on that. Someone on the inside. It hadn't just been Danny.

'This is Colin . . .' Trish went on, still trying. And the bloke sitting at the table – maybe mid-twenties, with dirty, cropped fair hair – raised resentful blue eyes from the makings of a smoke.

'You'd better count yourself lucky,' he muttered, as she had done before him. 'They're angry enough at the moment. You make them angrier, and we're the ones who fucking suffer.'

I shrugged helplessly. Colin held me with his stare for a moment longer, then returned his attention to the cigarette he was rolling. The collar of his shirt – one of those German army-surplus jobs – was open and I could see the metal pendant round his neck: a laughing – shrieking – skull impaled upon a sword. It wasn't the most encouraging of sights.

The third man was standing by the window, looking out; I glimpsed a narrow back garden. He was wearing a faded camouflage jacket; but it wasn't until he turned that I made the connection – and recognized his face. It was the bloke I'd spoken to that time in the department; the man with the dog. Even then they'd been watching me, through their servant's cold, assessing eyes . . .

'And this is Paul . . .' Trish said doggedly.

Now those eyes were on me once again: a lingering look, before he returned his attention to the gathering dusk. It left me feeling as if all this was somehow *my* fault; but before I could open my dry mouth to protest, I realized what else I'd sensed in his sombre expression. A sort of bitterness. A last faint hope betrayed.

Call yourself a Christian?

And here I was, in answer to the call of the Clinicians. Back myself in their unholy fold.

'. . . What time do you reckon they'll be here, then?' Colin asked, studiously ignoring me.

I sensed Steve shrug beside me. 'Fuck knows. I've got it all ready for them . . .'

'It had better be,' Paul muttered; while my mind fast-wound through all possible meanings, and found none of them pleasant. The fear was already clenching round my stomach like a fist.

'Okay,' Steve said; 'you want me to check it again, I'll check it.' He went past me and into the hall.

'Rachel? What'll you have?' Trish called from the kitchen. 'We've got coffee, or if you want –'

There was a brutal, slamming *thud* from right behind me. I almost jumped out of my skin.

So did young Steve, only more literally. He came flying

back past me, almost weightless in the air: giving vent to a geyser of brilliant red. His chest came open as I watched. His body hit the table full-on – and suddenly he had weight once more, smashing into it, upending it, as Colin gawped and tried to struggle upright, and Paul raised open, helpless hands.

The gun behind me kept on firing.

Its pounding filled the room: I felt as well as heard it through the numbness in my stinging ears as I ducked aside and cowered. Again, again – and all I could do was stare, while Steve slumped floorwards, the table collapsing beneath him as Colin went down behind it with a yell, and Paul was flung back hard against the wall. The shooting stopped – leaving the air as thick with smoke as our A&E relatives' room after a heavy session.

I found my gaze fixed on Paul as he slid painfully towards the floor: squirming once, convulsing, as if to smear his gore deeper into the tattered wallpaper. The blood – it was *everywhere* – put me horribly in mind of when I dropped a jar of sieved tomatoes while cooking the other week: the same scarlet, spattered mess . . . And then his frantic eyes found mine, and filled with helpless accusation.

I tried to shake my head. It wouldn't move.

A metallic rattle-rasp came from the passageway behind me. I lurched around.

The Angel of Death had come calling.

Razoxane. She came forward from the shadows of the hallway, the gloom from which she'd risen like a ghost. Her shotgun smouldered in her grip.

I shrank back as she came on in, the skeletal weapon still trained upon the bodies. Paul's gaze jerked round to meet her; he was still struggling to rise – or even move – from his sitting position as she turned towards him. Hopelessly he raised his hand.

She gave him a small circular wave in reply – and fired

one-handed. The recoil kicked the shotgun upwards; but at that range she couldn't really miss.

I made a small, damp moan of protest: my eyes almost starting from their sockets.

Razoxane turned away from the gutted corpse, already smiling – as if at some ghastly private joke. She nodded to me.

'Sorry I'm late.'

And before I could even think of a retort, I heard a gasp – and the second gun came out of nowhere, filling up her left hand as her arm snapped out straight. Aimed right at Trish, standing there in the kitchen doorway, agape at the carnage: so pale she looked about to faint.

'*No!*' I yelled. 'For Christ's sake . . .'

For a moment more she held her stance; I had time to study the pistol's every detail. An ugly, L-shaped automatic, with an oblong butt and short, stubby barrel . . . Then Razoxane gave me a sidelong glance.

'No need to shout, Rachel,' she admonished mildly.

I looked at Trish. Trish was staring into the gaping gun-muzzle with wide, wide eyes. There were tears on her pale, pretty cheeks.

'Leave her be,' I muttered.

A pause; then Razoxane shrugged. Her forefinger grew loose around the trigger.

Trish's shoulders slumped. She let out her breath with a sob.

Razoxane shot her in the face.

I watched in disbelief as Trish arched back into the kitchen, open-mouthed but with no breath left to scream with. Down she went, coming to rest in a heap against the cooker; thighs apart in final welcome. The splash her sagging head left all down the white enamel looked like pasta sauce this time: ripe tomatoes with greyish bits of mushroom . . .

That was the thought that nearly made me puke.

Razoxane lowered the smoking gun. She shrugged again. 'Second thoughts.'

'You *bitch*!' I almost screamed at her.

'Don't be stupid, Rachel,' she snapped back. 'We can't trust anyone, remember: not *one* of the people they've contaminated . . .'

I stepped unsteadily away, and over to the girl who'd tried to comfort me, despite her own distress. The girl who'd never dreamed she'd end up living in a real haunted house – much less dying in one. I stared down at the pinched, almost sullen look on her face – the eyes plastered closed with blood, and blood-soaked hair. Suddenly I wanted to shriek: to dig my fingers deep into my skull, and just let go.

'Forget her, Rachel,' Razoxane hissed behind me. 'One less life in this grieving, *grieving* age. Come on . . .'

I rounded on her. 'You dropped me right in it, didn't you?'

She'd already turned back, towards the hall. 'I'd managed to find out where they were based; I needed them trapped. What better lure than you turning up claiming you'd had second thoughts?'

'They didn't fall for it, though, did they?' I paused, then added bitterly, 'Or maybe you jumped the gun.'

She seemed unperturbed. 'It doesn't matter. We've hurt them badly, Rachel. This is their principal surgery, and they've lost it. There'll be an operating room upstairs, and somewhere for dissections . . . and a room for their rituals too. There will be stuff we can take, and use against them . . .' She thrust the shotgun towards me and unthinkingly I took it, keeping my fingers well clear of the trigger. Suddenly I felt as if I was handling a sleeping snake. And then a fresh chill went through me, and I almost dropped it anyway.

'Oh God . . . it's got my bloody fingerprints on it now . . .'

Razoxane grinned coldly. 'Whoops, that was careless of you, wasn't it?' She went on down the passageway – turning back to check that I was following. 'Rachel. Come on. Even a street like this one will think of calling the police eventually.'

'What . . . what're we looking for?' I asked, following her back up the staircase.

She was waiting at the top, and didn't reply. I stopped, and we both listened. Silence. The house so quiet, so still, that I fancied I could almost hear the dust-motes settling, all around us.

Razoxane's gun was on a level with her face: I saw her trigger-finger flexing. Then she pushed her hat back, let it drop to hang by a thong behind her neck; and took her shades off. Her pupils dilated to meet the darkness, becoming huge: fixed. It was like gazing into a dead girl's eyes. And I knew that mine looked just the same.

'Books,' she muttered, in answer to my question; and pushed in the nearest door – I glimpsed poor Trish's bedroom once again. 'Documents, manuscripts. Anything like that. What's in there?'

'Autopsy room, or something,' I said faintly, pausing outside the bathroom door but not opening it, not this time.

'This is more like it,' she called softly from the other end of the landing.

I went after her, very aware of how silent the house was above us, and below, and not wanting to be left alone. Not for a minute. She was standing on the threshold of what was probably the back bedroom, and went on in as I caught up. I followed her through.

It felt like a big room, but I was guessing. It was pitch-black in there.

And winter-cold.

I could hear Razoxane's breathing in the darkness: very close, and reassuringly even. I glanced back at the doorway, and the dim landing just visible beyond. It suddenly seemed very far away.

My flesh began to crawl.

This was an evil room: I sensed it. A defiled, unholy room. I could feel its creeping stillness all around us; its whispering silence . . .

'Razoxane . . .'

'What?' She'd moved further away than I'd thought.

'Can we . . . please . . . get out of here?'

'Hang on.' There was a sudden inspill of twilight as she located a curtain, and drew it back. Heavy, blackout material, I noted, and glanced around, no less jittery now that I could see. The room was completely empty: bare boards under our feet, and walls stripped of paint and paper. Unadorned, apart from the great heptagram laid out in chalk upon the floor: we'd smudged it slightly as we'd walked around.

'Ritual Room,' she murmured. 'They invoke power here, and think to use it. In fact it's using them . . .'

She broke off, and walked over to the corner. I noticed the small pile of books there, half-concealed by a fold of curtain.

Razoxane knelt – letting her pistol clunk down solidly on the floorboards – and picked one of them up: a hefty, black-bound volume, like a family Bible. She opened it to the title page – then glanced up at me.

'Know what this is?'

All out of sarcastic remarks, I shook my head.

'The *Chirurgia Noctis*; one of the key works of their Order. Compiled sometime before 1600, with maybe a half-dozen copies made since. Incredibly rare.' She sorted through the remaining three or four. 'Shit. They've got this one as well – *De Mysteriis Maleficarum*. A medieval book of ritual magic, suppressed by its own practitioners as being too dangerous to use . . .'

She gathered this and the *Chirurgia* under her arm, picking up her gun as she straightened up. 'We've got to hold on to these, Rachel.'

I was already heading for the door. 'Come on,' I almost pleaded. 'The police will be here soon.'

'Not soon enough.' She had a last look round before following me out. I made my way pointedly towards the stairs down to ground level; but she ignored the hint and started creeping up the flight to the second floor.

'*Razoxane*! For God's sake . . .' I hesitated, then followed.

She'd stopped again halfway up, and I didn't blame her: the higher we got, the darker and more claustrophobic the house became. I really hoped she didn't want to check the attic; if so, she'd be doing it on her own.

I'd almost reached her when she took a slow step backwards: feeling with her foot for the next stair down. Her gaze stayed fixed on the shadows above us.

'What?' I whispered nervously.

She didn't answer. There was silence. And in the silence, an icy thought came.

She's afraid, Razoxane's afraid.

The very idea brought panic to the boil; but I managed to keep the lid on as I backed stiffly down towards the landing. Razoxane followed; and I was staring over her shoulder all the time, but could see nothing up there.

I sensed the coldness, though. Heavier than the silence. Darker.

'. . . one of them . . . ?' I asked: my voice so small I scarcely heard it.

She moved her head left and right. 'Not a Clinician. Something else. Something they've attracted with their rites . . .'

I remembered then what she'd said about doors, and demons; recalled it with a fresh, keen thrill of dread. Something was waiting at the top of the house. Something hideous – like plague personified. And maybe even Angels of Death treated such with a wary respect.

'The place is infected now,' Razoxane murmured grimly. 'Ghost gangrene. Those downstairs were on borrowed time already . . .'

She drew back thoughtfully, and was about to turn away when we heard – so very faintly – a scraping of movement back down at ground level.

My heart crammed up into my throat. 'Oh God, they're here.' I didn't mean the police, either; we'd have heard the sirens.

Razoxane slid the pistol quickly under her coat, passed me the books – I was half-afraid to touch them – and took the shotgun back. 'Come on, then. Let's say hello.'

I watched her reloading with cartridges from her coat pocket: a calm, mechanical sequence as she listened. Silence from upstairs and down; but I felt as if we were caught between two fires now. Two freezing fires. The sounds came again – slow, and stealthy, and rising from the breakfast room.

Razoxane went down the stairs two at a time: so fast she stumbled, missed the banister, and tumbled the rest of the way headlong, to fetch up in a heap in the hall. She squirmed around at once – pointing the shotgun left-handed for one shot along the passageway. The blast broke glass, but the sounds continued through the echoes – a sudden rush, the back door creaking; boots on paving. The back gate crunching closed.

Razoxane swore and started clambering up as I came downstairs more slowly. Much more slowly. 'Losing your touch?' I sneered, before I could stop myself.

Her icicle gaze swung round to me, and for an instant I felt like someone on the edge of a precipice: one step from the plunge. For just an instant. Then she had control again, and the frosty mask of her face was thawing out. By the time I'd reached the bottom – step by wary step now, and so unnerved I was gripping the banister fiercely with my free hand — she'd put on her hat again, and her shades as well. And her chilling smile was just the same as ever.

'So one lives to die another day. So what?' She glanced back up the stairs one final time — I twisted nervously round, but nothing had followed us — then jerked her head. 'Let's get going.'

I followed her through into the breakfast room: already knowing what we'd find.

One of the bodies was missing. One of them had still been alive.

Trish, Steve and Paul all lay slumped and bloody where they'd fallen; but Colin, who'd gone down behind the table, was no longer there. I guessed the wood — and the flesh of his friends — had taken most of the blasts meant for him, leaving him wounded but far from finished . . .

'They'll know I'm involved with you, now,' I muttered. 'He'll tell them . . .'

'We'll have to make sure he won't talk then, won't we? But come on . . .' She was already in the kitchen and turning on the gas-taps on the cooker; I grimaced as the stink washed over me. 'See if you can find anything inflammable around: fuel for that, for instance.' She indicated the old paraffin heater in the corner. 'This house is going to burn like Hell.'

I found a half-empty can under the stairs, and started sloshing it around. 'Make sure you soak the bodies,' she'd called; but when I came to them, I found I didn't have the nerve.

She materialized at my elbow: her dry voice in my ear like a personal demon.

'These are the lost ones, Rachel. We don't need them found just yet.' She jogged my arm. 'Go ahead . . .'

I swallowed.

Somewhere in the distance, on the hissing edge between sound and silence, I heard the wail of sirens.

Gritting my teeth, I splashed paraffin over Trish's slack face: saw it overflow her open mouth, and spread the staining on her bloody blouse . . .

Then Paul. Then Steve.

Spaghetti bolognese I thought, and swayed.

A hand on my shoulder. 'Let's go.'

We got out the back way, fast. I laid a paraffin trail almost to the garden gate, and tossed the can aside as we stumbled out into the dingy back lane. Exhaustion and nausea almost overcame me then: I could only slump back against the gatepost and stare as Razoxane knelt and fumbled in her pocket.

The sirens were coming, racing closer. I could picture the cars, leapfrogging the rush-hour traffic: sun-bright headlamps and flaring blue strobes . . .

Razoxane struck a match over the final splash of paraffin. Its flame reflected from her shades: and photophobe or no, I glimpsed naked pyromania in her grin. Then bluish-yellow flame licked the spillage thirstily up, and raced away.

We both slipped into the gloom, and ran for it.

We didn't even pause to look back as the Clinicians' lair burst open, and began to burn.

Twenty-five

'How's the bloke in Minor Theatre?' I asked, as Karen came wandering back from that direction.

'I think Kath's nearly finished. Anything else going?' She looked at the central blackboard; most of the panels were now wiped clean.

'The RTA's still round in X-ray,' Mike said. 'Other than that, we're clear.'

Four-forty-five, a.m. From here on it should be a straight run through to dawn, if we were lucky. I glanced across at Mike. 'Time for another coffee, I think.'

'Be there in a minute,' Karen said.

I felt vaguely surprised at how easy it was getting: living this double life. Here I was, every inch the professional nurse, going about my job only hours after witnessing a multiple murder – and burning down the house where it had happened . . .

Maybe it was just my mind's way of coping: riding with each successive punch of shock and horror, because the alternative would be total breakdown. And I had to stay sane in order to survive.

I meant to survive, all right.

'You believe his story?' Mike asked as I followed him through into the duty room.

'Who – the one in theatre?'

'Yeah. If he's tellin' the truth · . . he ought to report it.'

I shrugged. 'Up to him.' I doubted if he would, though. Somehow.

He switched on the kettle, sat down, stretched. 'This

town's gettin' more like bloody Belfast every day. Hear about the fire in Fenner Street?'

I nodded. 'Karen said it was on the local radio. How many died?'

'Three: two men and a woman. And the police reckon foul play.'

'Arson, you mean?'

'Must be. It all adds up, doesn't it: a firebombin' down there. Part of this gang war that no one will admit is goin' on.'

I'd picked up a copy of *the Nursing Times* and was leafing through it; I grunted without looking up. The bodies would be up here in our mortuary, of course, awaiting post-mortem; once they discovered the gunshot wounds they'd know there'd been foul play, all right. And my mouth tightened as I thought of Trish, her pretty face burned beyond recognition, zipped up in a body bag labelled Unknown Female. An anonymous corpse . . .

'Rachel . . .'

He had to say it again before I glanced up. 'Hmmm?'

Mike grinned. 'You were miles away then . . .'

Oh God, Mike, I wish I was.

'You know the Charge Nurse job in Preston I told you about?' he went on evenly. 'Well . . . I've decided to apply.'

I'd thought he would: he'd been after an upgrading for some time. I had mixed feelings, really – wishing him well, and knowing that I'd miss him. We all would . . .

'Go for it,' I told him. 'We'd be sorry to lose you, but . . . I know you'll go far, Mike. You've got it in you. We need good nurses like you in management.'

He gestured noncommittally. 'I'm not aimin' that high, Rachel. I don't want to lose the patient-contact – or my clinical skills.'

'Oh, same here,' I admitted. 'But I sometimes think, we need nurse managers who feel that way . . . and who'll fight our corner properly.'

The kettle boiled, and there was a pause while he made

the coffee. Handed me the chipped mug with my name on it. I'd drunk from it a hundred times; but tonight its very homeliness sent a tight little pang through my stomach.

'Not too strong, is it?' he asked, smiling.

I shook my head; slopped in some more milk. And – in the absence of any clean spoons – just watched while Brownian Motion took its course.

As I approached the half-open door of Minor Theatre, I heard something metallic rattle into a kidney bowl, and Kathy saying: 'That's it, the last one.'

The patient mumbled something.

'You really should report this to the police, you know,' she added. 'You've been very lucky. The injuries could have been far more serious.'

'You reckon the cops'll give a shit?' the man came back morosely. 'Probably give the guy a medal. They've been trying hard enough themselves to move us on.'

'Which farmer did you say it was?' Fran's voice: she was doing the stitching.

'Dunno. One of the ones north of town.'

'And he shot at you deliberately?'

'I wasn't born with them pellets in me,' I heard him mutter.

'Suit yourself, then,' Kathy said, with a brittle briskness that told me how long a night she'd had already. I heard her stripping off her surgical gloves, followed by the creak of the pedal-bin. 'Right; we just need to dress those wounds, and give you a tetanus booster.' A moment later she emerged, and rolled her eyes at me, with an expression that said *bloody Travellers*.

'The RTA's back from X-ray,' I told her. 'Cubicle one.'

I watched her walk off down the corridor, then glanced in through the door. I could see the drab army blouse with the German flag on its sleeve, draped over a chair.

Fran moved round into my field of vision, the better to

reach the last of the wounds; still gloved-up, and with a white disposable apron on over her dress. She glimpsed me standing there and looked around. 'Hiya.'

'I'll finish up in here if you want,' I told her. 'Mike's just made coffee.'

She grinned. 'Thanks; I'll just finish suturing this one . . .'

I lingered there, just outside the door; hoping it didn't look too obvious. My heart was pounding: slogging away in my chest.

After a minute or so – it seemed like ten – I heard the snip of her scissors for the last time; then the elastic, twanging sound as she tugged off her gloves. 'There you go,' she told the man, as she binned them and went on to scrub her hands. 'Sister will do your dressings, and give you your injection. How's the pain now?'

'Not so bad,' he admitted, grudgingly.

'All right. Soon be finished now. 'Night, then,' she added cheerfully as she came on out, renewing her smile of thanks to me as she passed.

I glanced after her, watching until she was round the corner and out of sight. Even then I stayed where I was: waiting until Razoxane had emerged from one of the empty side-rooms and moved up beside me.

'Look,' I murmured. 'Just the questions, okay? Promise me you won't kill him.'

'He's seen your face, Rachel,' she said, reasonably enough.

'I don't care,' I almost hissed. 'You've done enough already.'

She appeared to consider it; then nodded, and stepped in through the door. I heard the click of her switchblade as she slid it closed behind her.

And I turned away, and leaned back against the wall: closed my eyes in sheer, sick weariness – and wished I could close my ears to the sudden muffled noises that came from the room behind me. The gasp of horrified disbelief . . . and the stifled sounds of pain.

It was hitting me now, at last. I felt like what I was: a nurse who'd betrayed her patient. The very role the Clinicians had wanted me to play. And in seeking to elude them, I'd ended up playing it after all.

After a few edgy minutes, the door slid open again a fraction. 'All clear?' her calm voice asked.

I glanced down the empty corridor. 'Yeah.'

Razoxane emerged, folding away the blade of her knife. 'He's all yours,' she told me drily.

'You haven't killed him, have you?' I asked dully, half-expecting the answer to be yes. But she shook her head.

'He was co-operative; he gave me useful information on his former masters. I think we can let him live.'

Big of you, I thought.

Aloud, I said: 'What'd he say?'

'Enough – but it can wait till later. I need to get back to Fenner Street, Rachel. There's a chance they might try scavenging something from the rubble.'

I heard a faint moan from the room behind us, and glanced back uncomfortably.

'Don't worry,' Razoxane said. 'I can find my own way out.'

I didn't doubt it; but my stomach still did a backflip as she just turned and walked calmly off down the corridor towards the trolley bay at the far end and beyond it the ambulance doors. Kathy was busy round in cubicle one, of course, and the others were still finishing coffee in the duty room. Our police protection had been discontinued, and night security was as non-existent as before. No one would see her leave. But my heart was still thudding in my throat for the few moments it took her unhurriedly to cover the distance and disappear out into the night.

Someone could have crossed her path, I knew; someone

could have chosen just the wrong moment to emerge. Someone could have died just then.

I swallowed down the bitterness in my mouth, and got a grip on myself, before sliding the door to Minor Theatre fully open.

The pallid young man who'd turned up at our department an hour before, peppered with shot and claiming a farmer had tried to blast him off his land, was now lying limply on his back, arms dangling over the sides of the ops table. His bare chest, left shoulder and cheek were bright with blood: an oozing mass of knife-cuts. Razoxane had clearly dug the point of her blade into each of Kathy's excavations, doubtless bearing down on his face with her free hand; choking his cries until he was ready to talk. Having reopened all his wounds, she'd gone on to make some of her own — tracing that razor-edge across his face and throat and stomach. And with each cold, methodical incision would have come the questions.

It hadn't taken her long to get some answers. Which wasn't surprising, really.

His eyes flickered open as I came through; he gasped hoarsely, and tried to raise himself. I glimpsed the panic in his staring eyes. Then he recognized my uniform, and let himself slump back with a sound that was more sob than sigh.

'Sister . . . Christ, help me. Someone . . .'

That was as far as he got before he remembered my face. And froze.

I already had the tetanus syringe in my hands, and his gaze locked on to it, on the glinting needle-point, as I lifted it to check the dose. I knew what he was thinking, of course; the look of desperate, dazed betrayal was clear on his face. He'd come to our hospital believing he'd be safe — only to find me working there. In league with the woman who'd murdered his friends and tortured him; and now about to administer the *coup de grâce*.

Blue angel. Death angel.

I couldn't help myself. I gave him a ghoulish little smile. 'Hello, Colin.'

He looked about ready to shit himself.

'Don't worry.' I said it softly – but felt the heady surge of confidence within me: the awareness of this sudden, awful power I had. 'I'm not going to hurt you. Just clean you up, and give you a tetanus shot – and a word of advice.

'That woman, you see: she's a psychopath. Completely mad. She's already killed half a dozen people – and two Clinicians besides. Even *they* are afraid of her. She let you live tonight – but she could change her mind any time. So get away: right away from this place, this town . . . this bloody *country*, if you can. And never speak of it to anyone or . . .' And I permitted myself that little-ghoul-lost smile again before adding: 'She'll come after you. Find you. And autopsy you alive.

'Clear?'

Speechless, saucer-eyed, he nodded; and I smiled again, more gently this time. A nurse's smile once more.

'All right,' I told him brightly. 'Let's get you cleaned up then, shall we?'

Twenty-six

The phone was ringing as I got in.

I closed the front door firmly on the wet grey morning, and fitted the chain before walking over to answer it, my coat dripping quietly on the carpet. I'd unhooked the receiver and was bringing it to my ear before I realized that this might well be Razoxane; the thought dried my mouth clean out.

'Hello?' someone asked. A woman; not her.

I swallowed, and said hello back.

'Is Sarah Hollis there, please? It's the hospital.'

Sarah kept a note of her Off-duty pinned to the corkboard in the kitchen: she tended to forget it otherwise. I knew she was on an Early this morning. 'Have you tried her ward?'

'This is her ward ... Staff Nurse Taylor. She hasn't shown up yet. I wondered if she was sick?'

I glanced at my watch. Twenty to nine. She should have begun her shift at quarter-past seven.

The flat was quiet.

'I don't know, I've only just got in,' I told her. 'If you'd like to hang on, I'll check her room.'

I put down the receiver, and for a moment stood quite still: listening. Then I went down the passage to her door and gently knocked.

'Sarah? It's me. You in?'

There was no reply. After a pause I opened the door and put my head round.

Her room, seen in the dimness retained by half-drawn curtains, was empty, and in the usual disarray; clothes strewn casually across the floor, along with members of her soft-toy collection. One of her posters had tugged clear of its blu-tack and was curling downwards at one corner. The bed was slept-in, and unmade.

I shrugged to myself, and returned to the phone. 'Hello? No, no sign of her. Sorry.' I remembered she'd been going out with her boyfriend again last night; but they'd clearly been back. So where had they gone from here?

Staff Nurse Taylor realized she was up against a dead end; she thanked me, rather grudgingly, and hung up. So did I, frowning: feeling the first, gnawing pang of concern as I turned away, towards the open doorway of the lounge.

And saw that someone had been watching me all the while.

For an instant, as the adrenaline thumped through me, I thought it was Razoxane; I'd half-expected her, after all. But as my eyes grew accustomed to the murky light in there, I saw that the figure sitting slouched in the chair facing me was a man. I recognized Terry, Sarah's boy-friend.

And realized he was dead.

It was obvious really, of course; clear from the way he sat or rather slumped, like some unstuffed dummy, quite devoid of life. His face was partly in shadow, but now I saw how slack it was – and glimpsed the whites of blind, half-open eyes.

I took a small, reluctant step across the threshold, into the curtained gloom. It never crossed my mind to try and get away: there wouldn't be any point. I had already real-ized, with an awful, sinking feeling, what had happened.

Razoxane had been here, meaning to meet me – and had found herself facing this unexpected guest. She'd reacted as all her madness had primed her to react.

And sure enough, she'd taken out his brain.

For all my nausea, I still found myself drawn closer to look, to see, to take in every grisly detail. She'd done a very neat job, in fact: running her blade round the top of his head in a scalping incision, and peeling back flesh and hair to bare the skull. She'd hacked out a circular section of bone, and removed the brain; then fitted the literal skull-cap into place again, and drawn the hood of scalp back over it. I could tell all this by the way the top of his head, like an ill-fitting hairpiece, no longer lay quite snug over the roughly reconstituted bone. That, and the cut, and the blood that had dribbled down to stain his collar here and there . . .

'Oh shit . . .' I muttered, backing away; I was afraid to say more in case the puke came with it. And then I thought of Sarah, and almost threw up anyway, in sheer, sick dread. What the hell had Razoxane done with her . . . ?

We all jump to conclusions, of course. I realized I was no exception when I suddenly smelled him, there behind me – and heard his mocking voice.

'Rachel,' Melphalan said drily. 'We meet again.'

I whirled, but far too late.

He'd emerged from the kitchen, as silently as a ghost, and was already between me and the front door: though even if I'd been able to reach it, I would never get past deadlock and chain in time. I'd come in here and sealed my own cell behind me. Or my own grave.

Planting his boots, the Lord of the Black Physicians parted his greatcoat with rubber-gloved hands, and hooked the thumbs casually into his waistband. The gesture revealed a grim assortment of clinical tools – scalpels and scissors and probes tucked into custom-made pockets; but what really yanked my attention downwards was the ugly meat-hook suspended from his wide leather belt. It summed up all the savagery behind their façade of medical finesse.

Slowly, reluctantly, I raised my eyes once more. Melphalan's face was mostly shadow in the dull light; but I could see that he was smiling.

Behind me, at the end of the passageway, I heard the bathroom door creak open. Hopelessly, I turned again. Glaukostyx stood framed there in the doorway, watching me with head on one side: his face like a mudpack on a month-old corpse. And then, even closer, Vokaine leaned slouching into view through the doorway of my own bedroom, to regard me with his goggles and death's-head leer.

I just stood there, and felt like a little kid cornered in the park by Strange Men.

'You are late, Rachel,' Melphalan continued at my back. 'We have been waiting.'

'We . . . had an emergency come in right at the end of the shift,' I mumbled, as if the explanation would do me any good.

'No matter: as you have seen, we were able to amuse ourselves until you arrived . . .'

In trying to avoid their eyes, I glanced into the kitchen – and saw the lump of pinkish-grey tissue on the table there. It took only a second to overcome my own desperate disbelief and recognize it as a human brain. It sat on the breadboard; someone had used our breadknife to cut part of it into neat, sticky slices . . .

I pressed my palm to my mouth.

'And as for your charming young friend,' Melphalan's voice continued, softly, insidiously, 'she has been entertaining us the while. 'He prodded me in the shoulder: the physical contact made me jump. 'Come. Come and see.'

I stumbled forward, towards the bathroom. As I passed Vokaine, he hissed, 'Weep for this!' once more, in my ear – but this time with ghastly amusement. And Glaukostyx stepped aside to let me through.

Sarah was in the bath; judging by the dressing-gown lying heaped beside the tub, she'd decided on a refreshing soak just after getting up. The water had drained away now, but her bare skin was still damp, still sticky with drying foam. I could tell at a glance that she was dead.

Her body was an acupuncturist's pincushion.

I looked, and my legs gave way, and I slumped down beside the tub, grasping hold of the side for support.

Sarah.

There were scores of needles in her: more than I could count. They pierced the flesh of her arms and thighs; her breasts and throat. Her stomach. Her open palms. Even her feet. And I knew she'd have felt every single penetrating jab – lying there doomed and helpless as the Clinicians wove their spiky web of agony around her.

'You are familiar with the technique of acupuncture?' Melphalan said, from somewhere overhead. 'We have a refined version of the art: one calculated to cause excruciating pain. The body's most sensitive, most exquisitely tender nerve-endings are mapped out – and the needles driven into every one . . .'

I was only half-listening. Almost dazedly, I reached out for Sarah, brushing my fingertips over her damp cheek . . . touching the wet-darkened blonde of her slicked-back hair. Her eyes were closed, her expression almost sulky; but there was a slackness there that meant her pain, at last, had ended . . .

'An added amusement,' Melphalan went on, 'was this: one of the needles was tipped with a powerful biotoxin, quick-acting but . . .' he paused, as if to savour the words '. . . extremely painful. She knew this – but not which one. Knew only that each jab could be the one that brought her death.

'Neither did we know; that would have made it so much less interesting. Out of two hundred needles, it turned out to be the ninety-seventh . . .'

She'd have been desperate to die by then. The final agony would have been a pleasure. I felt the tears flood my eyes as I looked at her. Sarah. Always so cheerful, a little ray of sunshine. And killed horribly just because she'd shared a flat with me, and been my friend.

Abruptly Melphalan's rubber fingers were in my hair and clenching to a fist: my mouth opened in a breathless, silent scream as he dragged me upright and wrenched me around — then flung me back down the passageway. I landed in a heap on the carpet, close to the toes of Vokaine's muddy boots. Glancing upwards, I saw the scalpel already drawn and gleaming in the Clinician's hand.

'You have been disobedient, Rachel,' Melphalan said grimly, following. 'You thought to defy us. Such behaviour will not be tolerated. You are a strong-willed woman, but we have remedies for that. Perhaps a hysterectomy will bring you to your senses . . .'

Vokaine, still grinning down at me, brought the scalpel to his mouth, and kissed the blade.

I wanted to scream — but could barely whisper, 'Please . . .'

There was a pause then; and looking fearfully over and up at Melphalan, I saw him remove his hat, and run a hand back through his lank black hair. Suddenly — through all my fright — it dawned on me that he looked weary. The realization came with a jolt: a sudden impact on the image I still had of the Clinicians as inhuman, invincible ghouls. Melphalan was tired.

'You are fortunate,' he continued after a moment, more quietly. 'You chose to return to us — a wise decision. Very wise.' He turned his gaze on me again, and I shuddered beneath his scrutiny. 'Last night . . . What did you see?'

I gulped air, my mind whirling. They still didn't know, then; still hadn't guessed. 'When I got to the house, it was all on fire,' I said off the top of my head. 'There were police everywhere . . . I ran away.'

He nodded, his stare unwavering.

Not quite sure whether I'd convinced him or not, I asked: 'What happened?'

Another pause, during which he seemed to consider what

– if anything – to tell me; then he said: 'An enemy has done this.'

I lay there on my side, propped on one elbow and staring up at him; struggling to keep my expression blank. 'Enemy?'

He nodded, the thin, bitter smile back on his face. 'Yes, Rachel. We have enemies. Even we. Someone has been hunting us for a long time now. It is time we put an end to them.'

I wondered if they could; and dreaded that the answer might be yes.

'But in the meantime,' Melphalan continued flatly, 'we have immediate need of new premises from which to operate. Your closed hospital wards will prove ideal. You will provide cover for us, and help arrange the move – and act to keep us supplied with subjects as soon as we are established.'

I just gawped at him.

'I will not bargain with you, Rachel,' the Clinician said. 'I made that error before. Now I demand. And if you try to defy us again . . . your friends will suffer for it, as they have today. Staff Nurse Shannon . . . Staff Nurse Kane . . . Dr Jones, and Dr Drew . . . We know them all. We know where they live. For every act of disobedience, one of them will die – *shrieking*. Do you understand?'

I nodded. I understood.

'Now get up.'

I struggled to comply; Vokaine grasping the sleeve of my coat to haul rather than assist me upright. I made it finally, and stood there swaying while their malodorous bodies closed in around me.

Melphalan leaned forward, frighteningly without expression: that close to, I could see the open pores like worm-holes in the grey flesh of his face.

'Take your cross off,' he told me.

My hand twitched, began instinctively to comply – and just as instinctively hesitated.

'Take it off,' he repeated. 'Throw it away. You know there is no god. There was no one to save your innocent friend. There is no one to save you.'

I had no words to answer him. Up until this dismal morning, I'd still believed in some vague yet infallible divine protection: believed in it strongly enough to unsettle even them. But now I realized sickly it had all been a façade – and they'd seen through it to the emptiness beyond. My mind filled with memories of Jenny, and Trish, and now Sarah: all of them savagely, senselessly killed. But the world just went on turning, and I was all alone.

Maybe Razoxane could save me. But right now Razoxane might as well have been a million miles away.

Slowly I reached behind my neck, delving inside my collar to find the clasp of the neck-chain and unclip it. I lifted out my crucifix, and placed it in Melphalan's waiting palm.

He didn't even flinch; but it was only a piece of metal, after all. I was surprised it had kept them at bay for so long.

Real faith makes them doubt, as Razoxane said. And for a while, over the past couple of weeks, I'd felt that mine had almost been renewed. But its victories had been illusory. In reality, my faith was waning: had been sickening for a long time; and now I felt it die.

Melphalan's fist closed tight around the cross. The leer on his face was one of wolfish satisfaction. In a way, I didn't blame him.

'Now what?' I muttered.

'Be patient, Rachel,' he almost purred. 'We will contact you again, when your services are needed. In the meantime, leave us here. Go walking under the rain. We will ensure the bodies are disposed of before you get back.'

I swallowed. 'How . . . ?'

'There are ways,' he answered darkly.

I tried not to think of Sarah's body hacked to bits and stuffed into a suitcase. Tried, and failed. The tears began again. And Melphalan reached out with his slick, rubber fingers to stroke my dripping cheek.

'Rachel,' he said, in soft admonishment. 'What do you cry for? The comedy is only just beginning . . .'

PART THREE

Night Sisters

Twenty-seven

'So Will was just raring to go,' the woman said; 'but when he took his out, it dropped off . . .'

A fragment of overheard conversation as I hurried back through the waiting area; my mind snagged on it for just a moment, then wiped it clean away as I re-entered the corridor down to Resus. Mark was in the doorway, holding it open as he talked with Mike. Over his shoulder I could see the activity within; the luminous jackets of the ambulance crew; a glimpse of Fran's pale face . . .

Thursday night was proving busy.

Mark held the door wider for me as I squeezed back through. Everyone was crowding round the woman on the trolley as the ambulancemen finished transferring her across. 'Legs, watch her legs!' someone had shouted, and I could see why. Her jeans were soaked with blood, and snagging here and there on the splinters of bone pushed out from her shattered legs.

Mike would have gone to help get Theatre ready. It would take the rest of the night, and more, to piece those limbs together again.

'Motorcyclist?' One of the ambulancemen nodded, and I turned to Fran. 'Okay, let's get her clothes off.'

She and Simon – this month's student on night-rotation – set calmly to work, slicing and scissoring off the outer layers, while I selected an airway and inserted it into her slack mouth; the old routine, unfolding once again. People talked or worked in silence; came and went around me. We took pulse and b/p, bloods for cross-matching, and got a drip up while Mark explored the bruising of her abdomen and chest.

It suddenly occurred to me that I hadn't thought about the Clinicians for over an hour now . . .

The ghastly memory of their visitation and their promise was already two days old; I'd seen nothing of them since. When I'd finally returned to the flat, soaked through after hours of aimless wandering in the drizzling rain, the place had been empty: lifeless. No sign of Sarah or Terry. They'd even mopped up the blood.

Most of it . . .

'Ortho reg?' I asked, checking the drip.

'On his way down,' Mark said, still probing. 'I think we may be luckier with this one.'

Luckier than with the bloke on the other trolley, anyway: parked askew on the other side of the room. The night's first RTA. The week's first death. We'd draped a once-white sheet across the mess.

The orthopaedics registrar appeared right on cue, pushing his way in through the doors: his white coat hanging open to reveal clothes that looked as though they'd been slept in. 'Evening all.'

Mark glanced up in some surprise, then moved aside as the other medic joined him at the trolley. 'That was quick.'

'My parachute failed to open.'

'Rachel!' June called from the doorway.

I rubbed an arm across my forehead. 'What?'

She gestured towards the sheeted form. 'The relatives have arrived.'

'Shit. Right. Put them in the Quiet Room, will you?' I followed her gaze towards the corpse. 'Do they know?'

She nodded. 'Police brought them up.'

'All right. I'll be out to talk to them in a minute.' I glanced back. 'How're we doing?'

'Okay at the moment,' Mark said over his shoulder.

I peeled off my gloves and binned them, and started untying my plastic pinny.

'Hey, it's still only half-past eleven, you know,' Simon informed us all cheerfully.

I glanced at the clock myself, and grimaced. I'd thought it was later – and hoped it was later still.

I was already feeling rotten as it was.

The dead man's relatives – his wife and son – listened in stunned disbelief as I explained how we'd tried, and failed, to save the patient's life. Not that it's ever easy to assimilate news like that. Lives can be shattered in an instant; minds take a little longer to catch up.

I went through the Coroner's procedure, asked if they wanted another cup of tea (they'd barely touched the first one), and closed the door carefully on their paper-thin control.

Walking back to Resus, I felt suddenly light-headed, and had to pause until I was sure I had my balance back. The dull, nauseous ache that had been resting like a weight in my stomach for most of the evening was definitely getting worse.

Brilliant. All I bloody needed.

I heard the phone start ringing in my office, and made a detour to answer it. It was a middle-aged-sounding woman calling to say she'd developed a rash of some sort, and should she come in? I advised her to wait until tomorrow and go and see her own GP. Better to check, though, wasn't it? Yes, I agreed, it was.

Hanging up, I found myself staring at the Garfield poster on the back of my door: our hero festooned with party detritus. *Are we having fun yet?*

No.

By the time I got back to Resus, the woman – we still hadn't learned her name – had been moved along to

Theatre, and the late James Buckingham had the place to himself. Simon had just finished bagging the clothes we'd scissored off him. He glanced up, readjusting his spectacles. 'What shall I do with these? Give them to the relis?'

I peered into the bag; the smell of blood and worse wafted up to clog my nostrils and throat, and turn my stomach sourer still.

'God, no.' I closed the bag for him. 'Don't give his wife those, she'll go bloody AWOL. Send them downstairs with him when he goes. If they want them later, they've got seven days to claim. Any valuables?' He shook his head. 'Right. You'd better get him cleaned up, they'll want to see him.'

'Raitch. Are you okay?' Fran asked.

'Not really. Why?'

She was looking quite concerned. 'You're really pale . . .' And she knew me well enough to know it wasn't the blood and bereavement, either.

I shrugged. 'I've got a stomach ache, I feel a bit sick – I'll survive.'

'I've heard there's something going round,' Simon murmured.

Someone always says that.

I left them to it, meaning to see how the backlog of non-urgent patients was building up. I'd got about ten feet before I realized I needed the toilet, now. I barged in through the door, stumbled over to a cubicle and was very sick. And each heave sent a stab of pain through my tautened stomach muscles.

Finished, I straightened up, and gingerly touched my palm to my lower belly. The slightest pressure brought a twinge. I tightened my lips and kept on pressing, as if that would somehow wear away the pain. But the pain persisted, lurking there just above my belt. Central, tending to lower right quadrant. I knew what it was. I just didn't believe it.

I wondered if I should mention it to Mark, or just keep quiet and see what happened.

I rinsed my mouth out before re-emerging into the fray, and was walking slowly in the direction of the waiting area when the matter was abruptly taken out of my hands.

Sudden, searing pain ripped me open inside. Transfixed, unable even to groan, I fell to my knees, grimacing in silent agony, and then collapsed completely. My impact with the floor seemed to jar all my insides loose. A fresh surge of pain engulfed me. I gasped, and wept, and writhed.

Dimly I heard a shout, and running feet, and then someone was kneeling beside me and calling my name: I thought I recognized Fran's voice through the queasy, burning haze. In another moment there were people all around me, and I felt their hands on me, lifting me clear of the floor. I was suddenly weightless, drifting: the ceiling lights swayed past overhead. Then there was a soft sheet under me, and green curtains being drawn closed around. I lay as still as I could, and the burning claws in my stomach began slowly to relax their grip. But they didn't let go. And I felt about ready to puke blood.

Mark leaned into view above me, smiling. I managed to grin back – but couldn't hold it, as his hands moved down over my stomach, bare now that someone had unfastened the front of my dress. His fingers quickly found the pain. I winced, and gasped aloud.

'Sorry.' He probed a couple more times, as gently as he could; then met my eyes again. 'Diagnosis, Sister Young?'

I swallowed. 'Acute appendicitis. Probably – *ah!* – ruptured.'

'Congratulations. Consider yourself admitted.' He checked my tongue and fingertips too, but only to confirm it; then moved aside as Fran appeared with a caz-card, to go through the formal process of admission. Once again.

Being treated in my own department was getting to be a habit.

She checked my full name, date of birth, address, GP . . . I answered dully, automatically, my eyes on the ceiling; thinking how ironic it all was. No sooner had I submitted to the Clinicians than I'd been put suddenly and completely out of action. For the next week, and longer, I'd be useless to them.

And, if they lost patience, completely at their mercy.

The realization filled my mind like a slow black sunrise. It was all I could do to choke back a sob, and pinch my lips tight shut to stop them trembling.

'Hang in there,' I heard Mark saying. 'We'll have you upstairs in no time . . .'

The pain was beginning to rise in me again. I closed my eyes, and waited hopelessly for it to go away.

Twenty-eight

I must have passed out at some stage, because my next conscious recollection was of corridor lights sliding past overhead, and the squeaking wheels of the trolley filling my ears, very loud in the small-hours silence. I lay motionless, my breathing shallow; keeping the pain dormant. I realized I was still wearing my uniform, apart from shoes and cap; my bare head rested comfortably on a pillow. A strand of hair was in my eyes, but I didn't dare raise my hand to brush it clear.

The wheels creaked onwards. Plodding, scuffing footfalls sounded on the linoleum. No one spoke. We turned a corner, into a dimmer corridor, where only every other light was on. And I felt the trolley begin to veer.

For a moment I assumed my escort would correct it; and a moment was all it took for the side of the trolley to collide with the wall, rebounding with a jolt that spilled white fire through my insides. I sucked in air with a gasp, which hurt some more, and gritted my teeth.

We kept moving as though nothing had happened. No one apologized, or asked if I was all right. I rolled my head to one side . . . then the other. No one was walking beside me, to whisper encouragement or hold my hand. I could only hear one person's footsteps, and those were up ahead.

We passed a couple of linen skips, haphazardly parked – and just failed to clear them. The corner of the trolley caught the nearer one, jarring me again: I almost cried out. The trolley slewed to the left, then straightened out once more as it was towed on down the corridor.

Groaning, I struggled up on to my elbows. Despite the agony in my stomach, I had to see . . .

His back. I saw his back. The dusty coat. The muffler. The battered hat. A rope had been lashed to the trolley frame and he was tugging on this to drag it along behind him.

My elbows gave way and I fell back, gasping frantically at the ceiling. I wanted to scream, or scramble clear; I had no strength left for either. All I could do was lie there, as if on my own bier, as the Clinician laboured onwards, careless of his steering and quite heedless of me; hauling me deeper into the darkness at the hospital's heart. I could see the onset of decay in the walls and ceiling now: the crumbled plaster and peeling paint. We were entering the old obstetric unit: the wards long since closed through lack of funding. I felt the change in the atmosphere itself: it grew danker and colder by the minute.

This is just another dream, I decided desperately, as he pushed through a pair of doors that should have been locked and drew the trolley bumpily through after him. Just a nightmare unleashed under anaesthetic. My mind was freewheeling, its every buried fear unbound; but in reality I must be on the table by now, in clean and sterile surroundings — and in the care of dedicated NHS doctors and nurses, some of whom I probably even knew . . .

I tried to cling to that thought as we went on down a corridor that was all but in darkness. I really tried. But of course it was useless.

Because deep down I knew perfectly well I wasn't dreaming.

We negotiated a veritable logjam of derelict beds, barely visible in the dimness; stripped of their mattresses to supply other parts of the hospital. Some of the empty rooms we passed were blue with moonlight, filtering in through dust-grimed windows. Another set of doors loomed up ahead: we rattled through them, and I found myself being wheeled into a windowless room, and a darkness that engulfed me.

The trolley juddered to a halt; in the silence that followed, quite breathless with terror, I heard the thud as the rope lead was casually dropped. The Clinician's footsteps moved around to my left, echoing hollowly through emptiness. And then the lights came on — bleak and bluish, like a midwinter sun. A bank of theatre lamps, suspended right above me: a glaring compound eye. Squinting, I turned my face away.

And found Melphalan standing there beside me.

Straight away I noticed the surgical mask he wore loose and ready at his throat.

'Welcome, Rachel,' the Lord of Physicians said gravely. 'I said we would call for you again; and so we have.'

I stared up at him, my breathing coming raggedly now, and cold sweat on my forehead. I couldn't think of a single thing to say. And then the pain flared up again, a pitiless reminder that if someone didn't help me soon, peritonitis would set in, and I would begin to die. Horribly.

'Why . . . are you doing this?' I managed. 'I said I'd help you. I promised . . .'

'Indeed you did,' he nodded. 'But you have proved untrustworthy before, Rachel Young. So we have to make sure.'

I glimpsed Glaukostyx walk round behind him. He too had a mask slung round his neck — and a green rubber apron on over his filthy clothes. There was a clink of metal to my left, and I rolled my head that way: saw Vokaine, who'd pulled the trolley, now sorting through a sharp and ugly range of instruments.

I began to realize what was going to happen.

With sudden, desperate strength, I tried to struggle up.

Melphalan shoved me back down again, with contemptuous ease; more pain tore through my abdomen, and I gave a stifled, wailing cry. He leaned forward, his palm resting heavily on my chest: holding me down until my breathing eased. The light was behind him now, his face in shadow. But I could see the glitter of his eyes.

'You must not excite yourself,' he told me drily. 'You have a ruptured appendix. It is only to be expected: we added one of our more specialized drugs to sundry items in your refrigerator. This particular substance causes rapid and catastrophic inflammation of the lower digestive tract. It was only a matter of time before you were admitted for some manner of surgery. We have been waiting.'

'No,' I said. I suddenly had no breath left to scream it.

'Oh, yes,' was all his answer. And before I could react to Vokaine closing in on my left, I felt a needle digging deep into my trailing forearm, spiking a vein.

The punch of pain was followed by a giddy, tingling numbness – and I found I couldn't move at all.

'Muscle relaxant,' Melphalan explained conversationally, unfastening my uniform to bare my stomach once again. He brushed his hand over the tender curve of my belly – I could still feel pain, and almost gagged even at that gentle contact – then glanced across at Vokaine. 'Let us begin.'

I managed to force my eyes sideways: glimpsed a trayful of knives at the blurred edge of my vision. They had a sour, chemical cleanliness about them that whispered *surgical*; but with their long blades and worn black handles, they wouldn't have looked out of place in a kitchen. Or a butcher's shop . . .

When I looked back at Melphalan, his mouth was smiling. Just his mouth.

'Liston knives,' he told me drily. 'A military surgeon's set. I had them in the Crimea, following in your army's wake. Such a rich harvest of flesh that was. We rode behind farmcarts full of wounded . . .' His smile split open across the teeth. 'You would call us ambulance chasers, perhaps . . .' The split quickly healed to a scar. 'There is

268

much to be learned from human suffering. And its infliction.'

He extended his gloved hand. Vokaine placed the first knife in it.

'Wait . . .' I slurred. 'Still . . . awake.'

'So you are,' Melphalan said, without looking up.

'Please . . .'

With his free hand he pulled the mask up over his lower face. Hardly to protect me from infection; more likely he didn't want the contents of my bowels contaminating him. His colleagues followed suit, like phantom outlaws, and closed right in around me.

I began silently to cry – and suddenly Vokaine was pressing a thick pad of cloth against my mouth and nose. For a moment I even thought it might be chloroform, the final mercy of an anaesthetic, and gratefully inhaled. But all I smelt was starch. Just something to stifle my shrieks.

'Observe, gentlemen,' came Melphalan's muffled voice. 'I shall make my first incision . . . *here*.'

And he proceeded, without further preamble, to cut me open.

The pain was instant and blinding white, but my scream couldn't get out past the gag: it backed up inside me until I thought my chest would burst. And even through the heat, I felt the cold invade my belly as Melphalan kept cutting: parting flesh and fat to bare my entrails. And then his living fingers were inside me, and groping deeper.

Vokaine's pitiless hand renewed its pressure.

It's just a nightmare, my mind insisted in the distance. *Nightmare. Night. Mare.*

An awful, throttled, keening sound was in my ears – and after a moment, I realized it was me. My cloth-stuffed voice. The filtered remnants of my anguish.

Melphalan straightened, and spread his hand: the fingers

red and dripping. I mewled something mindless at the sight; half expecting to taste my own blood soaking the gag as I haemorrhaged and died . . .

'Open wounds . . .' he almost mused '. . . are so dangerous, Rachel. They so easily become *infected* . . .'

And even through my agony and tears, I sensed a change in the room around us. A thickening chill: as cold as a north wind from out of the night.

I could see the scowl around Melphalan's eyes: a fierce concentration. He murmured something thickly: it wasn't English.

Then he shoved his hand back into my open belly – right up to the elbow.

That was when I *really* screamed.

And woke.

Bed. I was in a hospital bed. One of a four-bedded bay in a well-lit ward. And it was daylight.

I found I was sitting bolt-upright, hands pressed to my mouth: blocking the screams that had been queueing up behind the first one. Damp hair clung to my forehead. The white surgical gown I wore felt as though it had been pasted to my skin.

The three other women in the bay were looking on in consternation. One of them must have rung for a nurse, because an auxiliary walked in a moment later and came quickly to my bedside. 'All right,' I heard her soft voice saying, 'it's all right. All over now . . .'

I gestured urgently towards my bedside table. She understood, and passed me the vomit bowl. I grasped it, retched and threw up one final time, the puke bubbling thickly into the grey papier-mâché. I spat out the last, trailing spittle, and lay back exhaustedly as she took it away.

My fellow patients were all rather older than me, and seemed most concerned. Maybe seeing sickness in one so young brought out the mothers in them. I forced a wan smile, and felt a little sheepish.

With the nausea now quickly subsiding, I felt a bit better; I tried to shift in bed, but my muscles felt stiff, and my stomach very sore.

Tentatively I raised the sheet and peered under. My gown had rucked up to reveal skin painted bright pink with disinfectant. Folding the sheet back a little way, I saw down to where a slightly puckered line, dark with dried blood and pinched closed with clamps, marred the smoothness of my lower stomach. A classic appendicectomy scar.

That much I hadn't dreamed.

I sighed, and lay carefully back once more: settling down amid fresh, starched linen. Luxuriating in the feel and smell of the real world again – the clean, warm sterility of the everyday ward, a million miles away from the dark and foulness of my nightmare. At long, long last I began to feel safe. At least for the moment.

A Staff Nurse came in then, a red-haired girl I vaguely recognized. She gave me a bright and genuine smile.

'Hi: welcome to Parker Ward. I'm Alison.' She picked up my bed-end clipboard and glanced through the charts. 'Well, now . . . Rachel Mary Maureen Young. You work down in A&E, don't you?'

I nodded.

'Thought I'd seen you before. We'll see if we can't get you a side-room of your own. Staff have to have some perks . . .' She came round to the bedside and poured a glass of water from the jug on the locker. I took it gratefully and drank, swilling the water round my mouth before swallowing: washing the last of the bitterness away.

She had a thermometer out and ready. Finished, I opened wide and took it under my tongue. She found my pulse, and lifted her fob-watch with her free hand to measure it.

'Mr Allan did your op last night,' she went on cheerfully. 'I don't suppose you've met him? Locum surgical reg.'

The brittle glass of the thermometer precluded comment, so I shook my head.

'There were no complications, anyway. Routine appendicectomy, according to the notes. You'll be out in a few days. There we are.' She drew the thermometer out, checked the reading and nodded with satisfaction.

'Who'm I under?' I asked, interested. The consultant surgeons had varying reputations.

'Stevens. His ward round's at half-nine, he'll see you then.'

I could have done worse, I supposed. Like Mr McNeill, whose bedside manner was reputed to be along the lines of 'Hello, Mrs Jones, you've got cancer, goodbye.' Fran, who'd come down to us from Surgical, reckoned they'd needed extra nurses just to pick up the pieces of shattered lives . . .

The auxiliary appeared again behind her. 'You've got a visitor, if you feel up to it.'

'What, already?' I sat up a little – and grinned at Mark as he came into the bay. From the look of him he'd been up most of the night: dark stubble showed up against the paleness of his face, and he was clearly tired. But not too tired to smile back – and I saw the relief in his eyes.

'Rachel, how are you?'

'Okay. Better now. Much better.'

He nodded. 'I got someone to bleep me as soon as you were out; just so we all knew you were okay. Christ, we had a shock . . .'

'I was quite surprised myself,' I pointed out. 'Still . . . I suppose it couldn't have happened in a better place, could it? And I'm glad you were on. I mean that, Mark.'

He shrugged; then became aware of Alison and friend, hovering meaningfully in the background. 'Anyway . . . I'd best be getting on: get myself cleaned up before Kessler arrives.'

'You on for the weekend?'

'No, thank God. That's Graham's pleasure. I've just got to make it through today.'

'Have fun.'

He gave me a mock-pained look as he left.

'I expect you'll be glad of the rest,' Alison said, moving in again to plump up my pillows. 'Couple of weeks off work with your feet up: sounds good to me.'

It would do. She didn't have the Clinicians to worry about. Nor an empty flat to go back to, still full of the presence of an occupant who'd never return there again. Sarah's room was still as she'd left it; the remnants of one of her cooking experiments was gradually solidifying in the fridge. And pretty soon, of course, her ward, and friends and family would start to get increasingly concerned: I wasn't looking forward to fending off their questions, either.

As I settled back and tried to relax, my restless mind abruptly latched on to something Melphalan had told me; and refused to let go. Unwillingly I recalled him boasting of how he and his brotherhood could come and go at will: slipping through the hospital like ghosts. Even here, in a bay with three other people and under the watchful eye of nurses like Alison, I might not be safe. In a room of my own I'd be a sitting duck.

But at least I wouldn't be putting innocent lives at risk; it would be just them and me. And I knew things would have to be settled soon; whichever way.

Twenty-nine

'Fran,' I said, as she was about to leave. 'Could you . . . do me a favour?'

She grinned at my slightly hesitant tone. 'Like what?'

I glanced round in a conspiratorial sort of way, then lowered my voice. 'Get us a packet of Players, will you?'

'Rachel!' she said, with delighted mock-horror. 'You're not about to join the lighting-up-in-the-loo brigade, I hope.'

'Sshhhh!' I looked over at the nurses' station: there was one Staff Nurse at the desk, but she was head down over her care plans, oblivious to what was going on during Saturday visiting hours.

'Didn't you have any in your bag?' Fran asked, more reasonably.

'I think so; but God knows where they've put it. It's not in my locker. Didn't get left downstairs, did it?'

She shook her head; her eyes on me still bright with amusement.

'Just one packet, okay? And a lighter.'

'This whole bloody *floor* is a no-smoking zone, Raitch,' she whispered back. 'Mrs H's really strict about it, an' all. Just before I left she was talking about installing smoke alarms in the toilets to catch people at it . . .'

'Oh for God's sake. Did they?'

She shook her head. 'Couldn't afford it.'

'Well if they catch me,' I said nobly, 'I promise I won't reveal my supplier. They can torture me as much as they like . . .' Torture. I suddenly remembered what that meant

274

– and just about managed to stop my smile congealing. But there was still a trace of desperation in my voice – and maybe my eyes – as I added: 'Please, Fran. I really need it.'

She studied me for a moment; then clicked her tongue. 'You're setting a really bad example for your Staff Nurse, I hope you know. Fortunately, I'm already corrupted. One packet of Players it is, then. You can buy me a drink when you get out.'

'Thanks,' I said, and meant it.

'Glad you're liking Surgical, anyway,' Fran continued cheerfully. 'I used to work on Lister: next one along. You share a flat with Sarah Hollis, don't you? I used to work with her. Lovely girl.'

I nodded, speechless.

'How is she?'

I gestured. '. . . Fine,' I managed, noncommittally.

Fran didn't seem to notice my reticence; she got to her feet, adjusting her denim jacket, and slipped her shoulderbag on. 'Now is there anything else you need, apart from – shhh – you know what?'

I pulled a face.

'I take it that means no,' she grinned. The expression faded to a fond little smile. 'Take care, Raitch. We're thinking about you a lot.'

'Thanks. I'll see you,' I said, and watched her walk off down the corridor, dodging the newspaper trolley as it came in this direction.

I bought a copy of the local, and scanned it for any further news – as opposed to speculation – about what had happened in Fenner Street at the beginning of the week. There was plenty to read: it seemed as if the paper's entire staff were queueing up to cover some aspect of our town's transformation from post-industrial eyesore to urban combat zone. I supposed it made a change from writing about petty crime, school fêtes, and minor RTAs where no one got hurt . . .

POLICE PROBE SECRETS OF HORROR HOUSE ran the front-page headline, above a photo of the cordoned-off ruin. According to the report, they'd already found far more than they'd bargained for. Fragmented human remains, for one thing: buried beneath the floorboards, or silting up the sewers. 'A spokeswoman confirmed that parts of up to nine different bodies had so far been identified, but refused to comment on speculation that the house had been the scene of numerous murders over a period of time, reminiscent of the Dennis Nilsen case. Nor was she prepared to confirm that the police are planning to reopen a number of their missing persons files dating back over two years . . .'

I wondered grimly how long they'd been at it; and how many people had died in fear and misery behind the grimy windows of that dark, forbidding house. Lonely, faceless people, whom no one much had missed. Who'd died alone, and been forgotten. It was a sobering thought. If Hell is oblivion, then these were the damned.

I grazed through the next couple of paragraphs, which covered old ground: the bodies with gunshot wounds, and the melted skeleton of a shotgun thought to have been used in the latest murders. I wondered if they'd sifted out any surgical instruments yet – and what they'd make of them.

Victim's Mother Speaks to Press – page four. Aware of a sudden dryness in my mouth, I turned the pages and looked for the headline.

'The mother of Patricia Owens, 19, one of the two victims so far identified following Monday night's killings, spoke today from her home in Newcastle. Fighting back tears, Mrs Annie Owens told how she'd last heard from her daughter two months ago. "Tricia wrote to say she'd managed to find a job, she was happy, she didn't need anything. But she was such a trusting girl – I knew she would fall in with the wrong people if there was no one there to watch out for her . . ." Police (the reporter added pitilessly) confirmed that Patricia had been working as a prostitute for some time . . .'

Sorry, Trish. Wrong job.

I sensed someone standing beside my bed – and lowered the paper a shade too quickly. Alison raised her eyebrows. 'Sorry, did I startle you?'

I shook my head, and managed to smile.

'We've got a side-room for you, if you want it.'

For a moment I hesitated; then looked around at the other patients. All three were chatting happily with their families or friends. I took in the smiles, the flowers, the cards, before returning my gaze to Alison. And nodding.

'Please.'

There. I'd said it. I'd made my decision. When they came for me – whenever they came – I'd face them alone: and no more innocent people would die because they were simply in the way.

Karen dropped by to see me just before six that evening; back on Days, and taking her supper break. 'Hi. How are we?'

'Bored,' I said morosely.

'Here's something to cheer you up, then.' She glanced back at the doorway, then fished in the pocket of her cardigan and brought out a disposable lighter and a packet of Players. 'Fran said your willpower had collapsed again.'

I gave a little squeal, snatched them and stowed them away in my locker. 'Thanks.'

'"Designer coffin-nails", she called them . . .'

'Tell her I love her,' I grinned.

'I will. I prefer Marlboro myself, but there you go . . .' She inspected my growing selection of get-well cards; giggled at Mike's. 'When are they letting you out?'

I shrugged. 'Couple of days.'

'Don't rush back, now: you need a rest.'

'That's what you told me last time,' I protested.

'Well it's true. You work bloody hard, Rachel. I mean, the place is just collapsing without you. Sheer anarchy . . .'

'Get away,' I said, as her smirk broke through.

'Seriously, though . . . You do push yourself; it's time you took it easy for a bit. Got spoiled.'

I shrugged again, without replying. Relaxation wasn't really on the agenda – especially now that night was drawing in.

'Anyway, got to go.' She nodded towards my locker. 'Don't set the place on fire now.'

I smiled sweetly. 'So nice to see you, Nurse Kane.'

She was still grinning as she left.

My own smile lingered, too: it was good to have friends. People who stuck by you, and cared. If ever the Clinicians took me back with them, into the dark, at least I wouldn't go faceless and forgotten. Even if I died, the grief of others would keep my memory alive. The thought felt vaguely selfish, but oddly comforting too. Right now it was the only immortality I could imagine.

If – when they came for me – I defied them again, it would be Karen who'd suffer, and Mike, and God knew who else. I'd die to stop that happening.

I decided I needed a cigarette.

I wrapped myself in my hospital dressing-gown, slipped smokes and lighter into the pocket, and ventured out into the corridor. The passage was bright and empty. Glancing down towards the nurses' station, I saw a Sister leaning over the worktop, chatting with the duty staff. To judge by the bleep clipped to her belt, she was on for the Floor tonight. She didn't look round as I walked across to the toilet, the polished vinyl cold beneath my bare feet.

The two toilets were single cubicles, built into the walls of a small alcove off the main corridor. The doors were full-length, which suited my purpose admirably. I slipped into the nearer one and locked the door, then lowered the lid and sat down: still wary of the soreness in my midriff. I felt a bit like a junkie preparing for an overdue fix as I fumbled to peel off the cellophane and flip the packet open. I had the cigarette in my mouth, and was fiddling with the lighter, when someone tapped lightly at the door.

Oh shit.

I just sat there, with the unlit fag protruding from my mouth, and hoped whoever it was would go away. I'd been caught in the act, and knew it. And maybe it wasn't an ill-mannered patient with a weak bladder, but a suspicious little nurse . . .

The tapping came again.

I swallowed to clear my throat. 'Look, do you mind?'

'Going to be long?' a muffled voice asked.

'A few minutes, maybe. Can't you use the other one?' I sat back, glowering at the door; but he seemed to accept he'd have to wait. I waited until I felt sure he'd wandered off, then snapped on the flame and sucked it into the tip of my cigarette. The smoke filled my lungs, and I breathed it out with a sense of pure relief, resting my head against the wall behind me . . .

Something heavy pounded on the door.

The noise was deafening in the enclosed space; I jerked back upright, staring. And as I watched, wide-eyed, the very wood of the door itself seemed to bulge perceptibly towards me.

The cigarette dropped from my nerveless fingers. My jaw dropped with it.

Slam . . . slam . . . slam . . . slam. And then, just as I thought the door would burst inwards off its hinges, the pounding stopped.

In the silence that followed, I heard a woman's unhurried footsteps passing down the corridor outside. One of the nurses on her way somewhere . . .

And somehow she hadn't heard a thing.

I sat rock-still, my heart hammering.

After a pause of many minutes, I heard someone else come shuffling past the door and enter the adjacent toilet. The lock clicked.

Silence again.

Slowly, warily, I got to my feet; my smouldering cigarette forgotten between them. Almost despite myself, I reached out to unlock my own door.

When I peered out, and finally emerged, the alcove was empty.

There were footsteps approaching down the corridor as I stepped into it, but it was only the Staff Nurse coming back. She glanced at me, smiling; then stopped, and looked concerned. 'Are you all right, Rachel?'

I nodded, suddenly aware that I still had the lighter clenched in one fist, and the crumpled packet of Players in the other. She didn't seem to notice.

'Yes, thanks. Just felt a bit faint . . .'

'You'd better get back to bed. Give me a call if you don't feel any better . . .'

I nodded again, and watched her walk on towards the station; then stumbled back to my room, and closed the door behind me, leaning against it to catch my breath. The evening sky was deep blue beyond the window; the daylight all but gone. The room was slate-grey with shadow.

And there in the corner, where the gloom was at its thickest, the Lord of Physicians was waiting once again.

Thirty

My breathing slowed ... stopped. I just stood there, petrified, with only the door at my back to keep me from falling.

'Come over here,' said Melphalan softly.

In silent dread I obeyed him – and he gestured to the bed. 'Please,' he insisted, with mocking courtesy. 'You are not a well woman, Rachel Young. You must rest.'

I shrugged out of my dressing-gown, and climbed warily between the sheets, my eyes never leaving his darkened face.

Tonight he was dressed as a doctor.

A real doctor this time, with clean trousers and shirt and even tie, beneath a white coat so pristine it seemed to glow with the last of the light – a ghostly blur in the midst of the gathering dusk.

'Perhaps I should introduce myself once more,' he continued drily. 'I am Mr Allan, a locum registrar on Mr Stevens's firm. I performed your operation on Thursday night.'

I'd thought I couldn't turn any colder. I was wrong.

'You ... couldn't have,' I almost whispered. 'I dreamed that. It wasn't real. It *couldn't* have been real ...'

'You dreamed it?' He nodded, his expression still unreadable in the dimness. 'Very interesting. What did you dream, Rachel?'

I swallowed, twice, before I could reply. 'We were in the closed part of the hospital; Vokaine brought me on a trolley. One of the old obstetric theatres. You cut me *open* ...'

He considered that in silence for a moment; then nodded once more. 'Good. Very good.' There was a grim satisfaction in his tone as he continued. 'You are more of a sensitive than we thought, Rachel. Even while you slept, your mind sensed the truth of what was happening to you . . .'

'What . . . truth?' I managed — and even as I spoke, I realized my wound had begun to throb. As if some infection from a dingy room and dirty instruments, lurking in my flesh the while, had flared up at his very words.

'What indeed?' came his sardonic reply. 'You were admitted to this ward, transferred direct to Theatre and operated on by the team on call. Those are facts. You could ask the nurses who were present; the anaesthetist who put you under. But your operation was performed by me; and my brothers and I had already met, on the disused ward where you dreamed us, to focus our powers in preparation . . .'

He came slowly over to my bedside and stood there, looking down.

'Mr Stevens's firm recently required the services of a locum surgical registrar; one duly appeared. The paperwork is all in order. I have already performed a number of operations. Some of the outcomes should prove . . . interesting.' He leaned forward then, and switched my bedhead light on. The sight of his face, revealed at last by the hooded yellow glow, almost forced me back against the pillows.

His hair, still long, was combed and tidy now; his beard neatly shaped. The image of urbanity his suave, cold tones had painted; but drawn now into a mask of terrifying intensity — of *zeal* — that made me cower inside. The reptile eyes were gleaming; the teeth bared in an expression that was much more sneer than smile.

'Remember what I told you once before,' he said. 'The human mind is a malleable thing. We can twist its perception as we will, and those we manipulate will never know it. The staff who assisted at your appendicectomy saw all they expected to see — and nothing more. They were blind to my true business. But your mind is more resilient than most we have encountered – and gifted with a sensitivity you have not even guessed at.'

There was a pause.

'How do you mean?' I asked in a small voice.

Melphalan chuckled softly: the mirth of a favourite uncle from that wolfish grin. 'The human brain has great potential, Rachel – greater than your so-called scientists have dreamed of. And yours has proved particularly receptive. From the very beginning you sensed us, did you not? Even while your conscious mind tried explaining us away, your spirit felt our coldness. During your operation, your inner self sensed the truth behind what it might please you to call my spell – and so pictured a version of that truth for you.'

Another pause, while I struggled to take all that in.

'You mean . . . you think I'm psychic or something?' It came out sounding less incredulous than I'd expected.

He gestured casually. 'I told you: the potential is common to all. Occurring naturally, it is more pronounced in some than in others. In only a few cases is it ever developed. In your case, with our help, it can be fully realized.'

To their benefit, not mine. I had no doubt of that.

But something else was nagging now. 'In the dream . . .' I ventured, 'you said you were going to make sure I'd do what you wanted . . .'

Again his chuckle came. It chilled me to the bone.

'Ah. Yes. The small matter of your obedience. We thought a time might come when you would be prepared to sacrifice even your friends in order to elude us. So during your operation I performed . . . certain rituals. Rites of insemination.'

For a moment I thought and hoped and almost prayed I hadn't heard him right.

'What . . . ?'

He nodded. 'Insemination. But not in the sense you

might expect it. Deeper than that. Much deeper. We have planted a seed, of sorts. A secret, sleeping thing.'

It was surely only my imagination – the faint stirring I felt then, somewhere beneath my navel. Or a rumble of stomach gas. Perhaps. I lay back against the pillows and scarcely dared to breathe.

'If you should defy us again,' Melphalan continued evenly, 'it will awaken. It will be hungry. Your suffering will be beyond belief.'

I stared helplessly back at him, open-mouthed. And then someone knocked casually on the door, and came in.

It was the nurse I'd seen in the corridor: come to check on me before settling down at the desk. She was smiling, and got as far as 'Feeling better . . . ?' before she noticed Melphalan; and Melphalan turned.

Her smile faltered. 'Sorry, Mr Allan, I didn't realize . . .'

'That's all right, nurse,' he answered smoothly. 'I was called in anyway; I just thought I'd see how Miss Young is doing . . .'

His hand was drifting downwards as he spoke: down to curl around one tail of his coat and brush it casually aside. From where I lay, I could see the grisly meat-hook still dangling from his belt. The coat-tail blocked the nurse's view.

She took a step forward. 'Anything I can do, or . . . ?'

He shook his head. 'Thank you. I shall be finished soon.'

'Fine,' she smiled again at me. 'I'll look in later, Rachel. Buzz me if you need anything.'

I nodded dumbly, and she was gone.

'A fortunate young woman,' Melphalan said musingly. Knowing how close she'd come, I had to nod.

'But enough of this talk: these measures we must take,' the Clinician resumed. 'You are strong-willed, yet confused, and frightened: instinctively you resist us. So we have to ensure your obedience. But it doesn't have to be this way, Rachel. Believe me.'

I watched dully as he sat down on the edge of my bed. 'If only I could convince you that we have common cause,' he went on quietly. 'Why did you become a nurse: was it not to heal the sick, and prolong their lives?' After a moment's hesitation, I silently nodded, and he nodded with me. 'Yes. For that reason too we became physicians. Healers. We took the oath of Hippocrates, and dedicated ourselves to our art. We knew if only we studied long enough, we would learn every secret of the living flesh, and thus gain the power that men crave above all else: the power to defeat death, and put an end to pain. As you see, we have succeeded in prolonging our own lives. Yet still we can die. We have cheated death for centuries – but still it dogs our steps. The final answer still eludes us. But we draw closer all the time.

'We have reanimated dead flesh more than once; but the results are still unpredictable, and temporary. One woman who served us died in this very hospital; we raised and summoned her, but she went astray. Who knows: perhaps she still walks your streets . . . ?'

His macabre musing completely failed to register: my head was swimming. My stomach plunged. All I could picture was poor Jenny laying out the haggard corpse of Mrs Lennox, bending forward, reluctantly close. And then the hands. Would they have reached up almost casually for her, as she froze in disbelieving horror; or would they have shot upwards, like striking snakes, to grasp her throat and *squeeze* . . . ?

I must have gone as white as the sheets; but Melphalan seemed not to notice. Still too involved in his vision – the vision he wanted me to share. 'One day, Rachel. One day the final secret will be disclosed. There will be no more need of superstitions then; this Earth will be all the paradise we need . . .'

If I'd had any sense, I would have just lain there, nodding vigorously the while. But of course I had to know more.

Had to know the reason why Jenny Thomas had died.

'But if you wanted to do good . . .' I said cautiously, 'why'd you get involved with . . . forbidden things?'

He snorted. 'What you would call magic? Sorcery? Communing with mythical beings, be they angels or demons? Such primitive notions are beneath us, Rachel.' He leaned forward. 'There *is* power to be had: most certainly. But it has its roots within us, or the natural order of the cosmos. It can be tapped, controlled and used by the wise. A few, who half-knew its secrets, used it for healing purposes and called it white magic. And we, sensing the deeper truth behind that superstition, did the same.

'We learned how the power could be focused and released. By trance and meditation; by pain and ecstasy: the raptures of suffering, and death, and sexual possession. Such transports opened us to the universe, and the universe to us. Of course there had to be sacrifices: we were forced to use women, and lesser men, in order to feed our power. But the things we learned, Rachel . . . The abilities we gained. No value could be placed on that.'

Staring blankly back at him, I remembered what Razoxane had told me: how the Clinicians had first thought to use their occult powers in order to heal and to create. And things had begun to go horribly awry. The means had become the ends. The white magic had become the black . . .

And still their obsessive thirst for knowledge was unquenched.

'Consider the Christian mythos you once believed in,' Melphalan was saying. 'Even those folk-tales make mention of magical healings and raisings from the dead . . .'

No reason for me to challenge that statement: not any more. But abruptly I found myself doing so.

'That wasn't magic.'

Melphalan paused; frowned slightly. 'Explain.'

I swallowed hard – but was able to continue. 'Magic,

sorcery, witchcraft – it's all using some source of power to alter the world the way you want. Miracles are different: they're letting God work through you to alter the world the way He wants . . .'

I dried up then, partly in surprise at what I'd just said. I could only stare at Melphalan's mocking little smile.

'Rachel. I see we have still not cured you of that affliction. Not quite. But you shall learn . . .'

He leaned in closer. 'After your convalescence is over . . . your initiation can begin. We have much to teach you; and you have much to learn. There is power that will be yours for the taking. Power on Earth . . .'

Suddenly his fingers were in my hair: I almost squealed. For a moment his grip felt tight enough to tear a fistful from the roots; then relaxed to a thoughtful fingering of the strands he held.

'I could enrapture you here and now,' he murmured, while I fought to keep from shuddering. 'Lay you down – and lift you to heights undreamed of. But we will wait, my bright angel; until the night is ripe.'

Withdrawing his hand, he gently stroked my cheek – as he'd done that time before, after they'd murdered Sarah. His dark eyes met mine, and he held my frozen gaze for a long time, before rising to his feet.

Oh God, I realized, belatedly. *The bastard fancies me.*

After he'd gone, I gathered the sheets up close around me and lay very still: listening to the silence of the sleeping ward. And feeling my cold flesh crawl.

Thirty-one

The nurse who came to see me after breakfast brought an infusion pump in with her.

I watched her wheel it in on its drip-stand: a routine piece of hospital hardware. But the fist of dread had balled tight inside my stomach before she'd even opened her mouth.

'Mr Allan wants you on this,' she told me brightly, walking over to plug it in; ignoring my whey-faced stare. 'Reckons you've picked up an infection. You were pretty sick last night, weren't you . . . ?'

There was just a tinge of reproach in her voice: as if it was my fault I hadn't quite made it to the bowl. Let alone the fact that it was Mr Allan's visit that had gutted me in the first place . . .

'What's . . . what's he put me on?' I asked faintly. Maybe he'd written up something to keep me doped and passive – but my fear had a deeper seat than that. Just the thought of a cannula lodged in my vein – a direct line into my bloodstream for whoever chose to take advantage – made me want to cringe. And once I was hooked up to that contraption, I'd be stranded: unable to run. A prisoner on a hi-tech ball and chain . . .

'IV antibiotics: just penicillin . . .'

She was preparing the infusion set already – and even after all my years in hospitals, the sudden whiff of disinfectant caught me off-guard, pinching my nostrils like clean, stinging fingers. It brought back memories of blood-tests when I was small: waiting in the chair while my naked arm was wetly rubbed, and the gleaming needle brought in close . . . I wanted to protest, and found I'd neither words enough nor breath. Nor nerve simply to jerk my arm away.

She leaned forward, smiling: aware of my uneasiness now, and trying to reassure. I swallowed, and forced my eyes up from the two-inch needle.

'Listen . . . can't I have it orally?'

'IV's what he said. Sorry . . .'

'I mean . . .'

'Don't look if you don't want to,' she advised gently. And of course I didn't want to; but I looked. Watched the needle slide coldly in: more pressure than pain, but it stung.

'Ow.'

'Shh, that's the worst of it now.' She fixed the site with plasters, and set about programming the pump. It bleeped; lights flashed. The clear bag that hung above it looked as innocuous as something you brought goldfish home in.

'All done,' she said after a moment. 'Wasn't so bad, was it?' Her smile was almost indulgent now. 'Don't worry, Rachel: us nurses always make the worst patients.'

Ha bloody ha, I thought.

At least I could walk around the ward with it: the internal battery kept it going. That afternoon I went as far as the day-room, pushing it in front of me like a penance; the needle aching dully in my arm. The infusion wasn't affecting me much, but then it didn't need to. I was quite demoralized enough as it was.

Gazing out at the muddy sky, I found myself going over Melphalan's words again. Bringing them back up; chewing them over. Trying vainly to swallow them down once more.

A secret, sleeping thing . . .

Gingerly, unthinking, I made to touch my tummy – then jerked my hand away.

They had me now: I'd do anything they told me. Anything. My skin turned clammy as I remembered the lust in Melphalan's eyes, but it didn't change things. I hadn't any choice.

And what did he really want of me? Just my sex? Or my soul as well? Whatever heat I'd smelled on him, I knew the ice of intellect beneath would not have cracked. He was still seeking the key to death's doorway, just as he'd said. And now he had in his hands a spirit that he called special. Something he could cultivate, and study — and finally dissect.

Like that bloke in Razoxane's vision. The one they'd rendered senseless. Sense. Less. I tried to swallow my dread; but it went down the wrong way, and almost choked me.

I was wheeling the pump back towards my room — quite lost in my own misery — when a quiet voice said: 'Rachel.'

My head swung round.

Vokaine.

He was leaning comfortably against the wall, beside the sluice room: his faint smile showing yellowed teeth. The goggles fixed me like an insect's stare.

The scar on his cheek was infected now: a suppurating slash. Even as I watched, a fly buzzed in close, and tried to settle. His cheek twitched irritably, but the grim smile didn't waver.

Physician, heal thyself.

In that moment, even through his vagabond veneer of coat and scarf and grimy hat, I sensed an echo of the past he had behind him: could almost glimpse the muddy, bloody, screaming hospitals of the Hundred Years War, where he'd doubtless learned his trade. Where the pain of others had become his pleasure. Where familiarity with flesh had led to a quest to know its every anguish . . .

'I see you have picked up your bed and walked,' he observed drily.

'I just stared back at him; clutching the drip-stand to

keep myself upright. And then I heard approaching foot-steps, and turned my head – to see a couple of nurses coming towards us, cardigans on, and shoulderbags slung: on their way to afternoon break.

Alison was one of them.

My mouth opened without sound: too late for warnings now. I waited for surprise, for sudden horror; for Vokaine to draw his knives, and start to kill. And I was still waiting when they walked between us both, and off the ward. Alison broke off her conversation to give me a lively smile – 'All right, Rachel?' – and nodded politely to Vokaine.

He turned his head to watch them go; still smiling. ' "For seeing, they shall not perceive . . ." ' he murmured. ' "And hearing, they shall not understand." ' When his gaze came back to me, the smile had become a grin.

I tried to shrink back as he crossed the corridor towards me, but the soles of my feet seemed stuck to the linoleum. I could only shiver as he reached out for the pump, and began to examine it with grubby fingers.

'These advances in the art of medicine . . .' he said con-versationally, peering at the red digital readout, '. . . are wondrous indeed. But all engines made by men are subject to malfunction, are they not?' His fingers grazed the pro-gramming panel, while I stood and shook. My arm was throbbing coldly now, in sheer anticipation of what might happen next.

Still idly tinkering, he looked at me askance. 'The phys-icians of this age are sadly misled, Rachel Young. The power of Mind under Will is greater than all their potions and machines.' He eased back, leering. 'As you will soon discover.'

I bit deep into my lip: watching as he turned away. Relief was just beginning to seep into my stomach when he swung back round, stepped forward: leaned in close. I felt his breath as well as smelled it when he spoke again.

'Remember this last thing, little angel. If you defy us

once again, you'll scream for days ... until we tear your *fucking heart out.*'

I just moaned, and closed my eyes, and listened to his footsteps fade away.

After a minute, I made myself look – and saw that he was gone. But it took a while longer before I'd mustered sufficient strength to continue on towards my room. Not that I felt any safer there; but it was still a sanctuary of sorts. Somewhere I could sit and wait, in dismal silence, and count the minutes to nightfall.

Late in the afternoon, the storm that had been all day brewing broke at last.

And Razoxane came with it.

Thunder rumbled dully, somewhere up there amid the creeping grey clouds. The rain was coming down in stair-rods now, splashing the window, but I still craned forward, peering upwards through the glass: looking for the light-ning. It's strange, but I've always loved thunderstorms – ever since I was a little girl, when Mum used to tell me it was God taking photos with a flash.

Behind me in the lightless room, Razoxane said, 'What else did he tell you? Melphalan, I mean.'

I kept on staring at the cloud ceiling for a moment, then turned reluctantly back to her, shrugging deeper into my dressing-gown. She was still sat there in the bedside chair, legs casually crossed; helping herself to some of my grapes.

For once she was bare-headed, her hat resting on one knee. She'd taken off her shades again too, now that the daylight had dimmed to a tolerable level. I still wasn't used to the sight of her eyes: their coldness chilled me all the more for that.

'Look . . .' I hedged, putting off the evil moment, 'you're taking a hell of a risk coming here. What if someone comes in . . . ?'

'Well it's visiting time, isn't it? And believe me, they wouldn't give me a second glance. It's not just Clinicians who can mould unwary minds...' Her lips twitched. 'They'll just think you've got some rather unsavoury friends.'

'All right, then. He said...' I moistened my lips '...something about a rite of insemination. Planting something inside me...'

She nodded once, expressionless. 'Like what?'

I shrugged. 'Christ knows. Something sleeping, he said. Something that... mustn't be wakened...' I felt another vertiginous surge of dread then, and lapsed into silence: staring helplessly back at her.

'Anything else?'

'Only that... they met in the closed wing beforehand. The old labour ward: just like I'd dreamed them. To make their preparations, he said...'

Again she nodded. 'Yes. They would have focused it there; the final ritual taking place during your operation, performed by Melphalan alone...'

I grimaced. 'Focused *what*?'

'A taste of their power, Rachel,' she answered evenly. 'Some form of parasitic energy, sealed inside you.' Her lips stirred again, into a mirthless smile. 'Literally, a phantom pregnancy...'

'Oh, for God's sake...' I stopped, and swallowed the bile that was suddenly coating my throat. Then: 'You mean I've been *possessed*?'

'Not really. I told you, they've probably contaminated you with some sort of psychomorph. An implant of energy,' she elaborated, seeing my blank, scared look; 'something that feeds off the life-force of its host. In this case it's dormant; but if roused... Basically it would disrupt the genetics of your body cells and flood your whole system with cancer: secondaries all over. Within hours.'

Oh Jesus. I sat down heavily on the end of the bed, and

ran both hands back through my hair – then gave Razoxane a sidelong look.

'It's not . . . not a demon, then?'

Her moment's hesitation stopped my breath – like an
ice-cube lodging in my throat. Then she spread her hands.

'I've come up against rites like this before,' she said
steadily, her eyes fixing mine. 'They're a focus of psychic
power – of malevolent *will*. It could be that . . . they've
actually invoked some spirit, without knowing it; but if
they have, it will be a primitive thing – as blind as a bacil-
lus. Nothing that could consciously control you . . .'

I made a tiny, frightened sound; I felt like *wailing*. 'So
what the hell do I do now . . . ?'

'Trust me,' she said simply. 'I know how to get it out.'

I blinked: not quite daring to believe that it was going
to be that simple. 'How . . . ?'

In the pause that followed, a flicker of distant lightning
tinged the room with bluish-white – an instant so brief it
might have been imagined.

'What we have to do . . .' said Razoxane slowly, 'is find
their Ritual Room – the theatre they used – and reverse
the invocation. We need to do it there.'

I made a face. 'Can't we do it here . . . ?'

She shook her head. 'It has to be there: the conditions,
the polarities, must be the same. That room will already
be charged with power; we'll need to use it.'

'Reversing the . . . What'll that mean?'

'It's a matter of performing a counter-ritual, to draw the
thing back out of you. Not exactly an exorcism; I told you,
it's scarcely an entity as such. Purging might be a better
word. It won't be pleasant – but you'll not be harmed. I
can promise you that.'

Promises, promises, I thought grimly. But right now I
didn't have much choice. I took a deep breath, and nodded.

'All right, then. I should be out in the next couple of
days, and then –'

Once more she shook her head. 'We daren't wait even that long, Rachel. These things can prove unstable. A sudden change in mental or emotional activity could be enough to unleash it. Even a bad dream might set it off.' She paused, rubbing a hand back through her Greenham Common haircut; then looked at me directly. 'I want to do it tonight.'

Tonight. I almost echoed the word. For all that I wanted to be free of whatever slept inside me, the prospect filled me with awful trepidation.

'How do we know they won't be there?' I asked faintly.

She smiled thinly. 'Don't worry, I'll make sure. Besides, they don't perform their examinations that often. Quite apart from the limited supply of subjects, it drains their power . . .' She paused again, looking me over as I sat there wrapped up naked in my dressing-gown. 'You have clothes?'

I shook my head. 'My uniform went down to the laundry; I haven't got anything else to walk around in.'

'Right, I'll see what I can find. Next question: how easy will it be for you to slip away?'

I shrugged. 'I could always say I'm going to visit someone on another ward or something. I mean, how long is this going to take?'

'Hopefully not long. Perhaps an hour.'

'Right. Okay. They're quite short-staffed on this ward, so I doubt if anyone will get round to thinking I've gone AWOL.' I nodded to myself – and glanced at her again. 'But what if Vokaine comes back?'

'We'll have to hope he doesn't, won't we?' she murmured.

Despite myself, and all my self-control, I felt a quick shiver go through my flesh. I glanced out into the rain.

When I looked back, she had her pistol in her lap: fingering its lines like a lover. Watching me quizzically.

'Know anything about guns?' she asked.

I thought about it. 'No.'

She lifted the pistol and studied it, as if for the first time; then flicked her eyes back to me. 'Astra 400. Made in 1921. I had it when it was new . . .' In the pause that followed I sensed her gaze tip backwards, into the past. Maybe seeing again the faces of all the people that gun had killed since. Right up to Trish . . .

'I'm not putting that under my pillow,' I muttered.

'Just an idea. Slow him down . . .' She angled it thoughtfully towards the ceiling. 'You need to know it, though. It's heavy, the trigger's stiffened up . . .' She smiled faintly, before adding: 'And the safety catch is not what it was . . .'

For an instant I could picture the scene: the corridor outside, a nurse chatting with some relatives – and then the backfire bang from my room, shattering glass along with the silence . . . 'Put it *away*,' I hissed.

Still smiling, she pulled up her jersey, and tucked the automatic down between waistband and shirt. 'They're crude tools, anyway,' she admitted. 'Too detached. With a knife, now, you're close enough to feel the soul quit the body. You can feel it kiss your *face* . . .'

I knew I was going to start shaking in a minute.

Razoxane sat back comfortably. 'Oh, yes . . . Something else you should know. Everyone else does, but they haven't told you yet. Don't want to upset you . . .'

I waited uneasily.

'Your friend Sarah, and her young gentleman. You knew they'd been rowing quite a bit recently . . .'

As if it mattered now. I gave an affirmative sort of shrug.

'Well . . .' she went on brightly. 'It seems he just lost control the other night, and killed her: then himself . . .'

I just sat there, open-mouthed.

'It got quite unpleasant, by all accounts. He really carved the poor girl up. Put her in the boot of his car, and drove up into the woods. Then poured petrol over himself and her and everything, sat in the driving seat (*oh, she was enjoying this)*, put a shotgun in his mouth and pulled the trigger. The muzzle-flash set off the petrol, and . . . well, *vwamph*.' She grinned. 'Dental records, apparently.'

I almost moaned; but managed to ask: 'You think they'll believe it?'

'I reckon they should. Melphalan probably galvanized the bloke's own finger on the trigger. No other likely explanation: case closed . . .'

I felt the bitterness of sobs welling thickly up my throat: bit my lip and lowered my gaze, so as not to give her the satisfaction of seeing. And suddenly Razoxane had left her chair, and was kneeling down beside me, her hand on my arm.

'There's blue skies waiting at the end of the night, Rachel.' She whispered softly: urgently. 'Remember that. *Remember*.'

It was a side of her I hadn't seen before: one mercurial change I hadn't expected. I just nodded; and after a moment she rose, and returned to her chair.

'After supper, then,' she suggested, a minute later. 'Say half-past six. I'll meet you by the doors into the old labour ward. But I'll get some clothes to you before that.' She leaned forward, meeting my gaze and holding it. 'Believe me, Rachel. It's almost over now.'

Silence then, apart from the rain against the window.

At length I had to ask it: 'What are we really up against here? I mean . . . are they into Satanism and things, without knowing it?'

Razoxane gestured vaguely. 'It's true they've twisted themselves beyond humanity with the powers they use. And yes, they've slaughtered and violated so many innocents, in their ritualized ways, that the Benighted have been drawn to them, like moths to a candle in the dark . . .'

'The Benighted?' I asked warily.

'The Spirits Who Walk in Darkness. What you'd call demons. Such things exist, Rachel. And whenever

297

Melphalan and his black brotherhood have breached the spirit barrier with their rituals of lust and torture – their ecstasies of rape and violence – some more of them have come creeping out. Like whatever was back at Fenner Street; and worse. All power has its price.'

I stared at her; dry-mouthed, yet reluctant even to swallow. 'So . . . we're taking on the Devil here, is that right?'

'Depends on what you conceive him to be,' she answered calmly. 'Look up any work of occult lore, you'll get a whole string of demonic names. The Babylonians had a spectre for every sickness. Even in medieval times, there were devils too numerous to count. Every age has sensed the same evil entities – and called them its own. It's even been suggested that the serpent motif the Clinicians use – the sign of Asklepios – is somehow linked in with Livyathan: the fallen angel who is King over all the Children of Pride. So yes, there are things out there: shadows behind the superstitions. And they'll use the sorcerers who invoke them, whether knowingly or otherwise.'

Now I swallowed. 'Razoxane . . .'

'Believe me, Rachel,' she insisted. 'Trust me. You'll be quite safe as long as you keep your faith. Even demons have a healthy respect for that.'

'Razoxane. I don't believe, not really, not any more . . .'

She studied me for a moment. 'Why not?'

I shrugged, helplessly. 'It's just . . . I feel like I've died inside. Or he has. I can't feel him. I can't imagine a loving creator any more; nor any power for good watching over me. Oh, I still want it all to be true. But I can't *believe* it.' I said the last with something approaching frustration.

She nodded slowly. 'All right, Rachel. All right. Then you can believe in me. And in this . . .' She let the switchblade slide into her palm and flicked the weapon open, turning the blade to catch the light along its razored edge.

For a long time after she'd gone I just sat there, silent. Watching the lightning; listening for the thunder. And hearing the rain come down.

Thirty-two

It was Alison who came in for my tray.

'Finished?' she asked brightly. I glanced at the meal on my overbed table and nodded. She took a step closer, then hesitated, her smile fading somewhat.

'Rachel. You've hardly touched it.' She gave me a concerned look. 'You feeling okay?'

I nodded again. 'I just don't have much of an appetite tonight, that's all. Sorry.'

In fact I'd touched it quite a lot: picked at it, toyed with it, pushed it round the plate. I just hadn't eaten any of it. Hospital cooking didn't do much for me at the best of times; but now, with my stomach knotted tight and a taste like ashes on my tongue, I couldn't face the prospect of a single mouthful.

Alison shrugged, and picked up the tray. I noticed the bunch of keys pinned to her dress above the name-badge.

'You got the ward tonight?'

'For my sins.'

'Busy?'

'Fairly.' She paused, adjusting the cruet, then looked at me again. 'We're one trained nurse down tonight. Plus someone just rang to tell us there's a query bowel obstruction coming in . . .'

'Is it all right if I pop over and see someone on Lister?' I asked, managing to keep my tone casual. 'Friend of mine's just come in for a sinus op . . .'

'Sure, no problem.'

'We'll probably watch some TV in the day-room or something . . .' I elaborated anyway.

300

'See you later then,' Alison said, already turning to the door. 'Don't get too tired,' she added over her shoulder as she left.

I checked my watch. Just gone six-fifteen. I swallowed, and swung my legs out of bed.

Time to go.

Carefully I closed the plastic valve on the cannula in my vein, and pulled the IV line out. The vase of flowers on my locker seemed the best bet, so I left it to drain away in there, and pushed the stand into the corner, behind the door. At least the carnations would benefit. When all this was over, I might even find it funny.

Opening the locker, I took out the clothes Razoxane had surreptitiously brought round an hour or so before. A set of lime-green theatre pyjamas, a white coat and a plain pair of trainers. I hadn't asked where she'd got them – whether from the laundry downstairs, or from the Theatre changing room itself – and didn't much care. Just so long as she hadn't killed the previous owner in the process . . .

I dressed quickly, and looked myself over in the mirror. The sleeves of the coat were too short, so I rolled them back to the elbows and just hoped no one would notice the cannula site, and the patient's ID wristband I still wore. Other than that, I looked the image of a Recovery Room nurse, on her supper break and presumably heading for the canteen.

After a moment's thought, I also retrieved the half-empty packet of ciggies from the back of the locker, along with the lighter, and dropped them into one of the coat pockets. If this ceremony proved to be anything like as unpleasant as Razoxane had suggested, I was probably going to need them.

Opening my door an inch or two, I listened for footsteps. There were none. I peered cautiously out and glanced up and down the empty corridor; then made my move, walking briskly down past the office, off the ward and round the corner into the central thoroughfare. For a moment my back burned, as I thought of all the eyes that might be watching. But I heard no outcry behind me, no raised voice or running feet; and as I kept walking, so the sensation faded to a tingling, and was gone. My heart was still thudding painfully fast as I got to the lifts, but once I was inside one and the door was closing off my view of the surgical unit reception area, I felt a whole lot better.

I thumbed the button for the fourth floor, felt the lift shudder and begin to move, and leaned back against the wall to release a gasp of pent-up breath: my eyes on the indicator lights above the doors. They flicked from one number to the next with what seemed like painful slowness. But we got there in the end.

The lift shuddered again, positioning itself; then the door slid open, and I stepped warily out.

There was no one there to meet me.

To my left, a well-lit corridor led on to the modern maternity and gynae units; but on the right there was only a padlocked set of double doors, shutting off access to the old north wing. That whole corner of the building had been closed for longer than I'd been here: whether through straightforward cuts or structural decay, I'd never really known. The sign on the doors just said *No Entry*; and inner dimness pressed against their windows.

There was no sign of Razoxane; I hadn't the nerve to walk over and peer in at one of those windows, cupping my eyes against the glass . . . I looked at my watch.

Nearly half-past.

I began pacing nervously up and down. Knowing my luck, I was going to get accosted by some security-conscious member of staff who'd want to know what I was doing up here and where my name-badge was. Either that or I'd run into somebody I knew. Almost unconsciously I reached for the smokes in my pocket, then thought better of it.

Beyond the closest windows, the day was fading fast.

I could hear the sounds that drifted my way from the nearest ward: footsteps, a snatch of laughter; the rattle of cutlery as trays were collected. The porters would be up for the meal trolleys any time now – and most of them I knew . . .

When I glanced towards the locked doors again, there was a face at one of the windows, staring out at me.

I sucked in a scream's worth of air – then realized it was Razoxane, and almost reluctantly let it go. With a sardonic smile she beckoned me, then pushed one door open. The secure-looking padlock slipped apart, to hang by its chain from the door-handle.

'Going to stand there all night?' Razoxane asked drily.

I joined her with unseemly haste – as though seeking refuge from the light of the living wards behind me. The gloom ahead put me grimly in mind of that vision thing I'd had under anaesthetic: the dark corridors down which Vokaine had drawn me. My mind had picked and mixed the details, but the reality was recognizable enough. The shadow-damp in the plaster; the old, unlovely paint. The ceiling tiles still missing overhead, exposing naked pipe-work in the crawlways.

And what might already be crawling up there . . . ?

I was still peering nervously upwards as Razoxane closed the doors behind us, reaching through the last crack to readjust the padlock until it once again seemed to be sealing the entrance. Then she turned to me.

'I've found where it happened.'

I moistened my dry lips. 'Look . . . What if they come back?'

'Don't worry, Rachel. They're nowhere near. Not tonight.' She grasped my shoulder. 'Trust me.'

I stared back at her; stared into those inscrutable lenses. Sure I trusted her – about as much as I'd trust the Yorkshire Ripper; but I nodded dumbly anyway.

'Come on,' she almost whispered. 'Let's get it done.'

The passage was stripped and dingy; the smell of mouldy plaster spiked the air. We went quickly on down it, past empty bays and side-rooms, and turned left through a second set of doors. *Labour Ward*, announced a faded sign above them.

The corridor here lay in junkyard dimness, choked with shadows and the skeletons of beds. Again, much as I'd dreamed it: as if my subconscious mind, in picturing the essence of a past reality, had somehow glimpsed a future one as well. I wondered drearily if it had after all been an omen of sorts: a warning about ending up in this graveyard ward. A warning unheeded – for here I was now, with Razoxane tugging on my sleeve, drawing me deeper into the stale and dusty gloom.

And, for all my misgivings, I followed her.

Dust had settled like a grey skin over everything we passed: equipment left undisturbed for months that had become years. It hung in the air around us, a motionless haze – indistinguishable from the dusk, but prickling my nostrils and throat with every breath I took. The floor would be thick with it; but it was already too dark to see the footprints of those who'd come here before us – or the ones we left ourselves.

I touched Razoxane's shoulder. 'Won't they know we've been here?'

'It won't matter,' was her calm reply; 'they'll not be using this room again . . .'

That brought me up short. 'Hey . . . You're not going to set fire to the bloody *hospital* are you?'

She turned back to me. 'No I'm not. We don't have to physically destroy a place like this to make it useless to them. Believe me, Rachel: I know what I'm doing.'

That, at least, I didn't doubt. But knowing the ruthlessness with which she'd been pursuing her vendetta against the Clinicians, I wasn't entirely reassured. She'd risked my life before. I suddenly wondered when she might decide I was expendable . . .

'Come on,' she said softly, and pushed her way in through a pair of doors marked *Delivery Room 1*.

I followed her through.

In contrast to the other rooms we'd passed – all lightless glory-holes of junk and jumble – the theatre beyond was empty: quite bare, apart from a single trolley in the centre of the floor, and a lighting unit suspended above it. The shape of the latter really unnerved me: like an iron mantis crouching in the murk.

I stopped again on the threshold, and hugged myself: squeezed my own body tight in an effort to suppress the shiver that ran through me now. The room had an atmosphere, and I felt it straight away: a sort of stagnant coldness, like the one I'd felt in the Ritual Room at the house on Fenner Street. Maybe Melphalan had spoken the truth, and I was somehow sensitive to these things. Or maybe anyone would have felt the cold here: the eerie, unnatural, evil chill.

There was an unsettling sense of *déjà vu* as well; I'd been here once before, in spirit if not in body.

Razoxane had already walked over to the wall-switch; and as the lighting head flickered coldly into life, tinging the room with its bluish phosphorescence, I saw that the trolley was parked at the centre of a seven-pointed star within concentric circles: a chalked design that covered most of the floor. The basic design was interlaced with masses of detail: runes and symbols and scribbled words. In the shadow of the trolley itself, I glimpsed the twisted coils of the physician's serpent.

'Don't be afraid,' Razoxane said. 'The power's dormant now. It's not going to erupt spontaneously just because we're here.' She gestured to the trolley. 'Come and lie down.'

I did so, walking carefully: trying with heart in mouth

to avoid treading on any of the lines, like a superstitious little kid avoiding cracks in the pavement. Bears will get you if you do that. Or worse than bears . . . I reached the trolley, and tested its brakes – strained against them – before sitting on its edge; then glanced round again at the heptagram. 'This is . . . going to be a magical ceremony, isn't it?'

She nodded.

I swallowed. 'And you're sure it's safe?'

She met my frightened gaze, and nodded again. 'Like I told you: it won't be nice, but you'll feel better after it's done. Don't worry about the heptagram: it focuses power, but has protective qualities as well. We'll both be safe inside it.'

I almost asked, *Safe from what?* but didn't have the nerve. Instead I lay stiffly down, and waited, while she stooped and reached for something under the trolley.

When she straightened up again, I saw she was holding a book: a black-bound tome with a worn, unlettered cover. For a moment she stood quite still; then, murmuring something that might have been a prayer, she opened the book, gave me an empty smile, and began thumbing through it.

I swallowed again, with more difficulty. 'That's . . .'

'Their secret book, remember?' She walked around behind me, and placed it on the table just above my head. The rustle of paper sounded very loud in my ears as she turned another page, and another.

I stared up into the chilly light, and bit my lip to stop myself asking the obvious, awful questions. Questions like *How many times have you tried this before? And how many times did it work?* I really didn't want to know.

The rustling of pages slowed to silence, a stillness broken only by Razoxane's breathing as she studied the book before her. At length she spoke again. 'Right: we're ready to begin. Roll your top up, so I can see your stomach.'

Reluctantly I complied, and felt the cold air settle upon my skin. My scar tingled with the contact.

'Now, you have to lie quite still,' she continued. 'Still and quiet. In a while you'll feel it begin to move; *don't fight it*. Just let go. Let everything go.' She paused again. 'Are you ready?'

'Yes . . .' I managed weakly.

'Good.' I heard the rustle of movement, then the metallic snap of her switchblade flicking open. My stomach lurched then, as sudden images of ritual sacrifice crammed my brain; but she was already walking back round into view, and extending the blade towards my bare midriff. I felt the cold point prick my navel, and lay perfectly still: not daring even to breathe.

And Razoxane began to speak, in what I instinctively knew was a long-dead tongue, no longer spoken or studied or even remembered: an ancient, ugly language.

It was like a mantra, I realized as I lay there sweating beneath her knife, pinned to the table top by its minuscule, piercing pressure. The words were rhythmic and measured; I thought I detected a pattern of repetition within them. Abruptly she'd lifted the knife from my belly and was brandishing it above me, weaving it back and forth in time to her incantation. I stared up with wide, anxious eyes, watching the blade catch the pitiless light.

And felt something move inside me.

I gasped in horror, went rigid. And as I lay there, paralysed, the sense of movement came again.

It didn't feel like something physical within me, nestling in my gut; the sensation was much deeper, more horribly intimate than that. As though part of my own body was somehow rejecting me: seething and squirming to tear free. Ignoring Razoxane's warning – and her whirling knife – I managed to struggle up on to my elbows, staring down at my stomach, half-expecting to see the skin bulging out-wards as my very flesh rebelled; but the taut smoothness of my belly was unmarred.

The pain hit me then: the fundamental agony of rending tissue. I gave a little shriek and slumped back down on to the table top, gasping for air and quite unable to fill my lungs. A second, burning surge followed close on the first, and this time my scream was soundless as my body arched. Razoxane's blade was back against my stomach, and drew blood as I thrust upwards against it. Her cold, harsh chant-ing never wavered.

I hit the table top again and lay there, panting helplessly, while she described a single, endless pattern on my stomach with the point of her knife, too lightly to break the skin. It felt like a pentagram, drawn over and again with a con-tinuous stroke, my navel at its centre. And now she was speaking English once again, cajoling like some grim mid-wife: 'Let go, Rachel, let go . . . you're nearly there . . . let go . . .'

I let myself go limp: forced my locked muscles to loosen by sheer strength of will. And suddenly I felt – or sensed – an awful, freezing pressure in the depths of my belly, cold enough to chill the shit in my bowels. As I gritted my teeth, I felt it tighten, like a clutching hand: grip me like a fist; and gradually begin to slacken.

I lay there, gasping, my own fists clenched tightly at my sides; not daring to believe I felt it fading.

Razoxane snarled a final sentence in that alien language, touched the point of her blade to my navel once again, then raised the knife towards the ceiling – and I abruptly felt as if I'd been gutted. Groaning, I watched her raise her eyeless face, and spit.

The lamps went out.

There wasn't even a flicker, a dwindling spark; they died like burst lightbulbs, and let the pent-up darkness flood back in. For a panicked, freezing moment I was blinded.

Then, as my staring eyes began to adjust, dim light from the corridor outside showed me Razoxane once more. She hadn't moved an inch.

'*Consummatum est*,' I heard her breathe; and that, at least, I recognized as Latin.

Slowly she lowered the knife to her side, and stood there for a minute with head bowed: her face a pit of shadow. At last she looked at me again; and the wasted light caught the bared teeth of her grin.

'At least you can say you've discovered a cure for cancer,' she told me drily.

I just lay and stared back at her; feeling my sweat soak slowly through my greens. The hair was clinging to my damp forehead, but I was too drained even to wipe it aside.

Eventually, absurdly, I managed to say: 'Is that it?'

She nodded. 'All over. You're clean now.'

'But . . .' I tried unsuccessfully to raise my head. 'It felt like something tore . . . inside.'

'I know. Rooting out something like that always hurts like hell; as far as your nerves are aware, you're being ripped to pieces. But don't worry: there are no internal injuries. It didn't even reopen your wound. Did you feel it? At the end?'

I nodded gingerly. 'Something cold; sort of clinging on to me inside . . .'

'Well it's gone now: unfocused again. No threat to anyone any more.'

I took a deep breath, and tried again to rise; I could scarcely move. 'Shit . . . My muscles feel like water . . .'

'Relax,' she advised softly. 'Anyone's going to feel drained after a rite like that. You're going to need a while to get your strength back.'

'Yeah, but . . .' I lay back, grimacing. 'What if they come back now, or . . . ?'

'Oh, they'll come, all right,' Razoxane said calmly. 'Innocence will always lure them.'

It took an endless moment for her meaning to sink in. When it did, the only reaction I could think of was to scream.

I didn't, though. There really wouldn't have been much point.

Thirty-three

'Please . . .' I almost whimpered. 'Please, just let me go. You don't need me, not now . . .'

'Oh, but I do,' she answered pleasantly. 'Melphalan will require some promise of libation before he meets me face to face. You'll serve the purpose admirably. Virgin flesh — and innocent blood.'

'But . . .' I hesitated, summoning the strength to continue. 'Melphalan needs me. He fancies me, for God's sake.'

'Yes. But you've been betraying him all along, haven't you? Conspiring with his oldest enemy. His opinion of you may well go down a notch or two when he learns that . . .' She smiled her soulless smile once more. 'Don't you think?'

I made another vain attempt to sit up. The effort left me breathless. 'But you just saved me,' I protested, in between gulps of air. 'Why?'

She shrugged. 'I said I would purge you of that thing, and so I did. I keep my word, Rachel.'

Great, I thought, and almost giggled: the first slip and slither down towards hysteria. A serial killer, sociopath and schizophrenic, to be sure; but not a liar. Even fallen angels have their honour.

I could barely see her in the dimness; the grey light beyond the doors had deepened to slaty blue. Evening had already crept into the building; and night now followed close behind.

'When . . . do you think they'll come?' I ventured, hopelessly.

'When I choose to summon them,' was her calm reply. She walked slowly round behind me, and I heard the leaves of the black book rustling again. 'The *Ars Goetica* has much to say on the convocation of sorcerers. They will answer the call.'

For all my despair, I felt a new dread creeping over me. 'That book you're using. You said . . .'

'That it was their secret one, yes. But not the *Chirurgia*; rather, the older and more powerful volume. *De Mysteriis Maleficarum*. On the Mysteries of Witches.'

My stomach shrank painfully tight. 'But . . . you told me that even black magicians thought that one was too dangerous to use.'

'Not for someone who has truly mastered the art,' she said evenly. 'As my cleansing of your body demonstrated. Melphalan has long delved into this book, and tried to decipher its secrets; but even he does not know how to use its power as I do.'

'And you. Are you a witch, then?' Asking the question, I already knew the answer; and only a few short weeks ago, I'd still have thought of witches as old women in pointy hats: the stuff of superstition . . .

'Depends what you mean,' Razoxane said drily. She turned another page – as if even in the dark she saw the words. 'Some so-called witches worship the earth, and even think to do good. But if your idea of a witch is someone skilled in the practice of what was once called *maleficium*, then yes, I suppose I am.'

'*Maleficium?*' It even sounded sinister.

'The uninitiated would call it the working of evil by supernatural means. But like all moral judgements, that is a relative one. It's simply a power, to be used or abused like any other: to edify and strengthen the user – and bring ruin to his or her enemies.'

'You sound like one of them,' I muttered sourly.

Though I couldn't see her face, I sensed her cold,

sardonic smile in the pause that followed, before she even spoke.

'I *am* one of them,' she said.

'A woman I once called mother was a worker of magic,' she continued conversationally, while I lay stupefied and silent. 'She practised what you'd call white witchcraft: used it to strengthen and heal. There was much she taught me; but I was always hungry to know more. The city called me out of the country, in search of a tale that a traveller told. A secret house where physicians used wisdom and magical spells to make men whole.

'I found ghosts of rumours haunting the streets. Solomon's Surgery, they called it: a guild of the elect. The barber surgeon in Keller Street had access to them, so it was said – which should have warned me from the first, for he took a butcher's pleasure in his work. Thomas Mulloch, his name was then. Nowadays you know him as Vokaine.'

I listened, frozen: panting softly.

'So I disguised myself as a youth,' Razoxane went on, 'and was able to pass myself off as a student of medicine from the university. I also revealed some of my learning, and impressed him and his fellows sufficiently to be admitted as a novice to their Surgery. Their Hermetical Order of High Physicians, as it was truly called. This was in the year 1700 or thereabouts.'

She turned another page, and smoothed it down.

'At length, of course, they discovered their error – by which time I'd already discovered mine. They were healers no longer: their science had consumed them – and their magic – and made them sorcerers. Destroyers. But I'd already learned too many of their secrets. I am precocious, Rachel: I learn quickly. And I had advantages over other members of the Order – not least because I was also an ardent student of the witchcraft they'd long since come to despise and ignore.

'When my identity was known, I begged leave to remain within the Order: I wanted somehow to guide it back towards the white ways. But Melphalan – who was then calling himself Johannes Klein – opposed me, on the grounds that there was no place for women within the Order. The Brotherhood agreed, and I was expelled: living on borrowed time, I knew, because of the secrets I'd learned.

'Then, one night, everything changed.

'I dreamed, Rachel. And in my dream, remembered. I had lived before, and before that. Memories awoke that had lain buried for centuries – for millennia – in the depths of my soul. I saw back as far as Egypt, and Sumer, where first I learned the practice of magic; and further back still – to the shadow times when the angels walked the earth. And I saw how I had first been one of them.'

Oh, Jesus, I thought. A Clinician was bad enough. But a Clinician with psychotic delusions . . .

'In the beginning,' she went on softly – half to herself, I guessed – 'there was Paradise: so far back that even in the dream of my first life it strained my mind to think of it. I and my kind were cast out, for some transgression we can no longer even recall, and we are still in search of our redemption. And now I realized that if I took it upon myself to cleanse the earth of workers of evil such as Melphalan and his kind, I might someday find my way back to the gates of Paradise again . . . I have stalked and slaughtered the Black Physicians since that day.'

After a pause – I wasn't about to try interrupting – she added: 'Do not suppose that just because I use their art against them I'm damned like they are. I know a dozen Spells of Desolation – it was so easy to crash your switchboard, that first night – but whenever I can, I'll use guns and knives: you can wash the blood off your hands a lot more easily than out of your mind. Of course, I've had to draw on my learning in order to hunt and trap them – and to prolong my own life in doing so. But the *maleficium* I practise is directed towards the greater good, Rachel. It's fighting fire with fire.'

Sure, I thought grimly. *Sure it is.* The Clinicians had tried harnessing magical power to edify and heal; Razoxane had started using it to exterminate evildoers for God. And sorcery had sucked all of them down, into a darkness that had consumed their humanity, and a blind private war that left innocent corpses wherever it was fought. She was one of them all right; that was one irony she hadn't seen herself.

And here she was now, a healer turned insane destroyer. Still searching for the promised gift of God.

Eventually I asked: 'So tonight . . . you're going to finish the last of them off?'

'God willing.'

'You think God's got anything to do with this?' I muttered bitterly.

'Only fear of the *Lord* can bind the powers of the night, Rachel; you'd better believe it.'

'*They* don't, though, do they? So how . . . ?'

'I wasn't talking about Clinicians,' she cut in quietly.

There was a freezing pause. Amplified by silence, the pages of the book of black magic rustled like withered leaves as she turned them one by one.

'Then . . . what?' I asked, unwillingly; already suspecting the answer.

She paused to read, and didn't bother to reply.

'Oh no,' I finally whispered. 'You're not . . . You can't –'

'They never accepted the true nature of the powers they came to wield,' she murmured, as though I hadn't spoken. 'They don't believe in demons. But we do: don't we, Rachel?'

I felt as if I was suffocating; as if the fear had made my

lungs seize up. I'd always accepted the Church's teaching – and my own superstitions – that some kind of evil power existed, somewhere 'out there', in the distant dark. Once or twice, as I dogged Razoxane's steps, I'd caught a whiff of its watchful coldness. But such forebodings had hardly prepared me for the horror I was facing now: trapped in a darkened room with someone about to raise Hell . . .

'It's the only way,' Razoxane went on remorselessly. 'If we're going to convoke a cabal of sorcerers as powerful as Melphalan's, we'll need the strongest, darkest power there is. Power from the Void . . .'

'Please . . .' I said desperately.

'There are certain entities to be invoked: shadows that men have named down the centuries. They answer to those names now: and we can bind them to our will . . .'

'Razoxane, for Christ's sake, you'll kill us both!'

Or worse, some pitiless part of my mind insisted. *Or worse . . .*

Now she paused. Tipping my head back, I saw she'd braced herself against the table, one gloved hand on either side of the open book, as though still reading its darkened pages. Her head was bowed once more; face lost completely in her hat-brim's shadow.

'Lie still, Rachel,' her disembodied voice advised me drily. 'Wait a while. Discover all of *night's* surprises.'

I wanted to shut my eyes.

I didn't dare.

I lay there, and began to shiver as Razoxane once more began speaking in that grim, unearthly language.

After some moments, she raised her arms and spread them, like a priest saying Mass; her head still inclined towards the book. On and on she spoke, and now her knife was in her hand again, glinting in the dimness as she carved signs and patterns in the air.

My heart was thumping bruisingly, as I strained my

senses for the first warning of some other presence with us in the room: something out there beyond the circle, and drawing near us in the dark.

Razoxane paused – I thought I heard her swallowing – then lapsed back into comprehensible English. 'In the Name above names, *Adonai*, Yehovah *Saboath*, Lord of Spirits, I summon to my aid the four Archangels of God. Behind me and before me, on my left hand and my right. I summon Michael, angel of Peace; Gabriel, angel of Justice; Raphael, angel of Healing; Uriel, angel of Light. Come hold this inner ring against the powers of the dark. *Amen, so let it be.*'

There was no appreciable change in the air around us; the room was as dim and draughty as before. And if her call upon God was vaguely reassuring in the context, the hope I clutched at slipped away with the thought that maybe she'd miscalculated, and got it wrong, and that even if such things as angels existed after all, they wouldn't save us from whatever she was going to bring up next . . .

'In the Name of the Lord Almighty, the Most High God,' Razoxane resumed, her voice cold and strong, 'I summon from the Void the Shadows of Sickness, to stand at each point of the seven-pointed Seal of the Serpent. Come in fearful memory of Marduk, Master of Magic and First Lord of all Physicians. Come from your dominions of decay; gather to greet the enemies who mock you. I invoke and bind you, Nergal . . . Namtar . . . Asukku. I conjure and constrain you, Irra . . . Suruppu . . . Lamashtu . . . *Livyathan.*'

Again no movement, not a stirring, in the shadows around. But as I lay there, breathless with dread, I thought I felt the temperature begin to fall.

'Good. . . .' Razoxane murmured. 'Good.' She turned a page, and my heaving mind threw up, of all things, a joke, something someone once told me about the Kama Sutra: *if two pages stick together you can break a leg* . . . And if that happened to Razoxane, or she missed her place, or lost her concentration, what would happen then?

I wished, I really wished I hadn't thought that.

'In the protection of the holy Angels,' Razoxane persisted, 'and by the power of the seven Shadows, I convoke the Clinicians. May they come to us, and pass unharmed into our circle. *Amen,* so let it be . . .'

She spread her hands wide once more, then brought them together, raising the knife over her head and mine until I thought, with sudden, plunging horror that she was going to thrust it into me: to sacrifice me then. But after an endless moment she lowered the weapon, and placed her double-clenched fists against her shadowed mouth.

'Omega: it is ended,' she murmured. 'Alpha: it is beginning.'

Silence in the room.

As far as I could see or sense, the two of us were still alone.

I was breathing raggedly, and so was she; I guessed the ritual, whether successful or not, had taken a lot out of her. Cautiously I raised my head.

There was the faintest gleam of moonlight in the room. This windowless room . . .

I felt the prickle of rising hairs all over me.

It was a light that showed nothing: as dim and diffuse as the fluorescence of rotting fish. After a moment I realized it was coming from the floor, as though the heptagram had sucked in every last thin glimmer of the day and focused it here around us: a blue watchfire to keep back the night. Beyond the outer circle there was blackness now; and I could make out no dark shapes – much less bright ones – lurking in those dense, oppressive shadows.

Minutes passed.

'Now what?' I whispered, with vague surprise that my vocal cords still worked.

'Patience, Rachel: haven't I told you that before? They are coming.'

Surreptitiously I tried flexing some muscles; they were responding better now, but I was still desperately weak. With no prospect of escape, I tried reasoning with her again. 'Look ... If you're using these ... shadow things to bring them here, why do you need *me*?'

'There has to be a focus, Rachel,' she explained, as though clarifying some academic point. 'Something to draw them in. They think they're coming willingly. And like I said, the prospect of despoiling innocence is the greatest lure of all. It gives them *power*.'

I almost let it pass, but couldn't quite resist the dark temptation. 'And despoiling means ... ?'

She shrugged. 'Violation. Desecration. Torture. Rape. Murder ...'

I *won't* cry, I told myself fiercely. I won't. Biting my lip to steady it, I asked: 'And you're going to let it happen?'

'I told you to trust me, Rachel ...'

'Is that a joke, Razoxane? Is it? Well ha ha fucking ha!' My voice cracked as I said it.

Somewhere beyond the doors, a bed was shoved violently aside.

I almost bit my tongue off. The corridor out there was empty; we'd heard no footfalls. No movement to explain that clank and crash, and bedheads rattling like bones. Silence. Then another bed moved, more slowly. I heard the verminous squeak of its unoiled wheels.

'Oh God ...' I gasped out. 'Oh Jesus, no ...'

More sounds, from the room next door: like something clumsy blundering through the long-forgotten furniture. The dinning clatter of something falling to the floor. The scrape of metal. Then sudden silence once again.

It was broken by a muffled knocking sound – like cold air trapped in pipes. Like the central heating turning over.

But the pipes to this part of the building had been stopped up long ago.

I twisted my head back, looking frantically for Razoxane. And Razoxane was waiting, calm as ever; her face lit from below in ghostly cyanosis. Watching the darkness. Watching the doors.

The thumps and rattles were suddenly redoubled. The stale air thickened. I caught just a whiff of something that made me gag: a stink like the discharge from a rotting rectum. And when that numbing silence fell again, there were others in here with us.

I couldn't see them: they'd neither forms nor faces. Nothing moved. But I knew without a doubt that they were there. I felt their *misery*.

'Razoxane . . .' I moaned.

'Quiet now,' she came back evenly. 'Our friends are almost here.'

And as if on cue, I heard the distant slamming of a door.

Hospital doors have a sound all their own: a fireproofed weight swinging closed on an empty corridor. A hollow boom that echoes in the stairwells. It was that sombre sound that reached us now: not from the way we'd come ourselves, but from even deeper in the empty wing.

I wanted to curl up in a ball: draw my knees to my chin and just hug them. But I hadn't even the strength for that.

Another set of fire-doors banged closed: louder this time. Nearer.

'They can smell you already,' Razoxane murmured drily. 'The very core of their convocation . . .'

My tingling ears could hear the footsteps now: relentlessly closing the distance.

'Damn you, Razoxane,' I whispered helplessly. '*Damn* you . . .'

'Shh,' she chided softly. 'It's time to pray . . .'

My bitterness evaporated like smoke. 'Oh *shit* . . .'

'Can't you feel them?' she almost breathed; and suddenly

I could. A new, far deeper coldness was *congealing* on the other side of the doors.

Hopelessly I raised my head once more. Through the gloom I could just discern the two dim windows in the theatre doors – staring back at me like empty eyes, with only void behind them. But the cold was seeping through the crack now, and I felt it settle over me: stiffening the hairs on my flesh. I felt its dank, invasive chill in my mouth, and against my eyeballs, and between my parted thighs. Even the dismal presences around us seemed to fade before it: drawing back against the walls, as though to give our smothered spirits room to breathe.

And then the doors were pushed creaking open, and the cold came gusting in.

Melphalan came through first.

He was little more than a silhouette in the murk, but I recognized him by his height, and his wide-brimmed hat. The wan ghost-light wasn't bright enough to illuminate his features; but his eyes caught the gleam, and reflected it back at us like a cat's.

Slowly he advanced across the room towards us, and now I saw Vokaine and Glaukostyx come in behind him, following their lord to right and left, like misplaced, malodorous shadows. I caught the glint of light off the former's goggles – and the blade in the latter's hand.

I lay as if dead. I knew I was already.

Melphalan halted at the end of the trolley: close enough to grasp my feet and yank me down towards him, into his clutches one final time. But it seemed that he ignored me. From the lift of his head, he was studying Razoxane.

His brother Clinicians took their stance to either side, within the circle: one pace behind his back.

The tableau held for what seemed like minutes – as if frozen by the very coldness of the room. I'd even begun to wonder if they were all somehow communing telepathically, when Razoxane said softly: 'Greetings, Lord

Melphalan. It has been a long time since last we talked.'

Another pause. Then, wordlessly, the Clinician nodded.

'You recall our last meeting . . .' Razoxane went on.

'You summoned us here,' came Melphalan's dry and pitiless voice. 'A convocation. Why?'

'I have libation to offer, as you see,' Razoxane said calmly. 'A woman who betrayed you, and conspired to see you all destroyed. I trust the excruciation of her flesh will be pleasing to you . . . ?'

Now Melphalan glanced down at me. I felt my skin shrink beneath that luminous gaze. I sensed the lust in it: but no longer lust for me as a woman. Rather it was lust for my body and soul, and for power over both; the real horror of rape . . .

'May this be accepted as a token of my submission,' Razoxane said, and inclined her head. 'Once more I humbly petition my Lord for readmission to the Order.'

Oh God, I thought. *That wasn't in the script.*

Melphalan's gaze rose slowly back to her. 'What place has the Order for such as you?' he grated.

'You will recall the circumstances of my expulsion,' came her reply: 'You swore then that the only way a woman would gain entry into your cabal of seven was to slay one of the existing Brotherhood. And so I did – but you never honoured your word. So the ordeals went on, and now I have bested four. Once again I submit that I am worthy to join your number; I do most humbly seek admission to the Order of Clinical Judges.'

I just lay there, staring at the ceiling and thinking, *oh fuck*.

Melphalan seemed to be considering her proposal. At length he said. 'The woman, Rachel Young. She is entirely beyond trusting?'

'I fear so.'

'Then we will dispatch her now,' the Clinician said

coldly. 'And you may make the first incision. We shall see how your technique compares with ours . . .'

'I am honoured, Lord.' Razoxane's knife was lifting even as she spoke. For a moment I thought – and hoped – she would simply stab me; rip open my throat, and drown my thoughts in blood. But then, with a flick of her wrist she'd turned it in her hand, and now she was holding it like a precision instrument, a surgeon's blade, something with which she might carve for long and loving *hours* . . .

I gaped despairingly up at her, as Melphalan selected a scalpel of his own from beneath his coat, flexing his fingers round the handle as he ran his gaze up the length of my body. He took a step around the trolley.

And then Razoxane seemed to hesitate; I saw the knife-blade waver. She raised her head again – and looked away, towards one corner of the room. Through the blue-stained dimness, I sensed her frown.

'You,' she said. 'I did not summon you. What do you want here?'

Whoever she was speaking to gave no reply, and I rolled my head to look.

There was someone else with us in the room: someone standing out there in the shadows, beyond the circle's edge – just a blur in the gloom. Someone watching us.

Despite my terror, I felt my stomach surge afresh as I realized it must after all be one of the angels or demons that Razoxane had called upon. Whichever it was had taken the form of a woman: I could tell as much by her dimly-glimpsed figure, the way that she stood; the fall of her curling hair. She seemed dressed – or wrapped – in something white; hugging the garment close about her. As if she too felt the cold . . .

'Leave us,' commanded Razoxane grimly.

There was a pause. Then the wraith-woman shook her head.

'What trickery is this?' Melphalan growled; but I

scarcely heard him. Something about the watcher had grasped my full attention now; stirred the ghost of a memory in my mind. Something about her was so unsettlingly familiar . . .

'Leave us,' Razoxane repeated. 'Return to the Void whence you came . . .'

'Rachel,' the shadow-face said.

In the voice of Jenny Thomas.

My hand went instinctively to my mouth, stifling the sound that suddenly welled up there; the sound that might have been a scream. Wide-eyed with disbelieving horror, I watched her take a step closer, so that the faintest glimmer of light fell upon the shadow of her face.

The Clinicians had conjured up the form of Jenny Thomas once before, of course, and hoped to trap me; but I knew at once that this was not their doing. Their image of Jenny had been mine as I recalled her: the loving nurse who'd been my closest friend. But there was nothing lovely about the girl who stood there now. Her hair was lank and long-unwashed; her face pale, and smudged with shadow around the eyes. The cruel marks of strangulation still stood out lividly around her throat. And she was wearing nothing but a hospital shroud . . .

My eyes grew wider; my palm pressed tighter to my lips.

'Rachel,' she said again, so quietly I barely heard her. 'Come with me. Come with me now . . .'

And with a sudden strength I didn't know I had, I began to struggle up; drawing my legs jerkily back out of Melphalan's reach, though he and his brothers remained motionless. I'd managed to sit up, and was preparing to swing my feet towards the floor, when Razoxane's voice in my ear said: 'Don't.'

I froze.

'It's a trick, can't you see that?' she continued tightly. 'The powers outside the circle want you, Rachel; they're trying to lure you out. One step outside the heptagram and they'll tear you to pieces . . .'

Still staring at that haggard apparition, I tried to swallow, to speak, and was unable. My mind was a whirl of awe and apprehension, of wonder and dread. In horrid indecision I hesitated, watching as she extended one hand towards me.

'Come with me, Rachel. You have to come now.' She sounded almost pleading.

I *knew* it was Jenny. Choked and dead and buried, yet somehow she'd come back. *Somehow* . . . I slid down from the trolley, my eyes so intent on her half-shadowed face that I only remembered Melphalan when he made a lunging grab for me – and missed.

I half-turned, and almost lost my balance; but Melphalan was groping uselessly now, as though something held him back, there at the far end of the trolley. Whatever power had suddenly transfixed him, I sensed him fight it – returning his gaze to Razoxane as Vokaine and Glaukostyx tensed up behind him. And Razoxane herself went rigid, staring bitterly back at him, and I saw then how they were battling each other: each holding the other bound by sheer strength of will . . .

With neither faction about to intervene, I took a step towards the circle's outer edge.

'No, Rachel,' Razoxane managed from the corner of her mouth. 'It's . . . a trap . . .'

I glanced back at her, then turned my face towards the deepest dark once more. And again I hesitated. Remembering the litany of demons that Razoxane had called on – and the wintry spectres that had come in silent answer.

The girl with Jenny's face stood there before me, almost close enough to touch; one step outside the circle. One small step. I stared beyond her proffered hand, into her lacklustre eyes – and sudden *fear* squeezed my stomach tight.

'Come on,' she whispered. 'Please . . .'

'You can't survive out there,' I rasped out suddenly. 'You're not *real* – '

'The angels of God guard us through the night,' she came back softly.

My racing heart stumbled, and skipped a beat. I recognized the form of words, the prayer I'd sometimes heard at midnight Mass. Almost instinctively I made the ritual response.

'. . . And quieten the powers of darkness.'

'The spirit of God be our guide,' she responded in turn.

'. . . And lead us to faith and to glory,' I said – and, grasping her icy hand in mine, let her pull me out of the circle.

Close by in the darkness, something *moved*.

The gag reflex of terror almost choked me; but her grip stayed firm, and I returned it with desperate strength. 'Hold tight, Rachel,' she said, and drew me on towards the doors. 'Hold tight, and don't look back.'

Helplessly I stumbled after her. We'd almost reached the doors when Razoxane spoke again, grinding out the words behind us.

'Rachel. Forgive me. Pray for me . . .'

And as we forced our way out, into the relative warmth of the unheated corridor beyond, I heard her speak four final words. I thought it was the garbled, mystic language she'd used before – then realized she was speaking backwards: the angelic names reversed. Unravelling the protective inner circle to let the darkness in.

The theatre behind us imploded.

I felt it happen: the suction was instant and appalling. Yet the equipment and litter and floating dust around us never stirred. It was our souls that felt the vacuum, the vortex that had opened up behind us and now strained to suck us under.

I only heard one scream: a sound so anguished I couldn't

even tell if it was Razoxane or a Clinician. It peaked at the limits of human hearing, and was snatched away.

We blundered into a bed; groaning, I stumbled and slumped towards the floor. But Jenny's grip never slackened. She hauled me back up against the opposite wall, and I clung to her, felt her cold bare arms hug me tight, as the doors slammed closed on what Razoxane had called the Void. It was as if a cosmic black hole had opened in the room behind us, just across the event horizon of its threshold. The physical world it left untouched; but intangible things like light and heat and human sanity it strained to swallow down. I felt my senses reeling, my thoughts being wrenched away ... And then, just as I thought I would lose my mind completely, the suction stopped.

And the night was silent.

In the breathless stillness that followed, as I struggled to piece my fractured thoughts together, Jenny gently disengaged herself, and took a step back. When I raised my eyes to hers once more, she glanced down, and didn't meet my gaze. As if ashamed that I should see her dead ...

I was speechless, not surprisingly; still wide-eyed with disbelief. And sick to my stomach with fright. She was dead all right; stone-cold dead – and standing there before me. Surely not her physical body, some detached part of me reasoned – that was already rotting beneath six feet of earth – but a tangible manifestation none the less: the ghost of her own cadaver.

So what do you say to someone you've loved, and lost for ever; a girl whose murder you're still mourning? In the end, all I dared ask was: 'Is it ... over now?'

She nodded, her face sliding down into the shadows. 'Yes. One final trap. She breached the barrier of the Void – and dragged them down with her.' There was a strange huskiness in her voice, I noticed now – and realized it was a ghostly legacy of her bruised larynx: her strangulation. The thought almost made me shudder.

'This much she told you was true,' her dim mouth whispered. 'She lived for their deaths. In the end she sacrificed herself to see it done.'

'It was nearly her and me both,' I muttered.

She shrugged. 'You were the bait, Rachel. You always were. She'd use anyone, without scruple. Psychopaths don't feel guilt.'

And that was true enough: a psychopath was what she'd really been, for all her witchcraft. A sorceress as old as Melphalan, and ultimately just as twisted. She'd come to him with a vision – to marry healing magic with medical wisdom – and he'd spurned her. And the rejection had sent her mad. She'd fallen in her dreams – to rise like a nightmare. A self-made morbid angel: just like the ones the first physicians feared.

One more irony in life's rich pattern. Or death's.

I stared numbly back at Jenny for a moment longer; then turned back towards the delivery-room doors. 'And . . . where is she now?'

'The Void took them all: body and soul.'

The bluish glow had gone; but by the faint light in the corridor, I could see for myself that the room was completely empty. Slowly, warily, I walked over and peered in through one of the windows. There where the maelstrom's heart had been, the power of the Void had disrupted the physical world as well. The protective heptagram had been smudged and smeared and practically erased from the floor, and the trolley at its centre had been flung aside. It lay now in one corner, mangled and warped beyond recognition, like a piece of abstract sculpture – or the jetsam of a nuclear blast.

And I'd been lying on that . . .

I swallowed hard, then glanced at Jenny once more. 'And the . . . demons? Have they all gone?'

'Now they have. A sorcerer as powerful as Melphalan might have been able to resist them – so Razoxane bound

328

him with all her will. Think of it like wrapping your arms round someone and jumping into the sea. Holding on until both of you drown . . .'

There was a long pause. Then, almost without thinking, I reached out to her, reached out to touch her face. She didn't flinch – but my hand halted in mid-air, and wavered there; before I let it drop reluctantly to my side once more.

'Oh Jenny, Jenny . . .' I whispered.

She shook her head. 'I'm *dead*, Raitch. I don't belong here any more. I have to go back now . . .'

'Back where?' I asked urgently – just the first of all the questions now surging through my mind. But her reply was to reach out herself, placing a cool finger on my lips to silence them all.

'Don't ask, Rachel. Just don't. I couldn't explain in any way you'd understand. She didn't call me; I came of my own free will. But I can't stay any longer.'

Chilly fear knifed into me then: the dread of being left alone in the dark. 'Please, Jen –'

She stepped up close and kissed me – on the cheek, like the friend she'd always been. 'Don't be afraid, Rachel,' she said softly. 'Just remember you're not alone. You'll never be alone.'

I blinked – then blinked again, to dilute the tears. 'How . . . how do you mean . . . ?'

But she never answered that one; just said 'Goodbye, Raitch,' and smiled, and turned away into the dark.

I just stood there, watching – and saw her hesitate, and suddenly hug herself, and seem to cringe.

A new unease began to rise like nausea within me. 'Jen? What . . . what's wrong?'

'I can feel him, Rachel . . .' she said dully, head down.

'Who? Feel who?'

'In the Void . . . Rising.' She looked at me then, and her eyes were bright and fearful in the dimness. 'Razoxane's strong, but Melphalan is stronger. *Melphalan's getting out.*'

'Oh . . . Jesus.'

'Run, Rachel. Get away . . .' Her voice was fading as she said it, and so was she: as though the deeper gloom at the heart of the ward was sucking her back to the darkness from which she'd come. Her pale shroud fluttered and swelled in a phantom wind – and even then she stretched out her hand towards me, mouth still open in soundless warning. And she was gone.

And I was on my own.

I turned around, and around again. There was silence all about me. But down this corridor and the next one, through two more sets of doors, the lights of the living hospital were already waiting to welcome me back.

All I had to do was get there.

I started towards the doors at the corridor's end, shoving through the scrapyard of shadows: cursing as my coat snagged on a bedhead and almost tore; cursing, and praying too. I had nearly reached them, and the straight run to safety and sanity beyond, when behind me I heard the delivery-room doors burst suddenly open, emitting a gust of stinking cold – and something that came gasping and stumbling and snarling down the corridor after me.

Thirty-four

I hit the last doors running and stumbled through them, hearing the rattle of the chain as the padlock dropped apart. And the flat glare of hospital fluorescents hit my eyes full on, leaving me blinking like a mole emerging from the darkness, squinting to clear my stinging gaze . . .

Behind me – right behind me – I heard his hoarse and phlegmy breathing. The sounds impelled me onwards: without pausing to look back, or even draw breath, I began to run again. Launching myself towards the fire-doors into Gynae where there would be people, and phones, and somewhere to hide; then abruptly veering off, and shoving through the adjacent doorway and on to the stairs – just as my pursuer came crashing into view behind me. I glimpsed him once, and almost fell over my feet in redoubled haste: descending three steps with every leap I took.

The occupied wards had never really been an option, of course. Sure there were people there, but that wouldn't bother Melphalan, or stop him. Nurses, doctors, patients – he'd carve his way through all of them to get at me.

I swung myself across the landing – my trainers were worn, and I almost skidded – and down the next flight, and Melphalan was already descending after me. Gasping for breath, cold with perspiration, I kept on going – faster and faster, until it seemed that I must fall. And then, above the rasp and thunder of heart and lungs, I heard voices on the stairs below me, and footsteps coming up.

They were out of sight around the corner, still on the next flight down, but I could tell from the voices that they were several — and some of them were kids. Visitors, of course — after the endless nightmare I'd just lived through, it was with a jolt that I realized it was still only mid-evening: and the hospital was busy.

I couldn't run on into them; even if I'd had breath to scream a warning, they'd be too stunned to react before Melphalan too was upon them. Which left no option but the doors on to the next level, whichever one that was. I knew Melphalan was close enough to see and follow. The upcoming group just caught my eye as I barged through into the reception area. They'd probably be quite impressed: running people in hospitals always mean something exciting's going on . . .

The fire-doors were still open on this level, and I ran on down the central corridor for half its length before glancing round again. And Melphalan was still there behind me, but slowing to a walk now, and limping slightly as he came: more dishevelled than I'd ever seen him, his hair hanging into his eyes. He was mumbling something, and suddenly weaved to one side and back again, like some malevolent drunk. I knew what had happened, of course: the demons of the Void had sunk in their claws, and ripped his mind apart. Melphalan had been wise once, a wizard indeed, but his plunge into Hell had destroyed that suave, sadistic intellect and left a shambling wreck, a creature without a mind; but still with two good eyes, and at least one surgical blade, gripped tight and gleaming in his rubber-fingered hand.

I'd slowed to a wary walk myself and was backing steadily away from him; breathing in short, sharp gasps. Behind me the corridor formed a T-junction, with wards in either direction. I'd recognized the Medical floor by now, and knew they would probably both be full; but there was nowhere else to go.

Melphalan halted, and peered at me through a veil of straggling hair; then bared his clenched, discoloured teeth.

'Rachel . . .' he gritted. 'Rachel . . . Mary . . . Maureen . . . Young. *Bitch*. I'll take you there. You'll scream for ever . . .' And he resumed his slow advance.

I didn't wait for him to start running; I pre-empted him on that. Whirling, I ran myself, reached the junction and turned right – on to Jenner Ward once again.

I passed the open door of a side-room; glimpsed the patient, and two relatives in chairs at the bedside, all chatting comfortably, and glancing up as I stumbled by. The corridor ahead of me was empty, all the way to the desk at the corner. There were usually only three nurses covering the Late shift, and they'd probably all be busy. I was making a single-minded beeline for the phone at the station when someone emerged from the sluice room just as I was passing it, and nearly knocked me flying.

It was a male Staff Nurse; he almost swore, and reached out a hand to steady me. 'Whoops . . . Sorry.' He glanced down, taking in my greens. 'Help you . . . ?'

I swallowed to lubricate my throat. 'Please . . . there's someone after me, he's got a knife . . .' I glanced back fearfully as I spoke – but of Melphalan there was no sign. I turned to the nurse again: and found him staring at the ID bracelet on my wrist. And then the IV site. His eyes flicked up to study my face, and I knew what he was thinking.

'Look . . . I'm a nurse, a Sister in A&E, you can check with them . . .'

He nodded understandingly. 'Yes, of course. Which ward were you on?' His tone was low, reassuring, reasonable – and I realized with a surge of near despair that he thought I was a psychiatric patient who'd gone for a wander: someone quite out of her tree, who might need sectioning for her own protection.

Still no sign of my pursuer. I'd have almost welcomed an appearance, just to prove I was telling the truth . . .

'Won't you tell me where you've come from?' the Staff

Nurse was saying. 'People might be worried about you . . .'
Actually I thought he was quite good at it; or would be,
if he got the right bloody person.

'Please,' I said again, as calmly as I could. 'I'm not a
psychie patient or anything. It's just – ' Another nurse
emerged from one of the bays at that point, and he glanced
at her with a meaningful *get-over-here* sort of expression,
which was a bit off-putting. ' – Listen, we've got a . . .
patient emergency, someone with a knife . . .'

'Okay.' He nodded. 'You're saying someone on your
ward threatened you, is that right?' That was probably for
the other girl's benefit; he still didn't believe me. And why
should he, after all?

'Would you like to come to the office and talk about it?'
he suggested gently.

'But . . . he followed me here!'

'Don't worry, you'll be safe with us. Quite safe.' He
risked a look at my wristband. 'Rachel, is it? Come on, it's
just along here . . .'

I thought about making a break for it.

The other nurse's gaze switched to something over my
shoulder. Her colour faded as I watched.

An icy finger stroked my spine. I knew, before I'd even
turned, that Melphalan was coming.

'Who the hell . . .' she muttered.

I reached out, and grasped each of them by a shoulder,
and tried to force them with me. 'Come on, run, for God's
sake . . .' But the bloke shook free, and after giving him a
scared glance, his companion – who was still only a third-
year student, to judge by her belt – did the same. Pushing
past them, I twisted round. Melphalan was bearing down
on us like some wino who'd wandered in: no sign of his
knife now, and he seemed dazed and disoriented. The first
nurse took a step forward to meet him, hands spread:
blocking his way, but without threat. 'Evening. Can I help
you . . . ?'

334

'Oh God, no, no . . .' I muttered, then shouted: 'Get *away* from him!'

He glanced back at me, a little irritably; then returned his attention to Melphalan again, just in time to receive the scalpel stroke across his throat.

It happened so fast I could only gawp; he seemed stupefied himself. And then the wound yawned open like a slavering mouth, and blood splashed out everywhere as Melphalan grasped him by the collar of his once-white jacket and slammed him up against the wall, then gripped his chin to force his head back, and complete the incision. The poor bloke had been virtually decapitated by the time the Clinician let him slither to the floor.

I clapped my hands to my mouth – even after all I'd been through, I wasn't past horror yet – and stumbled back. But the other nurse, ghost-white as she was with shock, still took a slow step forward. For a moment her gaze rested on her murdered colleague, and her eyes were huge and terrified; but then, with a clear effort, she looked at Melphalan again, standing there with the dripping blade in his bloody fist – and cautiously extended her hand.

'Please . . .' She paused to clear her throat. 'Please, give me the knife. No one's going to hurt you, I promise . . .'

I seized her from behind, and tried to drag her back; she struggled free. For all the horror she'd just witnessed, she was still reacting as her training told her to react: reasoning with a violent intruder, no matter how disturbed. Acting to protect her patients, with more guts than I thought I'd ever muster.

Ideally of course she should have urged him just to drop the knife, and avoided direct eye-contact in the asking; but that was academic – just the professional in me, unable to switch off. Whatever she'd said, it wouldn't have done any good.

I took another step back: wanting to break and run, but I knew I couldn't leave her – just as she knew she couldn't leave the ward. Hopelessly I watched as she moved towards him; and Melphalan himself stood still and watched her come, as though transfixed. Maybe even he was impressed. Maybe, I thought desperately, she'll even drive him back . . .

'Please,' she almost whispered. 'Just give it to me . . .'

Melphalan did so. Her shriek almost split my eardrums. Choking, I spun around and ran.

The Lord of Physicians followed.

We were right into the ward now: patients and relatives staring out at us from every bay, confused and frightened. He was almost breathing down my neck as I reached the utility room, just this side of the station – and grasped the door-jamb to swing myself inside. He overshot, and stumbled to a halt, but he knew I was cornered now, and stepped back fast to block the doorway, his whole face twisted into a pained but savage grin.

Maybe it was the ordeal he had gone through that slowed his reactions; or maybe he was just too convinced of final victory. Either way, he was still grinning when the sphygmomanometer I'd snatched up crunched into his face with all my strength behind it.

A simple blood-pressure gauge: my only weapon. But it was hard and heavy metal and it knocked his head askew. Glass smashed; mercury spewed out. He lurched back; and almost whooping to refill my lungs, I lifted the sphyg and clobbered him again.

Melphalan went down on one knee; his face bubbling with blackish ooze, like septic blood. I stood over him, swaying, and suddenly the sphyg seemed too heavy to hold: it dragged my arms down straight, and I let it go, let it clatter to the floor.

Melphalan mopped his streaming face with one sleeve. The flesh was torn, the bone beneath surely fractured, but he wasn't blinded yet; and neither down nor out. As he began to struggle up I backed away – in the few square feet left me in this small and cluttered room. The shelves around me were crammed with ward stores: sealed sterile packages, and drip-bags, and treatment sets. But nothing else I could use as a weapon, nothing I could use even to slow his unstoppable advance.

He straightened up, and regarded me for a stomach-turning moment; then brought up the knife once more, and started in across the threshold.

I never dreamed I'd be able to say such a thing, much less believe it: not to a black butcher like Melphalan. But as he raised the scalpel and aimed his stroke, poised to slice through my breast and into my thudding heart, the words were suddenly there in my mind, and in my mouth: a total surrender to a power beyond us both. The same words Jesus spoke to Judas.

'Friend – do what you came here to do.'

The knife-blade wavered; for a moment, through his madness, he stared at me in disbelief.

And I glimpsed movement in the doorway behind him in the instant before someone slammed a metal bar across the base of his skull, and pitched him forward headlong.

It was one of the doctors standing there, his bespectacled face as pale as his clean white coat as he stared down at the vagrant he'd just floored. He'd got hold of a detachable drip-stand from somewhere on the ward, and was now gripping the T-shaped bar tightly in both his fists, as though he meant to bend the thing in half. Judging by the sick look on his face, and the sweat on his brow, he'd already seen what had happened to two of the ward's nurses. And even if this wasn't his first house job, he could never have been prepared for something like that.

I suddenly realized the scalpel was lying on the floor, close to my foot. Hastily I kicked it away.

Melphalan groaned, and began to stir.

I glanced round frantically, and my gaze locked on to one of the labelled shelves, and seemed to zero in. I snatched at a sealed package, tore it open and began fumbling with the tubing it contained – then looked at the medic again. He hadn't moved.

'We need to turn him over, now,' I said urgently, snapping him out of it. 'Come on, I need a hand.' And the two of us went down on our knees beside Melphalan's recumbent body, and between us managed to roll him over. His eyes were already open, shifting dazedly in their mask of gore. One hand pawed at me, the blood-slicked latex sliding down my forearm, leaving smears on my skin. Tight-mouthed, I finished readying the naso-gastric tube, and leaning forward, inserted it in one of the Clinician's nostrils. I pushed it in – and kept on pushing.

Melphalan's body jerked.

'Hold him down,' I gritted; my own knee was planted on his chest, and I bore down on him with all my weight as I fed the tube in deeper, through the nasal cavity, into the throat, and down the oesophagus towards the stomach. His flailing hand had found a purchase on my coat now; the fabric felt about to tear. His struggles were getting stronger.

Grimacing with nausea, I kept on pushing.

'What . . . what're you going to do?' the doctor asked hoarsely; but the NG tube was in position now, so I just said, 'Hold him,' and scrambled to my feet to examine the dangerous substance cupboard.

Controlled drugs were always securely locked away; other items were kept under lock and key as well, but in a glass-fronted cabinet. I picked up a metal kidney bowl and smashed the glass in, then reached through to finger the selection. A shard of glass raked my arm, and after a moment the blood began to come. I didn't even feel it.

I was turning bottles, checking labels; aware of Melphalan's muttering behind me, and the doctor's frantic breathing. The magic words *Highly Toxic* sprang out at me, and I yanked out the bottle of acetone and turned back to the struggle on the floor.

Melphalan was almost conscious now: the blow to his head would probably have brained a lesser mortal, but Clinicians were a different proposition altogether. Razoxane had said that complete evisceration was the only sure way to kill them; but maybe internal corrosion could put an end to them as well.

With that desperate thought in mind, I dropped to my knees again, wrenched the lid off the bottle, scooped up the trailing length of tube, and poured the liquid in.

Melphalan's scream was an awful, muffled sound. He thrashed and spasmed and arched his body upward. I rose to my feet above him, still pouring grimly, as he scrabbled at his face, and throat, and stomach, his boot-heels drumming on the floor. The doctor pulled himself clear and lurched back sickly; and as soon as the bottle was empty I dropped it and retreated with him. The protruding tube flopped back down, then flailed out wildly as Melphalan kicked and writhed halfway across the floor. And then, as he went into spasm again, I heard a death-rattle gurgle in the depths of his throat – and as we watched, his body slumped, and settled, and went finally limp.

The silence that followed was invaded by voices from the corridor outside; anxious patients and visitors, and members of staff trying hard to reassure. Someone – another nurse or doctor or whoever – must have summoned help; there would be nurses here from every other ward on the floor – and porters converging from every corner of the building. Not that we needed them now.

Or so I hoped.

I glanced at the doctor – Dr Rees, I noticed from his name-badge now – and he looked at me. He hadn't tried to stop me administering the lethal dose; I guessed the ghastliness of Melphalan's murders had precluded the niceties of medical ethics. But it was dawning on him now, I could tell: the fact that he'd assisted in a killing. Perhaps a murder in its own right.

'That was reasonable force,' I told him grimly. 'Believe me, it was . . .'

He grimaced, and glanced again at Melphalan's body. 'We'd disarmed him, though,' he muttered dully. 'We could have restrained him, till help arrived . . .'

I shook my head. 'No we couldn't.'

There was a pause. Someone round the corner at the station was on the phone and asking shakily for the police.

Dr Rees, who had clearly never seen a horror film in his life, took a step towards the body.

I grasped his sleeve and dragged him back. 'Wait! For Christ's sake don't go near him.'

He stared at me through his rimless glasses for a moment; then tugged his arm free. 'Look – whoever you are – he's dead, and I have to certify him . . .'

He turned again towards Melphalan.

And Melphalan sat bolt-upright, his face a rictus of agony and hate.

Dr Rees recoiled against me, then shoved past and out into the corridor. I stumbled back out after him, watching with horror as Melphalan clambered slowly but deliberately to his feet once more, the length of NG tube still dangling from his nostril and dripping to the floor. He stood there for a moment, getting his bearings; shaking his head to clear it – or in an animalistic response to pain. Then he noticed me still standing in the doorway: and met my stare with eyes that burned through the bloody black hair plastered across them.

'*Rayyyyy-chell*,' he hissed, as though calling for a playmate. And then his hand slid under his coat, and came out with another blade – a Liston knife out of my nightmare – and brandishing it he came staggering, slurring towards me.

I lunged backwards, missed my footing and fell, my head cracking against the handrail on the opposite wall. I came to rest slumped in a heap, half-sitting: my skull squeezed tight in a vice of pain. Dimly, through a blur of dizziness and tears, I saw Melphalan fill the doorway and come on out. There were people around us now, but no one dared restrain him as he approached me and, planting his boots astride my legs, leaned forward, extending the blade. The dangling tube swung in close, like a streamer of rubber snot. The reek of acetone pricked my nostrils.

Moving almost by instinct I fumbled in the pocket of my coat, and found the lighter I'd put there. Gripping it in near-nerveless fingers, I hauled it out, held it to the end of the tube and – as Melphalan, leering, slid his knife in under the angle of my jaw – snapped on the yellow flame.

The traces of acetone in the tubing were enough: they caught light at once, and the flame was sucked greedily up, and then down into Melphalan's body – straight to the reservoir of flammable liquid that had settled in his stomach. His stomach erupted.

For a moment it seemed his body might contain the fireball; but then the flames appeared, bursting out of him. I raised an arm to shield my face from the sudden, searing heat, but he was already staggering back, away from me, his arms flailing uselessly.

All around me there was screaming now, and a hideous stench; noxious smoke rose up and rolled across the ceiling, held against it by the heat. Someone tripped the fire alarm, which added its deafening clangour to the tumult.

Melphalan burned.

It wasn't just the acetone now, I realized; his whole body was afire. As if the very fact of his longevity had made his flesh more combustible, his blood more volatile. Still on his feet, he opened his jaws to scream, but only fire came out, an obscene tongue licking towards the ceiling. Even his brain, repository of all his learning, was ablaze: as I watched in mesmerized disgust, his eyeballs melted inwards, leaving two gaping sockets that glowed with a ghastly, fiery stare.

And then he toppled, arms frantically raised as if towards Heaven; still burning like a torch. As I scrambled whimpering away, I saw his blackening carcass struggle one last time to rise – then slump back, lying still to be consumed.

I hauled myself to my feet and staggered off down the corridor, making way for the beds being wheeled past and off the ward to safety. Once clear of the inferno – so intense that it already seemed to be burning itself out, like spontaneous combustion – my legs gave way, and I put my back to the wall and slid heavily down. A nurse broke away from the group of relatives she was shepherding towards the fire-doors, and came over to see if I was all right. And I nodded, and managed a smile of thanks, while the tears just came and came, and I never even realized I was crying.

Thirty-five

Mark stopped the engine, and for a moment the two of us just sat there in silence, staring through the windscreen and down the afternoon emptiness of Milston Road. I had my elbow propped against the windowframe, my fingers pushed into my hair. After a pause I glanced across at him, and grinned.

'Hey, cheer up, it might never happen.'

'It already did, Rachel . . .'

'I'll be all right: really.'

Now he smiled back, but it was still edged with concern. 'So long as you're sure . . .'

I nodded. 'It's something I need to do – and alone. It won't take long.'

Another pause. A car whooshed past.

'It's going to be really good to have you back, you know,' he murmured; I got the impression he'd been wanting to fit that in for quite a while.

'Just you wait,' I told him brightly, opening the door and sliding out. I leaned back in again. 'Thanks, Mark. I won't be long.'

'No hurry,' he insisted, and his gaze strayed briefly past me, towards the gates. 'Take as long as you need . . .'

I nodded once, slammed the door and didn't glance back as I walked briskly on into the cemetery.

I expect he thought it was my way of coming to terms with it all: the violence, blood and horror – and the know-ledge of how close death had really come. Certainly the people who'd counselled me afterwards had urged me not to bottle it up but to let it go, get it out of my system. He

343

must have reasoned that a good cry at my best friend's grave would do me the world of good: something that would bring acceptance of all that had happened – and with it a realization that I was still alive, and life could go on. He'd jumped at the chance to give me a lift here.

But I knew I wasn't going to cry today. There wasn't any need to.

The police reckoned they'd got everything sewn up, now. They were right, too; but not in any way they'd understand. The psychotic vagrant who'd got himself immolated up at the hospital was clearly the killer they'd been hunting, the spokespeople told us; he'd been carrying enough surgical steel on him to do a dozen autopsies. With the official body-count set at six, the press had been having a field day with this latest addition to the serial-killer cycle; it didn't take them long to draw the link with the *House of Death* on Fenner Street, where surgical implements and *other evidence* had also been found, and some projections of the death rate were already well into double figures. There was some talk of an accomplice, too – the mysterious *woman in black* who'd *terrorized the hospital* a month or so previously – but there were still no clues as to her whereabouts.

As a national story, it would be forgotten soon enough; there were plenty of other atrocities queueing up to take its place. Locally it would persist for a while longer, of course; and the locations of the murders would always have their morbid fascination. But the affair was ended now; its climax as spectacular and decisive as any fiction. Whatever rough edges remained were already being imaginatively sanded down – or conveniently ignored.

Oh, the papers had written about me as well, of course; the heroic nurse who'd finally put an end to the *Backstreet Butcher*'s rampage. What they wrote I had no idea. I didn't want to know.

So: that was it. A blood feud three centuries old had

finally been settled; the gates of Hell itself had opened, and closed again. And the world went back to business as usual, and no one was any the wiser – except for Jenny and me.

I came to the grave and halted there, my hands deep in the pockets of my coat. There were no flowers on the mound today, not even dead ones – and I hadn't brought any, either. She didn't need them now, I knew; and I didn't need to give them. It was time I directed my thoughts towards the living; and Jenny Thomas was alive. Not in the flesh of course: that still lay beneath my feet. But her mind, her essence, still survived: a state of being beyond death that I'd once taken unthinkingly for granted – and later despaired of altogether. She'd come back for me that night and saved me; and I knew she was somehow watching me now, aware of my thoughts, and gratitude, and all my love.

Standing there in silence, I thought of Razoxane as well, and where she might be now. It had taken a while for me to get over my nervous expectations that she might reappear at any moment: as scruffy, smelly and cheerfully vicious as before. For all the ruthlessness with which she'd used me and abused me, I still nursed a small, strange hope that she'd managed, against all odds, to cheat the Void; and that one day, as even in her madness she had dreamed, she would somehow find her way home.

This morning I'd been to church again: the first tentative step back across the threshold after so many months. The deep, dark, empty building had felt curiously welcoming, and I'd sat there for a long time, just absorbing the atmosphere until I was filled. On the way out I lit some candles, adding to the glowing yellow constellation in the corner. One for Jenny. One for Sarah. One for Razoxane.

Pray for me . . .

I felt better than I had in far too long.

At length I glanced up at the sky: there were more clouds now, thickening over the town like spilled, diluted ink. I took a deep breath and turned away, back towards the gate. There was someone else standing on the path, as though waiting her turn, and for a moment my heart leaped – then settled as I saw it was just some old woman, clutching a bunch of flowers and staring dully past me. I gave her a small, polite smile as I stepped towards her, my glance taking in her shabby coat, and bony frame; the dyed black hair escaping from beneath her headscarf, in weird contrast to the paleness of her face. I'd passed her before it finally registered about the flowers.

The flowers were dead.

I took the next three steps on automatic pilot, my mind a whirl of disbelief. Withered roses, shrivelled carnations, petals drying and discoloured – just like the flowers I'd seen here before. I'd suspected the Clinicians then, but the Clinicians were dead and gone now, and here was this gaunt old woman, whose dyed hair sounded chords of memory in my head, tying up with the description I'd read in the papers the day after Jenny died . . .

I spun around.

And the woman who Jenny had known – and dreaded – as Mrs Lennox looked back at me.

And slowly smiled.

Revelations
Clive Barker

Another Clive Barker story of living mayhem and dying faith adapted for the graphic form by Steve Niles and illustrated by Lionel Talaro.

A murder thirty years ago, to the night, haunts the motel room where it happened – and where evangelist John Geyer and his unhappy wife Virginia are staying. Virginia senses the ghosts of Buck and Sadie Durning are near. But her dependence on pills to alleviate the oppressive effect her husband's 'goodness' has on her lead her only to hideous dreams of violence. Observing her, the ghost Sadie, who was executed for the murder of her husband, is moved to sympathy. She is unrepentant, even though tonight she and the ghost of her husband have returned to the Cottonwood Motel to attempt a reconciliation beyond the grave. Virginia's problem is more compelling to her than Buck's lustful ghost. Before the clouds part to reveal a full moon, the bloodletting, the inevitable tragedy, will come to pass, again.

Clive Barker, the supreme fantasist, mixes life and death in a heady cocktail. Also included, an adaptation of his sinister story, Babel's Children, illustrated by Hector Gomez and adapted by Steve Niles.

ISBN 0 586 21756 8

Trapped
Dean Koontz

The first ever graphic adaptation of a story by the master of chilling fiction and chronicler of midnight's menace, Dean Koontz.

Laboratory rats locked in a cage together – originally they were kept in individual cages, but their aggressive behaviour was so disturbing that they were put together in the hope of quieting them. Instead it gives them the chance they've been waiting for. They break out on a stormy winter night. These are smart rats, bioengineered and hostile, for some reason, to humans. Perhaps because they were trapped . . .

But no longer. They take over the nearby house of Meg Lassiter, two years a widow, and mother to Tommy, aged ten and with his leg in plaster from a skiing fall. Meg and Tommy and trapped, now . . . the rat's first victims.

Dean Koontz's inimitable style permeates the graphic form, spreading evil and terror – and confronting them with the force of a mother's need to protect her child.

Adapted by Edward Gorman and illustrated by Bilau, this story of fear unleashed is realistic, unnerving and moving.

ISBN 0 586 21753 3

Clive Barker's
NIGHTBREED
The making of the film

CLIVE BARKER
Introduction by Mark Salisbury and John Gilbert

Nightbreed, based on his bestselling novel, *Cabal*, is the latest film from the astonishing imagination of the multi-talented writer and director Clive Barker. CLIVE BARKER'S NIGHTBREED – illustrated throughout with original sketches, storyboards, designs for sets and monsters, and photographs taken during filming – shows how the writer's vision is brought to the screen.

Clive Barker's foreword reveals his fascination with the horror genre, while his screenplay allows us to experience the terror of the film itself. In a special introduction by Mark Salisbury and John Gilbert, the concept behind the film is examined and actors, producers and designers talk about *Nightbreed* – destined to become a classic of *ciné-fantastique*.

ISBN 0 00 638136 7

Weaveworld
Clive Barker

Weaveworld is an epic adventure of the imagination. It begins with a carpet in which a world of rapture and enchantment is hiding; a world which comes back to life, alerting the dark forces from which it was hiding, and beginning a desperate battle to preserve the last vestiges of magic which Humankind still has access to.

Mysteriously drawn by the carpet and into the world it represents are Cal Mooney and Suzanna Parrish, two young people with no knowledge of what they are about to live through and confront. For the final conflict between the forces of good – the Seerkind – and of evil, embodied by the terrible Immacolata and her ravening twin wraith sisters, is about to take place.

Weaveworld is a book of visions and horrors, as real as the world we live and breathe in, yet opening doors to experiences, places and people that we all dream of, but daren't hope are real. It is a story of quest, of titanic struggles, of love and of hope. It is a triumph of imagination and storytelling, an adventure, a nightmare, a promise . . .

'Graphic, grotesque, and yet compellingly readable . . . its energy is unstoppable.'   *Washington Post*

'A powerful and fascinating writer with a brilliant imagination. *Weaveworld* reveals Clive Barker as an outstanding storyteller.'   J. G. Ballard

ISBN 0 00 617489 2